Miss Melville Returns

Now a successful artist, professional assassin Miss Susan Melville has the role of amateur sleuth thrust on her when a world-renowned artist is laid low by a knock'em dead speech which turns out to be just that.

The death, as Miss Melville quickly discovers, is not from natural causes – but is the inevitable result of the shady, dangerous dealings taking place in New York's art world...

Miss Melville Rides A Tiger

Former assassin Miss Melville is between jobs, charitably supporting the Rundle Home for Wayward Girls and trying to resist an invitation from the Government to assassinate the power-hungry Begum of Gandistan, a ruthless woman whose son has just ascended the throne following the unfortunate death of the rest of his family.

Although Miss Melville has her own reasons for undertaking this covert assignment, she also develops a fondness for the young Sultan, realizing he is an unwitting pawn in his mother's dangerous games...

By the same author

MISS MELVILLE REGRETS

Evelyn E. Smith

Miss Melville Returns
Miss Melville Rides a Tiger

Diamond Books
An Imprint of HarperCollins*Publishers*
77–85 Fulham Palace Road
Hammersmith, London W6 8JB

This Diamond Crime Two-In-One edition
published 1994

Miss Melville Returns© Evelyn E. Smith 1988
Miss Melville Rides a Tiger© Evelyn E. Smith 1991

The Author asserts the moral right to
be identified as the author of this work

ISBN 0261 66462 X

Cover photography by Monique Le Luhandre

Printed in Great Britain

Miss Melville Returns

To Christopher

CHAPTER 1

'He's dead!' Miss Melville cried before she could stop herself.

Everybody turned to look at her. Jill Turkel took firm hold of her client's arm. 'Don't be ridiculous, Susan. He just passed out.'

Susan Melville could see now, as Rafael Hoffmann's burly form was borne past her on 'Concupiscent Toad Crushed by Passion'— an artwork admirably adapted to serve as a stretcher—that the artist was not only breathing, but that there was a smile on his bearded face.

'Sorry,' she murmured, 'it—it must have been the shock of seeing him fall like that.'

Jill gave her arm a comforting squeeze. 'Everybody understands, Susan. You're not used to this kind of thing.'

Indeed I'm not, Miss Melville thought. Usually when I see them drop like that they're definitely dead. *Saw*, she reminded herself, *saw*. Her lethal days were behind her; she must take care not to let her memories of them become fond ones.

'I might have known something like this would happen to spoil my opening,' Roland DeMarnay wailed.

'Don't take it personally, Roland,' Jill advised him. 'At least he didn't get into a fight with any of the guests—which was what probably would have happened if he hadn't passed out.'

'I'll bet you were looking forward to it,' Alex Tabor suggested. Jill smiled and didn't reply.

'What do we do with him?' one of the two decorative young men staggering under the weight of the unconscious artist asked. Since he was wearing dark glasses, unusual at an art exhibit, particularly when worn by a member of the gallery staff, Miss Melville deduced him to be the unfortunate Damian, whom Rafael had assaulted earlier in the evening. 'We can't just stand here like live exhibits, slowly developing ruptures.'

'Don't be a fool, Damian,' Roland said. 'Put him on the couch in my office. But first take off his shoes so he doesn't mark the upholstery.'

The two youths trudged off. The musicians started playing again. The guests milled around and chattered. Damian and his colleague circulated bearing trays of champagne glasses; other young men went around with hors d'oeuvres and canapes. Nobody looked at the artworks. It was just another opening of another art gallery. Still Susan couldn't help feeling uneasy.

There had been a time, not too many years before, when nobody would have thought of inviting Susan Melville to speak at a gallery opening. There had been a time, too, when she would not have agreed to speak even if she had been asked. However, on this occasion Roland had asked her to speak and she had accepted and, she thought, done rather well. The guests were still applauding as she left the dais at the back of the gallery.

'Good show,' Roland said, as he passed her on his way to introduce the artist. Roland was a small, youngish man, good-looking in a blurry sort of way, with a British accent so thick as to seem improbable. His original request, conveyed through Alex, was to have a Susan Melville exhibit to open his gallery, but, 'There are over eight hundred art galleries in New York City alone,' Jill had declared, 'and there are at least seven hundred and ninety-nine I would take Susan's work to before Roland's.' She'd glared at Alex. 'I think you have a hell of a nerve suggesting such a thing, even if you are her half-brother.' If he had been Susan's full brother, her tone suggested, things might be different.

Susan wondered what Jill would think if she knew that Alex was not her brother even fractionally, that their relationship was a fictional one, hastily, almost accidentally, devised to obscure the fact that they had once been partners in crime. He'd been a professional assassin, she an unsuccessful artist. They had run into one another after she had on impulse killed an individual whom he had been assigned to dispose of. Recognizing talent when he saw it, Alex had

8

recruited the genteel, middle-aged lady into the organization for which he worked, and she had embarked on a successful new career—with the stipulation that she would kill only those she found truly deserving of that fate.

The identity of her employer had been kept from her as a matter of company policy. Originally she had agreed to work for him with the proviso that he take one of her paintings each time she made a hit. This was to explain her sudden modest affluence to the Internal Revenue Service, for she would never have dreamed of failing to pay taxes on her gains, no matter how ill-gotten. As she'd had no reason to suppose that her employer knew or cared anything about art, she had supposed that her paintings must be mouldering away in some dank basement, preserved only because he had established a corporation to take care of the payments and he too would be accountable to the IRS.

Only after his death did she learn that not only had he treasured her paintings, but he had enshrined them in a room of their own as the jewels of his collection. As soon as the news was out her work was in immediate demand. Now, little more than two years after her employer's death, when Roland had introduced her to the gallery guests as 'one of the brightest lights of the contemporary art scene', he spoke no more than what had come to be the truth.

As for Alex, by this time she had come to think of him as truly her brother. Since he had married the daughter of a long-time friend of hers, thus becoming inextricably en-meshed in her circle, it would have been difficult for her to repudiate him even if she had wanted to. Naturally, as a relative, he was going to seek favours for his friends. 'All I did was ask if Roland could open his gallery with a Melville exhibit,' he said. 'I didn't try to exert any pressure on you, Susan, did I?' Which was true. Clearly he couldn't understand why Jill was making such a fuss.

Susan, of course, could. She knew that Jill was right. By speaking at the gallery opening, Susan was, in a sense, giving her approval to both Rafael's work and Roland's gallery, neither of which deserved it. When she had refused to let her work be exhibited there, she'd unthinkingly agreed to speak as a graceful social gesture of atonement; and, by the time she realized it would seem like far more than that, it was too late to back out.

'You're letting the whole lot of them use you as an advertisement,' Jill grumbled. 'You're making a speech for Roland. You're wearing Baltasar's dress. God knows what else you're doing for them that you haven't told me about.'

As Susan Melville's artist's representative, Jill felt she should be consulted on all of her professional decisions. No argument with that; but Jill's definition of 'professional' seemed to be all-inclusive.

In Susan's youth, artists had always been represented by the galleries that showed their work. Today, however, some artists, like actors and writers, had representatives, but their field of operations was much wider in scope than literary or theatrical agents'. In addition to serving as dealers, artist's reps could also be press representatives, managers, investment advisers, guides, counsellors, and/or friends. So Hal Courtenay had told Susan, and, as Director of the Museum of American Art, he ought to know.

It was Hal who had introduced Jill to Susan. Even though she had great respect and even admiration for him, she did not take to Jill right away. Jill seemed more like a human dynamo than a normal, civilized young woman of thirty-three —which was the age Jill claimed, although she looked and acted much younger. She was aggressive, in fact, downright pushy, which at first put Susan off—unreasonable of her, she realized. A good businesswoman, a good agent, had to be pushy, if only to compensate for her client's deficiencies in that respect. Moreover, Susan was so beset by dealers anxious to represent her, and friends and acquaintances anxious to push the claims of favourite dealers, that the strain was growing unbearable. When Mimi Hunyadi (formerly Carruthers) took it upon herself to warn Susan against Jill—alleging that the girl was a vulgar little red-headed upstart who knew nothing about art—that did it. Susan signed with Jill.

Not out of spite. Spitefulness was a petty emotion, unworthy of a Melville. Even Black Buck Melville, her pirate ancestor, although charged by his enemies with every sin imaginable, had never been accused of spite. But, once she had decided to go with Jill, she could allow herself to take pleasure in the knowledge that it annoyed Mimi. It would be a long time before Susan could forgive Mimi for her despicable behaviour when, as chairman and loudest member of the MAA's Board of Trustees, she had been the moving spirit in selling out the Melville Wing.

Hal himself had had nothing to do with this, he assured Susan later. He had been in Europe at the time, tracking down some elusive Cassatts. 'Otherwise, I would have done my best to stop it.' Not, of course, that a curator, even a chief curator, as he had been then, would have had that much clout. Hal had been Director of the MAA for only the past year, ever since the previous director had expired among the statuary, so peacefully that it was some time before it was discovered that he was not part of the collection.

Before joining the Museum, half a dozen or so years earlier, Hal had been a freelance art expert and critic, teaching at various schools and contributing to most of the significant art journals. He also did an occasional piece for popular periodicals—all in all, a typical member of the city's resident *intelligentsia*. Not at all the sort of person Susan would have expected to be a friend of Jill's, but then art made strange bedfellows these days.

From the purely practical viewpoint, Susan seemed to have made a wise choice in going with Jill. Under Jill's aegis, the prices for her paintings quadrupled immediately and were still on their way up.

Susan had wondered whether whoever arranged for a speaker at an occasion like a gallery opening got some sort of commission or finder's fee. If so, Alex must be getting it, which might account for Jill's bad temper. However, Susan had a feeling it was something more, some personal animosity towards Roland. It couldn't be a question of money. The girl had to be doing very well, not only as Susan's rep, but also as representative of the late Darius Moffatt's estate —and possibly of other artists as well, for she was evasive when Susan tried to find out who Jill's other clients were.

11

When Susan asked Hal about it, he explained that an artist's rep whose clients were very high-priced usually handled only one or two in order to give them the personal attention they deserved. Susan sometimes felt she could do with a lot less personal attention. One thing you could say in a gallery's favour; it didn't keep breathing down your neck at every turn.

As for a commission, if anything like that were involved in getting Susan to speak gratis, it was less likely to take the shape of money than of a favour repaid or anticipated. And she certainly didn't begrudge it to Alex. Through Roland, he had made other arrangements as well. The Baltasar original she was wearing was worth thousands of dollars and there was no question of payment.

When Baltasar's offer had been made, she'd been reluctant to accept, not out of high-mindedness but because she was afraid she might be obligating herself to wear a dress that she wouldn't be caught in dead while she was still alive. She had never heard of Baltasar. His reputation had been achieved chiefly south of the border and in Madrid, and the stories about him she had read in the press convinced her only that he must have an excellent press agent.

Mimi assured her that the ladies she knew in Spain spoke very highly of his gowns and even more highly of his aristocratic connections. 'His wife is a *condesa* and he himself is related to the dukes of Astorga—on the wrong side of the blanket, of course, but who cares about that these days?'

'I don't care if he's related to the Duke of Plaza Toro,' Susan said. 'All I care about is whether I've committed myself to wearing a dress that'll make me want to hide in the ladies' room all evening.' But the dress turned out to be beautiful, a heavy dark grey silk shot with gold, that gave her the timeless elegance of a nineteenth-century portrait. So what if Baltasar was using her to help make a name for himself in New York. He deserved to have a name in New York.

Baltasar himself, a tall thin dark man who did indeed look like a Spanish grandee, came up to her now and kissed her hand, to Jill's undisguised disapproval. 'My dear Susan,' he said, 'your speech was truly an inspiration. And the dress looks divine. All the ladies are asking, "Who created that glorious gown for the glorious Miss Melville?" This is an evening of triumph, not only for Roland and Rafael, but also for me.'

'Shhh,' Jill whispered, 'Roland's speaking.' Maybe she thought Baltasar should have designed a dress for her too.

If the speech with which Roland had introduced Susan had seemed excessive to her, his introduction of Rafael Hoffmann was positively fulsome. But Susan Melville was merely a drawing card. Rafael Hoffmann was money in the pot, although, according to Jill, the ante in this case wasn't very high. 'Even if Roland couldn't get you, I would still have thought he could do better than Rafael Hoffmann for his opening show,' she'd said, looking at Rafael's work with disgust.

Rafael Hoffmann was a multimedia artist. His *oeuvre* combined painting, sculpture, and various crafts, with bits of photography, and, Susan supposed, mechanics or electronics, for some of the pieces moved in curious ways. Some even uttered remarks, most in bad taste, in the artist's own guttural accents whenever the unwary viewer got within a certain distance. There was one chair-shaped object ('Sitting Duck Incarnate') that made a rude noise if somebody was foolish enough to try to sit down on it.

How times had changed. When Susan had gone to the Hudson School—a world-famous institution that had finally cashed in its chips during the 1970s, after a glorious late-nineteenth-century, an eminent early-twentieth-century, and a respectable mid-twentieth-century past—a student would have been expelled for pulling something like that. Today they put it on exhibit.

Rafael himself, however, was a type that had been common enough when she went to art school, a type that had been common ever since art schools came into being; and before that probably there had been at least one in every old master's *atelier*. He was a huge, hairy young man—hard to judge his age because of the beard but she would place him in the mid-thirties—who looked like an ape and had manners that would have aroused comment among a tribe of baboons.

Not that she blamed him for having mistaken her for Alex's mother rather than his sister when they were introduced. After all, she was old enough to be Alex's mother, and had often considered herself lucky that fate had chosen to pass him off as her father's child (illegitimate) rather than her own. However, she resented Rafael's probing questions into how the disparity in age—and, indeed, in name—came to be.

'He kept asking questions about Father,' she told Alex, 'almost as if he . . . suspected something. You don't think he does, do you? After all, he's been working in Mexico, but, according to the catalogue, he comes from somewhere in South America.' The biographical essay in the front of the catalogue was oddly vague about his exact place of birth; and South America was where Buckley Melville had vanished after absconding with millions of dollars, most of them not his own, and where the man Susan loved had had a very unpleasant experience with a tribe of savages. She had been hypersensitive to that part of the world ever since.

'Pay no attention to Rafael,' Alex advised. 'He seems to have cultivated offensiveness into an art form. If there were awards for it, he'd take first prize.'

Roland had stopped speaking and was about to introduce Rafael with a flourish—except that Rafael wasn't there. Roland's young men scattered to all points of the gallery in search of the artist. At last he was brought forth from behind a door (which Jill had discovered led to the washrooms and to another door marked 'Private', that opened on to a stairway) and pushed on to the dais.

He started to speak. Although his English was good enough, his accent was so thick it was sometimes difficult to understand what he was saying. He seemed to be telling the assembled guests how wonderful he was. '. . . After years of degradation and neglect, at last I have the chance to reveal my genius in its true light. The world will recognize me as one of the greatest geniuses who has ever lived . . .'

'Do stop snorting like that, Jill,' Susan whispered. 'They can hear you all the way out in the foyer.'

14

CHAPTER 2

As soon as Rafael was well launched, Roland came over to where Alex, Susan, and the ubiquitous Jill were standing. Everything seemed to be going well. 'Don't you think everything's going very well, Alex? Susan, I can't thank you enough for agreeing to speak. Everybody who matters came, and I know I owe it all to you.'

Roland was wrong. Not everyone who mattered had come. Although Hal Courtenay had naturally been invited to the opening of the DeMarnay Gallery, he had not shown up. Perhaps it was too much to have expected him to dignify the occasion with his presence. But Susan couldn't help feeling disappointed. She'd looked forward to seeing him and hoped that this time they could manage to ditch Jill and go somewhere together afterward.

Baltasar's wife, the *condesa*, had not shown up either, although she had been expected. 'She was very sorry that she was unable to come,' Baltasar explained, 'but the doctor has ordered her to rest. She has a tendency to—how do you put it?—overdo things. But I promise you she will be at the Grand Drug Ball and Gala.'

'Promise Mimi Hunyadi, not me,' Roland said sulkily. Mimi was presiding genius of the Grand Art against Drug Abuse Gala and Ball that the Van Horn Foundation (Mimi had been born a Van Horn) was sponsoring in conjunction with the MAA and several large corporations. It was expected to be *the* event of the coming season, and she had succeeded in roping Susan into serving on one of the committees. Usually Susan avoided that sort of thing, but this time she could not refuse; the cause was too worthwhile. She was annoyed with Jill for saying approvingly, 'It'll add at least ten thousand dollars to your going price, more if you can possibly manage to be witty and charming so you'll be asked to serve on other committees.'

'But I don't want to serve on other committees. One's enough.'

'It isn't a question of what you want,' Jill said sternly. 'You can't live for pleasure alone. Getting the right people to see you in the right places is what's important. Don't forget to be especially nice to Brooke Astor, and maybe you'll get a one-woman show at the library.'

'What do you think of Rafael's work?' Roland whispered to Susan.

'If you try hard enough you can always find something nice to say without having to resort to a lie,' Susan's mother always used to say. Susan tried hard to find something nice to say about Rafael's work. 'He has great technical facility. That cat rubbing itself against "Hall Tree of Life" looks almost real.'

In keeping with what seemed to be Rafael's prevailing theme, 'Hall Tree of Life' had plastic replicas of women's breasts hanging on it instead of hats. However, in this instance Rafael had over-reached himself. Susan had never before realized how much a woman's breast looks like a pink pith helmet. The cat was black and without obvious symbolic significance, unless its gold collar, ornamented with what appeared to be green glass jewels, stood for something.

'The cat *is* real,' Roland exclaimed indignantly. 'Baltasar, I told you to keep that animal shut up!'

'I'm sorry, someone must have left the door open.' Baltasar picked up the cat and gave her into the charge of a middle-aged woman whom Susan had met previously at the fitting of her gown. Sanchia Guttierez had looked sad before. Now, wearing a couture gown in which she was obviously ill at ease, she looked miserable. 'Would you take Esmeralda upstairs and make sure she doesn't get out again?'

'Si, Señor Baltasar,' the woman said, 'but I am sure I locked the door. Someone must have let her out.' She carried the cat off in the direction of the stairway. Susan had a feeling that she was glad to have an excuse to escape from the festivities.

16

'Pity it wasn't a dog,' Jill murmured. 'That would have been really appropriate.'

Roland gave her a chilly look.

Rafael droned on and on. His accent was growing impenetrable, not that it mattered much because by this time no one was even pretending to listen to him. He also seemed to be unsteady on his feet. Nervousness? Susan wouldn't have thought he had a nervous bone in his body. She was always one to overlook the obvious. It was Jill who pointed out the truth. 'Rafael's loaded to the gunwales, Roland. You should have kept him away from the bar.'

'I tried,' Roland whined. 'I did the best I could, but I couldn't be everywhere at once, could I? I told Damian and Paul to keep an eye on him, but he was awful, especially to Damian.'

'So that's where Damian got his black eye,' Alex said. 'When I asked him, he said he'd run into "On the Horns of a Dilemma at Midnight". Which seemed entirely plausible,' he finished as he surveyed the art work in question, a pink phalluslike object ('Really, Roland,' Jill had said, 'somebody should tell Rafael that phalluses are passé') with a grandfather's clock painted on it and horns, both zoological and musical, protruding from it at odd angles. 'Which reminds me—' Alex glanced at the Gold Rolex on his slim olive wrist —'fascinating as Roland's speech is, I'm afraid I must tear myself away. I promised Tinsley I would be back early, and in her condition her every whim is my command. Since she has to keep up such a brave front at the office during the day, she feels she's entitled to go all Victorian of an evening.' For Tinsley was determined to work until the bitter end, less out of feminism, Susan thought, than because she did not quite trust Alex to keep his eye to the helm without her.

'Do make my apologies to anyone who's interested, Roland. I'll stop at the buffet and pick up some pickles. Do you provide doggie bags?'

'Pity your charming sister-in-law couldn't make it,' Roland observed, after Alex had gone, 'but naturally she would want to avoid crushes.'

'Of course it would be the ultimate act of creativity if she came to the opening and gave birth right here,' Jill said.

Roland tittered. 'That might do for the East Village perhaps but hardly for Madison Avenue.'

In point of fact, the DeMarnay Galleries were just off Madison, in one of the most opulent sections of this most opulent of cities, on the first floor of an elegant white limestone townhouse that Roland shared with Baltasar, who was about to establish a New York presence. 'It must be costing them both a fortune,' Jill had observed earlier, 'even if they're only renting. I understand Baltasar's a well-established couturier abroad, and he must be well fixed, but Roland's just a third-rate dealer, minor old masters, major modern disasters. Where would he get that kind of bread?'

'Maybe somebody's backing him,' Susan suggested, hoping it wasn't Alex, although he'd hardly be able to do that without Tinsley's knowledge, and Tinsley would know better than to invest their own or their clients' money in so dubious a venture. But what did Susan herself know about such things? Art was big business these days; possibly Roland's gallery was a sound investment. The location was good and the gallery itself a handsome showcase for any kind of art.

On the other hand, Roland himself did not impress her as a sound investment at all. I shouldn't let his appearance prejudice me, she told herself. Many of our most successful entrepreneurs look equally sleazy.

'More likely he borrowed the money from some sucker,' Jill said. 'Or—'

'Or what?' Susan asked.

'Oh, I don't know. Took out a bank loan, maybe.'

But Susan felt sure that wasn't what she had started to say.

Rafael had begun chanting in a language that Susan couldn't identify. Perhaps it was Indian; she'd heard Rafael had Aztec or Incan or something like that blood. If Peter had been there, she reflected, he would have been able to identify the language and to tell them more about it than anyone wanted to hear;

so perhaps it was just as well that he was away in Canada, teaching at the University of Saskatchewan, the only post he'd been able to get after his return from that ordeal in South America. Not that there was anything wrong with the University of Saskatchewan, an excellent institution, but he would have preferred somewhere closer to New York. And so would she. On the other hand, in Saskatchewan he couldn't be much further from the Indian tribe he'd been studying unless he went to the North Pole.

That suited him perfectly. For months after his return, he had awakened night after night screaming in a strange language, causing Susan distress and loss of sleep. She hoped that once he had settled down in his job he would not attempt to go out in the field again, this time wanting to turn his anthropological attentions to the Eskimos. She believed they had harpoons and would not hesitate to use them.

'Far be it from me to tell you your business, Roland,' Jill said, 'but don't you think you'd better turn Rafael off? People are beginning to laugh and once they start laughing at an artist it's only a matter of time before they start laughing at his work.

'You simply don't understand, Jill,' Roland said. 'His work is intended to be witty and amusing, even a trifle cheeky, but it is true, Rafael has spoken long enough.'

He started for the platform. But, before he could reach the artist, Rafael stopped in mid-chant and crumpled to the carpet with a thud that seemed to shake the entire gallery.

CHAPTER 3

Although the ambiance had lightened with Rafael's removal from the scene, the party had improved only by omission. Susan found herself growing bored, and so apparently did Jill. 'Well, now that the fun is over, time for us to fade into the sunset. Speaking of which, the evening is still young. Why don't I gather up Charlie or somebody and we can go on a club crawl. Unless you want to stay and circulate?'

It was clear that if Susan elected to stay and circulate, Jill felt it was her duty to stay and circulate with her.

'My only complaint,' Susan had told Hal, a few months after she'd signed with Jill, 'is that she seems to think she's my nursemaid as well as my rep. I can't seem to go anywhere without having her dogging my footsteps.'

To which Hal had smiled and said, 'She probably thinks you're so . . . unworldly you need looking after.'

Unworldly, indeed! How surprised both Jill and Hal would be if they knew how she had been making her living for the past few years. No, they wouldn't be surprised. They simply wouldn't believe it.

'Perhaps Jill is a bit overprotective,' Hal conceded. 'You need a chance to . . . er . . . spread your wings and fly on your own.'

She'd fancied he was about to suggest a trial flight in his company, but she never knew, because just then Jill had interrupted, as she always interrupted—deliberately, Susan sometimes thought. But why? To protect Susan from Hal? To protect Hal from Susan? Or was it simply that she had the instincts of a mother hen?

She was doing her mother-hen bit now. 'Thanks for the invitation,' Susan said, 'but I feel a little tired. I think I'll just go home.'

Jill nodded with an excess of understanding. 'I know. It must have been a rough day for you.'

Susan wasn't in the least tired; she was just bored. However, the prospect of being hauled by Jill and one of her young men from one disco to another seemed even more boring. Shortly after she'd become Jill's client, Peter had been called to a job interview in the South, leaving Susan tickets to an art film they had planned to see together. She went with Jill. She'd been under the impression that it was going to be an art film about chimpanzees. Instead, it was a film about chimpanzee art—all the arts, including music and the dance. The chimpanzees beat on hollow logs; they screamed; they stomped. Jill was enchanted. 'They'd go great at the Palladium,' she said.

Susan had agreed. Only Jill had meant her observation as a compliment. Susan had not.

So she left the gallery at the same time as Jill, but not with her. She half expected Roland to make a fuss when they made their farewells; however, although he expressed polite regret at her early departure (and none at all about Jill's), he made no effort to persuade her to stay. Rafael's collapse might have enlivened the party for everyone else, but it had spoiled it for Roland.

As she left, Susan couldn't help but gaze wistfully at the floral arrangements. Even if she stayed to the end, though, she had been forbidden to make off with them. 'That's tacky,' Jill had said when she caught Susan taking a bunch of bouquets at the conclusion of an earlier festivity. 'Even Eloise Charpentier doesn't stoop to that. If you want flowers, why, for heaven's sake, don't you just go out and buy them? At seventy-five thou and up per picture, depending on size and subject, you certainly can afford it.' Susan was well aware that she could afford all the floral arrangements she wanted—or needed, rather, for she was primarily a painter of flowers although she had expanded in new directions ever since changing her professional outlook. It was just that she appreciated them more if she picked them up herself.

Eloise Charpentier came out of the gallery right after them. 'Anybody going my way?' she asked brightly. One of the richest women in the world, she never paid for a taxi—or anything else—if she could help it.

'I'm going uptown,' Susan said, 'but I'm walking.'

'I'm going downtown,' Jill said, 'and I'm taking the subway.' Eloise looked disappointed. 'Oh, I'm going—er —east,' she said, 'so I'll bid you ladies good night.'

'I'm surprised that you didn't take a cab especially so you could give her a lift.'

'Normally I would,' Jill said, 'but it's been a rough night.'

The phone rang so early the next morning Susan thought it must be Peter having worked out the time differential incorrectly again. However, it was Alex with news. 'Rafael went into a coma last night and died before they could get him to a hospital. Roland called me up at the crack of dawn to tell me about it. He was positively gibbering—seems to take it as a personal affront.'

'Did somebody poison him?'

'Somebody's certainly going to do something drastic to him if he keeps carrying on like this . . . Oh, you mean Rafael?' Alex laughed. 'Of course not, it was a perfectly natural death—a perfectly natural accidental death, anyhow. Apparently Rafael drank a couple of gallons or so of whisky, and then shot himself up with heroin, which would have killed a moose, except that a moose would have more sense than to mix drugs and drink.'

'Was Rafael a drug addict?'

'I haven't the least idea. Why do you ask? Why do you care? I've always felt you needed a hobby, but I didn't expect you to start making an avocation out of sudden death. Death is like sex, you know. To kill is one thing, but to be a voyeur of death quite another. I never figured you for a voyeuse, Susan.'

'Don't be silly, Alex. I can't help being interested. After all, I was there.'

'So was I. So were a lot of other people. I'm sure they're all talking about nothing else. So far as I can tell, and I've read the morning papers, nobody so much has hinted it was murder—which is what you seem to have in mind.'

'Somebody could have deliberately injected him with heroin.'

'Why is it so hard for you to believe that he didn't inject himself?'

There was no reason at all why Rafael should not have injected himself. Not with suicidal intent—he'd been too boorishly triumphant in his gloating over glories to come —but without realizing that he was taking too much of everything. Many people had died of overdoses of heroin. Hadn't the artist Darius Moffatt died of a heroin overdose back in the seventies? Or had it been cocaine? No, cocaine hadn't been that potent then.

When Susan had been a hit woman, she'd never employed poison herself. The nature of her work had required immediate public recognition of the fact that each death was brought about by design and with lofty moral purpose. However, she had often thought that if one's aim was simply to get rid of someone without making a statement, poison would be quiet, efficient, and, providing you didn't go in for one of the imported alkaloids, economical. And, of course, a lethal dose of a narcotic would be poison: a lethal dose of anything would be poison.

She remained curious enough to follow the news accounts of Rafael's death. The post-mortem showed that the heroin Rafael had used was 'black tar', an unusually potent type from Mexico that had been sweeping the United States and had caused numerous fatalities, even among hardened addicts. The drug came from Mexico and Rafael came from Mexico; at any rate, he had been living and working there. Everything seemed to fit together. As for whether or not Rafael was a habitual drug user, there was no way of knowing. According to the newspapers, his arms were so covered with the nicks and scratches that were the normal accompaniment of the various crafts he used in his art that needlemarks might not have shown.

There seemed to be no ground at all for her suspicions. Even the most unlovable of us, she reminded herself, generally die of natural or accidental causes. Just because Rafael Hoffmann had been murder-worthy did not mean he had been murdered.

The death was officially posted as an accident and the city health commissioner took the opportunity to make a speech before a local civic organization warning against the dangers of drug use by the city's artists and artisans, although he was handicapped by the universal awareness that cocaine was currently the drug of choice among the members of the city's creative community. People weren't taking the drug problem seriously enough, he said.

'Obviously he hasn't heard about our Grand Gala,' Mimi Hunyadi said afterwards, and put him on her mailing list.

*

23

Susan was browbeaten into attending Rafael's funeral along with Alex, Roland, and Jill. There weren't too many mourners besides them: some of the young men from the gallery, Baltasar, Sanchia Guttierez, and a melancholy man with a drooping moustache who was introduced as her husband and seemed to speak no English. It snowed a little, as if Nature had started to add a touch of pathos to a scene deficient in that quality and gave up without really trying. Some of the flowers looked suspiciously like the bouquets Susan had passed up at the opening.

The DeMarnay Gallery closed for a week out of respect for the artist. When it reopened with what was now termed 'The Rafael Hoffmann Memorial Exhibit', everything sold immediately, which was to have been expected. Since the artist could work no more, his works automatically became more desirable. What was surprising was the amount of money they fetched.

'If you ask me,' Jill said, 'Roland didn't delay the opening out of respect for Rafael; he did it so he could go around and jack up all the prices.'

But wasn't that more or less what Jill had done with the second Darius Moffatt show, when she'd owned that little gallery in Soho? The Lord knew where she'd gotten the money to start it. She'd been fresh out of City College, she'd told Susan, and without assets or experience. She must have borrowed it, Susan thought, or been backed by a boyfriend.

The situation wasn't quite the same because Moffatt had been dead for some time when the first show opened, but, after its success, Jill had doubled—or was it tripled? —the prices for the second. It was simply a matter of sound economics, and just went to show that Roland was a better businessman than he looked.

'Well, at least there will be a nice little sum for the widow,' he said.

Susan was surprised to hear that there was a widow. The biographical essay had made no mention of a spouse. The bereaved Mrs Hoffmann, Roland said, lived in Mexico and had never been out of it in her life.

'I wanted to fly Lupe to New York for the opening, but

24

Rafael said no. He said she would feel out of place here, that she was just a simple peasant woman unaccustomed to the sophisticated life of the metropolis. I'm afraid he was ashamed of her.'

'Ashamed of her!' Jill exploded. '*He* had the gall to—!'

'Now, now, *de mortuis* and all that. I know it seems ridiculous that a . . . a rough diamond like Rafael should feel embarrassed by anyone else's behaviour, but we all have our little self-deceptions, don't we?' And Roland looked fixedly at Jill, who bit her lip and remained silent.

Susan remained silent too, although there were a number of questions she would have liked to ask. Why had Rafael's body not been sent back to Mexico or his native country for burial? Or at least why hadn't Roland arranged to have Lupe flown up for the funeral, since this time Rafael was in no position to object? It's none of my business, she told herself, resolving to get Alex aside and see if he could find out the answers.

However, Alex professed to know nothing at all about Rafael's private life, in fact very little about Rafael himself. 'I knew him only through Roland,' he said, 'and I don't know Roland all that well. We got acquainted because he used to sell pictures to the General from time to time. But we never really . . . palled around—is that the right expression? I like girls and he likes boys, and never the twain shall meet.'

She didn't believe that Alex's acquaintance with Roland was as slight as he professed. Granted that Alex was definitely heterosexual and Roland apparently homosexual, that did not prevent them from being friends, and it certainly did not keep them from having been mixed up in shady deals together. Or unshady deals, but shady seemed more likely. She remembered Hal's once saying that some of General Chomsky's acquisitions had proved to be forgeries, and wondered whether Roland—and possibly Alex, in the days before he had turned respectable—had been involved with them. Not that it mattered. If a collector couldn't tell the real thing from a fake, why waste the real thing on him?

She was surprised to learn that it was Baltasar who had bought the bulk of Rafael's works; she'd thought he had far better taste. However, it seemed that he was already a patron of Rafael's, having purchased some of the artist's works several years before, for his Acapulco salon.

'I felt the harsh aggressiveness of the pieces would provide an effective contrast to the elegant fluidity of my gowns,' he told Susan. 'Now, after the tragedy, I thought it would be appropriate to place his work in my salon here, as a permanent memorial to a genius that never did achieve its full potential.'

But ill luck seemed to follow anything to do with Rafael Hoffmann. His pieces were still in the gallery when a careless workman dropped a cigarette into a can of combustible material and the whole place went up in flames.

Luckily, the fire department was able to put them out before they could spread to Baltasar's part of the building. However, the works of an unfortunate artist whom Roland was planning to feature in his next show were ruined by smoke and water. Although, as Roland (rather cruelly, it seemed to Susan) pointed out, he would get more from the insurance than he could ever have hoped to gain from the sale of his works, he remained inconsolable. As for Rafael's pieces, they were totally destroyed.

CHAPTER 4

Some weeks after these events had taken place, Susan went out to dinner with a former colleague from the European-American Academy. Normally Susan would never have agreed to have dinner with Hortense Pomeroy, who, as a gym teacher (or games mistress as the Academy's brochure had it) had inhabited an entirely different sphere. A drink at most. However, Susan was feeling low. Hal Courtenay had called to cancel a dinner engagement he had with her and Jill for the ostensible purpose of discussing an artists' seminar to be held under the Museum's aegis.

Susan was interested in participating, because, as she told Jill, she felt she ought to become more a part of the comtemporary art world, rather than hold herself aloof as Jill seemed to want her to do. Jill denied any such thing. 'You're just paranoid. I am not deliberately trying to keep you away from other artists. Go to Hal's tacky little seminar if you want to. Spoil the image I'm trying to build up for you.'

In this particular instance, however, Susan was less interested in making herself a part of the art world than in making herself part of Hal's world. She found herself growing more and more interested in him. Not only was he one of the handsomest men she had ever met, but she had so much more in common with him than with any other man she knew—background, interests, even a bit of shared past; for it turned out that he'd been a classmate of Susan's at the Hudson. She hadn't recognized him when Mimi first introduced them at the Chomsky Memorial Exhibition, and he'd had to remind her. Who would have dreamed that the weedy, rather obnoxious adolescent could have developed into this suave, distinguished-looking scholar, with an accent—apparently acquired during his studies abroad—that was even fruitier than Roland's. He, however, claimed to have recognized her the instant he saw her again. 'I could never have forgotten you, Susan, even after twenty years.'

'Closer to thirty.'

'Ah, well, we were both very young then.'

'Do you still paint at all any more?' she asked.

He'd shaken his head with a mournful smile. 'I soon discovered that I had a certain technical facility, but no real talent. So I went back to Harvard, took my degrees in art history and became a hanger-on of the art world. Because that's all curators and critics and connoisseurs really are—art groupies. Unable to create, we worship at the muse's feet and sometimes, rendered mean-spirited by our inadequacies, nibble at her toes.'

She had an idea that she had read the same words

somewhere in one of his magazine pieces. Either that, or she was going to.

Despite the fact that Jill would be there, Susan had looked forward to that dinner. And now Hal said he had to fly to Houston to look at a reputed Whistler that had mysteriously turned up there and had to be inspected in a hurry, because the owner was impatient to sell.

'I'm sure it's a wild goose chase,' Hal told Susan over the phone. 'What would an unknown Whistler be doing in Houston? But I must go. Part of my job, you know.' There was amusement in his voice. Everyone knew museum directors didn't have jobs. They held positions.

Unreasonable of her to feel so disappointed, even after he said, 'I'll call you just as soon as I get back and perhaps we could have dinner without Jill; everything doesn't have to include Jill, does it?'

Wasn't that what she'd wanted? Yes, but he's just saying that, she told herself; he doesn't mean it, and even if he does ask me to dinner without Jill, she said to herself severely, I shouldn't accept because of Peter. Not that Peter would mind if she went to dinner with another man. It would never occur to him that Susan could be seriously interested in any man besides himself.

Susan couldn't help wondering about Hal's private life. His public life, of course, was a matter of record. A biography of him had been included in the Museum's Annual Report, together with a pipe-in-mouth picture that made Jill snigger every time she saw it—which might have been the reason why he'd apparently given up smoking.

Susan didn't like to ask questions about Hal. She didn't want anyone to get the idea that she was interested in him personally. Fortunately it took very little encouragement to get Mimi Hunyadi to tell all she knew about everyone who had the slightest connection with the Museum. Unfortunately it took a lot to stop Mimi, so Susan also had to listen to detailed accounts of the lurid (if Mimi were to be believed) lives led by the other members of the Board of Trustees, and in which she didn't take the least interest, although she never would have believed it of Ariel Slocum.

As for Hal, it seemed that he had left the Hudson to marry Cecily Flicker, who must have been at least twenty-five years his senior. She had financed Hal's studies, first at Harvard, then Oxford, and the Sorbonne. When he hit thirty, he became too old for her and she dumped him for a twenty-year-old minimalist. The parting was amicable and the settlement must have been substantial; otherwise, Mimi observed, he would hardly have been able to live as well as he did on a museum director's salary. His handsome apartment on Park Avenue belonged to the MAA, of course, but he also had a house in the Hamptons, a farm in Connecticut, 'And a villa somewhere or other—a Greek island, I think, although it might be Italian. One always thinks of the isles of Greece, but there are isles of Italy, too. Any country with a coast is apt to have islands.'

'He must be very comfortably off,' Susan said, not wanting to use a vulgar word like *rich*.

'Oh, Cissy was always very generous with her ex-husbands. After all, what else did she have to spend her money on?'

Neither Mimi nor the biography mentioned any subsequent wives, but if there had been any in the past, obviously there was none current or she would have been required to appear at Museum and related festivities. Rumour had it that he'd been involved with Peggy Guggenheim at one time, but then who hadn't? Sometimes Susan fancied she saw Eloise Charpentier look at him possessively, but then Eloise looked at everything possessively. When your family owns so much of the world it's easy to forget they don't own all of it.

When Hal had introduced Susan to Jill at an MAA benefit, Susan thought for a fleeting moment from the proprietary way he put his arm around the girl that there might be something between them. Then she decided there couldn't be, or Jill would scarcely have brought one or another of her young men to places where Hal was likely to turn up. She couldn't have been attempting to flaunt them in his face, because they were not the kind of young men to arouse jealousy in even the most insecure bosom. In the roughly two years that Susan had known Jill, the girl had run through at least half a dozen men. 'Searching for true love,' she had once explained to Susan, on imagining she discerned a raised eyebrow—which was not the case. Jill had merely been projecting the middle-class standards to which she'd been born, not understanding that in Susan's original milieu anything went that didn't frighten the horses. The trouble was that most of Jill's young men would by their appearance alone frighten any horse worthy of his oats. I must not be judgmental, Susan thought. Maybe Jill can't do any better.

Certainly Hal and Jill had known each other for a long time. They had met, she knew, after the first Darius Moffatt show, when Hal's enthusiastic review in *Muse* had launched the artist on a posthumous road to success.

But that must have been nine—no, ten—years ago. Had Jill and Hal become lovers then or later or never? Although curious to the point of nosiness about everyone else's affairs, Jill was reticent about her own past; and Susan was too entrenched in the mores of a more gracious era to do more than give vent to pointed hints, which were ignored with equal pointedness.

Hortense had rung up with her invitation soon after Hal had called to cancel his, and Susan had accepted, perhaps to punish herself for having thought of Hal in a romantic light. Ridiculous, at her age. Not that love and even sex were inappropriate for intelligent adults, but romance was strictly for teenagers and idiots.

However, the punishment she had inflicted on herself proved to be crueller and more unusual than she had anticipated. Like most gym teachers, Hortense considered herself a physical fitness expert, and, like most physical fitness experts, she was a bore. Susan was bitter, yes, but she had reason to be. Hortense had told Susan they were going to eat at a place called Sprouts 'n Stuff, and said, 'My treat,' before Susan had a chance to ask for a change of venue. Treat, indeed, Susan thought, as she studied the menu morosely.

Hortense had the athlete's typical disdain of subtlety. Hardly had they finished their zucchini zingers and started on their seaweed and soy lasagne when she started making her pitch. She was organizing a health club for middle-aged women and she wanted Susan's help.

'Seems to me there are plenty of health clubs around already,' Susan said, more brusquely than was her wont, but she resented having been put in the position of appearing in public with a lady of mature years and Wagnerian proportions who chose to attire herself in lavender sneakers, baggy purple pantaloons, an oversized greenish yellow shirt jacket, and a pink beret. The fact that this made Hortense in no way remarkable among the clientèle of Sprouts 'n Stuff did nothing to allay Susan's peevishness.

'Yes, but all of these health clubs are aimed at the young or the would-be young, and you know how distressing it is for the average middle-aged woman with the average middle-aged shape to have to work out alongside those skinny young things in their skimpy leotards.'

Susan didn't know, since she had never felt the least desire to 'work out' herself, stoutly resisting Jill's efforts to make her join in a morning jog. 'I myself run,' Jill had said, 'but I'd gladly slow down to a jog for you.'

'But why restrict your club to middle-aged women?' Susan asked. 'Isn't that discriminatory? Surely there are middle-aged men equally in need of physical improvement.'

Hortense shook her head with a superior smile. She seemed to have more teeth than most people, or perhaps it was that nature had equipped her with a set designed for a horse rather than a member of the human race. 'My dear, most middle-aged men who work out at health clubs go there specifically to look at the young girls jiggling around in those skimpy leotards—hopefully more than look at. Men are masters of self-deception. They see the sags and bulges of their wives as disfigurements, but regard their own paunches and protuberances as no more than slight and almost endearing flaws.'

Susan remembered that there had been talk around the Academy that in youth Hortense had been crossed in love,

31

her fiancé having run off with a lady mud wrestler. At the time she had dismissed it as part of the bitchery endemic to the cloistered ambiance. Perhaps there had been some truth to the story after all. Not that there wasn't a certain amount of truth in what Hortense was saying. Maybe the fault lies in my own upbringing, Susan thought. I still haven't accepted the idea that now women have acquired some power they can be allowed to age as ungracefully as men.

And, to be fair, men should be allowed to have face lifts without the kind of snide remark Jill had made about Hal. Why shouldn't Hal have had his face lifted if he felt the need? Not that Susan believed he had done any such thing. Some people simply aged better than others. I really must stop thinking of Hal, she thought. At least in that way.

'Anyhow,' Hortense was continuing, 'women of our age prefer to suffer and sweat in an all-female atmosphere, revealing ourselves in our glory to the opposite sex only after we have achieved our full physical potential.'

Hortense apparently felt she had achieved her full physical potential and was revealing herself to the world in all her glory. Susan wondered if Hortense were planning to use herself as an advertisement. If so, she was definitely not going to have anything to do with her health club.

'At first we didn't want to use the term "middle-aged" in our promotional literature, but we ran up against semantic difficulties. Today "adult" means dirty, and "mature" over the hill, so, since we didn't have much choice, we decided to be frank and open about it.' Hortense flung open her jacket to reveal a massive bosom draped in a pink T-shirt bearing the slogan, 'I'm Glad I'm a Muppie'.

'You're glad you're a *what*?'

'A Muppie. Middle-aged Urban Professional. As opposed to Yuppie—Young Urban Professional.' Hortense whinnied with laughter. 'Don't you think that's darling?'

'No, I do not. And I thought the U in Yuppie stood for—' Susan winced —'upwardly mobile.'

'"Upscale" in the case of Muppies, because by that age they'll have moved as far as they're likely to go. And the club certainly isn't going to be cheap. It's a very solid business proposition or I wouldn't have dreamed of bringing it to the attention of a busy professional woman like you.'

As if I were a dentist or an account executive, Susan thought, unreasonably irked. 'It could be inexpensive and still profitable,' she said.

'Now that you're rich, Susan, you can afford to be liberal. But those of us who have to work for a living have to take a more conservative approach.'

'I work for a living.'

'Oh, well, painting. You can hardly call that work.' Hortense went on quickly, in case she had given offence, which she had, 'We have a first-class group of instructors lined up, real pros, and, in addition to the usual aerobics, Nautilus machines, and so on—all geared to the specific requirements of the woman past forty—we're planning to offer some very unusual courses. For instance, Lady Daphne Merriwether has come back after spending years in the Himalayas—you know, where they used to practise polyandry, so a girl really had to be on her toes—with a really effective system of self-defence for ladies. "Nothing flashy, no threatening gestures or loud cries but simple low-key disablement, and, if need be, dismemberment, with a minimal extrusion of unpleasant body fluids, such as blood." I'm quoting from the prospectus, of course.'

'I rather thought you might be. Does this system have a name?'

'The Merriwether Method. As I've said, there's nothing showy or vulgar about it, and none of that psychological claptrap about releasing one's aggressions. It's completely functional: you hit me; I kill you. You must meet Lady Daphne. I know you'd like her, both of you coming out of the top drawer, as Lady Daphne herself might say.'

'I look forward to meeting her,' Susan said politely. 'However—'

'Since you're in the age group we're appealing to, and since you're doing so well now, I'm sure you'll want to invest in such a worthwhile as well as potentially profitable undertaking. In a way it's your duty.' She added temptingly, 'As soon as we're well under way, we could extend our range to include those of more modest means, even offer scholarships to the truly deserving. I daresay bag ladies stand as much in need of the Merriwether Method as the more privileged. We could call them the Melville Scholars and have a back door for them to come into the club by.'

It's not fair for her to appeal to my sense of duty, Susan thought. For people with her background and upbringing, the word 'duty' was like a trumpet to a warhorse. And Hortense knew it. She'd been exposed to enough of the Academy's fund-raising schemes to know how to arouse the guilt feelings in old money, and even though Susan's money was now new, she still had the old-money instincts.

'Here, let me give you some copies of our prospectus. Your friends might also be interested in investing.'

She handed Susan a surprisingly bulky envelope.

She whinnied. 'Tell your brother, the stockbroker, that, although men can't join the club, we're only too happy to accept their money.'

Susan wondered whether, once the club was under way, she might not take a course or two with Lady Daphne. She needed something to take the place of her shooting sessions with Alex. She missed them. Of course there was no longer any need for her to keep in practice, but she felt that once you had a skill you ought to keep it viable. You never knew when it might come in handy again. However, General Chomsky's estate was no longer available to them for target practice. The land had been sold and the art collection removed with all except the choicest items placed in storage while the Museum prepared a permanent home for them—something that, thanks to the General's will, it could now afford.

'The problem,' Hal Courtenay had confided in her, as he was giving her a private peep at the Cassatts prior to their public unveiling, 'is that our name is the Museum of *American* Art, while a number of the finest pieces in the collection are by foreign artists. The Board hasn't decided whether to try to get a zoning variation, enlarge the entire building, and rename it "The American Museum of Art" or to put up a separate but connecting building and call it "The Chomsky

Addition to the Museum of American Art", which would be considerably more expensive and mean we'd have to give up the parking lot. Meanwhile, we're going through the collection and deaccessioning the duds. The General made some very strange purchases as well as—' he smiled at her —'some very perspicacious ones. Your work in particular.'

She tried not to simper.

'Some, I fear, are out-and-out fakes.'

'The General bought fakes?' She was surprised. Of course she knew General Chomsky hadn't known anything about art, but she would have thought that as a good businessman he would have taken care to have his purchases vetted by someone who did.

'There are bound to be works of questionable authenticity in any major collection. Even experts have been fooled, you know. The Metropolitan has had its share of forgeries— more than its share, some would say,' he added with a meaning smile, for he had made no secret of the fact that he did not think much of the direction in which the Met had been going in recent years.

CHAPTER 5

Even though Susan and Hortense had dined at six— Hortense being a firm believer in early feeding—night had already fallen by the time Susan finally managed to detach herself. It was a pleasant evening in early spring, and, perhaps subliminally influenced by all Hortense's talk of fitness, Susan chose to walk the dozen or so blocks to her apartment.

Her route brought her past the DeMarnay Gallery, which had been closed to the public for almost a month now. Most of the neighbourhood—if you could call so elegant an ambiance by so plebeian a word as neighbourhood—shops were closed; most of the residents were presumably still at dinner. For a couple of minutes the street was deserted except for herself and a young man who emerged from the shadows under the front steps of the DeMarnay Gallery, came into the sunken area beyond, and mounted the steps that led to street level. She would have thought nothing of this except that, instead of opening the gate in the iron fence that separated the areaway from the street, he was climbing over it.

He seemed to be taking no particular care to avoid attracting attention, which would have been difficult for him to do, in any case, as he was accompanied by a beagle who was determined not to leave the areaway. Something under the front steps was fascinating him, and he had to be hoisted forcibly over the fence, struggling all the time.

The young man caught Susan's eye and grinned cheerfully. He gestured towards the massive padlock that fastened the gate. 'Forgot my key,' he said. It was not, Susan thought, an adequate explanation.

The young man set the dog down on the sidewalk. Losing interest in whatever fascinations lay down below, he rushed over to Susan and sniffed her with embarrassing thoroughness. Then, with a short, disappointed woof, he returned to his master.

'Don't let Brucie give you a feeling of rejection,' the young man said. 'He has very low tastes.'

Susan felt she should do something. But what? There were a few people on the street now, but no one had been there to see the young man make so unconventional an exit from the premises. It would be his word against hers, unless he told the truth, which was hardly likely. Anyhow, why should she care if somebody was burglarizing Roland's—or possibly Baltasar's—premises?

In the light of the street lamp, the young man certainly did not look like a burglar. However, these days when law-abiding citizens dressed like riffraff, malefactors might very well choose three-piece suits and ties. He had light hair cut rather short and an attractive, snub-nosed face of the all-American kind that used to prevail among movie leading men before sinister ethnic types became the fashion, and still could be seen in advertising, extolling wholesome products like cornflakes and mouthwash.

She looked down into the areaway. In the dimness, she could see boards and lumpy shapes under a tarpaulin, all presumably connected with the workmen who were renovating the place. There was also a grille which, from its size and shape, appeared to have been intended to close off the archway under the steps. However, instead of fulfilling its function, it was leaning against an adjacent wall.

Could the young man have gotten inside the house that way? No, there would be a door under the front steps as well as the grille.

She felt she should say something. 'The gallery's closed, you know. There's nobody around.'

'So I discovered.' He gave her a bright smile. 'Do you have any idea when the reopening's planned?'

'No, I'm afraid I don't.'

'I understand there was a fire.'

'Yes, there was.'

'Luckily there doesn't seem to have been any damage —to the exterior anyway. Except for those boarded-up windows, you couldn't tell anything had happened.'

As they turned to look at the windows, they saw, through a gap between the boards, a light go on. 'I see we were both wrong,' the young man said. 'Somebody is up there after all.'

'Perhaps you'd like to go back in. Only I'd suggest that this time you use the front door.'

'Oh, I don't think I'll bother. It's getting late and neither Brucie nor I have had our dinner. Another time perhaps.'

A cat emerged from the shadows under the steps. Apparently feeling secure now that man and dog were on the other side of the fence, it came halfway up the steps and hissed at them. The green-studded gold collar identified the animal: Baltasar's Esmeralda.

Brucie barked and attempted to squeeze through the bars back into the areaway. The young man snapped a leash on his collar. 'Come along, boy,' he said. 'Cats are not your game.'

He raised his hand to Susan in half salute. 'Have a nice

evening,' he said and strolled off with Brucie, looking like any honest citizen walking his dog.

Susan knew she should do *something*—at least ring the bell and advise whoever was inside of what she had seen. But she didn't know who might be inside. Perhaps this malefactor had left on discovering that the premises were already occupied by another, more dangerous one. It was true that someone who had no right to be there was hardly likely to answer the bell, but in New York anything was possible.

In the end she went home and called Alex for counsel. 'I wouldn't worry,' he said. 'Roland knows some very peculiar people.' Actually the young man had not looked at all peculiar, which was what made his behaviour especially strange.

'Then you don't think I should have called the police and told them about it?'

'You don't want to call the police,' he said. And he was right. She didn't. 'Anyhow, it's too late for that now. But if it would make you feel better give Roland a ring and tell him about it.'

That sounded like an excellent solution. Roland could decide for himself what, if anything, he wanted done about his nocturnal visitor. And, if he couldn't make up his mind, then the burden of indecision would rest upon him. 'Where is he staying?' she asked. 'What's his phone number?'

'Didn't you know? He has an apartment on one of the upstairs floors of the gallery building.'

'But surely it isn't habitable now.'

'He told me he's managed to get the place back into livable shape—lucky for him, as he's too broke to afford a hotel. He put everything he had into the gallery.'

'But doesn't Baltasar own the building? Why is Roland living there, then?'

'They were both supposed to live there at the beginning. Since the building is zoned for both residential and business use, it seemed like a practical idea. Baltasar has an apartment there, too, on the top floor; there's a sort of penthouse up there, Roland tells me. It was scheduled to be finished

38

by the time the gallery was opened, but apparently it didn't get done in time. So he's still at the Plaza. Lord knows when he'll ever be able to move into the apartment now.'

So the light she saw must have been in Roland's apartment—which still didn't explain the mysterious young man.

The gallery's phone rang and rang. She was beginning to think that either she'd been wrong and no one was there, or that Roland had a private number and wasn't answering the listed one. Finally she heard the sound of the receiver's being picked up, followed by heavy breathing. It's the caller who's supposed to do the heavy breathing, she thought, not the callee.

'Hello,' she said.

The only answer was a giggle. It didn't sound like Roland's.

'This is Susan Melville,' she said. 'I'd like to speak to Roland DeMarnay.'

There was the sound of whispering and more giggling. 'She wants to speak to Roly Poly,' a muffled voice sniggered.

The gigglers and whisperers—there seemed to be several of each—receded. Silence for a minute; then the sound of footsteps approaching, a clattering sound, and a sharp cry as the approacher fell over something. Somebody, not the faller, laughed; and somebody, presumably the faller—this did sound like Roland—swore.

Roland's voice came on the other end of the line, speaking very slowly and carefully. 'Shoo—Shoosan Melville. What a delightful shurprise.'

He was obviously drunk or on something, and it was none of her concern. 'I don't want to worry you,' she said, 'but I think there's something you ought to know.'

She told her story as succinctly as possible, because somebody in close proximity to Roland was making bubbling noises. 'I know it's probably nothing,' she finished, 'but—er—Alex thought I ought to tell you about it.'

Roland pulled himself together enough to master most of his consonants. 'Oh, it's something. Everything's something. Nothing is nothing.'

'Tha's really profound, Rollie,' a voice from behind him said.

'That's rollie profound, Really,' another voice added. Both voices giggled with glee.

'Are you going to call the police?' she asked.

'Oh, I don't think that's nesh—nesheshary.' He took a deep breath and enunciated his words very carefully. 'I know it's an imposition, but I would appreciate it if you could come over and show me exactly where you shaw—saw that man come out.'

He gave a faint shriek. 'Not now, you idiot!' he said in an undertone. 'Sorry,' he said to Susan. 'I don't mean tonight, of course; it's late and I have . . . uh . . . gueshts.'

There was a mad outbreak of giggling and one demoniac laugh. His voice became partly muffled, as if he had placed his hand inaccurately over the mouthpiece. 'Shut up, you bloody fools; this is important.'

Then, to Susan, 'Sorry again, I was talking to . . . to . . .' He seemed afflicted by a momentary aphasia.

'Your guests,' she finished helpfully.

'Right! If you could posh—possibly come over tomorrow and show me—tell me exactly what you saw—'

'Show and tell!' a voice burbled. 'What fun!'

'—I would be most grateful. Perhaps you would allow me to give you lunch. There are some other things I've been meaning to ask your advice about.'

'I already have a lunch date with Jill,' Susan said, pausing to give him the opportunity to include Jill in his invitation, but all he said was, 'Oh.'

'The gallery's not much out of our way. I'd be glad to stop off—say around eleven-thirty; Jill likes to eat early—and show you where I saw the man. Or I could come after lunch if that would be more convenient.'

'The earlier the merrier,' he said. 'And now, I'd better go check the door and make sure it's locked.'

'By the way,' Susan said, before he had a chance to hang up, 'does Baltasar know Esmeralda's down there in the areaway?'

'Eshmeralda?' Roland repeated. 'Eshmeralda who?'

40

'Baltasar's cat. He called her Esmeralda or something like that. You remember, she was there at the opening. I recognized her from her collar.'

'Oh, yes, his cat,' Roland said, as if he had trouble recollecting what a cat was. 'I'd better go out and collect her. I wonder how she got out there.'

'Maybe he lets her out at night,' Susan suggested. Then she remembered that Baltasar wouldn't be there to let Esmeralda out.

'Oh, he'd never do that. Those stones in her collar are real emeralds. First class all the way, that's Baltasar.' He didn't explain how it was that the cat was on the premises if Baltasar himself wasn't living there. Perhaps Roland was cat-sitting.

Later that evening Jill called to ask whether Susan would like to go to an auction of contemporary American art at Allardyce's on Wednesday. 'To the pre-sale exhibition in the morning; we don't have to go to the auction itself. The *Times* says one of the pictures up for sale is a Darius Moffatt. That's hardly likely, but I feel I should check it out. Interested?'

'Sure, why not.' Susan knew the prices that paintings fetched at auctions were important in setting future market prices, and, even though none of her work had or was likely to come up for auction any time soon, she felt she ought to keep up with these things. 'We can make definite arrangements tomorrow at lunch. We're going to have to make a stop first, though. I had a little adventure earlier this evening.'

'Met a handsome stranger, did you?'

'As a matter of fact, that's exactly what did happen.'

Once more she recounted the evening's events. Jill was a far more receptive audience than Alex, uttering little squeals and cries at appropriate points. 'So Roland's up to his old tricks again,' she observed after Susan had finished.

'What do you mean? What old tricks?'

'Carrying on with his friends like that,' Jill said quickly. 'But what do you suppose that guy was doing out there? And you actually spoke to him? Weren't you scared?'

It had never occurred to Susan to be frightened, but, now that Jill mentioned it, the man could have been dangerous. He hadn't looked like a killer, but then, Susan thought, neither do I. 'I hardly think a criminal would go skulking about with a dog. Especially not a beagle.'

'It doesn't seem likely. A Doberman would fit the picture much better. On the other hand, a Doberman would arouse instant suspicion.'

'Maybe he was just a nosy neighbour. I mean the man, not the dog. I hope I haven't alarmed Roland unnecessarily.'

'You can't alarm Roland unnecessarily. He needs to be shook up from time to time. Does him good.'

'He said he wasn't going to call the police,' Susan said.

'And spoil his party! Of course not. Anyhow, the man's gone. Even if Roland does find something missing, he might as well wait until morning. But I doubt that he'll find anything missing that he'd care to report to the police.'

'What do you mean?'

'I mean I doubt that he'll find anything missing. Glamour boy was probably just—what's the expression? —casing the joint. What I mean is who the hell cares if Roland was robbed? Serves him right for not asking me to lunch, too. He's a fantastic cook, you know. He should have opened a restaurant, but an art gallery was always his dream.'

'You seem to know him quite well,' Susan observed.

'Oh, in the art world everybody knows everybody else. Where shall I make our reservations for lunch?'

'Sprouts 'n Stuff,' Susan said. 'You'll love it.'

'*Where?*'

'Just a joke. We'll go to Leatherstocking's as usual. Wild gymnasts wouldn't drag me to Sprouts 'n Stuff again.'

She explained, expecting Jill to jeer at Hortense's project. But she'd forgotten that Jill was something of a health enthusiast herself. She approved of the idea. 'It might make a good investment. Health clubs are still very viable, and most of them aren't geared to the geriatric—to middle-aged women. Your friend—what's her name? Hortense? —just might have something there. Want me to look into it?'

'If you want to,' Susan said. 'I'll bring along the

42

prospectuses tomorrow and you can give the extras to your friends. I'm certainly not going to give them to mine.'

When she hung up she got the package of prospectuses with the intention of putting it on the table in her foyer so she'd remember to take it along the next day. The package had seemed unduly squishy. She opened it and saw why. In addition to a goodly supply of brochures, Hortense had enclosed a T-shirt with the 'I'm Glad I'm a Muppie' motto. Susan stuffed it back into the envelope. She would give that to Jill, too.

CHAPTER 6

There were plenty of signs of life about the DeMarnay Gallery next day as Susan and Jill approached. Workmen drifted in and out, carrying boards and pails and obscure implements of renovation. 'Hiya, Red!' one called to Jill and made a rude sucking noise with his lips.

She gave him such a dirty look that he advanced his pace from snail to turtle and disappeared into the building after one last languishing glance. The years may come and the years may go, Susan thought, but the American construction worker remains unchanging in his primaeval simplicity.

Jill expressed a similar thought aloud. 'Slime bag,' she said.

The two ladies climbed the short flight of steps that led to the massive front door, now restored to its original turn-of-the-century elegance—or perhaps it had never lost it. Other parts of Manhattan had their ups and downs; the strip between Fifth and Park Avenues from the sixties to the eighties had always been and probably always would be up. It was good to think there were some constants in this ever-changing, usually for the worse, city.

The door stood ajar. From inside came the merry sound of hammering, sawing, general banging, and voices raised in altercation. Jill would have walked right in, but, as the place wasn't officially open, Susan insisted on ringing the

43

bell, even though the disputants were standing in plain view in the foyer.

One was Roland, looking as if he rather than Esmeralda had been the one to be dragged in the night before, the other a handsome young woman with black hair streaming over her sable-clad shoulders. Susan could just imagine the effect she must have had on the workmen. The young woman—although she seemed to be about the same age as Jill, you would never think of calling her a girl—was stamping her booted foot, flashing her eyes, and otherwise exhibiting all the traditional signs of Latin temperament. 'I want my money,' she was saying, 'and I want it now!'

'But, Lupe, that's impossible. There are all sorts of legal formalities . . .'

At the sound of the bell and the sight of Susan and her companion, Roland smiled weakly and yanked at the open collar of his sports shirt, as if by pulling it together he could pull himself together. 'Susan, this is Lupe Hoffmann; Lupe, Susan Melville. And Jill Turkel,' he add grudgingly.

'Not Lupe Hoffmann,' the woman said, 'Lupe Montoya.' The rage vanished from her face as she turned to the two newcomers, to be replaced by a dazzling smile. 'I have never used any of my husbands' names. An artist must retain her own identity, don't you agree?'

'Definitely,' Jill said.

Lupe grasped both of Susan's hands in hers. She wore a great number of rings and had a very hearty grip. 'Susan Melville, I have heard so much about you. It is an honour and a privilege to meet so distinguished an artist.'

'You must be Rafael's wife,' Susan said, detaching her hands as sympathetically as possible. 'I'm so sorry about what happened to Rafael.'

'Pah, he was no good, as an artist and as a man. The world is better off without him.'

Although Susan couldn't have agreed with her more, she was a little shocked at the bereaved widow's forthrightness. I'm still the prisoner of my upbringing, she thought.

'But I should have been informed of his death,' Lupe said. 'I should have been advised of the funeral arrangements. I

44

should not have been left to read about it in the newspapers.'

'I certainly do agree,' Jill said. 'Why didn't you advise Lupe of the funeral arrangements, Roland?'

Roland's pale blue eyes looked waterier than ever. I do hope he's not going to burst into tears, Susan thought. 'I sent a telegram to Cancun,' he insisted. 'You can check with Western Union.'

'But I was not in Cancun,' she said. 'For the last six months I have been on tour in Australia. Everybody knew that.'

'Apparently nobody in Cancun did,' Roland said, 'or the telegram would have been forwarded.'

She simmered down a little. 'I have been travelling about a good deal. It is possible that it could have missed me,' she conceded. 'But Baltasar must have known I was not there.'

Roland looked guilty. 'I don't think I discussed your whereabouts with him. I just told him I was sending you a wire. Everything was in such a state—funeral arrangements and the gallery—and I had to cope with it all by myself.'

He looked around him for a sympathetic face and found none. Susan might have felt sorry for him if she hadn't recollected that he had Damian and Paul and other minions to help him cope.

'Rafael died months ago,' Jill said. 'How come you didn't get here until now?'

'Was Rafael a world-famous artist that the Australian papers should carry an account of his death on their front pages? No, it was not until I got to San Francisco, after cutting short my trip because they did not appreciate my art in Australia—such boors there, I tell you—and I went to pick up Fido and Rover (I had to leave them behind because of those stupid quarantine laws they have there) that I was told what had happened to Rafael.'

'I thought you said you read about it in the newspapers,' Jill pointed out.

'I never read the newspapers. As an artist, I am above such matters.'

*

There was a whirring sound. A door in the panelling of the wall opened, revealing a small elevator, from which Baltasar emerged, along with a small, bespectacled man carrying a clipboard. Baltasar wore a pullover and slacks that looked as if they had been designed for royalty; the other man was in shirt, vest, and trousers that looked as if he had slept in them. Both looked unhappy. They were followed by Esmeralda. She seemed to be in excellent spirits, weaving in and out of everybody's legs, carrying her tail erect like a flag.

'It is very discouraging, very,' Baltasar was saying. 'So much work to be done. I'm not sure I can afford it—emotionally, at least. And no amount of insurance could cover the cost of my gowns, and, of course, the Hoffmanns.'

'The Hoffmanns?' the little man repeated. 'Oh, yes, the art objects. Most regrettable.'

Baltasar's expression changed as he caught sight of the group in the foyer. 'My dear Susan, Jill, how nice to see you. And Lupe. What a lovely surprise.'

He kissed all the ladies' hands. Although he was a tall man, Lupe towered over him. Even if she had not been wearing stilt heels, she would still have topped him. This was a lady who obviously gloried in her physical proportions. Although Susan was beginning to do more and more figure work, Lupe was a subject she would not care to tackle. No matter how she painted her, Lupe was bound to come out looking like Wonder Woman. Leave her to Roy Lichtenstein.

'I was desolated not to see you at the funeral,' Baltasar said to Lupe, 'but not surprised. I know how things were between you and Rafael.'

'It is true that we had not spoken to each other for several years,' Lupe acknowledged, 'but I hope I know what is correct. No matter what the inconvenience, I would have made every effort to come to Rafael's funeral if I had been informed of it.'

Roland's voice rose to a whine. 'I didn't know she was in Australia. I wired Cancun. It was a mistake. I'm sorry. What more can I say?'

He was starting to say a good deal more when Baltasar

46

cut in gracefully, 'It was in part my fault. There was no reason why I should have assumed that you knew Lupe was in Australia. But, after all, what does it matter? Even if she had been able to come to the funeral it still would not have brought poor Rafael back.'

Susan expected Lupe to say something about the undesirability of bringing poor Rafael back, but she was silent. Apparently she was somewhat in awe of Baltasar. Susan could understand that. Although he might claim to be descended only from dukes, there was something definitely regal about him.

The man with the clipboard murmured something and disappeared through another little door in the panelling. Esmeralda stood on her hind legs and prepared to launch an attack on Lupe's boots. Baltasar bent over and picked her up. He turned to Susan. 'I must thank you for restoring my little Esmeralda to me. It worried me to have to keep leaving her here at night, but the Plaza does not accept pets. So uncivilized, so different from hotels in other countries. However, I thought she had been locked up securely.'

He certainly does have bad luck with his turnkeys, Susan thought, remembering that Esmeralda had made another unauthorized appearance on the night of the gallery opening.

'We had a prowler last night,' Roland said. 'I told you. I called you right away. Almost right away. This morning, anyhow. Susan—' he motioned towards her, as if by the gesture he was passing on some of the blame —'saw him. He must have let her out.'

'What I would like to know,' Baltasar said, 'was who let him in?'

Roland seemed to take this as an accusation. 'Prowlers don't have to be let in. They break in.'

'What about the alarm system?'

'The workmen had to disconnect it, so they could paint the grille. They said they wouldn't be able to put it back for a couple of days. I didn't think it mattered since there wasn't anything around now to—to interest a thief.'

Baltasar made a sound between his teeth that seemed to be the Spanish equivalent of 'Tcha!' 'Was there anything to show that anybody had actually broken in? Did you check?'

'Not exactly,' Roland admitted. 'I had to unlock the door when I went out to take Esmeralda in, so it must have been locked. But I didn't go out and actually look at the outside of the door. It was too dark.'

'There is a light under the stairs that can be turned on, I believe.'

'I didn't turn it on. I—I wasn't dressed. And I didn't look this morning. I figured I could wait until Susan came and we could look at it together.'

'In case something was waiting in the dark underneath the stairs, so it would get her first,' Jill put in.

'Jill, I don't think—' Susan tried to interrupt, but Jill continued, 'Anyhow, I don't see why you were so insistent that Susan come show you where and how it happened. Couldn't she just have given you the details over the phone? Why make her go to all this trouble?'

'No trouble at all,' Susan said. And it was true. Roland was merely an annoyance. It was Jill who was making trouble. 'As far as I could tell the man was just prowling. He may not have gotten in at all. Mightn't Esmeralda have sneaked out through an open window or something?'

'That must be it,' Roland said eagerly. 'I didn't think to look at the windows.'

'And you heard nothing?' Baltasar asked.

'I had the stereo on,' Roland said weakly.

Baltasar gave him a long look, then turned to Lupe. 'My dear, if there is anything I can do to help, please call on me.'

'That is what I am about to do. I am as a child when it comes to legal matters. Do you think I have grounds for a suit of law against Roland?' who uttered a protesting noise at this point, 'And how do I find out whether there is a life insurance policy?'

Baltasar patted her hand. 'Don't worry, Lupita. Leave it to me. I will see that everything is taken care of.'

*

'Well, shall we go take a look at the scene of the crime?'
Susan suggested, adding, 'Just a figure of speech,' as Roland
gave her a reproachful look.

Leaving Baltasar and Lupe, together with Esmeralda, in
the foyer, Susan, trailed by Jill, went out with Roland. By
this time the workmen had given up all pretence of working
and were sitting on the front steps of the gallery, eating and
drinking things out of brown paper bags. Several of them
made appreciative noises as Jill passed.

'Roland, can't you stop them?' she demanded.

He shook his head. 'I don't like it either, but it has
something to do with union rules, I think.'

'Union rules? Oh, you mean their sitting on the steps. I
meant about their passing sexist remarks.'

'I wouldn't be surprised if that didn't turn out to have
something to do with the union, too.'

The workmen laughed coarsely, and one of them made
a remark about Jill's physical attributes, that although
technically flattering, was of an explicitness that went beyond the boundaries of mere bad taste.

A sandwich was lying on the step next to the offender,
tastefully laid out on a paper napkin. Jill walked over,
brought up her foot, and stomped it.

The workmen stared at her open-mouthed.

'Next time, Buster, it'll be your hand.'

She swaggered back to her companions. She was clearly
pleased with herself. Roland wasn't. 'Did you have to do
that, Jill?' he complained, as he unlocked the gate and they
descended into the areaway. 'Don't I have enough trouble
with the men already?'

Before Jill could say anything, Susan jumped in with, 'You
wanted to hear about the man I saw last night, didn't you?'

She described the visitor's appearance.

'Doesn't sound like anyone I know,' Roland said.

'Sounds like somebody I'd like to know,' Jill said, 'and,
even though I'm not an animal person, I'd even be willing
to learn to love the dog.'

'Dog? What dog?' Roland yelped. 'You didn't say anything about a dog last night, Susan?'

Susan told him about Brucie. 'I didn't go into detail last night,' she said tactfully, 'because you seemed to be busy, but it did seem odd that a prowler should have a dog with him.'

Roland's face went ashen. 'Would you mind not saying anything about the dog to Baltasar? He—he has a thing about dogs. He can't stand them, and it would make him nervous to know that there'd been a dog anywhere near the place. *Please!*'

The poor man's really going off the deep end, Susan thought. 'Of course I won't say anything about the dog to Baltasar if you don't want me to,' she said. 'And neither will Jill; will you, Jill?'

'Oh, all right,' Jill said.

In the daylight, Susan could see the door behind the group of museum-quality garbage cans underneath the front steps, quite a handsome door, considering that it was, in effect, the tradesmen's entrance and would be all but concealed, once the grille (now with a 'Wet Paint' sign on it) was put back in place. There were no back doors for tradesmen on the block, because the buildings, like most of the buildings in Manhattan that had originally been designed as private residences, were all attached; no way of reaching the diminutive rear yards from the street.

Roland examined the lock on the door carefully. When he bent over, Susan noticed that, although he had combed his hair carefully to conceal it, he had the beginning of a bald spot. Poor Roland, Susan thought, he'll hate being bald.

'Any chance that your visitor did get inside?' Jill asked.

'The lock doesn't seem to have been tampered with, as far as I can see. But locks can be picked. And this is an old-fashioned one you could pick with a hairpin. I did have a new lock installed on the grille but the workmen took it off when they removed the grille.'

'How about the windows?' Susan asked.

They were generously proportioned, easily big enough for a man to get through; however, like all ground-level and below-ground-level windows in New York, they were heavily barred; in this instance, covered with ornamental ironwork that matched both the grille below and the gate above.

'You did check to see that nothing was taken?' Susan asked.

'Nothing was taken, I'm sure.'

But he still looked worried. 'What's in your basement, Roland?' Jill asked, trying to peer into a window, but the blinds were pulled all the way down to the sill.

'Nothing to interest a thief. Nothing to interest anybody. Just storage space and a workshop.'

'Why do you have a workshop?' Jill persisted, in spite of her client's frown. 'You've never been good with your hands.'

'I can hire people who are, can't I? I was going to use it to unpack and crate exhibits and frame pictures, that sort of thing, maybe even do a spot of restoration in the case of older works. I had such plans for the future. Now—' Roland sighed —'I—I feel the place is under a curse.'

'It does look that way, doesn't it?' Jill chirped. 'Don't worry, though. They say trouble comes in threes. First Rafael, then the fire; one more disaster and you'll be home free.'

'You've always been so supportive, Jill,' Roland said.

'Perhaps the handsome prowler could qualify as the third disaster,' Jill suggested. 'Or Lupe. She looks ready to make trouble.'

Roland addressed himself to Susan as if Jill were not there. 'It's not that I don't want to give Lupe the money from the sale of Rafael's work, but there are legal formalities to be observed. We're taking it for granted that, as his widow, she must be his heir, but supposing he made a will leaving his money to somebody else.'

'The money'll have to be put in escrow until the legal heir or heirs is determined,' Jill said.

'Something like that,' Roland muttered.

Susan got the impression that the money had not been placed in escrow, that Lupe would be lucky if she ever saw it.

Roland snapped the padlock on the gate shut behind them as they came out of the areaway. 'It's all too much. Sometimes I wish I had never—' he stopped.

'Never what, Roland?' Jill asked. 'What do you wish you never had done?'

'Opened that gallery at all. It's a big responsibility, a big responsibility.'

Susan tried to think of something reassuring to say to him. Nothing came to mind. Poor man, he was unpleasant, incompetent, and, she suspected, not altogether honest, but she did wish there were some way she could cheer him up.

He smiled faintly. Apparently he had thought of something to cheer himself. 'Jill, did you know there's a blob of chopped liver on your shoe? Charles Jourdan, isn't it? Too bad, I wouldn't be surprised if it was completely ruined.'

CHAPTER 7

Although Susan would have preferred to go directly to Leatherstocking's, Jill insisted that they go back inside the gallery to say goodbye to the others. 'It's only civil,' she said. Susan and Roland exchanged glances. Civility was not one of Jill's long suits. Obviously the girl was up to something.

Once again they ascended the front steps. The workmen had all vanished; probably they were hiding until Jill left. Or perhaps they were on strike. Was it possible that having one's sandwich stepped on by a friend of the management was grounds for a strike? That could be Roland's third disaster, Susan thought.

Roland held her back at the top of the steps while Jill galloped ahead. 'I must talk to you alone,' he said in a low voice. 'I need your advice. It's really quite important. Could we possibly have a drink later this afternoon? Or a spot of tea?'

Oh, dear, Susan thought, he's going to confide in me. People always were confiding in her, asking for advice, bending her ear. They thought that because she listened she was sympathetic, when actually she was merely being polite. Sometimes it paid to be rude. But here too she had been victimized by her upbringing.

'I'm sorry, Roland, but I'm afraid I can't make it tonight,' she said. 'I'm going to pick Alex up at his office, and then we're going over to his place for a family dinner.' Most likely Amy, Tinsley's mother and an old schoolfellow of Susan's, would be there; she was there most of the time now. Susan didn't look forward to an evening of prenatal conversation, but that was what came of acquiring a family.

'How about tomorrow then?' Roland persisted.

It would be unkind to put him off again. Moreover, if she pleaded another engagement, he would simply try to make another date. So difficult to reject someone who didn't expect to be accepted. Better to get it over with.

'I think I could make it tomorrow,' she said, 'although I'll have to go home and check my calendar just to make sure.' She had learned at a very early age always to leave herself an out. 'Shall we meet here?'

'That would be very convenient. Or I could come over to your place?'

'No, let's meet here.' Much easier for her to leave him than to get rid of him, in case he started telling her the story of his life, she thought.

'Super! I'll be working here all day, so how about dropping by around five or so?'

She wondered whether he intended to take her to some neighbourhood drinking place or whether he planned to dispense the beverage of her choice on the premises. She felt mildly curious about that apartment of his above the gallery and what Baltasar was doing with his part of the building. Perhaps she could persuade Roland to take her on a tour of the place.

'And you won't tell anybody—anybody at all—that you're going to meet me?'

'I won't tell a soul,' she promised, thinking poor, paranoid Roland, making such a big deal out of what was probably nothing, perhaps something as trivial as asking her advice on curtains. But no, Roland would know far more about curtains than she would.

By the time Susan and Roland came back into the foyer, Jill was already distributing copies of Hortense's brochures to Lupe and Baltasar and holding up the T-shirt for their admiration—Lupe's anyway, although it had to be explained to her just what a 'Moopie' might be.

Baltasar was looking disgusted. 'Why do people wear these silly little over-undershirts with the silly little mottos?' he wanted to know. 'Do they enjoy making themselves look ridiculous?'

'It gives them a sense of their identity,' Jill said.

Baltasar said something in Spanish. Lupe laughed and Roland gave a feeble titter.

Susan didn't know why she should feel surprised that Roland seemed to speak Spanish. Art dealers often were multilingual. And a lot of people in New York spoke Spanish. She wondered whether Jill did. She was certainly looking angry, but that could just as easily be because she didn't understand what he'd said as because she did.

Susan glanced at her watch. They had spent more time at the gallery than she'd figured on, what with the unexpected arrival of Lupe and Jill's brushes with practically everyone in sight. 'Leatherstocking's isn't going to hold our reservations much longer,' she reminded Jill. 'You know what M. Bumppo is like.'

'Like most restaurateurs,' Jill said. 'You've go to look 'em in the eye and stare them down. It's the only way to deal with them.'

But M. Bumppo was not like most restaurateurs. He was worse. A James Fenimore Cooper enthusiast, M. Auguste Benoit had come to the United States fired with the idea of creating a restaurant that would serve food that was both authentically Early American and *haute cuisine*. He called his place Leatherstocking's, after James Fenimore Cooper's tales of the same name; and, although he did not change his own name officially, he liked to be called M. Bumppo after the series' hero. Not Natty, though, that would be carrying democracy too far.

The restaurant was an immediate success, although Leatherstocking himself, and, indeed, James Fenimore Cooper, would not have recognized the food as native cuisine. (Nor would Leatherstocking have been allowed in the place. M. Bumppo enforced a strict dress code, and, although fringed deerskin shirts had come into fashion in Soho, they still were not *comme il faut* at Leatherstocking's, name or no name.) M. Bumppo's *pâté d'élan* (known as 'moose mousse' by the irreverent) received rave reviews from all the food critics except Mimi Sheraton, and his *ragoût de boufflon avec pissenlits* was the talk of the town.

The place was much favoured by such of the uptown art crowd as could afford it, for the prices were as *haute* as the *cuisine*—which meant that it was mostly dealers and museum people and the like who were its patrons (most of the artists whose works were shown in the uptown galleries being dead anyway). Although as a rule Susan tended to shun fashionable watering places when she was off duty, she made an exception of Leatherstocking's. Hal Courtenay often ate there. So, on the other hand, did Mimi Hunyadi.

As in most aspects of life you had to take the rough (Mimi) with the smooth (Hal).

'Why don't you join us for lunch?' Jill asked, as if the thought had just occurred to her, when, Susan realized, this was what she had been plotting ever since they got there. Why, Susan had no idea. Maybe she hoped to sell Baltasar a picture; maybe she hoped to acquire Lupe as a client. Or maybe she was simply suffering from the same insatiable curiosity that had done the Elephant's Child in.

'I am truly sorry,' Baltasar said. 'I would have loved to have lunch with you, and so, I am sure, would Lupe . . .' Lupe nodded and smiled and was about to speak, but he went on, 'Lupita and I are old friends, you know. She was one of my best models before she started her own artistic career. Now that she is here I hope to persuade her to model for me once again, at my fashion show for the charity ball in September.'

Lupe started to say something; then apparently thought better of it.

'This affair means such a lot to me. Of course the opportunity to present my work in New York for the first time is a great thing, but even greater is the chance to be able to do something for so splendid a cause.'

Jill snorted. She did not believe there was such a thing as disinterested altruism. Maybe she was right, Susan thought, but what was so bad about interested altruism if it got the job done? Of course it was grotesque to hold a Grand Ball and Gala in an art museum as a way of dealing with the growing problem of drug abuse; but if that was the only way of getting the money that was needed out of the people who could afford to give it, then it made sense. Not good sense, but sense.

'Other than holding a gun to somebody's head there's no better way to dig out the money than by throwing a party,' Pat Buckley had once said, throwing Susan into momentary panic before she realized that Mrs Buckley probably had not intended to suggest that she use her extra-artistic talents for fund-raising; although it was not beyond the bounds of probability that Mrs Buckley would have done so if she had known of their existence. Some society hostesses would stop at nothing in their relentless pursuit of the public weal.

At least there was one thing that could be said about the Grand Art against Drug Abuse Gala and Ball that did not apply to most other charitable events. You were likely to find a number of the individuals for whose particular problem (although not whose particular class) the affair had been arranged sitting at the table as paying guests—something not likely to be true of the homeless, the delinquent, and/or the disabled.

'I only hope I will be able to get a new collection together in time,' Baltasar said. 'The gowns I had planned to show were ruined by smoke and water. I will have to fly back to Madrid as soon as I can and attempt to recreate them in my *atelier* there. But there is so much to be done here as well. I am torn in all directions.'

'Such a misfortune,' Lupe said. 'But you will rise above

it, Baltasar, and create an even more glorious collection, I know. You have never let anything stop you.'

'You are too kind, Lupita,' he said, kissing her hand. 'You give me renewed hope.'

Jill was about to snort again, but caught her client's eye and desisted. Maybe charity doesn't begin at home any more, Susan thought, but good public relations still do.

'Baltasar has some nerve sneering at T-shirts,' Jill said, when Susan finally managed to tear her away and get her to the restaurant. M. Bumppo greeted them reproachfully and made it clear that if they had not been especially valued customers ('I always said he had an eye for you, Susan,' Jill said), they would have been forced to kick their heels at the bar along with the other sinners. Jill seemed to identify with messaged T-shirts. Perhaps to her they represented the spirit of her generation. As for Susan, she was inclined to agree with Baltasar, but she kept her counsel.

'He talks as if he'd been involved in *haute couture* all his life, when I understand he actually started out in quilted robes, fancy nightgowns, beaded sweaters, that kind of *shmatta*, from the Far East and the Caribbean. Strictly for the bargain basement trade—in the days when there were still bargain basements.'

'Don't be such a snob, Jill,' Susan said. 'The man had to start somewhere.'

'All right, all right,' Jill said, 'but tell me how his gowns got ruined? I thought only Roland's part of the building got hit by the fire.'

'Maybe he stored them there because the men were still working on his part. Who cares, anyway? I'm hungry.' Susan picked up the menu. 'I'm going to start with the *soupe à l'oseille*.'

'No sorrel soup for me,' Jill said. 'We used to eat that in the Bronx, before ethnic became fashionable. It tasted like something that came out of a goldfish bowl then and it still does. I'm going to have the clam chowder.'

'*Potage à la palourde* is not—ugh—clam chowder,

57

madame,' the waiter said severely. M. Bumppo did not care to have his menu trifled with.

'Whatever,' Jill said.

If he was going to poison anybody, Susan thought, and he certainly looked as if he would like to, she hoped he'd be careful to slip it in the *potage* and not the *soupe*. 'Why on earth did you ask them to join us?' she asked. 'I thought this was supposed to be a business lunch. We were going to discuss the where, when, and what of my next show, remember?'

'And so we shall, Susan, so we shall. We do want to deduct this lunch from our taxes, don't we?'

'Your taxes. We can't both deduct the bill.'

'Don't be silly. Of course we can. I am sorry we didn't get a chance to talk to Lupe, though. I have a feeling there's something funny going on. Roland knew damn well she wasn't a simple barefoot peasant. Did you get a look at those sables she was wearing? She must be doing very well at whatever it is she does.'

'Roland was probably just repeating what Rafael told him about her.'

'Why would he have told him anything?'

'To explain why she wasn't at the opening perhaps?' But Jill was right: why would Rafael have bothered to give any explanation at all?

'Anyhow, it's just as well they didn't accept my invitation,' Jill said. 'I wouldn't have had much chance to talk to Lupe with Roland and Baltasar around. And we'd have had to pick up the tab for the whole gang.'

'We? You were the one who issued the invitation. You would have had to pick up the tab.'

'Don't be so petty, Susan. Probably Baltasar would have insisted on paying. He's of the old school. So is Roland, but a different kind of old school. Incidentally, what did Roland want to talk to you about, anyway? When you two were whispering and giggling in the vestibule?'

Susan had no scruples about lying in a good cause, and thwarting her rep's snoopiness was an excellent cause. 'He had a message he wanted me to give Alex. And I may have been talking in a low tone of voice but I was not giggling. I never giggle.'

Nor had Roland—although he did giggle on occasion—been giggling at the time, she recalled. He'd acted nervous, almost frightened.

'Something wrong with Roland's phone? Or Alex's?'

'I didn't ask him.' Subtlety was wasted on Jill. 'I don't pry.'

'You must miss out on an awful lot that way.' Jill shook a warning finger. 'Just be sure you don't go and make any deals without me. Remember, we have a contract.' Her tone was joking but she was not.

'I'm well aware that we have a contract,' Susan said, wondering, not for the first time, if she might not have made a mistake in signing with Jill so precipitately. On the other hand, thinking of the other people in the art business whom she'd met subsequently, she could have done worse. Her old schoolmate, Dodo Pangborn, for example, was now running an art gallery and most anxious to represent her. However, Dodo had done time in the Bedford Hills Correctional Facility for Women (though for running a house of ill fame under the guise of a religious institution rather than any artistic misdeeds); and, even more of a drawback, her gallery was downtown. The downtown galleries might be currently fashionable, but to Susan there was no art south of Fifty-Seventh Street.

Besides Hal had recommended Jill, Susan reminded herself, so basically the girl must be sound.

'Speaking of contracts,' Jill said with a sigh, 'I guess we better get down to business. The Europeans are beginning to take an interest in your work and I think our next public showing should be abroad—at one of the international expositions.'

'You showed my work at an international exposition last year.'

'That was in Chicago. Chicago is in the United States. I was thinking of maybe Zurich. Meanwhile, I don't want you to be overexposed, like those artists who have gallery shows every two or three months. They're not going to last. The public will soon get tired of them; you'll see.'

Some of them had lasted for several decades and still seemed to be going strong, Susan thought. However, from the business point of view, Jill was probably right. It wouldn't do to take any chances. Jill was undoubtedly also right when she said that Susan's paintings would fetch higher prices if they were released gradually over a period of time rather than poured out in one great gush of art. Just the same, Susan would have preferred to flood the market and get as much as she could while she was hot. If her popularity had been based on her work itself, she would have been content to take her chances and let her career, however belated, develop naturally; but she had become fashionable by such a freak that she was afraid she would go out of fashion just as suddenly.

'Okay,' Jill had told her when she had voiced as many of her fears as she could discreetly, 'so you did get to be the rage because it turned out that old General Chomsky had been collecting your paintings secretly—because that way he got them cheap. People are going to keep on buying your stuff because you're good. Didn't Hal write that terrific review of your work before he'd even met you, so you can't say he did it because he likes you, which no reputable critic would do, anyway. Write a good review of an artist's work because he likes her,' she added, realizing her words needed clarifying.

That's right, Susan thought, he did write a very favourable piece about me, so he really must think I'm good. He wouldn't have praised my work simply because his museum had just inherited a sizeable collection of my paintings.

'And you would have become popular a lot sooner,' Jill went on, 'if you hadn't been such a wimp. No matter what you'd promised the General, as soon as you'd sold him a few pictures—so he had an investment in you—you could have let the word leak out.'

'I . . . just couldn't,' Susan said.

How could she explain to Jill that the General hadn't actually paid her for the paintings at all? He'd paid her to kill, and she'd insisted on giving him a painting each time she disposed of someone, so she could declare her income to the IRS.

Jill patted her hand. 'Of course you couldn't. You're too much of a lady. Which is where I come in. In addition, it takes hype to get an artist up into the six-figure bracket, and hype is my specialty.'

'I'm not in the six-figure bracket yet,' Susan pointed out.

'Do what I tell you and in your next show you will be. I think your next show should be private,' Jill said, as the waiter removed the remains of the soup and placed their *canard à la canneberge avec beignets à la citrouille* before them. ('What could be more authentically American than cranberry duck with pumpkin fritters!' M. Bumppo had roared at an unfortunate soul who had ventured to question the authenticity of his menu—after which the offender had been barred from Leatherstocking's for life.)

'It should be by invitation only—and only the extremely well-heeled invited.'

Avoiding her client's eye, Jill continued, 'That one in your apartment last fall was a great success. Collectors feel they're really getting their money's worth if they see the painters disporting themselves in their native habitat. An apartment on the upper East Side isn't their idea of an authentic artist's studio, though. Pity you don't have a loft in some artistic neighbourhood. Soho and the West Village are verging on the passé, though. Maybe the East Village; it's going upscale without becoming too respectable. Visitors can still feel a thrill of danger as they step out of their limos.'

'They can feel that anywhere in the city. And I don't want another show in my apartment. One was too much.'

That previous apartment show had been preceded by a month of relentless tidying up. Not so much for neatness's sake, although that counted, too, Jill said, but to make sure that the vast output of over two decades was removed from the premises and safely stored. 'I've known artists who were prolific, but they pale beside you. For you they're going to have to make up a new word.'

61

Susan felt mildly stung, as if Jill had suggested there was something rather vulgar about being prolific even though she knew Jill had no such thought in mind; and, indeed, would have seen nothing wrong with vulgarity, provided they kept it between themselves, so as not to spoil the image into which she was casting her client.

'If you add up all Darius Moffatt's canvases, I bet it'll turn out that he was more prolific than I am.'

'But you're still turning 'em out and he isn't, on account of being dead. That makes the difference. There are going to be a lot more Melvilles unless somebody puts a brake on you. There aren't going to be any more Moffatts ever.'

'Unless some more cousins in remote parts of the country turn up with more forgotten Moffatts,' Susan suggested.

Jill glanced at her sharply. Susan returned the look with bland composure.

CHAPTER 8

If ever I start feeling sorry for myself, Susan thought, I have only to think of Darius Moffatt and thank my lucky stars. For me it came late but for him it never came at all.

Everybody who could read knew the tragic history of Darius Moffatt. He had died in obscurity ten years before, apparently never having sold a picture in his life. Now he had become almost legendary, hailed by some as one of the most important artists of the twentieth century.

As a youth still in his teens, Darius Moffatt had come to New York to study art, first at the Hudson School and later at the Art Students League. Where he'd gotten the money to pay for his lessons and his keep never became entirely clear. He was not the type to go after scholarships or, if he had been, to win them. But he'd been unable to make a go of life in the city, and so he'd returned to the small New England village he came from to help his twice-widowed mother work the family farm. However, he continued to paint in his spare time, using an abandoned barn as his studio.

Then a real-estate developer had made an offer to Moffatt's mother that she could not refuse. She'd sold him most of the family land, keeping only the house, a couple of acres of land, and the barn. Now she was comfortably off, though by no means wealthy. But her son wasn't happy. Perhaps he missed the land; perhaps he didn't like the idea of living in the midst of a middle-income housing development.

And so he had left the village and drifted across the country, staying with various relatives at their farms, where he helped out in exchange for his keep and a place to paint and enough money to buy the materials with which to do so. They seemed to be an agrarian family. 'Very Early American,' Jill had put it in one of the early interviews. They also seemed, as it developed later, to be a very large family.

In the 1970s, with most small farms mechanized out of existence, he had drifted back to New York. It was possible that he had heard of the art boom and hoped he might be able to find a place for himself now; more likely he'd had no clear purpose in mind. At any rate, someone had apparently given him a shot of heroin—possibly his first—and he had died of it. His death had passed unremarked by the press. People were always dying of drugs in New York, sometimes from their first shot but always from their last. There might have been a story about him in his native village's paper, if it had one; but Jill, from whom all information about him emanated, steadfastly kept the name of the place a secret. For the same reason she also kept the name Darius's mother had acquired as the result of her second marriage a secret, although that had been her legal name for over thirty years. She was always referred to as Mrs Moffatt, at least in the beginning; it was only later that the sobriquet an irreverent reporter from the *Daily News* bestowed on her stuck and she became universally known as 'Old Mother Moffatt'.

'They're very private people up there,' Jill had explained in another early interview. 'Some of them, especially the older ones, know about Darius and his paintings, of course, but they protect their own. Before Mrs Moffatt let me handle

63

the pictures, she made me promise never to tell anybody where she lives.'

'Sounds more like Appalachia than New England,' the mathematics teacher at the European-American Academy, a thin dark girl whose name Susan could not now remember, had said.

'Sounds more like the Twilight Zone,' someone else had observed.

Susan had still been teaching at the Academy when Darius Moffatt's name first came into prominence. They had discussed him in the faculty lounge. As the school's artist-in-residence (which was how the brochure referred, rather embarrassingly, to her), Susan was expected to keep on top of the current art scene. She had not herself seen any great genius in the Moffatt works but was reluctant to admit it for fear of being thought out of step with the times. Fortunately the vocabulary of art appreciation enabled her to discuss the subject at length without ever making it clear what her actual opinion of the paintings was—not that she would have hesitated to lie in order to keep her job but she had found it was better to tell the truth whenever possible; it diminished the risk of being caught in a contradiction.

According to the stories in the press, Moffatt's mother had come down from the little town (or village; the two terms were used interchangeably) where he'd been born and raised to collect her son's body and pick up his meagre personal effects from the squalid East Village apartment in which he had passed his last days. She was quite old now, and inflation had cut down her income to minimal adequacy. She was poor. There were a number of canvases in the apartment and Mrs Moffatt brought a few to Jill Turkel's little Soho gallery for promising artists, to see if she might get something for them.

Susan remembered the mathematics teacher's wondering how an elderly New England widow who had never before set foot in New York had managed to make her way from the East Village to an obscure Soho gallery, carrying a bundle of rather large canvases. Someone suggested that perhaps each gallery that turned her down recommended another one, and so she had trudged across town until she reached Jill's. It was a touching, if somewhat improbable, picture.

Unlike the others, Jill had instantly recognized their genius, she told the press. She gave the artist a one-man show, selected from the best of the canvases. Hal Courtenay, assistant curator of the Museum of American Art, at that time an art critic and consultant, had stopped in at the gallery. He always made an effort to look at every art show, no matter how obscure, he said in an interview later. 'Most of it's dross, of course, but there's always the hope that one day you'll stumble upon a vein of pure gold to make it all worth while.'

This time he seemed to have hit pay dirt. He wrote a long laudatory piece about Moffatt for the *New York Art Journal*, as well as shorter pieces for the *Times* and other popular publications. This brought other reviewers to the Turkel Gallery. Although there were one or two dissenting voices (there always are dissenting voices, sometimes, Susan suspected, just for the sake of dissension) most were as enthusiastic as Hal. A few were even more laudatory; one went so far as to call Moffatt 'the greatest genius the second half of the twentieth century has as yet produced'.

'Which was, of course, absurd,' Hal told Susan at the MAA's second Moffatt Retrospective. 'There were several quite good, even if somewhat overrated, artists on the scene already. And, of course, nobody knew about you yet.'

And he had looked deeply into her eyes. His were very blue. Why hadn't she noticed back in the old days how blue his eyes were? He'd worn glasses then, she remembered, wire-framed ones. Probably they had obscured the blueness of his eyes. And, since she'd considered him a creep then, she'd had no reason to look deeply into his eyes. He must be wearing contact lenses now.

'Did you remember Darius Moffatt from school?' she asked. 'According to the dates, I must have been there around the same times as he was, but I must confess I can't remember him at all.'

Hal had shaken his handsome head. 'When I first saw the paintings in Jill's gallery his name didn't strike the faintest chord. There was a biography in that first little catalogue, but it was very sketchy. It did mention that he'd gone to the Hudson while he was still in his teens, but it didn't give a birth date so I had no way of knowing when those teens were. Then, later on, when Jill got those photographs from his mother, I began to remember him dimly.'

The snapshots, later reproduced in the daily papers, *Time*, *Newsweek*, *People*, and all the art journals, were themselves dim—imperfectly preserved Polaroids of a pale, long-haired, scraggly-bearded, youngish man in work clothes, scowling into the camera. When Susan looked at them with the knowledge that they were of someone she once must have seen at least, perhaps even spoken to, a faint sense of recognition seemed to stir in her mind. But I could simply be projecting, she thought.

The paintings at that first show had sold out immediately. A few months later Jill offered the rest of the paintings that had been in the East Village apartment for sale—at triple the prices of the first batch. This show sold out immediately as well.

And that seemed to be that. The paltry handful of paintings appeared to be all the artist had left behind him. Most of those collectors who had been astute enough to secure one or more of the paintings held on to them, but a few, either overanxious to cash in while he was still in the news, or in need of money, sold theirs. The prices they fetched were fantastic, especially considering that they had sold for a couple of thousand dollars apiece less than a year before.

Almost two years after the second show, great news burst upon the art world. Jill revealed that she had received a letter from old Mrs Moffatt saying that now she was well along in years she found the big old-fashioned farmhouse too much for her to cope with. She'd decided to sell it and move to a small cottage with all modern conveniences, which she described in detail in her chatty agrarian way. It took two handwritten pages (later reproduced in facsimile in *Art Notes*) before she got to the point. While clearing out the old barn, she'd discovered a number of her son's paintings stored there. Would Jill be interested in handling them?

Jill would, indeed. By this time rising rents had forced her to give up her little Soho gallery, so, acting as the late artist's representative now, she arranged to have them shown at the Stratton Gallery, at prices befitting 'one of the great geniuses of the twentieth century'. There were twice as many paintings on view as there had been in the previous two shows. Still not an enormous number, but enough to constitute a respectable *oeuvre*, so that his death, as Hal Courtenay pointed out in an article for the *Times Magazine*, seemed less a tragedy for the world of art, if not for the artist himself. All of them equalled and, in some cases, even surpassed the high standards set by the first group. All of them sold at prices ranging from fifty thousand dollars on up. Old Mother Moffatt must be a millionairess. And so must Jill.

The press clamoured for interviews with the old lady, or, at the least, with neighbours who had grown up with Darius. Jill remained adamant. She had promised the family that she would protect their privacy. Even though they were no longer her clients, as there were no more pictures to be sold, she was not going to betray them. An aura of quiet dignity and rectitude shone through the interviews, accounting for much of the surprise Susan later felt when she met Jill.

It must have been over a year after Old Mother Moffatt's happy discovery in the barn that one of her brothers died and left her everything he had. Among his effects was another dozen of Darius's paintings. It wasn't clear whether the artist had merely left them behind in the course of his peregrinations or had given them to his uncle, not that it mattered since his mother was the sole heir in either case.

By this time Hal Courtenay had become the MAA's curator of contemporary art. He took the discovery of the new paintings as an occasion for mounting a Moffatt Retrospective. Jill graciously lent the Museum the paintings, prior to their commercial exhibition.

The paintings were never exhibited commercially. The Charpentier Foundation acquired them all at prices that were never disclosed but were reported to be astronomic.

Simultaneously with the exhibition, Hal Courtenay published his monograph *Darius Moffatt, Man and Myth*, which became the definitive work on the artist. Although Hal was in a privileged position, having earned Jill's gratitude for the first rapturous review that put Moffatt on the map, even he was not allowed to interview old Mother Moffatt or even to know her location. All information had to come through Jill. He was, however, allowed access to the Moffatt letters, for Darius had written regularly to his mother. An inarticulate man verbally—though how Jill knew this was never made clear—Darius was not much better on paper.

A typical example of his letters was one he had written while he was staying with his cousins George and Mary (not their real names) who were cousins to each other as well as to him, and man and wife to boot. ('They're a very inbred family,' Jill had told an interviewer once, 'which may be why they're rather strange.')

Dear Ma,

I am well and hope you are the same. George and Mary and the kids send their love. They are all well except George Junior has the chicken pox but we are sure he will recover (ha ha). I have been painting a lot of pictures now that the crops are all in. Could you send me another half dozen pairs of sox from [name withheld]'s general store? You can't get that kind out here in [location deleted].

Your loving son,
Darry

His other letters were similar—little about his life, even less about his art. The only information the reader derived from them was that Darius had loved his mother. Dr Joyce Brothers devoted a column in the New York *Post* and, since she was syndicated, other papers, to him.

In the years that followed, it seemed that every few

months another group of Moffatt paintings would show up at the home of one or another of his kin. Not only was his family large, but it was scattered all over the country. He seemed to have relatives in every state except Hawaii and Alaska, and he apparently had left paintings with every one of them. As a writer for the *Village Voice* pointed out, rather than drift across the country, Darius must have rushed madly about to have stayed in so many places during the dozen or so years of his wandering.

The fact that the paintings were all beginning to show up, Jill had told that same writer, was not fortuitous. She had asked Old Mother Moffatt to write to every relative she could think of, asking whether they happened to have any of Darius's paintings. 'I wanted her to Xerox a form letter which she could just send around, but she said no; that wasn't proper. She insisted on sending a personal hand-written letter to each one, asking them to look in their closets and cellars and barns, and that's why it's taking so long to find them all, especially since her memory isn't what it was, and she keeps remembering third and fourth cousins she overlooked.'

Jill shook her head sadly, as the press duly noted. 'Lord knows how many paintings will never turn up, that are still mouldering somewhere or were just tossed in the garbage like so much junk.'

You could almost hear the readers' collective gasps of horror.

'Don't the relatives ever claim that the paintings belong to them?' a reporter from the *Post* asked, his nose twitching for scandal. 'That Darius *gave* them the paintings?'

'Even if that were true, it would be hard to prove,' Jill said. 'If they took her to court, they might lose everything. This way Mrs Moffatt gives them a share of what she gets. Besides, they don't sue their own kind. They're not that type of people.

But of course, the public had only Jill's word for that. And, as Susan began to realize later, for everything else concerning Darius Moffatt as well.

CHAPTER 9

'Too bad you don't have a barn or some place like that to store your paintings,' Jill had said, two years before, as she looked over her new client's total *oeuvre* for the first time. Canvases were stacked in every available part of the apartment, filling the rooms Susan didn't use—for it was a spacious pre-war apartment—and threatening to make those she lived in unliveable.

'Anyhow, you're going to have to store them somewhere and just release a few at a time. If so much as a hint escapes of how many there are already in existence, your prices are going to tumble, in spite of all the hoopla.'

'Shouldn't a painting's value be based on its inherent worth rather than its rarity?' Peter, who was in residence at the time, had asked.

'Worth has nothing to do with a painting's price,' Jill told him. 'Price depends on fashion, rarity, and good PR.' Here she patted her chest. 'Worth—well—there isn't any objective way of determining the inherent worth of a work of art, so why bother to try?'

'Critical approval?' Susan suggested without conviction.

'Among the Oupi,' Peter began, and embarked on a long anthropological narrative that neither of his companions paid any attention to.

Jill opened the door to a closet and closed it again just in time to escape being buried by an avalanche of art. Susan supposed the girl didn't know any better than to open other people's closets, but she couldn't help feeling annoyed. 'Well, I think you get the general idea,' she said, steering Jill back into the studio, which having originally been the living-room of the apartment, was not equipped with closets. 'I don't suppose you want to look at them one by one.'

'Not right now,' Jill said, subsiding into a chair, 'although I guess I'll have to eventually. Not that I'm not looking forward to it,' she added quickly. This was early in their relationship and she was still wary of offending her client.

'Yes, thank you, I would like something to drink,' she replied to Susan's offer of refreshment. 'And I hope it's stronger than tea.'

She seemed surprised to find that Susan not only had a well-stocked bar but that she joined Jill in a bourbon and soda. For some reason I seem to look the tea type to her, Susan thought. She should look at my paintings instead of at me.

'You know you have enough pictures here to make you a multi-millionaire without you ever lifting a brush again—providing they're carefully marketed. Which, of course, they will be.'

'But I want to keep on painting,' Susan protested. 'I paint because I want to, not because I want to be an artist.'

Jill gave her a pitying smile.

'I don't know why you find that so hard to understand,' Susan persisted. 'Darius Moffatt obviously liked to paint or he wouldn't have kept on painting.'

'Who knows what motivated Darius Moffatt, what compulsions moved him to keep on painting, even though he had no reason to expect anybody—except maybe his family—would ever see his work?' Jill asked. She was, whether consciously or not, quoting from *Darius Moffatt, Man and Myth*. 'But he was a throwback. Art for art's sake is pretty much obsolete these days, if it ever did hold good. Artists don't like art. Collectors like art. Artists paint so they can sell their pictures to collectors. The only painters who enjoy their work are chimpanzees, like in that movie you took me to, and what do they do with their paintings? They eat them.'

She was bitter, Susan thought. She must have had some really rough clients. 'I'm not sure I know what motivates me. It certainly hasn't been money because I didn't make any up until a few years ago.'

'But you hoped to, didn't you?'

'Well, I'd hoped to be able to support myself by painting,' Susan said. 'I never expected to make money, in the real sense, from it.'

71

'That's because you were born to money. The idea that you yourself could become rich through your own efforts probably never even occurred to you.'

Susan's pride was piqued. 'The family fortunes were founded by a man who most definitely made his own money.'

Jill laughed. 'You mean old Black Buck, the pirate? Oh, he's great PR, no mistake about it. But there are at least eight generations between you and him. There isn't much of his blood running in your veins, Susan. I can't see you making anyone walk the plank.'

Looking back later, Susan was to wish she had made Jill walk the plank then and there. But everybody makes mistakes, and there was no use crying over unspilt blood—metaphorically speaking, of course.

'All right, keep on painting if it makes you happy,' Jill said. 'A happy client is a . . . er . . . a happy client. But you can't keep the paintings here. It's not safe.'

'Are you suggesting that I should hire a barn? Like Darius Moffatt?'

'He didn't hire a barn; he had a barn, which is a whole other thing. You have to be born to a barn. You're not the barn type. And barns aren't safe, anyway. The family vault, maybe.'

'Even in the most elegant of circles,' Susan told her, 'to which you mistakenly seem to think I belong, it is not customary to store anything but bodies in the family vault.'

'Vaults are fireproof,' Jill said, apparently confusing funeral vaults with bank vaults. 'Sometimes I wake up in a cold sweat, imagining what could've happened to the Moffatt barn over the years. It could have been struck by lightning. Vandals could've set it on fire. The country could have been invaded by—by—'

'Giant fireflies perhaps? In any of those events you'd never even have known the pictures existed, so why worry now over what might have happened. Worry about what's to come.'

Jill looked agitated. 'What do you mean? Are you expecting any kind of trouble? You've got to tell me now.'

72

Susan was a little disconcerted by such an emotional response. 'No, it's only that man is born to trouble as the sparks fly upward. All this talk of fire made me think of it,' she apologized.

'Please don't quote the Bible at me,' Jill said. 'I'm an atheist. It makes me nervous. But we are going to have to store your pictures somewhere fireproof. And get them insured.'

Susan's once-a-week maid, now pensioned off ('How feudal,' Jill had sneered), had always worried about fire, but Susan hadn't paid much attention, since she hadn't had the money to put her paintings in storage, especially since they hadn't been worth anything to anyone but herself. Now that they had become so valuable, it made sense to take proper precautions; and so the paintings were duly removed to a fireproof warehouse in Long Island City, where Jill was already renting space for purposes she did not explain.

After Susan's apartment had been emptied of extraneous canvases, it was thoroughly cleaned by a crew of uniformed professionals, and somewhat refurbished, although not re-furnished—Susan drew an emphatic line there. 'All right, slipcovers, if you must,' she told Jill, 'although I personally think they're a little—' she searched for a tactful word —'dowdy, but no new furniture. It isn't a question of expense; it's a question of personal comfort.'

However, she joined Jill in persuading Peter to give up the loin cloth which he favoured as informal attire and have his hair trimmed. Jill also said he had to choose between growing a beard and moustache in time for the exhibit or shaving. 'The Don Johnson look might do for Hollywood or Miami, but it's definitely uncool in New York,' she'd pointed out. Thank heaven she didn't tell him it was 'uncool' for a man his age, Susan had thought, for, although he prided himself on being a detached social scientist, Peter was not without his share of male self-delusion.

'I do not like being treated like an exhibit,' he had said.

'Then stop acting like one,' Jill had retorted. They had not gotten on at all well. They were both difficult people.

It's unfair, Susan thought. I'm the artist; I should be the one with the temperament instead of the peacemaker, the moderator, the patsy. No wonder so few people with her background ever achieved success in the arts. True artistry requires passion while true social grace requires that passion, or at least its outward manifestation, be bred out of you.

The exhibit had been a success from the financial point of view. All the paintings on display had been sold for handsome sums—more, Jill confessed afterward, than she had dreamed of getting. 'I pushed the prices up because I know how rich people love to dicker. I didn't expect them to pay what I asked, practically without a murmur, or I would have asked more.' And she shook her head sadly.

The experience of being forced to act as a hostess combined with the despoliation of her apartment had been unnerving for Susan. It took a while before she could get back to painting in this suddenly alien environment. And her style of painting changed.

She did allow Jill to bring up individual clients from time to time, and tried to be gracious even to the really obnoxious ones, like Eloise Charpentier, who couldn't understand why Susan had chosen to convert her 'drawing-room' into a studio, instead of using one of the smaller rooms. 'It's the only room with a north light,' Susan had tried to explain.

'Well, can't you have a north light put in one of the bedrooms? Where do you entertain?'

'I don't do any large-scale entertaining,' Susan had said. She'd had enough of festivity during her days as party crasher cum hit woman; and even then she hadn't had to *give* the parties, just provide the surprise endings.

'Oh, you poor thing,' Eloise said, and invited Susan to lunch at the Quilted Giraffe, leaving Susan to pick up the cheque afterward. However, the Charpentier Foundation subsequently bought a million dollars' worth of Susan's paintings (for eight hundred thousand dollars; 'The Charpentiers always expect a discount,' Jill said), so she supposed it was time and money well spent. But she refused to let another full-scale exhibit be mounted in her apartment, in spite of all Jill's attempts to persuade her to repeat the event.

Today, however, Jill didn't press her. Susan would have liked to think that this was because she had learned that her client could be pushed just so far; however, she had a feeling that the girl had something else in mind from the start, and was just using Susan's apartment as a stalking horse.

And she was right. 'That charming Mrs Hunyadi offered to exhibit your work in her apartment,' Jill suggested, casually spooning her *coupé iroquoise* on to the tablecloth, instead of her mouth. She was nervous. She was plotting something.

'Mimi Hunyadi is a bitch,' Susan said.

'Of course she is. She also is a member of the board of directors of the MAA, the Van Horn of the Van Horn Foundation, a celebrated patron of the arts, your best girl-hood chum, and filthy rich.'

'She's all of that,' Susan agreed, 'but—'

'What's more, she knows all the right people. We can't let just anybody buy your paintings.'

'They're available to anyone who can afford to pay the price,' Susan said coldly. 'In fact—'

'You weren't thinking of offering them at reduced prices to people below a certain income level, were you?'

'Better than offering them at reduced prices to people who can well afford to pay full price.'

Jill shook her head. 'Susan, Susan, where would you be without me?'

Susan had been beginning to wonder about that herself. 'I suppose you think I shouldn't have agreed to let Mimi have a painting to be auctioned off at that confounded anti-drug ball of hers.'

'On the contrary, that's good publicity, as well as being a worthy cause,' she added, for, as she kept pointing out to her client, Jill was not heartless; she believed in charity as long as it benefited the giver more than the receiver.

'I, too, appreciate the value of publicity,' Susan said, 'so

I want my next show to be in a public gallery.' She knew why Jill wanted to avoid gallery shows. It would mean she would have to split her commissions. 'The show last fall at the Stratton went very well, I thought.'

It had gone better, in fact, than Jill knew. 'Why are you letting this snippet who knows nothing about art handle your work, Susan?' Gil Stratton had asked. 'This new-fangled idea of agents for artists won't last. It's galleries who should be handling them, the way they've always done. Come with me, Susan, we'll give you terms you wouldn't believe.'

'I have a contract with Jill.'

'Contract, shmontract. Think it over and, by the way, while you're thinking, you won't mention my little sugges-tion to Jill, will you? I wouldn't like to upset her.'

I'll bet you wouldn't, Susan thought. You'd never get another Melville show—or another Moffatt show, if any more distant relatives of Darius's show up with pictures. And you might get a brick through your window to boot.

She had never told Jill about Stratton's offer, and, although the temptation was strong, she didn't tell her now. 'If my paintings are shown in a public gallery, at least the general public will be able to see them, even if they can't afford to buy them.'

'Susan, the general public isn't interested in your paint-ings—as paintings, that is. Oh, they'll come to see them because you're in the news and because they hear they're going for astronomical sums, but not for love of art. They'd never have come in the days when you were an unknown.'

'You don't know that. When I was unknown, there was no way they could see my paintings because they weren't on view anywhere. I suppose if I had brought my pictures to your gallery, you wouldn't have shown them either.'

'I don't know what I would have done,' Jill said. 'For Pete's sake, Susan, that was a long time ago. Just between ourselves, I might not have accepted Darius Moffatt's paint-ings if I hadn't been desperate right then . . .'

'Desperate?' Susan asked. 'Come on! Gallery owners may

be desperate for money to pay the rent. They may be desperate for collectors to come and buy their pictures. But they are never desperate for artists.'

Jill swallowed. 'I guess I should have told you about it before, only I was ashamed. I wasn't running that gallery all by myself. Even though it was only a hole in the wall, I couldn't have afforded it. I had a partner. His name wasn't on the gallery because he'd gotten into trouble not too long before. It might have started us off on the wrong foot if people knew he had anything to do with the place.' She took a deep breath. 'It was Roland. He was my partner.'

'Roland!' For some time Susan had realized that there was some connection between the two, but it had never occurred to her that they might once have been business partners. No wonder they hated each other.

'How is it that he can open a gallery under his own name now, if he had such a bad reputation then?'

Jill looked annoyed, as if Susan had been supposed to sympathize, not ask questions. 'Oh, all that happened over ten years ago,' she said vaguely. 'People forget over the years, and he'd been working a lot outside the country. I guess he re-established himself abroad.'

'So that's how he got to know Baltasar?'

'Must've been,' Jill said.

'What kind of trouble had Roland gotten into?' Susan asked, wondering whether Baltasar had been charitable enough to overlook Roland's murky past or was simply unaware of it.

Jill looked uncomfortable. 'As you may have gathered, I'm not exactly a friend of Roland's. Just the same, I don't think I ought to snitch on the little prick.'

Susan remembered that Roland had sold paintings to General Chomsky. She remembered that fakes had turned up in the General's collection. 'Forged paintings, was that it?'

'You're a good guesser,' Jill said, after a pause. 'Or has somebody said something to you about it?'

Susan shrugged in an omniscient way and made a mental note to grille Alex on the subject at the earliest possible opportunity. He must have known all this and hadn't seen fit to tell her. What kind of a fake brother was he, anyway? But if he had told her, she wouldn't have agreed to make a speech at Roland's opening exhibit. He's still manipulating me, she thought.

'You're right; it was forged paintings,' Jill said. 'He swore he hadn't known the paintings were fakes. I believed him, because they were very good fakes. Of course it's easy to fake modern paintings; even experts have a hard time telling. There's no real craftsmanship to speak of, and the forger can get hold of the same type of paint and canvas the artist used. And, after the paintings have had a chance to dry, you can't tell whether a picture was painted five years or fifty years ago. So, when he said he'd bought them in good faith, I believed him.'

She stopped for breath. For some reason she was looking pleased with herself. 'But then when we opened our little gallery, after a while he started getting up to his old tricks again. I didn't want to expose him and have him maybe go to jail, but I couldn't keep on working with him. It would ruin my reputation before I'd even made one. So I borrowed money, and I bought him out. But that left me without an exhibit.'

'And that was when Mrs Moffatt turned up with her son's paintings?'

'Right. I grabbed them, figuring I'd show them for a few weeks, until I could line up another artist. But before I had a chance to start looking, Hal Courtenay stopped in and—' she gave a weak laugh —'the rest is art history.'

'I don't imagine Roland was too happy with the turn of events,' Susan said.

'He was spitting mad. Kept saying I had signed up Moffatt's mother *before* I bought him out, but that's ridiculous. For one thing, who could have imagined Moffatt's stuff was going to take off like that?'

That at least had the ring of truth. Why then was there something about the rest of the girl's story that didn't quite ring true?

I must have a very suspicious nature, Susan thought.

Still, she would have liked to hear Roland's side of the story. And perhaps tomorrow she would hear it. She began to look forward to the coming rendezvous.

CHAPTER 10

Jill's tone changed. 'Well, look who's here!'' Lupe Montoya was standing at the entrace to the restaurant, looking over the clientèle. The clientèle was looking her over with equal interest, some of the male customers going so far as to get out of their chairs on the pretext of summoning their waiters, so that they could get a better view. '*Saperlipopette!*' M. Bumppo exclaimed, and was about to brush aside the maître d' in order to welcome her personally, when Jill stood up and waved. 'Over here, Lupe!' she called.

'How did a bimbo like that ever team up with a jerk like Rafael Hoffmann?' Jill muttered in an undertone as Lupe strode magnificently to their table and flung herself into a chair.

'I have decided to join you after all,' she said.

'We've almost finished,' Susan said, 'but we'd be happy to wait while you eat.'

Lupe shook her head. 'I never eat lunch. For me it is very important to keep the figure.'

She pushed her sables over the back of her chair and leaned forward, as if to display to the fullest advantage the figure she was so anxious to keep. Her dress was very tight and her décolletage very low for lunchtime.

The waiter who had rushed up to take her order nearly burst into tears when he found out coffee was all she was having. 'Another time I will come back and have dinner here, I promise you,' she told him.

As the waiter drooped off, the youngest of three men who had been lunching at a nearby table got up and came over. 'Would you ladies—?'

'Beat it, Buster,' Jill said. 'This is a business lunch. And not funny business either.' Did it disturb her, Susan

79

wondered, that her own entrance had aroused only respectful admiration?

'What an interesting restaurant,' Lupe said, looking around, 'so very American. And such charming murals: pictures of Indians and—what do you call those people in the hats with tails—backwardsmen?'

'Backwoodsmen,' Susan said. 'The murals are supposed to be illustrations to the works of James Fenimore Cooper. *Leatherstocking Tales*.'

'Ah,' Lupe said, 'I have heard of these Leatherstocking places, and I admit I was surprised that someone like you, Susan, should go to one. But this is not at all what I expected. There are no masks, no whips, not even a chain, except on the *sommelier*.' The *sommelier*, hearing himself designated, started to spring forward but was waved back.

Susan tried to explain that James Fenimore Cooper was not an Early American pornographer but an author, a classic, read by generation after generation of children. ('No, not child abuse, Lupe.') Interesting that Lupe apparently would not have been surprised that Jill should frequent the sort of establishment she had fancied this to be—and flattering to neither Jill nor Susan.

'But I have not come to talk about literature,' Lupe said. 'I have come to talk about life; that is, death—Rafael's death. I need to talk to somebody who was there when he died, yet who was not—' she groped for the right word, —'concerned with him personally. Rafael meant nothing to you, yes?' she demanded of Susan.

'Nothing,' Susan said, 'except as a fellow artist, of course.' Jill closed her eyes and said something under her breath.

'Or you?' Lupe looked at Jill. 'You were not a friend of his either?'

Jill shook her head. 'I'd never even heard of him before the show.'

'Then I will tell you, both of you, what I think. I think there was something very fishlike about the way Rafael died. I think he was—' she paused for maximum effect—'I think he was *murdered*.'

Susan tried to look appropriately surprised and shocked but could not help feeling gratified that someone else, someone who was in a position to know, shared her earlier suspicions.

Jill looked surprised and shocked enough for two. 'He couldn't have been murdered. It was a drug overdose—combined with alcohol. Didn't Baltasar tell you?'

'That is as may be,' Lupe said darkly. 'I will not deny that Rafael took drugs once in a while like everybody else. But always cocaine, never heroin. And he would never, never drink at the same time. He was very careful of his health. He—can you believe this? —actually worked out, lifted the weights, the whole *manojo*. If he had died of a vitamin overdose, that I would have believed. But drugs, never. Somebody must have given it to him without his knowing.'

'Ridiculous,' Jill said. 'You don't understand. In New York people die of drug overdoses all the time. It's like getting run over or mugged in the park. It's normal.'

'You think so? Well, perhaps you are right. Maybe I am over-reactionary. You think I should do nothing about it then? Good. I will do nothing.'

'Maybe you should tell the police your suspicions,' Susan said. She didn't particularly like the idea, as the police might then interview everybody who'd been on the scene at the time of Rafael's death. However, it was the right thing to do and she owed it to Lupe, and to herself, to tell her that. If Lupe chose not to follow up on her suggestion, then the responsibility would be Lupe's.

'I wouldn't go talk to the police if I were you,' Jill advised. 'They wouldn't take you seriously without anything to back you up. And they can be pretty rough with foreigners, especially Spanish-speaking foreigners.'

Lupe nodded. 'That is what I thought. And Rafael was a most unpleasant man and a bad artist, so why should I worry even if someone did kill him, eh? All that should concern me is the money that is coming to me. Baltasar has very kindly given me the name of a lawyer to consult in the matter of my inheritance.'

'Maybe you should talk to the lawyer about your suspicions,' Susan said. Neither Jill nor Lupe seemed to think this was a good idea.

The coffee arrived. Susan and Jill each had another cup to keep Lupe company. 'You and Baltasar seem to have known each other a long time,' Jill said.

Lupe looked coy. 'Once we were very close, and we are still good friends.'

'That was before he married the *condesa*, was it?'

Lupe opened her eyes very wide. To Susan's surprise, they were not the black or brown she would have expected but blue. 'Of course, before. He is the most honourable of men.'

'What's the *condesa* like?' Jill asked.

Lupe shrugged. 'Most people say she is very beautiful, but they always say that if a woman has a title and is passable-looking.'

As for Lupe herself, she had been married to Rafael for six years, she told them, in response to Jill's questioning. Most of this time they had spent apart, partly for professional reasons, but mostly because they couldn't stand each other. 'Sometimes I find myself blaming Baltasar for having introduced him to me, but I know that is silly. Baltasar did not force me to marry Rafael, and, if he gave me away at the wedding, it was as a favour to me, not because he wanted to.'

Susan would have liked to ask why she had married Rafael in the first place but was too well bred to put such a question. Jill wasn't.

'He seemed so—so macho. I was very young then.' Susan could see Jill counting on her fingers and then shrug. 'But that is all water over the bridgework.'

She took a deep breath. 'What I do blame Baltasar for is disappointing me now. Since he has the whole top of this fine building which he is not using, I had hoped that he would let me keep little Rover and Fido there for a time. But he said no: I could stay there myself for a while, if I did not mind the discommodity, but the law did not permit wolves to be kept in the city. And he could not let me do it secretly, because of the howling. They are very sweet and good, but I must admit they do make a lot of noise.'

'Anyhow, Baltasar doesn't like dogs,' Jill said.

'Baltasar not like dogs; wherever did you get such an idea! Baltasar loves dogs. Back in his hacienda he has dozens of big dogs and in his castle he has dozens of little dogs. Also he has cats. He takes this Esmeralda of his everywhere he goes, can you believe it?' She rolled her eyes. 'But Fido and Rover are not dogs. They are wolves. You must meet them. They are adorable.'

'Roland says Baltasar hates dogs; that's why Susan wasn't supposed to tell him that the man she saw climbing over the fence had a dog with him,' Jill said, all in one breath.

'Jill, we promised—'

'We promised not to tell Baltasar, not Lupe.'

'I think that this Roland is *loco*; that is what I think,' Lupe declared.

'All the things that have been happening at the gallery are enough to upset anyone,' Susan said, wondering why she felt impelled to defend Roland. She didn't even like him. But then nobody seemed to. Perhaps that was it—Susan Melville, champion of the underdog. Or maybe it was underwolf. Why were they talking about animals anyway?

'Pah, Roland was always a little crazy,' Lupe said. 'That is to say, so Baltasar tells me. I do not understand why he chooses to—to let such a man share his building. But then, it is none of my concern.'

Susan had been wondering the same thing, wondering, too, if Lupe had any explanation to offer out of her knowledge of Baltasar. Obviously, she didn't or wasn't going to share it with them if she did. She took out a compact that looked like solid gold and examined her face in its mirror; then, satisfied that it could not be improved upon, snapped it shut.

'I don't suppose either of you ladies could provide accommodation for Rover and Fido? They are very good and almost house-broken.'

'It would be against the law even more for me than for Baltasar,' Susan said, 'since I live in an apartment.'

'I do, too,' Jill said quickly. 'They don't even allow children in my house. You need someone with a house in the country.'

'Baltasar has an assistant, a lady who has worked for him for years,' Lupe said. 'She is living in a house in a place called Johnson Heights. That is in the country, no?'

'If you mean Jackson Heights,' Jill said, 'it's in Queens, which is part of the city. I doubt that you'd be allowed to keep wolves even there, although, judging by the things that keep happening there, it does look as if anything goes in that borough.'

'Well, I could ask her anyway,' Lupe said optimistically. 'It is in a Spanish neighbourhood, Baltasar tells me, so they will not notice the howling.'

Susan wondered why Lupe had chosen to confide her suspicions about Rafael's death to a couple of strangers, even if they had been in at the death, so to speak. It's always easier to confide in strangers, true, but that's when you expect never to see them again. If Lupe stayed in New York, they were more than likely to run into her.

Susan had a feeling that Lupe was trying to ask for help of some kind. Possibly finding a temporary home for Rover and Fido really was all she wanted, but that didn't seem like enough to account for her intensity. Maybe she was just an intense person. Maybe, it was just her way of trying to make friends, although trying to foist off a pair of wolves on a new acquaintance is not the best way of making friends.

'Have you told Baltasar of your suspicions about Roland's death?' she asked.

'Well, no, there were so many people around.'

But there are more people around now, Susan thought, than there had been at the gallery. Was it possible Lupe suspected Roland of having killed her husband?

Of course, it would have been easy enough for him to have injected Rafael with a lethal dose of heroin while they were moving a statue or something. If Rafael had had enough to drink by that time, he probably wouldn't even have noticed it. But why? Could Rafael have been black-mailing Roland? If so, Roland must have committed other and possibly darker misdeeds than those they knew about, because his former ones were apparently no secret. Perhaps Roland had chosen Rafael's work for his opening exhibit because Rafael had blackmailed him into doing it. Perhaps blackmail was a regular way for an artist to get his work shown; certainly it could account for some of the exhibits she had seen in other galleries.

She was a little sorry now that she had put Roland off when she could as easily have told Alex and Tinsley she would skip the before-dinner drinks. Was it too late to change her mind? Roland must have other plans by this time. Besides, she'd feel a fool if it turned out all he wanted was to borrow money or something like that. I can wait until tomorrow, she told herself.

CHAPTER 11

'But what is it Lupe does, exactly?' Alex asked, when Susan came to the offices of Tabor, Tinsley & Tabor to pick him up for dinner. Otherwise, he would dilly-dally and leave her to have drinks with Tinsley and Amy, only turning up when they were halfway through the soup. Impending fatherhood was getting to him.

Although the firm's offices occupied only one floor of the state-of-the-art midtown skyscraper in which it paid top-of-the-market rents—for the firm was young yet—those offices were sumptuously appointed and equipped with the fine art collection without which no self-respecting concern would be found even moribund in these days. A number of the paintings hung on the walls were Melvilles—a few the property of the firm, but most on loan from the painter herself. Jill had acceded to this, albeit grudgingly, because, 'A lot of their customers are likely to be or become collectors. Not that you need any advertisement; still, it doesn't hurt to be seen hanging in the right places. Just make sure you have Alex sign papers to show they belong to you and weren't a gift.' But Susan had already taken care of that. She might be naïve in commercial terms, but she was not a fool.

She found her fictive brother sitting behind a desk piled high with papers, keening to himself, as he so often did these days. He attempted to express courteous interest in what she had to tell him, although it was plain that he had little concern for anything at the moment except his private woes. What a shame to see the once charming rogue reduced to a quivering lump of domesticity.

'What sort of performance does this Lupe put on then?' he asked drearily.

'She described it to us in detail, and I must say I'm dying to see it. First, she says, the performance area—stage or whatever is available—is totally dark. The howling of wolves is heard.'

'Recorded, I assume?'

'In Australia, yes, owing to the bigoted—her word—quarantine laws in force there. However, when she's in the western hemisphere, she travels with Rover and Fido, and they howl along with the records. Sometimes, she says, if the audience is really "heap—" I think she means "hip—" they howl along, too.'

'Rover and Fido are her dogs?'

'Actually, they're wolves, but, she says, it saves trouble, even when she travels in places where there are no bigoted quarantine laws, if they have dog names, because people tend to assume they're dogs, which saves a lot of fuss.'

'Is that all there is—a lot of howling?'

'No, indeed. Photographs of larger-than-life wolves flash or flicker—she couldn't decide which word she preferred—on and off. Strobe lights, I would guess. This is accompanied by more howling and music that she composed herself.'

'She's a musician then?'

'Among other things. She's a multimedia artist, though not in the same way Rafael was.'

'Good,' Alex said.

'Most of the music is on tape, although sometimes she has live musicians playing drums and other instruments, depending on what's available locally and whether union rules prevail. The lights come up on a giant figure of a wolf, "semi-abstract but menacing—" her words, not mine—also created by herself.'

'She's a sculptress then?' He sighed, as if he had hoped for something more interesting.

'I suppose you could call her that also,' Susan said, 'but those are only two of her talents.'

'Carrying the statue from place to place must present a problem,' he said, 'but I'm sure she has solved it, so there's no need to give me the details. If she should ever give a performance in town we must all go see it. Get up a little family party—you and Tinsley and I and Tinsley's mother, maybe even the twins if it takes her that long to get a booking. But, for the present—'

'She calls it a construct not a statue and there's no problem transporting it because it's made of papier mâché, although she could probably handle it if it were solid granite. She's built along the lines of a Norse goddess and she doesn't need wolves—four-legged ones, anyway— to get howls. The men in the restaurant were on their hind legs yammering at the sight of her.'

Alex began to look interested. 'I must really meet her. Only right I should express my condolences,' he explained.

'The construct comes apart. Piece by piece is slowly removed. At first she had Rover and Fido do the removing, when they were available, but they tended to slobber on the mâché which softened it and spoiled the fit. So now she does it herself.'

Alex looked even more interested. 'She's inside the statue —the construct—is she?'

'Eventually all the pieces are stripped away, leaving Lupe wearing a wolf mask and, I gather, nothing else.'

'Ah,' Alex said, 'and what happens then?'

'Like all true performance art, hers is participatory. She sings and does a dance in which she gets as many of the audience as she can to dance along with her after they get rid of their wolf's clothing—i. e., the trappings of civilization —and get down to bare essentials. She and selected male members of the audience then proceed to demonstrate other aspects of natural behaviour—with females free to participate ad lib. It is at this point that the performance, especially in less progressive areas, is often cut short by the arrival of the police.'

'When I was a boy they didn't use to call that sort of thing performance art,' Alex said pensively. 'I shall look forward to attending her next appearance in New York, though not, I think, in a family party. She should be a howling success.'

He gave a melancholy laugh. Susan smiled. Expectant fathers had to be humoured.

Alex got up and went over to the fashionably inoperative window (those who wanted to commit suicide had to go up to the roof) and stared out at the splendid Manhattan panorama below that added so much to the firm's rent. 'Another two months,' he said, pressing his forehead against the glass. 'I don't know how I'm going to be able to stand it.'

Susan refused to let the subject of the conversation be changed. 'But I haven't told you the important thing, which is that Lupe thinks there's something fishy about Rafael's death. Remember, I thought there was, too?'

'Two fishies do not make a fact.'

'She said Rafael always used cocaine, never heroin, and always in extreme moderation.'

'But you said she'd been out of touch with him for years. People change. Anyhow, if he had been murdered, she'd be the chief suspect, wouldn't she? Spouses always are.'

'Except that she wasn't around to murder him.'

'Oh, who cares if Rafael was murdered or not!' Alex said passionately. 'You know what the doctor told Tinsley? From now on she has to stay home all the time until the babies come.'

Susan already knew, having received a full account from Tinsley's mother, but she let Alex have the pleasure of telling it to her all over again. 'He said: "You've really been overdoing it, Mrs Tabor. You aren't a superwoman after all." But I married her in the belief that she was a superwoman. Only a superwoman could cope with all this paperwork.' And he swept his hand across the desk, knocking a pile of bonds to the floor.

'Alex, why didn't you tell me Roland had gotten into trouble over some forged paintings?'

'What art dealer hasn't gotten into trouble over a forged painting at one time or another? And I don't see why it should matter to you.'

'Jill tells me because of that he couldn't open a gallery under his own name, but had to use her as a front.'

'But he has opened a gallery under his own name.'

'No, no, the one he ran with her—eight or nine years ago.'

'I didn't even know they'd ever had a gallery together. But then I didn't know Jill until you turned up with her.'

He looked thoughtful. 'Come to think of it, I did meet her with Hal Courtenay years ago at some Chomp House jamboree. She wore her hair long then and kept her mouth shut; that's why I didn't remember until now.'

Susan was astounded. A Chomp House jamboree did not seem like Hal Courtenay's milieu at all. 'What on earth was Hal doing there?'

'I thought you knew: he used to vet pictures for the General on a pretty regular basis until that big blowup over the fake Picasso Roland sold the old man.'

'Then the big trouble Jill was talking about was with the General?'

'Might have been, or it might have been some other forged paintings. I haven't really been following Roland's career.'

Was he as uninterested as he sounded? She knew him as well as anyone, she supposed, and yet she couldn't be sure.

Bending over, he picked up the bonds and stacked them neatly on the desk. 'Well, shall we be on our way?'

They were out in the main corridor, waiting for the elevator when he said, 'Incidentally, I was talking to a fellow I know over at National Underwriters. He says they're not completely satisfied that the fire at Roland's Gallery was accidental. It's just a rumour, so I wouldn't mention it to anyone, if I were you. But I just thought you'd be interested.'

CHAPTER 12

When Susan joined Jill at Allardyce's Auction Galleries next morning, Jill told her she'd already heard the rumour and hadn't taken much stock in it. 'People always say there's something suspicious whenever there's a fire in New York. That doesn't mean anything. After all, who could possibly stand to gain? Roland? All he'll get is enough—maybe not even enough—to pay for repairs; that artist—whatshisname —will get most of the insurance.'

'Maybe it was whatshisname who set fire to the place,' Susan suggested.

'Naaah, if you expect to set the world on fire with your paintings, you don't set fire to the gallery that's going to show 'em.'

'Baltasar?'

But that seemed even more unlikely. A businessman might arrange to have his premises set on fire if his business were failing but Baltasar's business hadn't even started yet. He lost a lot more than he could possibly gain— irreplaceable artworks (and, no matter what she thought of them personally, she had to admit he would never be able to find their like again); gowns, which could be re-created only after a lot of trouble; furniture . . . but he hadn't moved in yet, so there couldn't have been any furniture. Besides, the fire had been limited to Roland's part of the building.

'They said it was an accident,' Jill reminded her. 'A careless workman. You've seen their workmen. I rest my case.'

She fanned herself vigorously with her catalogue. 'Gosh, they certainly keep this place hot, don't they?' She pulled off the three-quarter-length mink coat that she wore no

90

matter what the occasion, sometimes no matter what the season. It was the first fur coat she had ever owned; for Jill, as she was fond of saying, had been reared in humble circumstances ('. . . and if you tell me once more that's a small village outside Pittsburgh, I shall be forced to resort to unpleasantness,' Susan had said). Actually Jill had come from the Bronx. She'd told Susan this with an air of defiance, which Susan found inexplicable. People came from all sorts of weird places.

Now, with the money Jill must have been making, first as Darius Moffatt's rep and then as Susan's, she should be able to afford several fur coats if she wanted them. And she did. Greed had shone in her eyes the day before as she stared at Lupe's sables. 'If you like it so much, why don't you get yourself a coat like it?' Susan asked after Lupe had gone.

'Sable isn't practical,' Jill said. 'It sheds. Look, Lupe's left hairs all over her chair.'

Susan herself had had fur coats when she was young and unenlightened, but now she saw no reason to decorate her body with the bodies of dead animals. She did not have a similar prejudice against leather, though, and when she saw what Jill was wearing underneath her coat, she felt like skinning the girl alive.

'Jill, put your coat back on immediately!'

'But it's so hot in here. What's wrong?' She looked at Susan with wide green eyes, like grapes. Someday I'm going to paint her as a fruit salad, Susan thought. With wax fruit.

For the upper part of Jill's body was clad in the pink T-shirt with the message 'I'm Glad I'm a Muppie' emblazoned across her chest, which might more appropriately have been inscribed 'I'm Glad I'm a Mammal'.

'I'm wearing your gift. I thought you'd be pleased.'

'You know perfectly well I didn't expect you to wear it; I meant it as a joke. Especially not in Allardyce's. People are looking at us—at you.'

'I like people to look at me,' Jill said complacently. 'But if you think the shirt makes me too conspicuous, I'll take it off. Only, I should warn you, I don't have anything on under it.'

Which was all too obvious.

'You worry too much about appearances, Susan,' Jill said.

'You're the one who's always talking about image.'

'Image is one thing, appearances another.'

'You're not entitled to wear the shirt,' Susan said desperately. 'You're not a bona fide Muppie."

'But I will be one day—not too far off either,' Jill mourned. 'Only the other morning I found a grey hair.'

Susan refused to be diverted. 'Hortense may not like your jumping the gun like that. Giving away her ideas before she's even gotten started.'

'Oh, if that's all you're worrying about . . . I called her last night and she said she'd be delighted to have me wear it, and she'd be happy to give me a further supply of her brochures to hand out to anybody who asked. She was even more delighted to hear that you were planning to invest in her health club, and hopes to see you there as a patron as well as an investor. At reduced rates, natch?'

'Natch?'

'Little archaic expression which I hoped would strike a chord.'

'It strikes something, but not a chord. I haven't made up my mind whether or not I'm going to invest in her club, but I am sure that I am not going to patronize it.'

'How about if she called it a spa?'

'I still wouldn't patronize it.'

'It looks like a good investment to me,' Jill said. 'As a matter of fact, I'm thinking of taking a piece of the action myself.' That did impress Susan, for she knew how careful Jill was of her own money.

'Who else do you think I can interest?' Jill went on. 'Baltasar? Roland? Alex? Hortense promised me a commission on any other investors I can bring in. You don't count because she already worked on you herself. Besides, since I represent you, it might not be ethical. I wonder whether Lupe would care to invest her widow's mite? She seemed interested.'

'Just Old World courtesy,' Susan said. Isn't Jill making enough money as my representative, she wondered; why

92

does she have to hustle like that? 'Remember,' she said aloud, 'we came here to look at the Moffatt.'

'Alleged Moffatt. Alleged Darius Moffatt, that is. It could be another Moffatt entirely, or maybe even a Muffett, painting a tuffet.'

But the catalogue clearly said, 'Darius Moffatt, Portrait of Emmy.' The centrefold showed a small black-and-white photograph that gave no clear idea of the original.

'"Property of an individual collector," Jill read. 'I wonder just who that "individual collector" might be.'

'Can't you tell from the name of the picture who the original buyer was?'

'He was always doing portraits of Emmy; that is, if Emmy and Emma and Emily and Emilia and Em were the same person. You can't tell from the pictures themselves. They're not exactly representational.'

You couldn't tell, indeed. Not only were the pictures not exactly representational, they were not exactly abstract either. In fact, they seemed to be a mélange of the most egregious aspects of contemporary painting. The only thing worthy of remark was the skill with which they combined such seemingly disparate styles as neoexpressionism and minimalism with occasional sorties into pop art and constructivism; and, in what seemed to be his later pictures—for his work could be dated only by inference—an occasional flirtation with conceptualism. But the female forms which sometimes appeared in various degrees of fragmentation were too far removed from realism to give any idea of the original human Emmy (or Emma or Emilia or Emily).

'Who was Emmy?' Hal Courtenay had written. 'A real woman, a figment of the artist's imagination, or a combination of both, a woman whom he had once known and perhaps loved, and who came to represent his ideal of womanhood?'

Obviously, most if not all of the pictures must have been done from memory or imagination, because Darius could hardly have towed Emmy all across the country without exciting remark from his agrarian and probably Puritanical relatives.

'I'm afraid I can't remember which I sold to whom,' Jill confessed. 'Especially in the early days when I didn't care who bought the paintings as long as their cheques were good. I'll bet it's one of the first ones that went for next to nothing, and now it's estimated at—' she gave a low howl —'a hundred to a hundred and fifty thousand dollars.'

'More than I'd be estimated at,' Susan said.

'That's because you're still alive. Imagine what your paintings will fetch after you're dead.'

'Don't look so happy at the thought,' Susan said. 'You don't own any of my pictures and the contract between us automatically terminates on my death.'

'I have faith in you, Susan. You're going to live forever like Louise Nevelson.'

I really must make out a new will, Susan thought. She still hadn't gotten around to changing her old one, which had been made out in favour of her distant cousin Sophie von Eulenberg, who was by this time very old and very mad. She supposed she would leave her money to Peter, and perhaps some to Alex (it would look odd, otherwise), but it would have to be tied up in a trust. She would trust neither with the principal, especially since the bulk of her assets was still in the form of paintings. She would need to appoint someone knowledgeable about art to look after her estate. Dare she ask Hal Courtenay to act as a trustee, she wondered.

'Portrait of Emmy' looked to Susan like most of the other Moffatts she'd seen, but Jill declared, 'I've never seen this one before. I'm sure of it.'

'It could be one that was never sold through you at all,' Susan suggested. 'He might have sold it himself. I know his mother told you he'd never sold a picture in his life, but how could she be sure with him wandering all over the country like that? Besides, she's old; her memory might be going.'

'Sharp as a tack,' Jill said.

94

'He might have given the picture to somebody—perhaps Emmy herself.'

'That's not likely!' And, when Susan wanted to know why, Jill snapped, 'Because I say so, that's why.'

Susan had an idea of why Jill was so sure, and she was surprised that no one else seemed to have had any suspicions; but then they probably hadn't heard Jill expatiate on the subject of careful marketing and timed release. Darius Moffatt must have left some paintings in his East Village apartment, and his mother probably had brought them to the Turkel Gallery to see if they were worth anything. All the rest of them had been in the barn on the Moffatt place, although whether his mother had come upon them, as the press releases said, or had known they were there all along was a matter for conjecture.

To have disclosed their existence at the time would have been to reveal the whole body of work at once, no chance for the timed release that would step up the artist's prices each time a new group of pictures was put on the market—and which would come about naturally in the case of a still-living and still-painting artist. Susan was almost sure that Jill had fabricated the story of Darius's wanderings—and the relatives with whom he had left his paintings—to make sure that prices would rise in a steady progression.

If there were any remaining from the original store in the barn, no doubt they were cached in that Long Island City warehouse, along with Susan's paintings. Someday, Susan thought, there would be a brass plate on the building that said: 'Susan Melville's and Darius Moffatt's paintings were stored here.' That is, if the building hadn't been turned into condominiums in the interval.

But there must have been a friend to whom Darius actually had given a painting. And now that friend had decided to cash in, without benefit of Jill. Good for him or her or it, Susan thought.

Jill glared at a small boy who was staring at her chest. 'And what are you looking at?'

'Which Muppet are you, lady?' he asked. 'Are you Miss Piggy?'

Jill stuck her tongue out at him and put her coat back on, to Susan's immense relief.

The boy put an instrument to his lips that Susan, after a moment of memory-searching, identified as a kazoo, and blew a mighty blast. A woman in a purple fur coat appeared and, after an angry glance at Jill, dragged the child away.

'Why don't we go look at the other pictures,' Susan suggested.

'I don't want to go look at the other pictures,' Jill said. She took another look at the Moffatt. 'I'm going to find out the name of this individual collector. I'm going to insist that whoever's in charge here tell me exactly who that anonymous turd is!'

And she stomped off, leaving Susan standing in front of 'Portrait of Emmy'.

CHAPTER 13

'Your friend seems to have quite a temper,' a voice behind her said. 'Goes with the hair. Do you suppose there's some genetic basis or is it simply a self-fulfilling prophecy?'

Susan turned. The young man whom she had met climbing out of Roland's areaway the evening before last grinned at her. 'Remember me?'

'Indeed I do.'

'I'm afraid I didn't have a chance to introduce myself. I'm Andy Mackay.'

He handed her a card. It said, 'Andrew Mackay, Investigations.' It also gave a phone number—nothing else, not even a post office box number.

'No need to tell me who you are,' he added, although she hadn't had the slightest intention of introducing herself, 'the famous "Susan Melville, Late Bloomer", as *Time*, or was it *Newsweek*, put it.'

'What are you investigating?' she asked coldly.

'All sorts of things. You'd be surprised how much there is that needs to be investigated.'

'And on whose behalf are you conducting these investigations?'

'Forgive me, but I can't tell you that. Privileged information, you know.'

'Do you usually carry out your investigations accompanied by your dog?'

'Brucie isn't my dog. I was taking care of him for a friend. He's back home now. But I'm sure he would have sent his love, if he'd known I was going to run into you.'

He looked at 'Portrait of Emmy'. 'I know this is going to give you a very poor opinion of me, but I'm afraid I just can't seem to appreciate that kind of thing. The most I can say for it is that at least it doesn't have things sticking out of it. Now, your pictures I like. You can understand what they're supposed to be—flowers and things. Although lately you've been going heavier on the things and lighter on the flowers, haven't you?'

She tried to keep herself from warming towards him. Reputable private investigators, she told herself, no matter how excellent their taste in art, do not climb over locked gates. Nor do they break and enter—or whatever the legal term for picking locks is—because she was as sure as if she had seen him open the door underneath the stairs and come out, that he had been inside the DeMarnay Gallery the other night.

All he had shown her was his card, not his licence, she reminded herself. Anyone could have a card printed up, even with raised letters. He might not even be a disreputable private investigator; he might not be an investigator at all.

Jill came back, looking angrier than before. 'They say that the consignor wishes to keep his identity private. When I insisted, they said they had no authority to give me his name. They were so fucking polite I wanted to knock their fucking teeth down their fucking throats!'

'Jill,' Susan said, 'I'd like you to meet Andrew Mackay. Mr Mackay, this is Jill Turkel.'

Jill started to snap out a surly acknowledgement of the introduction. Then she stopped. She looked at Andrew Mackay. He looked at her. He smiled at her. She smiled back.

Oh, Lord, Susan thought, all it needs is a burst of Tschaikowsky to make the moment complete.

As if in answer to her thought, there was a discordant squawk practically in her ear. The inquisitive urchin had crept up unobserved and was serenading them on his kazoo.

A member of the gallery staff rushed up, along with the lady in purple fur. 'Madam,' he said to her, 'kazoos are not permitted in Allardyce's. I suggest you try Sotheby's.'

'I will,' she said. 'All you have here is junk, anyway.' And she swept out, to kazoo accompaniment.

'Well, really,' the Allardyce man said.

'Mr Mackay was Roland's late-night visitor,' Susan told Jill. 'The one with the dog.'

'Merely passing by,' Mr Mackay said. 'Brucie saw their cat in the yard and went after her and I went after Brucie.'

'Sounds reasonable to me,' Jill said.

'Mr Mackay says he's a private investigator.'

'Oh, and what is he investigating?'

'I've already asked him that. He won't say.'

Both ladies looked inquiringly at Mr Mackay who, in harmony with his surroundings, gave them a Mona Lisa smile.

'Did you manage to get inside?' Jill asked bluntly.

Mackay looked shocked. 'Of course not. Why would I have done such a thing? Besides, it would have been illegal.'

'Does the fact that you're talking to us have anything to do with your investigation?' Jill demanded.

He bowed with such elegance Susan couldn't help being impressed. 'Let us say that I'm combining business with pleasure.'

Jill didn't say anything. She stood there, looking at him with an expression on her face that was impossible, for Susan at least, to read. Susan took her by the arm and led her from the young man's immediate vicinity. 'Well, now that you've seen the picture, shall we go?'

'I think I'd like to stick around and watch the auction after all,' Jill said. 'It might be interesting to see how much it goes for. How about going out and having lunch and then coming back afterward?'

'Do you really want me to come back here with you,' Susan asked, 'or would you rather be alone with the charming Mr Mackay—whom I warn you against. Whatever he's investigating, he's up to no good.' Or, if he's up to good, maybe you're not, she thought.

'Don't be silly, Susan,' Jill said, 'of course I want you to come to the auction with me. And we don't know that he is going to be at the auction, do we? He must have other cases.'

Susan was startled. She hadn't thought of herself as part of a case. Jill looked back over her shoulder at Mackay who was standing in front of the Moffatt, as if he were testing Marcel Duchamp's dictum that anything becomes beautiful if you look at it long enough.

'He would have to be a detective,' she said.

'I'd be happy to come to lunch with you,' Susan said, 'and go to the auction, as long as I can get out by four-thirty.'

'Oh, the picture ought to come up long before that.'

Since there wasn't time to make reservations at a posh restaurant, they repaired to a nearby coffee shop. All the way there, Jill kept looking over her shoulder, but Mackay neither attempted to follow them or accompany them. Susan was relieved. It would be most unwise of Jill to get involved with him in any way; and it was no use telling her that because she was obviously aware of it. Pity though; he seemed so much more personable than Jill's general run of young men.

They settled into a booth. 'Why do you have to be out by four-thirty?' Jill asked. 'Date?'

'Yes.'

'Anyone I know?'

'I'll have the chicken salad on rye toast,' Susan told the waitress. 'No mayonnaise.'

'I'll have a cheeseburger, medium rare, with a double

helping of fries and cole slaw and a Coke. No gourmet food for me today!'

'All our food is gourmet,' the waitress said huffily. 'The cole slaw is subtly seasoned with fresh herbs and the cheese on the all-lean-beef hamburger is New York State Cheddar, aged to a mellow ripeness.'

'I know it's none of my business,' Jill said, when they finally got rid of the waitress (but not before she told them how the potatoes had been flown in from Idaho by gentle jet), 'but your date isn't with Hal Courtenay, by any chance, is it?'

'Hal said he was going out of town and wouldn't be back until the middle of the week. I told you. If he's back already, he hasn't gotten in touch with me. There wouldn't have been any reason.'

'All right, all right,' Jill said, 'I was just making conversation, not innuendos. Even if I am your rep, I don't have to know everyone you know, keep tabs on you wherever you go—although that might be a good idea. You never know when there might be a sudden call for your work.'

'Also, you're nosy.'

'Also, as you say, I'm nosy.'

'If I were nosy,' Susan said, trying to sound casual, 'I would ask whether there's anything between you and Hal.'

'And, being frank and open, I'd tell you that there was once, a long time ago, but he decided I was too young and uncouth for him and I decided he was too old and stuffy for me—so the field is clear for you.'

'Don't be silly, Jill.'

'I'm not being silly,' Jill said. 'He's been making a play for you; you must have noticed. But, if you'll take my advice, and I know you won't, you'll steer clear of him.'

'Mind telling me why?'

'Because he's a lying, cheating, stinking snake-in-the-grass, that's why,' Jill said.

She stopped and gave Susan a forced smile. 'As you can see, we do have our little differences. Nothing serious, of course. But I do think you owe it to Peter to stay away from Hal.'

'Since when have you been so concerned for Peter?'

'Maybe I don't show it, but I have always had the utmost respect for Peter. Are you going to have dessert? I'm going to have a banana split with hot fudge sauce, full steam ahead and damn the calories. I'm full of conflicting emotions and when my emotions are in conflict I eat.'

When they returned to the auction room, Mackay was there, to Jill's pleasure and Susan's regret. However, they had reason to be thankful to him, for he had saved them a couple of choice seats up front; otherwise they might not have gotten seats at all. The place was packed.

Jill looked around. 'I'm surprised not to see Roland here.'

'Why should he be here?' Susan asked.

'This is an important auction,' Jill explained. 'Most of the other dealers are here. And collectors. Look, there's Baltasar. I wonder why he's here.'

'Maybe he wants to buy some pictures,' Mackay suggested humbly.

'I know he did buy some of Rafael's pieces to decorate his place in Acapulco,' Jill said, 'but I didn't know he was a collector. This stuff is too expensive for mere decoration. Still, it's possible. Who knows what he has in his hacienda? Or his castle? Besides dogs, of course, and probably horses. People who live in castles always have horses.'

'That sounds like a proverb,' Susan said.

'In time it will be.'

'Do people buy art only because they want to decorate their places or because they're collectors?' Mackay asked. 'Don't they ever buy a picture or a statue just because they happen to like it?'

'Not at these prices,' Jill said. 'I can see you have a lot to learn about art.'

'Maybe you could find the time to teach me,' he suggested.

'Portrait of Emmy' didn't come up until a quarter to five. It sold for two hundred and fifty thousand dollars and went to one of Gil Stratton's associates.

When the gavel came down for the third time, Jill gave a

101

loud shriek, tore up her catalogue, jumped on it, and was requested to leave by the management. Susan left also, trying to act as if they were not together, that it was just chance that they happened to be leaving at the same time.

This time Mackay did follow them out. Brave man, Susan thought, but probably it's part of his job. He really did seem to like Jill, though.

'How about a drink?' he suggested. 'I should think you could use one.

'She has a date,' Jill said, 'but I certainly could use one. A drink, I mean. Maybe two, if your expense account can stand it.'

Susan didn't like the idea of Jill's going off alone with young Mr Mackay. For a moment she thought of breaking her date with Roland and tagging along, however undesired her presence might be, but she couldn't do that. It wouldn't be fair to Roland. And Jill probably would feel it wasn't fair to her either.

CHAPTER 14

What on earth could Roland have to say to her, Susan wondered again as she walked uptown. Was it something she would want to hear? Did he want her help in some way? Did he want to warn her against someone? Or had he simply chosen her to be a repository for his confidences?

And why had he been so insistent that nobody should know that they had arranged to meet? She felt a vague sense of unease, for which there was no rational explanation. The likelihood was that he wanted to tell her something about Jill; and, indeed, she was beginning to wonder about the girl herself. Yesterday she had given Susan to understand that Roland had originally gotten into trouble for dealing in forged paintings—and that she had parted company with him when she'd caught him 'up to his old tricks'.

All of which had sounded plausible enough while she was speaking. Now that Susan had time to think about it, she recalled that the two had been running a small Soho gallery that dealt in the work of little-known artists. Why would anyone bother to fake a painting by a little-known artist?

Could it be a question of stolen rather than fake paintings? If so, Roland could hardly have expected to exhibit them in the gallery. Had he gone in for theft as a sideline; and had Jill found out about it and wanted nothing to do with him? That made sense. But why hadn't Jill simply told Susan that Roland was a thief? Then she remembered that Jill hadn't been the one to suggest that Roland had been involved with forged paintings. Susan had, herself, and Jill had agreed. If Susan had suggested that Roland had been caught stealing paintings, perhaps Jill would have agreed to that too.

What was it Roland actually had done? Maybe I'll find out now, she thought, quickening her step.

Earlier the day had been warmish for the time of year, but since then a chilly wind had sprung up. It was quite cold now. Susan pulled the collar of her coat up around her ears.

As she reached the corner of Madison Avenue, she could see from across the street that a crowd had gathered on Roland's block—a quiet crowd rather than a demonstrative one, the kind of crowd that gathers whenever there is either trouble afoot or a film crew at work; that is, a crew making a movie, as distinguished from a television crew, which goes hand in hand with—and sometimes precedes—trouble.

There were cameras from two of the TV networks and one of the local stations and a number of police cars, plus a bunch of what appeared to be reporters, some with microphones, some with tape recorders, one traditionalist with a notebook. An ambulance drew away as she approached. Trouble, maybe even big trouble, but not major trouble, or all the networks would have been there.

She was strongly tempted to turn back. Later she could explain to Roland that she hadn't wanted to push her way through the throng. Provided, of course, that Roland was in a position where he could be explained to. Because the space the police had cleared was directly in front of the

DeMarnay gallery, and the uniformed policeman who was shooing passers-by away was standing at the bottom of the DeMarnay Gallery's steps. Another policeman was posted at the top, and she could see several more down in the areaway. Whatever had happened, had happened right there.

The uneasiness inside her stopped being a vague feeling and developed into something very specific. Prudence told her to turn back, go home, and wait until she heard about it, whatever it was, on the news. But prudence had never been one of her strong points.

She approached the steps. Several reporters glanced at her. Fortunately none appeared to be from the fine arts departments of their respective media, or she might have been recognized and pounced upon. 'Distinguished artist in front of gallery where [disaster] occurred' would be good for some kind of story even if she were only passing by on her way to the supermarket.

'Move along, please, miss,' the policeman said. 'There's been an accident. Nobody allowed inside.'

'I'm sorry to hear that. I had an appointment with Mr DeMarnay.'

Although she'd kept her voice low, she could see the reporters' ears prick up. From the expression on the policeman's face and the glance he exchanged with the policeman at the head of the stairs, she could tell that Roland was not going to be able to keep their appointment.

'Mr DeMarnay,' the policeman repeated. 'Mr Roland DeMarnay, would that be?'

'Yes, Roland DeMarnay. I do hope he hasn't been hurt or anything?'

But she knew, as surely as if there had been a wreath hanging on the gallery door and a heavenly chorus singing overhead, that Roland was dead. Poor Roland, she couldn't help thinking, he's never going to have to worry about getting bald after all.

One of the reporters took a tentative step in her direction. 'Just what was your business with DeMarnay—?' he began, when the policeman cut him off with, 'I'm sure Lieutenant Bracco would like to have a word with you, miss. If you wouldn't mind coming upstairs.'

What would he do if I said I did mind, she wondered. Seize me, handcuff me, and drag me up the stairs? But no question of her refusing. It was an honest citizen's duty to cooperate with the law; and, in spite of having committed some actions in the past that the law in its narrow-mindedness might frown upon, she remained an honest citizen in her own mind and heart, which was what counted.

The first policeman escorted her up the stairs and entrusted her to the second policeman, who opened the door and said to the plainclothesman who appeared, 'A lady come to see Mr DeMarnay,' in a manner reminiscent of the Frog Footman.

Inside, boards and buckets and sawhorses were stacked against the walls, but none of the workmen was in sight. No doubt it was the end of the working day; however, it seemed unlikely that they were going to be back any time soon.

'Please wait here, miss,' the detective said, indicating one of the two bronze and leather benches sited on opposite sides of the foyer. He went through the archway that led to the interior of the gallery and was now closed by a barrier, a cross between a curtain and a folding door, made of shining geometric shapes that broke the reflection of his body into fragments and repeated them in almost cubistic fashion, as he pushed one half aside and passed through. The barrier had been there on her previous visits, she recalled, but it had been folded back against the wall on either side, so that she had taken it to be a pair of ornamental pilasters.

A dishevelled-looking Damian and Paul were huddled on the other bench. They appeared to have been weeping. She could think of no tactful way of phrasing her question. 'What happened?'

'Oh, Miss Melville,' Damian whimpered, 'it—it's too terrible to talk about. Paul and I stopped in on our way to lunch to pick up some things we'd left—' here Paul burst into loud sobs —'we've been on hiatus you know, until the redecorating was finished—and we found Roland—

squashed to pieces . . . *strewn* all over the basement . . .'

'It was awful,' Paul sobbed, 'awful. I was sick all over the carpet.'

'I was sick, too,' Damian said. 'I was just as sick as you were, maybe even sicker.'

She was not interested in their relative degrees of nausea, particularly as she was beginning to feel a trifle queasy herself She couldn't help remembering 'Concupiscent Toad Crushed by Passion', and envisageing Roland in similar state. 'Roland is dead, then?'

'Is he ever,' Damian moaned.

'And the carpet is ruined,' Paul said.

'Don't be so heartless,' Damian admonished him. 'Carpets can be cleaned, but nothing will ever bring Rollie back.' Damian turned to Susan, 'They say he must have been beaten to death after a party, but he never would have had a party without inviting us.'

'You never know though, do you?' Paul said. 'You think you know somebody utterly, and then they go and do something like this behind your back.' He shook his head.

'A party?' Susan repeated.

'We never partied like that,' Damian said. 'It was just fun and games. I know some people do go in for pain, but it wasn't *our* thing. Besides, Roland had a very low pain threshold.'

'All those sinister-looking things he had hanging on the walls and around were just for decoration,' Paul said. 'That's what he told me when I wanted to—that's what he told me.'

'They were valuable antiques. He would never let us so much as touch them, let alone use them.'

'But he must have let someone else use them,' Paul sobbed. 'And they squashed him like a bug in the basement.'

'We mustn't speak ill of the dead. Maybe he didn't let someone use the things. Maybe, whoever it was simply took one and—and *bashed* him.'

Both of them burst into loud wails. I should try to comfort them, Susan thought, instead of wanting to take a blunt instrument and bash them myself.

*

The detective returned and, after casting a look at Damian and Paul which of itself was almost enough to lay him open to charges of police brutality, said, 'If you'll come this way, miss—'

She hesitated. 'You're not taking me to see the . . . er . . . Mr DeMarnay, are you?'

He looked shocked. 'No, no, of course not. The remains have been removed. Anyhow, the fatality took place in the basement. And that's where most of our people and the forensics people are right now.'

'But it's so quiet up here.' Surely with all that activity going on they should be able to hear . . . something.

'The basement's soundproofed,' he said.

'Of course. How naïve of me.'

'Lieutenant Bracco is up here in the office on this floor. All very nice and pleasant, except for the artwork and that can't be helped.'

'Philistine,' either Damian or Paul hissed.

Ignoring this, the detective waved Susan towards the back of the gallery. He pushed half of the shiny closure aside and they entered the alcove that led to Roland's office.

Lieutenant Bracco was sitting at Roland's desk underneath an enormous Italian Renaissance painting with a classical theme. Esmeralda was sitting on the blotter in front of him, washing her face. Each of them pretended that the other wasn't there, Esmeralda rather more successfully than the lieutenant.

On the night of the gallery's opening, the office had been dimly lit. From the brief glimpse Susan had had, she'd thought that the picture over Roland's desk depicted satyrs chasing nymphs. Now she could see the picture was of satyrs chasing other satyrs and, in some instances, catching them. A scene of a very intimate nature was taking place right over the detective's head. From the fact that he never once turned his head in the course of their conversation, it was clear that he was aware of it.

The picture appeared to have suffered no damage from the fire; it hadn't even been darkened by smoke. Or perhaps it had, and Roland had restored it. Pity, she thought.

The lieutenant got up to greet her with the courtesy due an upper-bracket taxpayer and a lady. 'Relative of the deceased?' he asked. He sounded more like an undertaker than a detective.

'No, just a friend.'

He looked surprised, either that Roland should have such respectable friends, or that she should have such unrespectable ones.

'A business friend. I'm a painter.'

He nodded, as if that made it better, but she still had the feeling that she had let him down somehow. 'Please sit down, Mrs —er—?' he said, sinking back into his seat and indicating a chair on the opposite side of the desk. The plainclothesman remained just outside the door—ready to spring to his chief's aid if she should turn violent, she supposed.

'Melville, Susan Melville. And it's Miss, not Mrs.'

Esmeralda started washing her toes meticulously, paying great attention to the spaces in between. There was something hypnotic about the ritual. Susan tore her eyes away with an effort.

'What happened to Mr DeMarnay?' she asked. 'Or can't you tell me?'

'It's a matter of public record, or will be as soon as we've given a statement to the media. Citizens have a right to know. He was battered to death. Looks like your standard sex crime, with things getting out of hand. No evidence of robbery, so far as we can tell.'

He hesitated; then went on, 'There's a room in the back of the basement, very . . . exotically furnished, and fitted up with all the usual appurtenances—whips, hoods, chains, leather garments, and what forensics tells me are old-fashioned torture instruments—so that sort of thing seems to have been a regular activity.'

'Damian and Paul say it wasn't.'

'Damian and Paul? Oh, the Bobbsey twins. Well, what would you expect them to say? You know them?'

'I've met them before. They work at the gallery. But of course you know that.'

'So they informed me,' he said. 'Anyhow, that's where it happened. I'm sure you've never been down there.'

'No,' Susan said, 'I never have.' And now she probably would never get the chance to, either. 'When did he die?' she asked. 'Do they know that yet?'

'The fellow from the ME's office says, at a rough estimate, sometime between midnight and three. They'll know more exactly when they get him in the lab. Those two said they found him at noon, and the workmen did see them come in. But they could have done it the night before and come back. On the other hand, that doesn't mean they did it, either. He probably knew other people of that . . . er . . . nature. And the alarm system was off, so it wouldn't have been too hard for anyone to get in, though there weren't any signs of forced entry.'

'What was it . . . er . . . done with?'

He seemed disappointed at her unladylike thirst for details, but citizens had a right to know. 'The murder weapon was a heavy piece of brass, shaped like—it was a heavy piece of brass that I understand is supposed to be a kind of sculpture. It was wiped clean, so there weren't any fingerprints.'

The mere fact that it had been wiped clean did not of itself mean that Roland's death had not been a crime of passion; simply that the killer had come to his senses after the deed was done and set about trying to cover his tracks. But she was already beginning to have doubts that Roland's death was just a simple hit-and-run S-and-M encounter.

'Now, I wonder whether you'd mind telling me what the exact nature of your business with Mr DeMarnay was,' Bracco asked. 'Not that it could be connected in any way with the unfortunate event, I'm sure, but we're going to have to ask the same thing of everybody who had the slightest connection with him. Matter of routine.'

'Of course. I quite understand. He asked me to come see him, but he didn't tell me why. I had an idea that he might want me to exhibit my pictures in his gallery, which wouldn't, of course, be up to me but to my representative.

She handles that kind of thing. I'm afraid I'm not much of a businesswoman.' The lieutenant looked approving. As she'd expected.

'But since Roland—Mr DeMarnay—put it as a personal favour, I didn't like to refuse.'

'Personal favour?' The lieutenant looked disapproving.

'He was a friend—an acquaintance—of my brother's.' Oh dear, she thought, now she'd brought Alex into it. Well, if they were going to ask questions of anyone who had anything to do with Roland, they were bound to get around to Alex sooner or later. So all she'd done was make it a little sooner.

'They weren't close. His wife—Alex's—is expecting a baby,' she added, hoping she'd made her meaning perfectly clear.

The lieutenant seemed satisfied. 'I think that's all I need to ask you right now. Unless you know something else that you think might be of help?'

I know that a man died of heroin poisoning here a couple of months ago and that his wife thinks it was murder. I know that there was a fire here a month ago, and the rumour is that it might have been arson. I know Roland was a dealer in forged paintings and God knows what else. It did not occur to her then that Darius Moffatt's death, although it had occurred almost ten years before, could have some connection with the things that had been going on in the gallery, or she might have added it to her mental list.

She shook her head. 'I'm afraid I can't think of anything. Really, I hardly knew the man.'

Let the police find out all these things and put them together for themselves. That was what they were paid for. Enough that she had thrown Alex to the wolves. She wondered whether Lupe had succeeded in establishing Rover and Fido in Jackson Heights, or whether she was still looking for a home for them. Should she tell the lieutenant about Lupe's arrival? No, let Baltasar. Lupe probably had nothing to do with all this. An unfortunate coincidence that she had happened to turn up yesterday.

*

'One thing more,' the lieutenant said, as Susan was about to get up, 'you don't happen to know where we might locate a Mr Baltasar who has the place upstairs, do you? Those two out there told us he's living at the Plaza, but, although he is registered there, we haven't been able to reach him.'

It was almost as if he had been reading her thoughts. 'Ordinarily, I wouldn't, because I hardly know him either, but I just came from an auction at Allardyce's. He was there, and he might still be there; the auction wasn't over when I left.'

'Thank you, you've been very helpful.' The lieutenant picked up the phone and gave instructions to someone at the other end to go to Allardyce's and pick up Baltasar, if he were still there. I hope they're not going to fetch him in a police car with sirens screaming, she thought. He won't like that at all. But then I'm not enjoying myself very much either.

This time she finally did rise, and Bracco rose along with her. 'By the way,' he said, acknowledging Esmeralda's presence for the first time, 'this cat—she does belong to someone in the building, doesn't she?'

Hearing herself mentioned, Esmeralda rolled over and waved her paws in the air as if to show she at least had no secrets. But she has, Susan thought. She must know everything that's been going on here. She probably even knows who killed Roland, might even have seen it happen.

'She belongs to Baltasar upstairs. Her name is Esmeralda.'

'Is that Mr Baltasar or Baltasar something? I mean, is Baltasar his first or last name?'

'It seems to be his only name, at least the only name he goes by. He's a dress designer. They often have only one name.'

'I don't suppose he would have participated in the . . . the festivities in the basement.'

'I would hardly think so.' Although, of course, you never could tell.

'Well, anyway, I'm glad to know the cat belongs here. I'd hate to think a stray got in somehow and we let her stay

111

and leave hairs all over everything and maybe make a mess.'

Esmeralda sat up and looked affronted.

'Oh, no, I'm sure Baltasar will be delighted that you're taking such good care of her.'

She would have liked to ask whether Esmeralda had been found on the actual scene of the crime or merely wandering about the place. But she had asked too many questions already. She tickled Esmeralda between the ears. Esmeralda purred.

'If you'll just give your name and address and your brother's name and address to Sergeant Collins—' he indicated the detective at the door —'we'll know where to get in touch with you, if it should turn out to be necessary. You will let us know if you're planning to go out of town, won't you?'

'Yes, certainly, but I'm not planning to go anywhere.'

'You might as well give him your representative's name and address, too, in case DeMarnay happened to tell her what he wanted to talk to you about.'

And if he checks into Roland's past, as he undoubtedly will, and finds out that my representative was once Roland's partner, what will he think then? Especially since it wasn't likely Jill would volunteer the information.

She started to go; then paused at the door. 'I've just remembered something. I don't know whether it'll be helpful or not.' And she told him about having met Andrew Mackay outside the DeMarnay Gallery, and then again at the auction gallery, behaving suspiciously in both instances. Him she was glad to sacrifice.

The lieutenant seemed a little annoyed. 'So they've had this place under surveillance, have they? I do wish they'd let us know what they're up to. I'll have to have a talk with him.'

'Who are "they"?'

He smiled. 'Come now, Miss Melville, I've been very frank and open with you, but you must allow us to have some secrets.'

'Mr Mackay went off with my representative,' Susan said. 'I think I ought to know who he is.'

'If she can't take care of herself, she isn't much of a representative, is she? I take it she's young and pretty.' Susan nodded. He shrugged. 'Well, you know what these private eyes are like.'

'So he's a real detective then?'

Bracco considered. 'He is an investigator,' he said finally. 'I suppose you could call him a detective.'

'And he does have a licence?'

'In a manner of speaking.'

She waited, but he offered no explanation. So Mackay was on the right side of the law. Right now she wasn't sure whether that was good or bad.

CHAPTER 15

Although the light on her answering machine was glowing when she got home, indicating that messages were waiting, they could keep on waiting, she thought, as she sat down to mourn Roland. He was a despicable little man but he deserved to be mourned, especially as she couldn't help feeling that if she had agreed to talk to him the evening before, he might be alive now. On the other hand, she too might be dead. Whatever secret he'd had to impart apparently was worth killing for, unless his death was the crime of passion it appeared to be.

She made herself a drink and turned on the radio. The news reports offered nothing new. Roland had been savagely beaten to death with a bronze statuette of, as the announcer put it, 'an erogenous nature', seemingly in the course of an orgy that had gotten out of hand. Such things were happening too often these days, a commentator said. It wasn't clear whether he was referring to orgies or murders.

The phone rang. Alex. 'I've been trying to reach you all afternoon,' he complained—which, she later discovered, was an exaggeration. There had been only one message from him, although there were so many messages from so many other people (routine these days), it was possible that he had tried her more than once and failed to get through.

'I've been with the police,' she said.

'Do they want you to give a course in graffiti appreciation to police cadets, or have you been up to something?'

'In connection with Roland's death. You must have heard about it by now.'

'I heard it on the radio,' he said. 'That's why I've been calling. Very sad about Roland, of course, but why were the police talking to you? You didn't do it, did you?'

She tried to indicate by her tone of voice that she felt this remark was not in the best of taste. 'I had an appointment to see Roland this afternoon. Since I had no idea anything had happened, I just walked in on the investigation.'

No point in letting him know that she hadn't simply stumbled into the investigation but had seen something was wrong and deliberately walked right into it. And could kick herself now. Otherwise, unless the police got in touch with everybody on Roland's address list, they might never have gotten around to her.

He sounded apprehensive. 'An appointment to see Roland! Why on earth would you want to see Roland?'

She explained once again that she hadn't wanted to see Roland. He had wanted to talk to her, and, no, she didn't know why and would probably never know now.

'You should have known better than to go see Roland,' Alex said.

'For heaven's sake, I didn't know he was going to be killed, did I? I went for the same reason I spoke at the opening of his gallery: I didn't want to refuse a request from a friend of yours.'

Spluttering sounds came from the telephone. 'And I suppose you told the police I was a bosom buddy of Roland's?'

'I told them you were the one who introduced me to him . . . Well, they wanted to know how I came to know Roland, and that's the truth, isn't it?'

'That doesn't mean you had to go and blab it to the police. You could have said you forgot who introduced you to him. You could have said he introduced himself to you at—at some art thing or other. You could have—'

114

'Alex, they're undoubtedly going to investigate his background, find out everybody he knew. It would look odd if I'd said I didn't remember who introduced us, when lots of people know he was a friend—all right, an acquaintance—of yours.'

'All right, all right. It's just that I hate getting mixed up in something like this when I haven't done anything. In all the years I worked for the General, the police never even knew I existed, except for the odd parking ticket. You really don't have any idea what Roland wanted to talk to you about?'

'None whatsoever. I do have a feeling, though, that he wasn't really beaten to death by a . . . a lover, I suppose you'd call it.'

'I'd call it a sex maniac,' he said firmly, 'and I should think they'd investigate all the sex maniacs of his acquaintance and not bother with anybody else. In fact, it was probably done by a stranger—somebody he just picked up. That's the way most of these sex murders happen.'

'You don't really believe that, do you, Alex? After everything else that's happened?'

'It could all have been a series of coincidences.'

'And that man I saw coming out of Roland's place that night and thought was a prowler could have been a coincidence, too, only he wasn't a prowler and I doubt that he was a coincidence either. He's a detective or something along that line and his name's Andrew Mackay.'

She told Alex what the lieutenant had said, and also not said, about Andrew Mackay. 'And why would he have been snooping around the gallery if he hadn't thought something was going on?' she concluded.

'Vice squad, maybe,' Alex suggested. 'Okay, okay, so they had suspicions about the gallery.'

'But who are "they", Alex? And what were they suspicious of?'

'Could be the Feds.'

'You mean Roland was a spy?' Somehow she couldn't see Roland as a KGB employee. She had more respect for the Russians than that.

'The Federal Government has its fingers in a number of pies—spies, drugs, tobacco, alcohol, firearms, immigration and naturalization, transporting stolen property and/or underage women (or, in this case, underage men) across state lines. This fellow—Mackay—didn't give you any clue what he was after?'

'Jill, as far as I could see. The last I saw of him he was going off with her. I must say he really seemed to like her.'

'Probably part of his cover,' Alex said. He was not a fan of Jill's.

'What cover? He said he was a detective—an investigator, anyhow. I mean today. He didn't say so when I met him with the dog, but then he didn't say anything about who he was then.'

'Ah, yes, the dog. I was forgetting the dog.' Alex sounded very thoughtful.

'Is there something significant about the dog? He did bark in the night, you know—although it was at Esmeralda. The cat,' she added, in case Alex had forgotten who Esmeralda was.

'Your guess is as good as mine,' Alex said. She knew that evasive note in his voice.

'And you're not going to tell me what your guess is?'

'No, because I could be wrong, and I hope I am.'

Sometimes he could be very exasperating. Later she realized that she had been very dense.

'Has it occurred to you that, if this is something more than a sex crime, Roland may have been killed to keep him from talking to you?'

'The thought had occurred to me,' she admitted.

Which would mean that the killer would have to be someone who knew she'd had an appointment with Roland. Roland had been careful not to let anyone hear what they were saying, but anyone who was on the premises or even outside in the street could have seen him draw her aside and talk to her confidentially. And anyone who had seen them could have passed on his observations to someone else. So far as knowledge, or at least suspicion, of their rendezvous was concerned, the field was wide open.

'I don't want to frighten you but you could be in danger,' Alex said.

'If you don't want to frighten me, then don't tell me I could be in danger. Anyhow if somebody killed Roland to keep him from talking to me, why should I be in danger? Roland was very effectively stopped from talking to me.'

'He might feel Roland had already told you too much.'

'But if Roland had told me anything, I could already have passed it on to someone else. Like you, for example. Or he could have talked to other people. Is he—or she—going to batter everyone in Roland's address book to death?'

He laughed. 'That would be a tall order. But "she"? I hardly think a woman would have been able to beat Roland to death.'

She didn't agree. So many of today's young women made a fetish of fitness, and often had as much muscular strength as men. And not only young women. Someone like Hortense Pomeroy, for example, could have battered Roland to death without exerting herself. Hortense wouldn't even have needed a brass statuette of an erogenous nature; she could have done it with her bare hands.

'Whatever it was he wanted to say to me might have nothing at all to do with the reason he was killed,' Susan said.

'Maybe so, but I still don't think it's a good idea for you to be there alone. Why don't you come stay with us? We have plenty of room and Tinsley would be glad of your company.'

Tinsley would be especially glad now. That very morning, her mother, who'd been spending most of her days at the Tabor domicile, had departed for California to visit her younger daughter who was due to give birth any day now. Alex and Tinsley did have a live-in housekeeper, personally selected (and salaried) by Amy herself, but they couldn't impose on her the way they could on a member of the family. No, on the whole Susan would rather take her chances with the murderer.

117

'It's kind of you to offer, Alex, but I'm sure I'm not in any danger. Besides, I can take care of myself.'

'I'm not so sure of that. Remember, you don't have a gun any more.'

'There are a couple of guns still left from Father's collection that I think I can lay my hands on.'

'But they're old. They might not work. You're out of practice.'

'The last one worked very well,' she reminded him. 'And I'd been out of practice then much longer than I am now.'

As soon as she got rid of Alex, she went to the closet shelf where she had stored the remaining guns in a suitcase, locked ever since Peter's return. Not that he was snoopy, but better safe than sorry. They were in excellent condition, which they should have been as she had devoted considerable time to their cleaning and polishing ever since she discovered her affinity for them. She had fresh ammunition for them now. She'd purchased it while she was attending a fine-arts conference at a university in a state with more liberal gun laws than New York's.

Why she'd picked up the ammunition she didn't know exactly, except that she hated things that were incomplete, and a gun without ammunition was like an unfinished canvas. And the conference had been very boring. Of course these guns were nothing like the state-of-the-art models she'd grown accustomed to when she'd been a professional, but they had been the finest obtainable in their day, certainly adequate for emergency use—and easier to explain if she should happen to be caught carrying a concealed weapon. Not that the fact that the gun had belonged to her father would make her possession of it any more legal; just that at least there would be no questions about the gun's provenance.

But she didn't intend to be caught carrying it, she thought, as she loaded the gun.

She got out one of the big handbags that she'd carried in her gun-toting days. After transferring her belongings (always such a nuisance, changing bags) she dropped in the gun. Amazing how much comfort it gave her to know that there was a gun within reach. It wasn't that she didn't believe in strict gun control laws. She knew, through vivid personal experience, how the mere possession of a gun could provoke the mildest of persons into violence. In her case her impulsive behaviour had had positive results, both for herself and society, but that was the exception. She had read and heard of too many instances where otherwise upstanding citizens who, piqued by loved ones or fellow motorists, had expressed that pique with a bullet, for her to feel that unrestricted ownership of handguns was a good thing. Some people just could not be trusted with guns. If that's an élitist viewpoint, so be it, she told herself.

Only after she had armed herself was she able to relax and play back the messages on her answering machine. There was one from Hal Courtenay. Was he back in town or had he called her from Houston? His message gave no idea of the time he had called or his reason for calling. It merely said he was sorry to have missed her and would she call him back. Since he gave no number for her to call him, that must mean he was back in New York and had called her immediately upon his return. She would need to find out why he had been so anxious to see her before she could let herself feel flattered.

She phoned the Museum. 'I'm afraid Mr Courtenay is out of town,' his secretary said.

'I know he went to Houston, but I thought he might be back.'

'Houston?' The secretary sounded puzzled. 'I was under the impression he'd gone to Litchfield. He has a farm up there. In any case, he's not expected back until tomorrow.'

It was none of her business whether he had gone to Houston or Connecticut. If he'd been out of town, he would have left an out-of-town number for her to call back. No, he must be back in town and simply hadn't checked in at the Museum. No reason why he should if he wasn't due until the next day.

She called his home number. An orchestra played several

119

bars of *Pictures at an Exhibition*; then Hal's mellifluous voice said, 'This is Hal Courtenay. I am so sorry not to be here to receive your call. However, if you will be good enough to leave your name, number, and a message, I will be only too happy to call you back, just as soon as I possibly can.'

Another few bars of *Pictures at an Exhibition*, followed by a chime—no beep for Hal Courtenay.

She gave her name and number and said, 'Returning your call.' That was one of the drawbacks of an answering machine. Two machines could chat back and forth indefinitely without their owners' ever making direct contact.

There were a lot of other messages, but nothing of real interest.

She didn't call any of them back. They could wait until tomorrow, or the next day, or, in the case of one or two, forever.

CHAPTER 16

Close to eight o'clock her phone rang. This would be Hal, she thought. On previous occasions the idea of hearing his voice could . . . well . . . not cause her heart to skip a beat —her heart didn't go in for that sort of thing—but arouse pleasurable emotions in her. Now she felt only mildly interested in discovering the purpose of his call. Of course Roland's death had put a damper on any pleasurable emotions she might be feeling in any connection. More than that, though, it was hard to believe that the director of a respected museum, someone who should be an arbiter of taste and elegance, would do anything so tacky as to have his answering machine respond with a burst of canned music. Next thing you knew, the elevators in the Museum would be playing Muzak.

She picked up the phone.

It wasn't Hal. It was Jill. She was practically gibbering. 'I just heard about what happened to Roland. Did you know? Why didn't you call me?'

120

It hadn't even occurred to Susan to call Jill. 'Calm down, you're hysterical. I knew you were out with Mr Mackay. I wouldn't have expected you to be back so soon.'

'Nor would I,' Jill acknowledged. 'We had a couple of drinks, and we were getting on very well, or so I thought. Turns out we have a lot in common. He doesn't run but he does play squash. And he likes sushi.'

She made it sound as if sushi were some kind of game. Well, in a way when you ate raw fish, you were playing Russian roulette. But she'd already told Jill that a number of times; no use telling her again. And no point. For all she knew Roland had never eaten raw fish and yet, there he was, dead as a mackerel.

'So things were going great,' Jill went on, 'and there was talk of dinner, but he said he had to call his answering service first. When he came back, he was looking very funny. Something had come up, he said, and he'd have to take a rain check on dinner. Naturally I thought it must be another woman.'

She brightened a little. 'Maybe somebody told him what had happened to Roland and that was what called him away. Why didn't he tell me, though?'

'A detective's work is confidential, Jill,' Susan said, knowing she sounded like a schoolteacher. She hated sounding like a schoolteacher, especially when she was imparting information that she had acquired from watching television rather than some more scholarly pursuit. 'Probably there are all sorts of things that come up in the course of his work that have to be attended to right away. It might have had nothing at all to do with Roland.'

'Maybe,' Jill said, 'but I still have a feeling that it did.'

So did Susan, but she saw no reason to tell Jill that. Nor did she feel it needful to mention that she had told the police about Mackay's presence at the scene of the crime earlier in the week; and that it was possibly as a result of that disclosure that the young man had received the message that took him away from Jill.

So she had spoiled Jill's date. Someone had spoiled

Roland. A life was more important than a date, though possibly not to Jill. Especially not Roland's.

'I went home wondering whether or not I'd been dumped,' Jill went on. 'Then I turned on the radio, and I heard about Roland. Oh, Susan, I'm so scared; I don't know what to do. Could I come over and stay with you tonight? Please?'

She seemed to be in a panic. Susan couldn't understand why. 'What do you have to be frightened about? He was beaten to death in an orgy. It could happen to anyone—anyone who went in for orgies, that is.'

'You know that's not true: that it was just a sex murder, I mean. There was too much funny stuff going on at the gallery before.'

Since that was precisely what she herself had told Alex, Susan could not in all honesty disagree. 'But why should that put you in such a panic, Jill? You haven't had anything to do with Roland for years, have you?'

'Anybody who's ever had anything to do with Roland, in any way, is in danger,' Jill insisted, without answering the question directly.

'Ridiculous. That would mean that I'm in danger. Baltasar, Lupe, even the workmen renovating the place are in danger.'

'But you especially could be in danger, after the way you and Roland were whispering together on Monday.'

Susan was annoyed. Jill was practically accusing her of conspiring with Roland. She wondered to whom else Jill might have been talking in similar vein. 'As I've already pointed out, we were not whispering, merely conversing in low tones. And the idea of either you or me being in danger is absurd.'

She made her words very firm to overcome the lack of conviction that lay behind them.

'Does that mean you won't let me stay over tonight?'

'Oh, if you're nervous, come over,' Susan said grudgingly. 'But I don't want to hear one word about how I ought to get new furniture.'

'I'm really grateful,' Jill said. 'You're the best client I've ever had.' Since the only other client Jill had apparently been able to hang on to had been dead from the start, the tribute was not as handsome as it might have been. 'I'll throw a few things together and be over there as soon as I can. And I promise not to say one word about your furniture, even if it collapses under me.'

I hope she understands it's just for tonight, Susan thought. I don't want her moving in here on a permanent basis. My days of poverty are over; I'm certainly not going to start taking in boarders now. And if Jill showed any signs of outstaying her limited welcome, Susan could always tell her Peter had decided to come back home for the spring break, instead of going on that field trip up north. No matter how edgy Jill was, she wouldn't want to stay if Peter were around.

But why is it me she chooses to stay with? Susan wondered. Surely she has people who are closer. Jill's parents, she knew, had retired to a condominium in Florida. Originally Jill hailed from the Bronx. Was there no place in the Bronx where she could find shelter? Well, perhaps seeking refuge in the Bronx was like fleeing the frying pan for the fire. But she must know people in the other boroughs, in the rest of the Metropolitan area, who would take her in.

The likelihood was that she didn't know anyone else who had as much room as Susan did. Spare bedrooms in New York City had gone out with the passenger pigeon. Only the very rich and those who had managed to hold on to the commodious flats of their forebears still had them.

Perhaps this was a ploy by Jill to achieve total possession of Susan by physically encompassing her. Was it possible that Jill might have killed Roland in order to give herself an excuse for moving in on her client? I'm getting to be as crazy as she is, Susan thought.

Suddenly she found herself wishing Peter had come home for the spring break after all. His presence, although maddening at times, was comforting in a way no one else's could be. As soon as all this is cleared up and the weather gets warmer, she thought, I'm going to fly up to Canada and spend some time with him. And maybe we can figure out some way he can come back to New York permanently, some way he can find a job here.

Of course Peter didn't have to work. She could support both of them. He wouldn't object at all to being supported in a style to which he'd had no trouble becoming accustomed. But she didn't like the idea of supporting him, not because she had any old-fashioned ideas about support being a male prerogative, but because that would mean he'd be around the apartment too much of the time. She couldn't count on his spending his days in the library.

Maybe I could establish a small foundation in an appropriate field, she thought, with him as the sole employee. I'll talk to Mimi about it; she knows all about establishing foundations. With the aid of a good accountant, perhaps things could be worked out so that it would cost Susan nothing to set up, even under the new tax laws.

The phone rang again. This time it was Hal. 'Susan, I'm so glad I finally reached you,' he said warmly. 'I suppose you've heard about Roland DeMarnay, although that isn't the reason I called. The first time I tried to get you I hadn't even heard the news yet. Shocking, isn't it?'

'Yes, it's awful,' she said. 'And sad, too. Such a waste,' she added, because she couldn't think of anything else to say.

'The waste of a human life is always sad.'

'I see you're back from Texas,' she said, wondering whether he'd tell her he'd changed his plans and gone to Connecticut. The secretary could have been wrong, of course. And what if she wasn't? What do I care where he was? In Houston, in Litchfield, or on that confounded Greek or Italian or whatever island of his?

'I got back early this afternoon. I called you from the airport—I was so anxious to hear your voice—but, alas, only your machine answered.'

'The machine answers in my voice,' she pointed out.

'Ah, yes, but it isn't really the same, is it?'

'I was at Allardyce's.'

'Oh, yes, the contemporary art auction. I took a look at

the catalogue before I left but there was nothing there we wanted, at least not at their estimates. Ridiculous the prices contemporary art is fetching these days, especially when so much of it is junk, don't you agree?'

She agreed.

'I suppose you and Jill were there about the Moffatt. What did it go for, do you happen to recall?'

'Two hundred and fifty thousand.'

He whistled. 'That's the highest a Moffatt's gone for yet.' For some reason the news seemed to please him; why, she couldn't understand, since to her Moffatt's work seemed a shining example of the junk movement. Of course that meant the value of the Moffatts in the Museum's collection would be increased; maybe he was pleased on the Museum's behalf.

'Pity he couldn't have seen some of the money when he was alive,' she observed.

'That's the way it's been with so many artists. They achieve fame and fortune only after they're dead. Only the fame doesn't do them much good and it's their heirs who get the fortune.'

'And the collectors and dealers.'

'And the collectors and dealers.'

'I wonder how much my paintings will sell for after I'm dead.'

'You mustn't look at it like that, Susan. One of James Rosenquist's pictures went for over two million dollars recently, and he's still alive. And a Jasper Johns sold for close to four million, and he's alive, too.'

'But the paintings were sold at auction by the people who owned them,' Susan pointed out. 'Neither of the artists gets any of the money.'

'That's true,' Hal said, 'but it certainly will make a difference in the prices they get for their paintings from now on. Listen, Susan, I know this is unpardonably last-minute of me, but I wondered whether you could have dinner with me tonight?'

'I haven't made any plans, but Jill's coming to stay overnight. Roland's death has made her nervous. I

125

don't know why.' She made the words clearly a question.

There was a pause before he answered. 'I believe she was associated with him in a business way some time ago.'

'She told me he was a partner with her in that gallery she was running in Soho.'

'She told you about that?' He sounded surprised and not altogether pleased. 'I wasn't sure whether she wanted you to know, so I never mentioned it,' he added. 'But that was such a long time ago, there couldn't be any connection. I'm sure they haven't had anything to do with each other for years. And his death was one of those sadomasochistic things, wasn't it? So why should there be any reason for her to be nervous?'

'I don't know. I just know that she sounded frightened.'

She wondered whether Hal knew why the partnership had broken up. But of course he must. He had become Jill's lover afterwards, so she was bound to tell him everything. Or was she? I've never told Peter everything. On the other hand, Peter never was all that interested.

There was a harsh cackle.

'What's that?' Hal said sharply.

He's on edge, too, she thought. 'The intercom's buzzing. Probably the doorman calling to tell me Jill's here. Why don't you come over, too? I doubt that Jill will be in any mood to go out but we could have dinner sent up.'

'Thank you,' he said, 'but I really wanted to have dinner with you alone. There are a number of things I wanted to talk to you about. Could we make it later this week? Perhaps at my apartment. I have a wonderful cook.'

As she waited for Jill to come upstairs, she remembered that Roland had also been insistent on seeing her alone. I'm getting as jumpy as Jill, she thought, suspecting everyone, imagining all sorts of wild things.

She got her handbag and looped the strap over her arm. Let the wild things come on, she thought; I'm ready for them.

CHAPTER 17

Jill came in looking like a wild thing herself, hair flying every which way, even the fur on her mink standing on end. She carried a small overnight case, which she set on the floor, and a large shopping bag with grease spots, which she handed to Susan. 'Little hostess gift. I don't know whether you've had dinner or not, but I'm starved, so I brought up some Chinese food. Why are you hanging on to your handbag like that?'

'I thought you might be a delivery boy,' Susan said, peering into the shopping bag, from which succulent odours issued. 'There's enough here to feed an army. Are you expecting anyone else?'

Jill shuddered. '*No*, I don't want to see anyone else as long as I live. Not until tomorrow, anyway, if I live that long. Anything left over would do for breakfast. Chinese food is good cold. And anything left over after that you can reheat for lunch. Are you expecting a delivery? What are you expecting?'

'Peter always sends me flowers on my birthday.'

'I thought your birthday wasn't until September.'

'Yes, but Peter's so absent-minded he always gets it mixed up with Ground Hog Day.'

'But Ground Hog Day was back in February.'

'I must be a little mixed up too.' She helped Jill out of her coat. The girl was shivering. Her terror was real enough, whatever else about her might be false.

'I felt eyes upon me all the way here,' she said.

'The eyes of admiration, no doubt.'

'Not that kind of eyes—creepy, crawly eyes, the kind of eyes that paranoids feel watching them all the time. There are canvases in that closet!' she said, as Susan opened the door to put away her coat. 'You're relapsing. You promised me that you would send your stuff to the warehouse as soon as it started spilling out of the studio.'

Even fear could not keep her from poking her nose into other people's closets. Susan shut the door firmly. 'It's my closet and I'll put what I want in it.'

'Even skeletons?'

'I keep my skeletons elsewhere. Now, let's get this food into the kitchen. There's so much of it, it's almost a pity Hal didn't accept my invitation to dinner.'

'What invitation?' Jill followed Susan into the big, old-fashioned kitchen. 'What Hal? Hal Courtenay? Why did you invite him?

'He called just after you did. I asked him to join us and we'd have dinner sent up. But he said he was busy.'

'He's back in town then?'

'I would hardly have asked him to fly in from Texas to take pot luck.'

'When did he get back?'

'Early this afternoon.'

'You mean he said he got back early this afternoon?'

'Well, I wasn't waiting for him at the airport. Does it matter when he got back?'

Jill didn't say anything. Why, Susan wondered, as she reached into cabinets and cupboards, was Jill so upset at the knowledge that Hal was back in town somewhat earlier than expected?

Was it possible Jill thought Hal might have something to do with Roland's death? Nonsense, Hal hardly knew the man.

Although knowing someone was hardly a prerequisite for killing him. Quite the opposite sometimes. She herself, for example, would have had great difficulty in killing someone with whom she was personally acquainted, no matter how unspeakably vile that person was; unless, of course, that person had done, or was attempting to do, something unpleasant to her. Other people might be less sensitive—less oversensitive, perhaps.

Come to think of it, she had no idea of the extent of Hal's actual acquaintance with Roland. They might have known each other very well. But that wouldn't account for Jill's fear, even if it was Hal she was afraid of.

*

'Shall we eat here or in the dining-room?' she asked.

'The dining-room of course.' Even in her current state of emotional dishevelment, Jill seemed shocked at the idea that anyone who had a dining-room would even dream of eating in the kitchen. Under other circumstances she would probably expect me to dress for dinner, Susan thought.

'I should think you'd have this place modernized,' Jill said, casting a disparaging glance around. 'I know—I know —I said I wasn't going to criticize your furniture, but this isn't furniture, it's—it's equipment,' she concluded triumphantly. 'With the money you're making, you can afford to get it fixed over. You could sell most of the stuff here as antiques, maybe even come out ahead. That stove is a collector's item if ever I saw one. And the sink—'

'Well, then, I'm in fashion. I have an antique kitchen.'

'It's not fashionable if that's the way your kitchen has always been. It's fashionable only if you have a modern kitchen to begin with and have all the appliances taken out and the antique ones put in.'

'How about if I make believe that's what I did?'

Jill shook her head. 'They look as if they belonged there. That's always a dead giveaway.'

Fear seemed to have increased rather than impaired Jill's appetite. She consumed prodigious quantities of food, but refused to open her fortune cookie afterwards. 'It would be tempting fate,' she said.

Susan didn't open her cookie either.

'Susan, do you think he really likes me?'

Susan didn't have to ask who 'he' was. 'Mr Mackay certainly does seem to be attracted to you, but I wouldn't have thought you'd be attracted to him. He doesn't seem like your type somehow.'

'Too clean-cut, you mean? Susan, I'll tell you a secret. Inside every woman, no matter how hip, there's a secret yearning for a man who looks like a toothpaste ad.' Giving Susan no time to meditate on this profundity, she patted her stomach. 'I do feel much better. It must have been too many drinks and too little food that made me so jittery. You're right, there's no reason to suppose Roland wasn't

129

beaten to death by an ordinary sex maniac, just because a couple of other things happened in the same place.'

'I never said Roland was beaten to death by a sex maniac,' Susan protested. 'It was just that when you said—'

'Forget I ever said anything. I'm not responsible for what I say. I always get the jitters whenever somebody I know gets murdered.'

'Look, Jill, if you know something that you think could make you a threat to anyone, you'd better tell the police about it. Then you wouldn't be a threat any more.'

Unless, she thought, you yourself killed Roland, or had a hand in his killing, in which case I could not in all good conscience advise you to go to the police.

There was a stubborn look on Jill's face. 'I don't know anything, so there's nothing to tell. Let's turn on the TV and listen to the terrible things they say about Roland on the news.'

Roland's death had been so overwhelming to them, it was almost a shock to realize that it was not the lead story. There had been a failed attempt to assassinate a South American dictator (really they should have hired a professional, Susan thought, as pictures of the mess the unfortunate amateur had made appeared on the screen), several bombings in various parts of the world, and a fresh political scandal in Queens—all of which took precedence over Roland's demise.

The scenes of carnage and calumny were interrupted by the simultaneous buzzing of the intercom and the ringing of the phone. 'Jill, would you ask whoever's on the phone to hold on while I answer the buzzer?'

'Gen'lman on his way up,' the doorman announced. He was a new man and he still hadn't got it through his head that he was supposed to discover the name of a caller and find out whether he was welcome before letting him up. Susan tried to explain correct procedure to him once again.

'It's a young gen'lman,' he said, as if Susan ought to be glad to have such a caller, no matter who it was, no matter what time it was. Not that eleven-twenty was late in absolute terms, just late for an unexpected caller.

'It must be Alex,' she said to Jill. 'He was worried about me.'

'Aha, see, I'm not the only one who's paranoid.'

But paranoia implies irrational fears. Susan was afraid that Jill's fears might have a very rational basis. And she began to feel a little afraid herself.

'Who is it on the phone?' she asked.

'Who was it, you mean? He hung up. It was Baltasar. He wouldn't tell me what it was about. He said never mind; it wasn't important. He'd call again. What do you suppose he wanted?'

'I have no idea.'

But Susan did have an idea of what he must want—to speak to her alone, like everybody else. Why he wanted to speak to her she didn't know. It was unlikely he would want to weep on her shoulder; he didn't seem the type. Just the same, remembering what had happened to Roland, she resolved to call Baltasar as soon as Alex left. She would sleep easier that way.

The doorbell rang. Susan opened the door. The merry quip about fatherhood she'd had prepared faded on her lips.

Because it wasn't Alex standing outside. It was Andrew Mackay, looking both apologetic and determined.

'Forgive my dropping in on you like this, but I had to talk to you alone.'

'Come in, but before you say anything I ought to warn you that I am not alone. Jill is here.'

'And why shouldn't Jill be here?' Jill asked, erupting into the foyer. 'Oh, it's you.'

'Yes, it's me,' he said.

They stared at each other. For once Mackay wasn't smiling. This calls for music, too, Susan thought, something tragic this time, about two lovers about to be sundered by cruel fate. There probably was something suitable in *Tristan*. There probably was something suitable in most operas. They wouldn't be operas without it. She couldn't see Jill as an operatic heroine, though, not even in a modern opera.

'Look,' Jill said, 'if I'm in the way, I can always leave.

I'll probably get murdered on my way out, but who cares.'

Andrew opened his mouth and shut it. He cares, Susan thought; the more fool, he.

'No need for you to leave, Jill,' she said. 'If Mr Mackay wants to talk to me alone in his official capacity . . .?'

'Professional capacity,' he corrected her. 'I have no official standing. Call Lieutenant Bracco; he'll tell you the same thing. You don't have to talk to me if you don't want to.'

'You heard what he said, Susan. Don't talk to him.' Jill clutched her client's arm. 'Please, please, don't talk to him. Send him away.'

Susan disengaged her arm. 'We can go into the library. Jill can amuse herself watching television, or listening to the radio, or throwing a tantrum.'

'I could read a good book,' Jill said, 'but all the books are in the library.' Her voice was shaky.

'All right, Mr Mackay and I can talk in the kitchen.'

'You don't have to go that far. I'll be a good girl and wait in the studio. I can always brood.'

CHAPTER 18

Mackay took off his coat. Susan did not offer to take it from him, so he carried it over his arm as he followed her into the library, which she used as a sitting-room when she had need of one. It was a smallish room by the standards of the rest of the place, good-sized by today's norms, lined with a miscellany of well-read books, the old rare editions and leather-bound sets having fallen under the auctioneer's hammer years before. There was a working fireplace in which a fire was burning. Mackay looked at it suspiciously. Probably thinks I'm burning evidence, Susan thought.

She gestured him to an easy chair covered with dark red leather so worn it had passed beyond the boundaries of comfortable shabbiness and looked as if it were moulting. He looked around him and, finding no better place, threw his coat on the adjacent ottoman, then sat down himself.

She prepared herself for interrogation.

'She's mad at me,' he said.

When it came to police matters, she would cooperate with him, but she wasn't going to make things easier when it came to matters of the heart. 'Do you blame her?' she asked.

'But she knew I was an investigator from the start. I never tried to hide that from her, so why should she be so upset to find me . . . uh . . .'

'Investigating,' she finished for him.

'Yes, investigating.'

'Perhaps she didn't think you'd invited her out to investigate her.'

'But I didn't. Well, not exactly. Anyhow, we never did get around to talk about—about anything that had to do with anything. We just talked about us. I was open and aboveboard from the start. So why is she acting like this?' He looked honestly bewildered.

Susan resisted the temptation to tell him to write to Dear Abby. It would be unkind as well as unwise. Although he himself might have no official standing—and she didn't really believe that—he was undoubtedly associated with those who did.

'I don't know why I took it for granted you would be home alone,' he said. 'Probably I should have called first to check.'

'Probably you should. Everybody else who wanted to talk to me alone did.'

He looked alert; the bloodhound sniffing on the trail. 'Who else wanted to talk to you alone?'

Well, maybe it was his business. But she saw no reason to spare his feelings. 'Jill to begin with . . .'

'Besides Jill?'

'Hal Courtenay and Baltasar . . .' Should she tell him the names of her other callers? No, they hadn't said they wanted to speak to her alone, only that they wanted to speak to her.

'I know who Baltasar is. Should I know Hal Courtenay?'

'Hal Courtenay's the Director of the Museum of American Art.'

133

He frowned. 'I think I remember coming across the name somewhere.'

'Hal's quite well known, gets in the papers often, new acquisitions, membership drives, authoritative opinions, articles on art. There was a piece by him in the *New York Times* a couple of months ago and one about him in *Connoisseur* last year. And, of course, he goes to parties a lot—part of his job—so he's often in the society (excuse me, *style*) columns.'

He shook his head.

'Perhaps you saw him on TV? He often appears on Channel 13 and sometimes on 31.'

'That's not it, either. Tell me, would Courtenay have known DeMarnay?'

'Museum people are bound to know dealers. They buy pictures from them.'

'They do!' He looked surprised. Where did he think museums got their pictures from, anyway? The tooth fairy?

'Hal was the one who introduced Jill to me and suggested that I sign up with her,' she added.

He appeared to consider this and dismiss it. However, she could see he was thinking about it, even though he went off on a different tack. 'Tell me, why did you really go to see DeMarnay this afternoon?'

'Surely Lieutenant Bracco told you.'

'He told me what you told him, but . . .'

'But you don't believe it was the truth?' She arched her eyebrows. Pity they didn't use lorgnettes any more, she thought, or she could have looked at him through hers.

He put out his hand, as if to disclaim any lack of faith in her integrity. 'No, no, I'm sure you wouldn't lie to the police. But I had a feeling that you might not have told him . . . uh . . . the whole truth. In other words—' he gave her a smile that was intended to be disarming, but didn't quite make it —'that you might have been holding out on him.'

'You said you had no official standing,' she reminded him. 'So, if I had been holding out on the lieutenant, which, of course, I wouldn't have dreamed of doing, why wouldn't I hold out on you?'

'You mean you're not going to answer my questions?' He looked disappointed, as if she had failed him somehow.

'I didn't say that. I might answer your questions, if you'll answer mine first.'

She doubted that she actually had any concrete information that could be of use either to him or the police in their investigations; all she had were some vague suspicions that she had no intention of passing on in their present nebulous state, but he didn't know that. And she wanted to know what was going on, not simply out of a citizen's right to know, i.e., vulgar curiosity, but because this was her concern. She herself might not be involved, but people she knew were—Jill, for one, and Hal, even Baltasar (although him she hardly knew). And then there was the nagging fear that Alex might be somehow caught up in this.

'My dear Miss Melville—Susan—are you suggesting a deal?'

'I understand bargains are not unheard of even in official police circles, to which, I take it, you don't belong—or do you?'

He didn't answer, but leaned back in the moulting armchair with a sigh, and put his hand in front of his eyes. In the lamplight the lines in his face deepened and he looked older and even handsomer. Poor Jill, she thought.

'I can't promise you anything,' he said finally, 'but I'll tell you as much as I can. And you'll tell me whatever you know. Promise?'

'I promise.'

'Go ahead, ask your questions.'

'That night I ran into you outside the gallery, did you actually manage to get inside?'

He took his hand away from his eyes. 'You don't really expect me to answer that?'

'Oh, but I do. I know that as a licensed investigator, whether public or private, you had no business being inside; so officially you were not there, even if you were. So there's no reason why you shouldn't tell me about something that you didn't do.'

It took him a while to figure this out, or at least to realize that he never would be able to figure it out. 'All right. Off the record and strictly between ourselves I did get inside—something which I'll deny even under torture if ever I'm accused of it. But, if you're expecting startling revelations, you'll be disappointed. I didn't get very far inside. It was my bad luck to hit a night when DeMarnay and his friends were having a . . . a . . .'

'Party. That's what Damian called it.'

'Damian? Oh, yes, Damian Schwimmer.'

She wondered how he knew Damian's last name. But of course, he was a detective. Detectives knew how to ferret out such arcane bits of information. She wondered what else he might have discovered about other people in Roland's orbit. The idea made her uncomfortable. It would make anyone uncomfortable. Everyone has secrets they don't want out in the open, she thought, but some are more secret than others.

'They were rampaging all over the place,' he went on, 'so I couldn't get a look around. I was afraid they might catch me and—'

'And prevail upon you to join in?'

He smiled weakly. 'That was the least of my worries.' She didn't believe him. 'Do you want the details or will a broad general outline do?'

She fought back an unworthy desire to ask for details. 'I have a pretty good idea of what must have been going on, gained from literature and the news; and, of course, as I told the lieutenant, I spoke to Roland on the phone not long after I saw you, so I heard them.'

'I know,' he said. 'You reported suspicious character leaving premises, or at least you said you did. We have only your word for it that you did tell DeMarnay that you saw me.'

He was watching her carefully. Why? What could he possibly suspect her of? At least what could he possibly suspect her of that had any connection with this particular crime or, as she was beginning to think, series of crimes? Why wouldn't she have told Roland? Was Mackay trying to make her nervous so she would say more than she had intended?

'Oh, I'm sure he mentioned to whoever was there with him at the time that a possible intruder had been sighted. And, oh, yes, I remember he told Baltasar the next day, and there were other people around. I'm sure they'll confirm it.'

'I'm sure they will, too,' he said. 'Not, of course, that I doubted your word.'

'Nice of you to say so,' she said, 'but I understand. Of course, you have to doubt everyone's word. Even Jill's.'

Hitting below the belt, she knew, but she was observing Merriwether rather than Queensberry rules. I really must meet Lady Daphne, she thought. I could learn a lot from her and who knows, she thought modestly, I might have something to teach her myself.

'How did DeMarnay act when you spoke to him on the phone? Was he sober?'

'He and the others—I could hear them in the background —did seem to be high on 'something. They didn't sound violent. They sounded . . . affectionate. But it was still early.'

'It was later than when I saw them. They were certainly affectionate when I was there. Very affectionate. And also high. But this was the night before he was killed so it isn't really relevant, is it? Just . . . just . . .'

'Indicative of a general pattern,' she suggested.

'Indicative of something, anyway. They were running around naked, except for some sort of spicy gook they'd smeared on themselves. One of them had put on so much he left a trail of slime, like a snail. They were drinking wine and snorting coke, which, incidentally, was why I couldn't do anything with Brucie.'

'Brucie?' She was surprised. 'I didn't know dogs could be such prudes.'

Mackay stared at her. 'You're serious? You really don't know why I brought Brucie along? I thought that was obvious—or at least would be later, when you'd had time to think about it.'

The truth of the matter was that she had been exceedingly obtuse. 'You mean Brucie is one of those drug-sniffing dogs?' So that was why Roland had been upset when she'd told him about Brucie's presence on the scene. 'I didn't know that the police or Customs or whatever took dogs to parties to sniff out drugs.'

'They don't. The dogs are used to sniff out large quantities of drugs, amounts a dealer might have on hand. If they took them to every party in New York where drugs might be used, New York would be the canine capital of the world. Not that it isn't already. I never saw so many dogs in my life as there are here.'

So he was from out of town. Washington? She didn't ask because she knew he wouldn't tell her.

'Brucie was trained for quality not quantity. As soon as he sniffs the slightest amount of coke he starts demonstrating. Luckily Roland and his friends were yipping and whining so much themselves, they didn't notice, and we were able to get away, but there was one close call—' He shuddered.

Again she would have liked to hear the details, but she didn't like to ask. And he probably wouldn't tell her anyway. He was a curiously old-fashioned young man. She might have deduced that from his appearance, but she'd been under the impression that it was some sort of disguise.

She still didn't understand why Roland should have been suspected of drug dealing when she'd been given to understand that forged paintings were his line. Not that criminals were necessarily specialists but Roland hadn't looked like someone who could chew gum and walk at the same time, let alone deal in drugs and forged paintings simultaneously. Or even alternately.

Roland had started out as an art dealer, Andrew told her, possibly even an honest dealer. Certainly nothing had been known against him until General Chomsky got upset over that fake Picasso Roland had sold him (the one Alex had told her about). How he'd found out it was a fake wasn't clear. Perhaps Picasso himself had spilled the beans. She tried to remember just when Picasso had died.

Roland had insisted that he'd bought the picture from a private party whose name he refused to divulge, believing it to be genuine, and had sold it in good faith. He'd offered to take it back and make full restitution. The General had accepted and dropped all charges. Technically, Roland's record was still clean. Nevertheless, Mackay said, the General had been angry and he hadn't kept the matter secret. Everybody in the art world knew about it. Mackay seemed to think that this represented a permanent blot on Roland's escutcheon. Susan knew better than that.

Roland hadn't come to the attention of the police again until a few years later, when he and Jill opened their art gallery under her name. Mackay seemed to feel that their suppression of Roland's role was entirely understandable. Susan did not. As far as she could see, there was no reason why they should not have used Roland's name as well as Jill's (granted the lack of euphony that the combination would have involved). Roland had no criminal record and his slightly tarnished reputation was hardly likely to frighten away the kind of artists and collectors that would fall within the gallery's purview. If the gallery had been set up on a grander scale, like the DeMarnay Gallery, it wouldn't have frightened away any kind of artist or collector.

'I gather that the police continued to keep an eye on him,' Susan said.

Mackay looked embarrassed for his colleagues. 'As a matter of fact, they didn't. It's true there seems to be a lot of hanky-panky going on in the art world, but that's not one of the New York police's prime concerns. Oh, they deal with art crimes when they've been committed, but they don't go around checking artwork and antiques to make sure they're authentic.'

He looked disapproving. He wasn't going to criticize the New York police; at least not to a civilian. Neither was he going to give them an A for effort.

CHAPTER 19

What had happened to turn the authorities' attention to the Turkel Gallery, he told her, was that Customs had found cocaine in the frames of some paintings consigned to the gallery by an artist from Colombia.

'I suppose the sniffer dogs detected the drugs?'

'Well, not exactly. Not at first, anyway. Customs is always a little leery of anything that comes from Colombia, and these seemed a little heavy for pictures of that size. So they opened one or two crates. But all they found were pictures, in heavy, old-fashioned frames, the kind I'm told they don't use much any more here, but that could have been what they like in South America.'

'So Customs broke open one of the frames?'

He shook his head. 'They couldn't do that just on vague suspicions. They re-crated the pictures. But, just as they were about to be taken away, a clumsy workman happened to drop a crate.'

'Purely by accident.'

'Purely by accident,' he said firmly. 'The crate broke, and so did one of the frames. The dogs started barking their heads off. That's when they broke open all the frames, and found them loaded with coke.'

'Jill told me she bought Roland out when she found he was dealing in forged paintings.'

'Did she say that? Maybe she didn't want to tell you what really happened because she was ashamed of being connected with drugs, no matter how innocently.'

'How can you be so sure she was innocent?'

There was a long pause before he answered. 'I—they couldn't be absolutely sure of anything, of course. But there was nothing to show that either she or the other partner was involved. DeMarnay set up the deal. He handled all the paintings. He did all the paperwork. Jill didn't have much to do with the business end of things. She was a kid, right out of school, not much more than a receptionist, really. Okay, so they named the gallery after her—'

'Wait a minute!' Susan finally managed to break into his monologue. 'I thought there were only two partners.'

'Both Jill and DeMarnay ran it; that is, he ran it and she—'

'Was actually a glorified receptionist, I know, I know. But tell me about the third partner.'

'I forget what his name was. Anyhow, he was a silent partner. All he did was put up most of the money. He had nothing to do with the gallery's operations.'

'You're sure of that?'

He seemed surprised at her interest. She was surprised at his apparent lack of it. 'There never was anything to show that he even came near the place. Lots of businesses do get started that way. Somebody puts up the money; somebody else supplies the expertise.'

'Was this the Turkel Gallery's first show?' she asked.

'I think there were two, maybe three, before. All by local artists. No question of smuggling.'

She was curious about those early shows, but he had no further information about them. The authorities had been interested in drugs, not art. If she was really curious, she could always look them up, she thought.

Roland had gotten a clever lawyer, Mackay told her, who managed to keep him from being formally charged. Although the police hadn't had much doubt that he'd been guilty of trying to smuggle drugs, they couldn't prove that the whole thing hadn't been the artist's own idea— especially since he'd paid for the privilege of being exhibited in New York, something which was not an unusual practice, though, Susan felt, highly deplorable.

'If Customs hadn't been so eager, they would have fixed up that first frame, re-crated the picture and waited to see who bought the paintings after they'd been put on exhibit. Because that would have been the fellow they were after— maybe even the guy behind the whole thing.'

He shook his head. 'They really blew that one.'

141

'Could it have been the silent partner?' Susan asked.

'It could have been anybody. Why pick on him?' He grinned suddenly. 'Or even her. There have been lady criminals, you know. If you can be a criminal and a lady at the same time.'

'I don't see why not,' she said.

Jill and the other partner had bought Roland out; that much at least was true. They then went on to make a success with the Moffatt paintings, while Roland went back to dealing on his own. For the past few years he had been working mostly abroad, south of the border, and in Europe. Although the New York police had dutifully informed their foreign colleagues of Roland's questionable background through Interpol, his record with the local police forces seemed to be clear in all respects. However, although Andrew didn't say so outright, Susan gathered that he felt foreign police forces might not be as devoted to duty as their American counterparts.

'He must have met Baltasar while he was dealing abroad,' Susan deduced, 'and I suppose to Baltasar Roland might have seemed like a reputable dealer.'

'Maybe so. And the fact that Baltasar was born in Colombia is probably only a coincidence.'

'I thought Baltasar came from Spain, of noble blood.'

'His family came from Spain way back. As for noble blood . . .' Mackay shrugged. 'He is a Spanish citizen now. But he was born in Colombia.'

'Don't you think you're being a bit bigoted? I'm sure most Colombians are honest, decent people.'

'I'm sure they are, too,' he said. 'They also export coffee. And pickpockets.'

She refused to dignify that with any comment. 'Was Rafael Colombian, too?'

'No, he was born in Argentina. And he'd been working in Mexico.'

When Roland came back to New York to open his gallery, Andrew told her, the authorities did take an immediate interest in him. They'd gotten a tip that one of the big international drug dealers they'd been anxious to get their hands on for a long time was planning to send a huge shipment of drugs up from Mexico. Rumour had it that this could be as much as two hundred kilos, a quarter of a ton.

'That's a lot, isn't it?'

'Worth a small fortune.' He seemed to figure in his head. 'A large fortune, actually. It could come to more than fifteen million dollars wholesale.'

She was impressed. She would have liked to ask how much that would be retail, but he might think she was interested in getting into the business, herself.

'DeMarnay's first exhibit was coming from Mexico. A lot of drugs have been coming in from Mexico. It did look as if he might have been playing the same old trick. So we kept an eye on him—and a lot of other people, as well,' he added. 'There was always the possibility that he was straight.' A remote possibility, his tone indicated.

'Wouldn't it have been foolish of him to do something like that for his opening show, when he must have known he'd come under suspicion? Especially since they'd set up such an elaborate installation. Wouldn't it have been wiser to wait?'

'Look,' he said, 'I can't second-guess them.' He got up and walked over to the fireplace and then back. He seemed restless. 'Maybe they made a mistake. That's how we catch 'em—by their mistakes or through informants. DeMarnay might have thought the police had forgotten all about him. Or he might not have had a choice.'

She considered this. 'Blackmail, you mean?'

'That's a possibility, if somebody had proof that he'd done some of the things he'd been accused of.' Catching Susan's eye, he said, 'Jill couldn't possibly have had anything to do with something like that.'

But what if Jill had, Susan wondered. What if, for some reason Susan couldn't imagine, Jill had killed Roland; although, if she had been blackmailing him, it would be much more likely that he would kill her. Would Mackay try to cover up for her? He couldn't be that far gone. Why, he had only met the girl that morning. Love at first sight happened only in books. This was real life.

'More likely, if he was working for a drug dealer, he might simply have to do what he was told. He'd have no choice.'

But everyone has a choice, she thought. When she'd worked as an assassin for General Chomsky (only, of course, she hadn't known the identity of her employer), she would never have accepted an assignment unless her target was a thoroughly evil person. On the other hand, maybe Roland had decided that he did have a choice. Maybe he had made that choice . . . and that was why he was dead now.

She wondered whether, if he had not been an acquaintance of hers, she would have accepted him as an assignment. She couldn't make up her mind about that, but she knew that she certainly would have killed his putative employer without a qualm. Drugs were bad medicine.

'Do sit down, you're making me nervous.'

Mackay sat, but he kept shifting uneasily in the chair, anxious to be gone, not from the apartment but from the library. 'I hope my coming here didn't scare Jill away,' he blurted.

'She's here for the night. She's frightened all right, but not of you, as far as I can see. It's Roland's death—it seems to have terrified her.'

'Did she say why?'

Susan shook her head. 'No, she refused to talk about it. And—' as he started to get up —'she's even less likely to talk about it to you than to me.'

He subsided in the chair, muttering to himself.

'I wonder if Rafael's death had anything to do with all this,' Susan mused.

Apparently that point had not occurred to him. 'That's right, Hoffmann did die of an overdose on the night the gallery opened. But there wasn't anything suspicious about it. That kind of thing happens every day in New York.'

'His wife thinks he was murdered.'

He was all attention. 'How do you know that?'

'She told me when she was in the gallery yesterday. She'd just come back from Australia.'

'Lieutenant Bracco didn't say anything about her to me!'

144

Susan did a spirited impersonation of someone cudgelling her brains. 'I don't remember whether or not I mentioned her to Lieutenant Bracco. He didn't ask me who'd been in the gallery the last time I saw Roland, and I was so shocked I—well—I just couldn't think.'

He regarded her with a sceptical eye.

'But surely Lupe—that's her name, Lupe Montoya— told him, herself.'

'As far as I know, he doesn't even know she exists. Which he wouldn't, if nobody had told him about her.'

'Didn't Baltasar mention her arrival?'

'Apparently not.'

'Maybe you spoke to the lieutenant before he spoke to Baltasar.'

He shook his head. 'After.'

'Then he must have been acting like a gallant Spanish gentleman, keeping her out of it, since she didn't seem to have any connection with the murder.'

'Maybe so, but that's for the lieutenant to judge. Still,' he sighed, 'Baltasar's a foreigner.' It wasn't clear whether he meant one must make allowances for foreigners or whether foreigners were not to be trusted.

The authorities had figured Roland might have been stupid enough to try the same trick twice. They made plans to open the frames of the Hoffmann pieces in Customs, but there turned out not to be any frames. 'It was all—would you call it sculpture?'

There were a number of things she could have called Rafael Hoffmann's work, but she desisted out of respect for a man who, however despicable, had not only been a fellow artist but was dead. 'It's as good a name as any.'

'The pieces were very heavy, but sculpture usually is heavy. We couldn't figure out how heavy they should have been because they were made up of all kinds of different stuff —wood, metal, stone, paper, plastic, all mixed together.'

His voice held a note of grievance as if he felt the main object of multimedia art was to confound the law. Wouldn't it be interesting, she thought, if that had been the original purpose of that type of art, originated because Customs had grown too sophisticated for sculptors simply to stuff their bronzes with illegal substances. (She wondered whether during the Prohibition Era—but, no, even the most innocent revenue agent would be bound to suspect statues that gurgled.) Then, the style could have caught on with collectors and now be produced for its own sake. Mere speculation, of course, but the theory pleased her. It would explain so much.

'Customs couldn't go ahead and destroy a valuable art collection just on suspicion. What if they'd been wrong? Can you imagine how the Civil Liberties Union would have carried on?'

'The same way they would have carried on if Customs had been right,' she said. 'What about using Brucie and his colleagues?'

'They tried sniffer dogs, of course, but the cocaine, if it was there, would have been hermetically sealed and then covered by layers of non-porous stuff—metal, fibreglass, various synthetics, God knows what else, with tons of paint and varnish piled on top. Even a superdog couldn't sniff through that.'

'How would they get the cocaine out then?'

'The pieces would have to be broken up. Roland and his associates could do it, of course. It was their property.'

'You mean Rafael would have gone to all that work just to see his things destroyed?' Little though she thought of Rafael's *oeuvre*, she was shocked. Maybe it didn't represent art in her eyes, but it certainly represented a lot of effort.

Mackay looked at her as if she had started to show signs of mental deficiency. 'That's what he would have made them for. And that's what he would have been paid for.'

'But he seemed so sincere in thinking he was going to make his reputation as one of the world's greatest artists with this show.'

'Maybe he was a good actor.'

But she didn't think so. She knew artists. Rafael had been genuinely dedicated to his profession and to himself. He had

146

truly thought he was the greatest thing since Michelangelo. In fact, that was too modest a claim. Shortly before the opening (which was to become his closing) he had confided to her that he had always felt Michelangelo to be highly overrated.

The authorities had been watching the gallery, waiting to see who would take possession of the pieces. That was all they could do. It was entirely possible that the stuff was clean, that Roland had either gone straight—or been smart enough not to try any tricks with his opening exhibit.

And then the gallery caught—or more likely was set—on fire, and the pieces were completely destroyed without ever having left the place. Which made it almost certain that the authorities' suspicions had been correct.

They might have had grounds for a warrant now, but what was the use of searching the place? The drugs were certain to be gone by this time. The pieces would have been broken up and the drugs removed long before the fire; then taken away little by little to a 'safe house', where they would be readied for distribution.

Since work was still being done on the top floors of the gallery, there were always people going in and out, carrying things. They could easily have taken away a quarter of a ton, a few pounds at a time—only it would be kilos, of course. Mackay seemed to think the spread of the metric system had some connection with the rise of drug-related crime.

'You should have sneaked in sooner, since you were going to do it anyway.'

He looked at her. 'Do you think I wouldn't have liked to? The alarm system was always on before. And there were always a couple of tough-looking guards on duty. They never came back after the fire, which made us even more sure that there had been drugs in the statues. We tried to get in before the fire. We sent in men as building inspectors, as meter readers, as people from the EPA looking for radon contamination. The guards followed them wherever they went. We tried to get some of our men in as construction

147

workers, but we ran up against the unions. You'd think people engaged in illegal activities would hire non-union help, but no. It was a closed shop in every sense of the word.'

'Why did you bother to sneak in after the fire?' she wanted to know.

'When I saw the alarm system was off I thought I'd take a look around to see if there was any evidence that drugs had been there, and also to get the lie of the land. This was too expensive a set-up for a one-shot operation. They had to be planning to use the gallery again.'

'It must have occurred to them that if they had to set a fire each time they got in a new shipment, the police would be bound to get suspicious. Not to speak of the fire department.'

'I don't know what they had in mind. Maybe next time they were planning to bomb the block, and place the blame on subversives. There's a consulate across the street. Maybe they would have tied it in with that somehow.'

But all that didn't explain why Roland had been killed. The drugs had been successfully removed from the artworks; the finger of suspicion had rested on no one; what reason was there to kill Roland?

'Drug dealers are always killing each other. It's an occupational hazard. And it is possible that his death wasn't drug-related. That sex maniac could still have done it.'

'Which sex maniac?'

'Any sex maniac. I mean Roland could have been a drug dealer who was killed by an unrelated sex maniac.'

'I'm beginning to wonder whether Darius Moffatt's death was really an accident.'

'Darius Moffatt!' He seemed startled by this sudden addition to the cast of characters. 'Oh, yes, the guy who painted that picture we saw today? Did he die too?'

'Yes, of a shot of heroin. Like Rafael. Except that Rafael was also drunk, and, as far as I know, Darius wasn't.'

'When did it happen?'

'About ten years ago, just before Roland and Jill started their gallery. Or just after. I'm not sure which.'

He didn't seem struck by the coincidence. She got up and took her copy of *Darius Moffatt, Man and Myth* (autographed, of course) from its shelf. 'Here, this will tell you about him.'

Andrew got up, too, and took the book without eagerness. He's humouring me, she thought. Well, I'm a taxpayer.

He studied the picture on the back. 'I take it that's Moffatt. Good-looking fellow.'

'No,' she said, 'that's a picture of the author. Hal Courtenay. The director of the MAA. There's a picture of Moffatt somewhere inside.'

He sighed. 'Well, it was all a long time ago, and I think the connection's a little far-fetched, but I'll look into it. You never know.'

It was late, he said, and he had to be running along, but first he would go into the studio to say good night to Jill. Susan tactfully remained in the library. He came back so soon it appeared that their parting had not been an amicable one, and picked up his coat, brushing more leather crumbs off it before he put it on. It's a nuisance, she thought, but I suppose Jill is right; I will have to get the furniture reupholstered. Or get new furniture. After Roland's murder had been settled. She wouldn't be able to keep her mind on furniture now.

She escorted him into the foyer.

'You understand, I'm going to have to tell Bracco all you've told me—which isn't all that much,' he added to make it clear he felt he had given more than he had received. 'He'll probably want to talk to you again.'

'Maybe it won't be necessary,' she said hopefully. 'You'll be able to tell him everything I know.'

He smiled. She was going to have to see the lieutenant again, she gathered.

'Good night, Susan. I'll be in touch.' The door closed behind him.

An instant later the bell rang. She opened the door. 'Sorry to bother you again, but this Hal Courtenay—would Hal be short for Henry?

'It usually is,' she said, 'although he always uses Hal, even on his professional papers.'

'I just remembered where I ran across the name before. He was the third partner in the Turkel Gallery.'

CHAPTER 20

'I can see from your face that he's been telling you things about me,' Jill said. 'Bad things. Things he had no business telling you, or even knowing.'

Her own face was tear-streaked and her mascara had run. She was a sorry sight, but Susan could not feel sorry for her. 'He told me things I had a right to know,' she said.

'Roland always spoiled everything,' Jill said. 'If only he hadn't gone and died, nobody would ever have dug up those old stories and you'd never have known about them.'

But Mackay had been watching Roland for some time. He must have known about the Turkel Gallery and Jill's connection with Roland long before he had met Jill. It was just that now Roland's death had given that knowledge immediacy. His past would become of interest to the press. They would dig and they would find a rich lode of definite scandal and alleged crime—a veritable embarrassment of riches for the tabloids and a springboard for pontification for the *Times*.

Susan had never really fancied Jill as a candidate for Roland's murderer. However, even if it turned out that she had killed the art dealer, Susan would not necessarily have held that against her. Whoever killed Roland might have had very good reason for the act. But Jill had lied to her. And that Susan could not forgive. Neither could she forgive Hal. He had been the one who introduced Jill to her, and not, she was beginning to suspect, out of disinterested kindness towards either of them.

'If you have some explanation, I'm willing to hear it,' she told Jill.

'First tell me what Andy told you—' Jill began; then

150

changed her mind. 'I don't want to talk about it. Besides, you wouldn't believe me.'

'I believed the other stories you told me. Who knows, maybe I'll swallow this one too. But it's going to have to be a lot better than the other ones because I'm a lot more suspicious.'

Jill shook her head. 'It's no use. I'm going to bed. Just show me where I'm supposed to sleep. Unless you're throwing me out?'

Once a visitor had been invited to stay, you didn't throw him or her out unless he (or she) did nasty things on the carpet. That was the code by which Susan had been brought up, and she did not intend to violate it. 'No, you can stay here tonight.' If Jill didn't want to talk, Susan wasn't going to insist. It would save a lot of awkwardness.

'Aren't you afraid I might creep in and kill you or something?' Jill asked bitterly.

'Don't be silly. There's no reason for you to kill me. I don't know anything that the police don't know, and I'm not the one who's frightened out of her wits.'

'Does that mean you trust me?'

'Not in the least,' Susan said. 'It's a long way from not thinking you're a killer to trusting you.' Besides, she thought, just in case I'm wrong, I have a gun in my bag. However, there was no point in sharing that information with Jill, and frightening her even more—unless it became necessary to shoot her.

She showed Jill to one of the spare bedrooms that still had a bed in it. 'You can sleep here. I'll get some fresh linen.'

'That's all right,' Jill said. 'I can sleep on the floor.'

'I can also get you a hair shirt to sleep in, unless you'd like to go get that suitcase of yours out of the foyer. I assume you have nightclothes in it.' Perhaps Jill slept in the nude. She'd be sorry if she did. The heat in the apartment tended to go down at night.

Jill made a sound that was a cross between a sob and a grunt.

Susan went to the back of the apartment and got clean

linen out of a closet. How worn and thin the sheets had become. It hadn't occurred to her before that she could ever need new ones, that sheets were not forever. But any sheets she bought now—no matter how much she paid for them —would never last as long as the old ones had. Nothing was made to last any more. It was probably because of the atom bomb. Why manufacture sheets that would last for future generations when there was a good chance there weren't going to be any future generations? Might as well buy seconds, she thought.

When she came back with her arms full of sheets and pillowcases (fragrant with the lavender she always put between them because lavender was what you put between sheets), the door to the bedroom she had allotted to Jill was closed. She could hear Jill inside, fumbling at the lock. 'There's no key,' she complained, as Susan said, 'Here's the linen,' and, unable to knock because her arms were full, pushed open the door, and Jill along with it.

'What's the sense of having locks on your doors if there aren't any keys to them?' Jill demanded.

'Do you have a key to your bedroom door?'

'I don't have a separate bedroom. I have a studio apartment—a small, rent-stabilized studio apartment in an un-gentrified walk up,' Jill said in what Susan's mother would have described as 'a socialist tone of voice'.

But Jill had no right to talk like a downtrodden member of the proletariat. She ought to be making plenty of money, more perhaps than Susan, herself, since Jill's commissions from both the Moffatt and the Melville works together, plus any odd jobs she might take on the side, should amount to more than Susan was making. Of course, in spite of Jill's cutting every possible corner as well as a few impossible ones, there were a lot of expenses that had to come out of her share of the take. Nevertheless, she ought to be very comfortably off, and well able to afford a decent if not a luxurious apartment, even at today's outrageous prices.

Susan had never seen Jill's apartment, never been invited

there. All she knew was that it was in Brooklyn, but she'd been told that there were some very nice places in Brooklyn. Jill might be lying again. But why?

Susan dumped the linen on the bed. 'There must have been keys once, but I can't remember ever seeing any.' Her family had been occupying the apartment since before she'd been born. It had been their New York *pied à terre* at first and, after her father had decamped, their principal, and then their sole, residence. Now she owned it. In all that time she had never seen any keys. There had been no need for them. Privacy had been understood.

She remembered an old boarding-school trick. 'You can always hook a chair under the doorknob if it makes you feel safer.'

'I'm not afraid of you,' Jill declared angrily, as if the very idea were absurd. 'I just want to be left alone.'

'Don't worry. I won't intrude on your privacy.' Susan turned at the door. 'There's one question I must ask you. Is Hal—?'

'I don't want to discuss the matter. You want to know anything about Hal, you ask him.'

'I intend to,' Susan said.

Jill gave a choked sob. 'He'll say it was all my fault somehow.'

'Roland's death, too?'

Jill's only answer was to slam the door.

'Well, good night then,' Susan called through the door. 'Maybe you'll feel different in the morning, after you've had a chance to sleep on it.'

What an asinine thing to say. Sleep on what? By morning Jill would have had a chance to think up more lies, and Susan would have had a chance to grow even more suspicious. At least I didn't tell her things were bound to look better in the morning, Susan thought, because, as far as I can see, they're going to look worse.

She went into the studio and turned on the answering machine. If Baltasar called again, he would have to leave a message, and the same went for anyone else who tried to

153

speak to her. But the phone didn't ring again that night, or, if it did, she didn't hear it.

She went to bed, but she'd known before she lay down that the chances of her getting much sleep were slight. Pieces of a picture began to come together but they did not fit neatly. The edges were ragged, like the parts of Lupe's construct after Rover and Fido had been chewing on it.

If Hal Courtenay had been one of the partners in the Turkel Gallery, it would seem to indicate that Roland had been right, providing Jill had reported his suspicions accurately: they'd had the Darius Moffatt paintings lined up from the start. It had been planned in advance for Hal to give Moffatt an enthusiastic review and set the ball rolling. But who could have envisaged that the ball would roll so fast and so far?

Why would a man like Hal have gotten involved in such a scheme? Possibly the whole thing could have been a joke, Hal's desire to thumb his nose at the art establishment by secretly backing this decidedly inferior artist; then setting him up as a genius. But, no, it was too costly a set-up even for a rich man—and too dangerous for a man in his position. Not only had he been a museum curator (assistant curator, anyhow), but also a distinguished art historian, critic, and expert with a reputation to uphold. He would hardly have laid that reputation on the line for a joke that a lot of people wouldn't think was funny.

And there would have been nothing to tempt Roland to join in the operation. No, they must have expected to make money out of the gallery, but not more than a modest profit as the pictures were gradually released over the years. Possibly they had planned to do the same thing with other artists as well. If one didn't take off, they'd try another and, little by little, build the gallery up. Why, it was almost legitimate. In fact, except that Hal would be using his status to puff the pictures, it was legitimate.

When Roland's dabblings in the drug world had been found out, the other two (or rather Hal, because Jill obviously had

154

had only a small financial stake, if that, in the venture) had bought him out. They couldn't have been involved in the drug deal themselves or why would they have bothered with the Moffatt scheme? Which would seem to indicate that Hal could not be, as she had half feared, the shadowy figure that loomed behind the whole picture—the international drug dealer whom Mackay had mentioned in connection with the Hoffmann exhibit, and who might have been the same individual who had involved Roland the first time and for whom Roland might have been working ever since.

It was ridiculous, anyway, to think that a man of such culture and distinction, a museum director, no matter how flawed his character, how tacky his answering-machine messages, should be a trafficker in drugs. Yet what better front for an international drug dealer than that of a museum director, travelling all over the world in search of art and artifacts; moreover, an individual with an Italian or Greek island of his very own, perfect headquarters from which to conduct nefarious activities. She recalled that her own ancestor, Black Buck Melville, had owned such an island, although it had been in the Caribbean, a more convenient location for a man in his line of work.

However, the mere fact of owning an island did not automatically make a person suspect of being an international drug dealer, any more than having an apartment in Jackson Heights made a person suspect of being a national one. Jackson Heights . . . What had made her think of Jackson Heights? Where had she heard it mentioned recently? She couldn't recall. It didn't seem relevant.

There was a fourth party involved in the Hal-Jill-Roland relationship. Someone she had been overlooking in her speculations. What about Darius Moffatt himself? Had he been an innocent, or part of the plan to exploit his pictures beyond the bounds of legitimate hype?

Had it been a coincidence that he'd died just before the exhibit opened? Surely, in spite of what she'd told Mackay, his death must have been an accident. Hal and Jill were hardly likely to have killed the goose that could lay more

155

golden—no silver—eggs. They couldn't have expected that his works would turn into pure gold. But eggs were eggs. Even if you're selling plain goose eggs, you don't make pâté de foie gras out of the goose.

Perhaps they'd been forced to kill him. Perhaps he had refused to go along with the scheme? Not likely. As far as he would be concerned, it would simply seem like a good way of getting his work before the public. To him, as to most unsuccessful or undersuccessful artists, all critics would seem axiomatically prejudiced, cronyistic, venal, devoid of a genuine appreciation of true art, too ready to pander to fashion and flattery. A rave review, no matter how obtained, would be no more than his just due. No, they wouldn't have killed Moffatt for that reason. He would have been eager to go along with the scheme.

He must simply have died of natural causes. (In New York death from a drug overdose counts as a natural cause.) How had they managed to gain possession of his work after he died? Or had it already been in their possession at the time of his death? The story of Old Mother Moffatt and her barn was, as she had already realized, probably fictitious, the creation of Jill's fertile brain.

So, it was likely, was Old Mother Moffatt herself. Darius might have had a mother; in fact, he must have had a mother, because they hadn't started breeding babies in test tubes until years after his birth. It seemed doubtful, however, that she was getting anything out of this if she were still alive. And that seemed doubtful, too. They must have made sure that the dead artist had no heirs to haunt them, or they would not have embarked on such an elaborate deception, with its chain of paintings, interviews, magazine articles, books, and so on.

What fun they must have had, she thought, a little wistfully. And, provided they hadn't killed Darius himself, and had a legitimate claim to his works, all of it was legal or as near legal as made no difference.

So everything had worked out well, with Darius's paintings dwindling to their inevitable end. And then that painting had turned up at Allardyce's.

Apparently they had made a mistake. Moffatt must have sold a painting during his lifetime or given one away. Possibly there was an heir after all. How frightened Jill and Hal must have been. But Jill hadn't seemed frightened at the auction, just angry. She became frightened only after she'd learned of Roland's death.

Had Roland somehow hung on to one of the Moffatt paintings? Was that why he had been killed? For just one picture? There had been hundreds before, but none before had commanded such a price.

Susan felt as victimized as Roland, though not, of course, as drastically. It was possible that Jill was doing a good job in her capacity as Susan's representative. Nevertheless, Susan didn't like being represented by someone whose only other client was a myth. Would I feel so strongly about it, she wondered, if I didn't feel that I myself am, in a sense, a myth?

CHAPTER 21

Susan finally did fall asleep, but she was awakened after what seemed like only a few hours, by a sound that she could not at first identify. Then she realized what it had been—a door closing somewhere inside the apartment. An intruder? Picking up the handbag with the gun in it, she went to Jill's room.

It was empty. Pinned to the pillow was a sheet of paper torn from one of her sketch pads. On it was scrawled, 'I'm not staying where I'm not wanted—Jill . . . PS. You need some new sheets.'

It was the front door she had heard closing, which meant now it was locked only on the snap latch. If I hadn't heard her leave, she thought crossly, any one of the neighbours could have come in with a credit card and killed me.

She thought of calling down to the doorman to tell him to stop Jill, in case Jill hadn't passed him yet. But he could hardly restrain the girl bodily. If he tried, Jill would probably put up a fight. And then both of them would sue Susan.

Let her go, she thought. Why should I care, anyway? But a line from an old song rang in her head: 'Let her go, let her go, God bless her . . .'

Saint James Infirmary, that was where the line came from. She thought of Jill's body stretched out 'on a long white table, so young, so cold, so fair . . .' and she shuddered. If she had felt Jill deserved it, there was a time when she might have killed the girl herself, but she didn't want her to die as the result of her own inaction.

She was being silly. That was what often happened when you woke up in the small hours of the night and started thinking.

She looked at the clock. Not so small as all that—almost six. By this hour Jill should have no trouble finding a cab —a lot more easily than she would two or three hours later when the streets would be full of strong young men with attaché cases pushing little old ladies aside and grabbing their cabs. Jill would be all right, she told herself.

She tried to go back to sleep, but she couldn't. Suppose someone had really been after Jill, and had been lurking in the street all night waiting for a chance to get at her. Supposing Jill simply got killed by a casual mugger for her fur coat. Supposing she had felt so repentant over past misdeeds, that she had gone and thrown herself into the river—conveniently situated only a few blocks to the east. That was one of the troubles with New York, Susan thought; it had too many rivers and they were all too handy for anyone who didn't mind drowning in a stream of effluvium.

Nonsense, she told herself. Now that it's daylight, Jill has probably realized how groundless her fears were and simply gone home. Except that, and it came back to the beginning again, her fears might not have been groundless.

Susan got up and dressed; then called Jill's number. Jill's machine answered. Perhaps she hadn't had enough time to get home. Or she hadn't gone home but to some other place of refuge—some friend who might be even at that moment engaged in the act of killing her.

Jill might have stopped somewhere for breakfast. She might simply not be answering her phone. 'Jill, if you're there I insist that you speak to me,' Susan told the machine. 'It's urgent. Gil Stratton is trying to get me to be his client.'

But the machine went on whirring. Nobody picked it up. Jill was not home.

Hal might know where Jill had gone, but he might also be the one, or one of the ones, of whom she was afraid; in which case Susan didn't want to let him know that Jill was no longer safely ensconced in her apartment. Besides, even though he was a fraud and possibly a murderer, he didn't know she knew that, so it was too early to call him.

Perhaps Andrew Mackay might have some idea of where Jill might be, or at least could find out. He's a detective, she thought, let's see how well he can detect. Anyhow, it was never too early or too late to call a detective.

She rooted around in the bag she had been carrying the day before until she found Mackay's card. She didn't know whether the number was of his home or his office—or whether, in fact, he had an office (or, for that matter, a home), but she called it. Again, only a machine answered. Am I the only living person left in the city, she wondered. Has everyone else left for another planet, leaving only their machines behind to take messages until their tapes run out?

'Andrew,' she said into the phone, 'this is Susan Melville. Jill has disappeared.'

There, she said to herself with satisfaction, that ought to get him going.

By this time it was seven o'clock, not too early to call Alex, a relative by blood if not by consanguinity. He whistled when she gave him a recap of all that had happened since she had last spoken to him, rather, of all that she'd learned, for in actual fact nothing had happened. It only seemed that way.

'The worms certainly seem to have emerged from the canister with a vengeance,' he said. 'Whatever possessed

159

you to let her come over? It could have been dangerous.'

'Well, she's gone and I haven't come to any harm, so it's all water over the bridgework, as Lupe would say. That's right, I wonder where Lupe fits in in all this, if she fits in at all. Andrew seemed to think she might be connected in some way, but as far as I can see she's just an innocent bystander.'

'If you can call a lady who travels with a pack of wolves innocent in any sense of the word. Listen, Susan, why don't you come over to breakfast and then we can talk about it and decide what to do or, better yet, what not to do. Do nothing is my instinctive reaction, but I agree that the matter needs discussion. Oh, by the way, I have the *Times* and the *Wall Street Journal,* of course, but would you mind picking up the *News* on your way? And *Newsday* and the *Post* if they're out. Oh, yes, and a dozen eggs, if you would be so good. The far-from-efficient Mrs Liebling has slipped up again.'

Tinsley was still asleep when Susan arrived, so she and Alex had breakfast alone together, in the Tabors' pleasant breakfast room overlooking Central Park. Tinsley's family counted among the superrich and so their handsome penthouse condominium on Fifth Avenue (a wedding gift from the bride's family), while being up to date in every respect, was well equipped with such relics of a bygone era as both breakfast and dining-rooms and 'more baths,' as Jill had observed, 'than you can shake a mahl stick at.'

Alex prepared breakfast. The housekeeper didn't come on duty officially until eight, except in case of emergencies —for which she generally exacted a pound of flesh in addition to overtime, so that Tinsley and Alex were wary of seeking any extra services. 'It isn't the money,' Tinsley said, 'it's the martyrdom.'

Alex was a much better cook than Mrs Liebling, anyway, Susan thought, but he nearly spoiled her breakfast by informing her that, while she was on her way over, Lieutenant Bracco had called. 'He wanted to come over here to talk to me, but I told him my wife was pregnant and easily upset, so I'd stop down and see him at his office before I went to mine. I figured that would touch a chord. Civil servants have a high regard for motherhood.'

'Why don't you consolidate your standing by taking him an apple pie?'

'I'll leave that to you. He said he wanted to "have another chat—" his words—with you, and that he'd left a message to that effect on your machine; but, if I happened to talk to you before you picked it up, I should let you know. He has a few more questions he wants to put to you.'

Even though Mackay had warned her that she was likely to get a call from the lieutenant, she was nonetheless un-nerved. 'Did you tell him I was coming over here?'

Alex was shocked. 'What kind of brother do you take me for? I told him I had no idea of where you might be, but that only the other day you had spoken of longing to paint the sun coming up over the Himalayas, and I wouldn't be surprised if you had packed up your palette and impulsively dashed off to Nepal.'

'And what did he say to that?'

'He said he'd told you to let him know if you were planning to leave town and he had no doubt you would have gotten in touch with him if you intended to go to Nepal. He seems to have formed a very favourable impression of you. I wouldn't be surprised if you'd made another conquest.'

Mrs Liebling appeared at the breakfast room door, breath-ing fire, with a touch of brimstone for Susan. 'You should have called me,' she said. 'I would have been only too happy—'

'There was no need to disturb you. I am perfectly capable of making breakfast for my sister and myself.'

'It's not right for a man to do the cooking,' she said, glaring at Susan.

There were a number of French chefs, including M. Bumppo, who would be interested to hear that, Susan thought, but she held her tongue, not wanting to roil Alex's domestic waters.

'Mrs Liebling,' he began ominously, 'I have told you before—'

'At least I can clear away,' she said, making a grab for the dishes.

'We haven't finished yet,' Alex said. 'Why don't you go see if Mrs Tabor wants anything. I'm not going to apologize for her,' he told Susan, after the housekeeper had left with a parting sniff. One of these days I'm going to do a picture of her as a dragon, Susan thought, no, a fire-breathing toad sitting under a canopy of poison ivy leaves. 'Amy hired her and Amy is your friend.'

'If Amy hadn't been, you wouldn't be where you are now,' Susan reminded him.

He hesitated before he said, 'All right, I apologize for her. How about putting a bad word for her in my dear mother-in-law's ear? I don't want to seem ungrateful, but you have no reason for gratitude.'

Together Alex and Susan scanned the relevant parts of the papers. Because of the other events in the news (plus a small war that had started up during the wee hours), Roland's death got no more than a cover line in the tabloids, plus an inside story on the third page of the *Post* and the fourth of the *News*, while the *Times* relegated it to the Metropolitan Section as if it were merely a routine local event, which she supposed it was to the *Times*. All of the people she had killed, she couldn't help remembering, had hit the front page, even though some had been carried over to Section D (Business and Obituaries).

Otherwise there was nothing in the papers about Roland's demise that she didn't already know. There really hadn't been time for them to do much digging. Tomorrow, especially after the drug angle had been brought out into the open, there would be more background information, and she would learn more about Roland's past from presumably reliable sources.

She wondered how soon and how much of what Mackay had told her about Hal's and Jill's enterprise would get in the papers. If they unearthed Hal's direct connection with the Turkel Gallery, which they might well do, since it was presumably no secret—it was just that there had been no

reason before for anyone to take the trouble to look it up—
Hal would find himself in a very unenviable position.

As they went through the papers, her attention was caught
by a small item in the *Times* and larger ones in the other
papers concerning a Lady Daphne Merriwether who, after
having been struck by a bicyclist who had not stopped for
a red light, had attacked and nearly killed him with her
bare hands. The bicyclist, who was nineteen, was in the
hospital. Lady Daphne, who was seventy-five, was in police
custody. Bully for Lady Daphne, Susan thought, and decided against calling the episode to Alex's attention. He had
enough to think about.

Alex seemed genuinely surprised to learn that Hal had been
the principal backer of the Turkel Gallery. She'd been
half afraid he'd known and hadn't told her. 'That's right,
Courtenay did stop working for the General about the same
time as he gave Roland the boot,' Alex said thoughtfully.
'Could be they were in the thing together. I'd just started
working for the organization then, so I really wasn't in on
things. In fact, I didn't have too much to do with the art
side until I recruited you. But I wouldn't be at all surprised
to find out Courtenay authenticated that Picasso. What does
surprise me, though, is to find out Courtenay's apparently
a crook. He always seemed so stuffy. But then there's no
law saying crooks have to be free spirits. What puzzles me
is why this fellow Mackay should be interested in them at
all, if he's decided they have nothing to do with the drug
aspect of the matter. He seems, from what you tell me, to
be some kind of narc.'

'Drugs would make him a federal agent, then?' she asked.

'Not necessarily. The city and state police have narcotics
divisions. He could even be a private detective. The cops
sometimes use private eyes to do things they can't do themselves.'

He spoke authoritatively. He had spent most of his adult
life and the latter part of his adolescence working against
the law. The fact that he had never been caught should give
him authority.

163

'I thought the police resented private detectives.'

Alex laughed. 'I see you're still keeping up with the television shows.'

She hadn't had a chance to watch television, except for the news, in weeks. And she missed it. Fictional crime was always so much more satisfactory than real-life crime, if only because it had to be solved by the end of the hour, while real-life crime often never got solved at all.

'Do you think Roland could have been blackmailing Jill and Hal?'

'Why would he stick his neck out like that?' Alex said. 'He wasn't a courageous man, you know. And, if he had wanted to blackmail them, why now, when he had this big drug deal going?'

'Then why is Jill so afraid?' Susan asked. 'And of whom?'

'Good questions,' he said. 'I only wish I had some equally good answers. The only one I can think of is Hal, and the Moffatt thing doesn't seem like enough to kill for, unless he killed Moffatt. Besides, he doesn't seem the killer type to me. Not that that means anything, of course.' He smiled and patted her hand.

She pulled her hand away.

'And, of course, we don't know what else Roland was up to or who he was up to it with. But don't worry about Jill. That's one lady who can take care of herself.'

Susan didn't agree. In spite of Jill's tough exterior, she was extremely vulnerable.

Alex got up. 'Well, it's time for me to go pay my respects to the lieutenant. Like to come with me and save everybody trouble?'

'No, thanks,' she said, 'I'll wait until I hear from him directly.' Which wouldn't be very soon, if she had any choice in the matter.

CHAPTER 22

They parted at the front door of Alex's building. He gave her a searching look. 'You're carrying one of those big bags you used to carry when you were doing jobs for the General.'

She had not expected him to be so observant. 'Waste not, want not,' she said. 'It's a good bag. Lots of wear left in it.'

'You aren't carrying a gun in there, are you?'

She couldn't lie about it. Much too embarrassing later if she should happen to find herself obliged to shoot somebody. She didn't say anything.

'But that's ridiculous. There's no reason for you to carry a gun any more.'

'It makes me feel more comfortable. Isn't that reason enough?'

'No, it is not. Do you mean to say you're planning to carry a gun when you go to see Lieutenant Bracco?'

Since she hadn't had any intention of seeing the lieutenant when she set out that morning, she hadn't made any plans with respect to the gun. But she wasn't going to traipse all the way back to her apartment simply to put it away.

'The police are hardly likely to search me. Anyhow, why should you worry? It's one of father's old guns; it has no connection with you.'

'But he's my father, too, now,' Alex explained patiently, 'and you're my sister. How would it look in the papers: "Stockbroker's sister charged with illegal possession of concealed weapon"?'

'How would it look: "Well-known artist charged, etcetera"?'

He laughed. 'Not nearly as bad from my point of view. You're right, of course, I'm not my sister's keeper. I can't tell you what to do; that is, I can tell you, but I don't have any way of making you do it any more.'

And he sighed, no doubt thinking of the past, when he'd been in a position to coerce her into doing his bidding. But even that hadn't always worked, she remembered with pride. She'd been her own woman then—far more than she was now. Part of the price one had to pay for success, she supposed. Had it all been worth it? Although there were some aspects of her new life she could do without, the overall answer was an emphatic yes.

Alex offered to give her a lift in his cab to wherever she was going, but, having no particular destination in mind, she was in no hurry to get there. All she knew was that she didn't want to go home and pick up her messages. The answering machine did have a remote control system whereby messages could, in theory at least, be picked up from any phone, but she never used it; as she explained over and over again to Jill who felt that whenever her client was away from home, her constant concern should be to get to a phone at periodic intervals to pick up messages from her representative. Jill couldn't get it through her head that sometimes one of the reasons Susan left her apartment was just to get away from the phone.

Of course Susan could and sometimes did stay at home and simply not pick up the phone, especially when she was painting and could not be disturbed, letting messages collect until she was in a receptive mode. Or she would listen to them and not answer. But, whenever she did that, she found herself feeling guilty—a hangover from the past of which she had been unable to rid herself. This way she hadn't actually received the lieutenant's message, so she felt no obligation to act upon it.

Why was she so anxious to avoid the lieutenant? He had been perfectly affable at their previous interview. Why would he be less affable now? She had given him all the information he had asked for; and, if she had neglected to give him further information that might have been pertinent, how on earth was she to know what did and did not pertain? Was she a mind reader? Besides, how could she have been expected to think of details in the stress of the moment?

In any case, everything she'd told Mackay should have been readily obtainable elsewhere. In fact, by this time the lieutenant probably had found out all she could tell him from other sources. Probably all he wanted from her was to check out a few things.

In due time she would go home and pick up her messages; then she would call the office and go down and have a chat with the lieutenant, over a cup of tea, perhaps. No, that was the British police. American police served coffee in plastic cups.

Only there were other things she had to do before she went home. Important things. As, for instance, go to see Baltasar. How could she have forgotten how worried she had been about him the night before?

She must check immediately to make sure that he was all right. It was the decent, human, time-consuming thing to do.

She'd go to the nearest telephone and call him. But it was always so difficult to communicate on one of those street phones. Every passer-by could hear what you were saying, while you couldn't hear the person on the other end, because a heavy truck or a fire engine or a car with a loud radio invariably went by just as you made your connection. Once she had dropped in a quarter just as a particularly noisy parade had marched down the street. Her money had run out before the person on the other end had been able to hear anything but a brass band playing a medley of folk songs from some unidentified nation.

What she would do was go to the Plaza and call Baltasar on one of the house phones. He would ask her to have breakfast with him, and she'd join him for a cup of coffee —which would not be served in a plastic cup. The Plaza's standards had not deteriorated that far. The police would never think of tracking her down in the Palm Court. After that, she might—yes, she would go to the MAA and beard Hal in his den.

She decided to stroll down Fifth Avenue to the Plaza. It was a nice day for a walk, brisk and invigorating—so brisk and invigorating it was hard for her to keep her pace down to the stroll necessary if she was not going to reach the hotel too early.

167

She rang Baltasar's room. There was no answer. He seemed to be an early riser. Not that ten o'clock was so very early, just that she'd been under the impression that natives of Spanish-speaking countries kept late hours, although, she supposed, there was no reason why your mother tongue should affect your circadian rhythm.

Baltasar could be anywhere. How did she know what his haunts might be? However, there was a good chance that he might be at his building. There was a better than good chance that the police might be there, too. Not Lieutenant Bracco, though. He would be at his office, talking to Alex. The likelihood was that they would simply have left a man on guard at the scene of the crime, someone who didn't even know that the lieutenant wanted to see her; or who, even if he did, probably would not be able to identify her by sight.

And what if he did recognize her and inform her that she was being sought for further questioning? So she would go and be questioned further. It isn't as if I were a fugitive or even a material witness, she thought.

There was a policeman stationed outside the gallery. He was standing in front of the gate that led to the basement steps, flapping his arms, although it didn't seem to her the day was all that cold, and muttering to himself. Clearly he didn't like his present post and didn't care who knew it. He glanced at her without apparent interest as she paused in front of the gallery.

She smiled at him. 'Could you tell me if Mr Baltasar is inside?'

'You can ring the bell and ask,' he said. 'I'm a policeman not a doorman.'

He seemed to have a cold in his nose, poor man. Or perhaps he was coming down with the flu. She hoped he was. Bed rest would do him so much good.

To her surprise, it was Damian Schwimmer who answered the door. The 'Schwimmer' seemed to give him a whole new dimension. 'Do come in,' he said hospitably.

Esmeralda came forward with a cordial meow and twined herself around Susan's legs as she entered. Both Damian and Esmeralda seemed glad to see her. She was touched. She bent over and patted Esmeralda's head. Damian looked as if he would have liked to have his head patted, too, but there she drew the line.

'Baltasar asked us to stay on for a bit and look after things,' Damian explained. 'We're staying in Rollie's apartment.'

It wasn't clear whether he meant himself and Esmeralda or himself and Paul. 'Since it wasn't the actual scene of the crime, which is sealed off, not that wild unicorns would drag me down there—' and he shuddered, —'the police had no objection. First they searched the place with frightening thoroughness. All of Rollie's little secrets revealed. Too sickening for him, only, of course, he's in no position to be sickened any more.'

He looked sad. She looked sad, too. They shared a moment of respectful silence. *I suppose I'll be expected to go to his funeral,* she thought. *I do hope there aren't going to be any more murders. I hate wearing black.*

'Paul and I were absolutely terrified that the police would search us, too. They didn't, though.' Damian didn't look terrified, even in retrospect. He looked disappointed.

'Do you know they found a secret room in the sub-basement? More of a secret storage closet than a secret room. A large walk-in type of closet. And not so secret because the police found it right away.'

She had never even thought of the sub-basement, but, of course, all those old buildings had sub-basements below ground level—where they had used to keep coal in the old days, before oil heat took over. It would have been a perfect spot for a concealed cache, except that it was one of the first places the police would look. They knew about these old buildings too.

'Did they find anything there?' she asked. 'I mean anything that would shed any light on what happened to Roland?'

'It was absolutely empty, not even a skeleton. But, a very sweet boy on the DA's staff told me, one of those little men with microscopes found traces of coke there. They seem to think Rollie was a drug dealer or smuggler or something.

Which is ridiculous. He may have used coke once in a while —everybody does—but he couldn't have been trading in it. That would be immoral. I'm sure Rollie didn't have the least idea the room was there. What I think is the previous occupant of the building must have been a drug dealer.' He nodded firmly.

Esmeralda butted her head against Susan's legs. Susan obediently bent over and patted her again. Why is this cat making up to me, she wondered. And then she laughed at herself. I'm beginning to suspect everyone of having ulterior motives, even the cat.

'Anyhow I must admit it's a blessing that Baltasar's letting us stay here, because I don't know how Paul and I would have been able to go on paying the rent at our hotel, now Rollie's gone and our jobs with him.'

'Well, perhaps whoever takes over the gallery will keep you on,' Susan suggested.

Damian shook his sleek head. 'I'm afraid Baltasar has other ideas. He's suddenly decided not to have a gallery here at all. Thinks there's a curse on the place or something like that. But if there should be a curse—although, mind you, I don't believe in such things—it would be on anything that set up here, not just an art gallery. So why not leave it as a gallery?'

'Maybe he'll decide to keep it as a gallery once he gets over the shock.'

Damian shook his head. 'He's set things in motion.' Lowering his voice, he said, 'He's been going over the place with the strangest lady, who seems to be thinking of renting it. And I'm afraid she has something a lot different from an art gallery in mind.'

He made such a face that Susan leaped to erotic and erroneous conclusions. 'A brothel, do you mean?'

He laughed. 'Oh, no, that would be fun—and there might even be spots for Paul and me. I'd love to work in a brothel. You meet—you must meet such fascinating people there.'

Susan felt a little embarrassed at having entertained such an unseemly thought. That was the result of association, however casual, with Dodo Pangborn. No, if she left Jill,

170

she definitely would not become a client of Dodo's. Not that she had ever considered the prospect seriously.

'I'm not sure what Baltasar's prospective tenant is actually planning,' Damian said. 'That is, I know what it sounds like, but I can't believe my ears. She seems to be—but I hear the elevator. I'd better be discreet, or I won't be kept on even temporarily.'

If only Damian had said, 'But hark, I hear the elevator,' or—better yet—'hark, I hear the lift,' it would have sounded like a line from an old melodrama.

CHAPTER 23

The little door in the woodwork opened and Baltasar came out. This time, instead of being accompanied by the contractor, he handed out—Susan blinked—Hortense Pomeroy, of all people! Today she was dressed for business in a hairy purple and green culotte suit. Atop her head was the pink beret, or perhaps another pink beret; it did look fuzzier than the one she'd worn to Sprouts 'n Stuff. Attached to it by what looked vaguely like a Girl Scout badge was a jaunty lavender feather.

Never had anyone seemed so out of place in an art gallery. No, that wasn't true. She looked like something perpetrated by a pop artist of the sixties. But what was she doing here? '. . . Should have taken the stairs,' she was saying. 'Greatest exercise in the world for man, woman, and child. Beast too. Bet *she* never takes the elevator.'

At first Susan thought Hortense was talking about Susan herself. For a moment she wondered what she had done to arouse the physical educator's disapproval. Then she realized it was Esmeralda to whom Hortense referred. Esmeralda stretched sinuously, as if to indicate she needed no physical fitness classes to keep in condition.

There was a look of strain on Baltasar's face—either from too much of Hortense's society or from the series of disasters with which he'd been forced to cope. Somehow she could not

171

feel sorry for him; he was not the sort of person who aroused sympathy. A sort of reverse *noblesse oblige*, she supposed.

'I assure you, Miss Pomeroy—'

'Hortense, please.'

'—Hortense, that if Esmeralda were able to open the door and reach the buttons she would be taking the lift more often than any one of us. There is no animal lazier than a cat.'

He saw Susan and his dark face seemed to light up. 'My dear Susan, how nice to see you. I tried to get in touch with you last night.'

'I know, Jill gave me your message. That's why I came over—'

'Susan, I can't begin to thank you enough!' Hortense interrupted. Striding across the foyer, she grasped both of the other woman's hands and pumped them up and down, as if she were trying to start her engine. 'I always knew you'd go to bat for an old school chum, but I never thought you'd hit a homer like this.'

As if they had gone to school together, instead of merely teaching at the same place. And what was the woman talking about, anyway? 'I didn't know you two knew each other,' Susan said.

'Never actually met until this morning. Phone chums—' Baltasar winced —'that was all. But we know each other now, thanks to you.' She patted Susan on the shoulder with a hand like a slab of meat loaf.

Susan looked inquiringly at Baltasar.

He rubbed the back of his neck with his hand. 'After the terrible things that have happened at this place, I felt certain that no art dealer would wish to have a gallery here, nor would any artist want to exhibit his works in such a place.'

'I don't see any reason why not,' Susan objected. 'It's a good space at a good address. I'm sure there are any number of dealers who would jump at the chance to take it over.'

Behind Baltasar's back Damian raised a circled thumb and forefinger in encouragement; then, either out of delicacy or boredom, he vanished behind the shiny curtain that still closed off the back regions of the gallery.

Hortense waggled a roguish finger. 'Now, now, Susie, don't spoil the good work. Of course no artist who had the least . . . uh . . . sensitivity would want to show his work in a place with such a—a dark cloud hanging over it.'

'Please call me Susan, not Susie.' Sensitivity indeed. What did someone as boorish as Hortense know about sensitivity? And she didn't understand what Hortense was talking about. What was she doing here? And why did Baltasar feel the place could no longer function as an art gallery? Did he think Roland was going to come back and haunt it? Even if he did, that was hardly likely to bother the average art dealer. If Roland's ghost tried to haunt Gil Stratton, for example, Gil would just laugh in its face. As for an artist, he would probably try to tie-dye its sheet.

'Jill—I'm afraid I have forgotten her surname, that charming young representative of yours—gave me one of this lady's brochures the other day,' Baltasar explained. 'I found it of enormous interest. Such a worthy-sounding enterprise.'

'Turkel. Her name's Jill Turkel, and she was acting on her own, not as my representative, when she gave you that brochure.'

'Oh, I understood that, of course. I knew you would not personally be involved with so commercial a project.'

For some reason Susan couldn't quite put her finger on, she felt vaguely insulted.

'I, too, really must thank Jill,' Hortense said. 'I tried to get her on the phone this morning, but only her machine answered.'

'She's disappeared.'

'Oh, well, these artistic people . . .' Hortense said. Apparently she didn't make Baltasar's distinction between art and commerce. 'I tried to call you, too, and only your machine answered. And here you are, so at least *you* haven't disappeared.'

'Speaking of disappearances,' Baltasar said, 'you do not happen to know where Lupe has gotten to, do you, Susan?'

'Lupe!' Susan was startled. 'I'd have thought you would know, if anyone did.'

He shook his head. 'I would have thought so myself, but didn't. She left the gallery the day before yesterday—not long after you and Jill had gone—promising to call and let me know where she would be staying. Since then I have heard not a word from her. I am beginning to feel concerned. I know she seems very ... very much in possession of herself, but she is a young woman alone in a strange city.'

Should she tell him that Lupe had come to Leatherstocking's after she had left the gallery? No reason to bring it up; for some reason Lupe might not want him to know. 'Wasn't she supposed to get in touch with your lawyer?'

He looked at her with faint reproach. 'That idea did occur to me, of course. But he says he has not heard from her either. Incidentally, while Lupe was here at the gallery, she asked for your address and telephone number and also Jill's. I secured them from poor Roland ...'

He paused. Susan wondered if they were in for another moment of respectful silence; then Hortense boomed, 'Roland, wasn't that the fellow who got bashed?' and the opportunity for such a moment was over.

'I hope you do not mind that I gave Lupe your addresses. It seemed to me a good thing that since she was a stranger in a strange country she should make friends with some nice ladies.'

'Of course, I don't mind. I wish she had called me.' Or Jill, Susan was about to add, but, for all she knew Lupe *had* called Jill.

'If this lady you're talking about is from out of town, maybe she registered at a hotel,' Hortense offered.

Baltasar seemed struck by this suggestion, which, Susan had to admit (grudgingly) to herself, was a sensible one. 'She might be at a hotel, yes, and did not call me because she heard about what had happened here, and it made her nervous.'

That didn't make sense. If Lupe was nervous, it seemed to Susan the first thing she would do would be to call the only real friend she had in the city. Susan had a suspicion that Baltasar was being less than candid with her, that he

174

knew perfectly well where Lupe was and, for some reason of his own, did not choose to admit it.

'How would one go about checking the hotels?' Baltasar asked. 'There must be a great many of them here. There seems to be a great many of everything here.'

'I imagine the police will be doing that for you,' Susan told him.

'Ah yes, the police.' Baltasar looked as if he had smelled something bad. 'They must be demons of efficiency, your police. One of them came to fetch me from Allardyce's yesterday. I cannot imagine how they knew I was there. But I suppose they must have their methods.'

'Well,' Susan said, glad she had long since gotten over such *gaucheries* as blushing, 'they're not called New York's Finest for nothing.'

'They questioned me quite extensively at the time, and then this morning, I was called down to their offices at an incredible hour. The lieutenant had found out about Lupe's existence somehow—' Susan tried to keep her face blank —'and he was displeased that I had not thought to inform him about her advent. But what, for Heaven's sake, could she have to do with Roland? She had never so much as set eyes on him before.'

'The police undoubtedly want to talk to everyone who had been in the gallery that day,' Susan told him. 'It's routine.'

If he'd been a television watcher, he would have known that. But perhaps Spanish TV was different.

'But, if it was a sex crime, surely there would be no need to question women,' Hortense said.

'This morning the lieutenant told me that they are beginning to think that perhaps it was not a sex crime, after all,' Baltasar said, 'that perhaps some enemy of Roland's killed him in that manner in order to divert suspicion from his real reason.'

Baltasar must have learned about the drug angle by this time, Susan thought. However, she could understand his reluctance to mention it in front of Hortense. You don't tell a prospective tenant that she may be taking over a former drug den.

'Ah,' Hortense said, 'a man like that must have many enemies.'

'A man like what?' Susan asked.

'Oh, you know,' Hortense said.

Susan did know, but she wondered how Hortense did.

'The police were annoyed with me, too, because I hadn't mentioned Lupe,' Susan told Baltasar. 'I must admit I was so . . . so upset I'd forgotten about her. But you, as an old friend, couldn't have forgotten—'

'I saw no need to drag her into it. She is a foreigner. It is frightening to be questioned by the authorities when one is not in one's own country. I know; I am a foreigner myself. You cannot imagine the trouble I have had with your building inspectors, your sewer inspectors, and now, your police inspectors. Can you imagine! That detective said I must not leave the city without letting him know where I was going.'

'That wasn't because you're a foreigner. He told me the same thing.'

'That makes it even more insufferable. To think that they would treat you, dear lady, in such a manner; it is almost beyond belief.'

'The police always tend to take such an authoritarian approach, Lady Daphne always says, and I suppose you could call her a foreigner. She's British, you know. She's gotten into trouble with them, again. Dear Lady Daphne, always so impetuous. One of our instructors,' Hortense explained to Baltasar.

'Lady Daphne? That means she is of the nobility? Good, that will lend prestige to the undertaking.'

'I understand your dear wife is also of the nobility. I hope she will lend her name to the undertaking. That will give us even greater prestige.'

Baltasar looked taken aback for a moment; then he recovered his aplomb. 'If she ever decides to leave Spain and visit this country, I am sure she will be only too delighted to do whatever she can to help. But she is of rather a retiring nature, like so many Spanish ladies of old family.'

That wasn't how the *condesa*'s friends had described her, according to Mimi. One of the most celebrated hostesses in Madrid, they'd said. And hadn't she been supposed to come to the opening of the gallery? Even if she hadn't been able to make it, still she had planned to be there, so she couldn't be all that retiring. Probably Baltasar was painting a fictitious picture in order to keep Hortense at bay, and she could hardly blame him. But why then had he chosen to get involved with Hortense in the first place? Or hadn't he realized what he was getting into?

'I read about Lady Daphne's little brush with the law in the papers,' Susan said to Hortense. 'If she needs help posting bail, anything like that . . .?'

'Sweet of you to offer, but she's out on bail already. Thousands have rallied to her side, and one of the top women lawyers in the city has volunteered her services. We're going to make a cause out of this. First, ban the bicycle; then, the bomb.'

Susan would have thought that Hortense, as a fitness buff, would be pro-bicycle. Perhaps she had been, before the invasion of the bicycle monsters had turned the city into a three-way battlefield, with the pedestrian losing out to both bicycle and automobile. 'They accused her of using excessive force,' Hortense said, 'as if you could use too much force against a rogue bicyclist.' Susan nodded.

Baltasar looked dismayed. 'Violence, violence, is there no getting away from it! I thought a health club would be so quiet, so peaceful.'

Obviously he didn't understand about health clubs. 'After all,' Susan pointed out, 'Lady Daphne does teach unarmed combat. You could look on this in the light of a testimonial to her expertise.'

'Hear, hear,' Hortense said.

Baltasar looked ill.

'Wasn't it rather a sudden decision to turn the gallery into a health club?' Susan asked Baltasar.

'Do you think so? I suppose it does appear that way. But I was interested in the club from the moment I read the brochure. I had been looking for some sound local invest-ments. It is so important for a businessman to diversify these days, you know. And the idea of a health club for ladies of a certain age seemed so right, so American, so attuned to your national passion for physical fitness. It seemed to me it could not fail to succeed.'

'And it will succeed,' Hortense beamed.

'And so I telephoned Miss Pomeroy—'

'Hortense.'

'—Hortense, later that day. When I spoke to her, she happened to mention that she had not as yet found a suitable location.'

'Everything was either too expensive or too awful. Some-times both.'

But what could be more expensive than this place? Unless Baltasar was giving Hortense a spectacular break on the rent. And why should he do that, even if he was taking a piece of the action? Was he so anxious to get rid of the place to anyone who had no connection with the art world that he was willing to lose money on it?

'Last evening,' he explained, almost as if he had been able to read her mind—not that it was difficult to know what she or what any intelligent person must be thinking, 'after I had been told what had happened to poor Roland, I found I could not bear the thought of having another art gallery take the place of this one. It would always remind me of him.'

'Great pals, were you?' Hortense asked sympathetically.

'Merely professional associates,' he said, moving just enough so that her meaty hand missed his shoulder. 'Still . . . well . . . I suppose we Spaniards are more . . . sentimental— is that the right word?—than you Americans.'

Hortense murmured something to the effect that it did them credit.

'Then I had my inspiration. Why should we not turn this place into a health club? It would be perfect. All the ladies who come to make themselves beautiful will want beautiful gowns.'

The idea was ridiculous. All those middle-aged pink berets trooping in and out were hardly likely to enhance the couturier image. And what about the T-shirts and the bag-lady scholarships? The scholarships had probably been just a come-on to draw Susan into the fold, but Hortense would never give up her T-shirts, at least not without a fight.

Well, Susan told herself, it was none of her business what Baltasar decided to do with his gallery. Whatever arrangement he might have had with Roland, it was unquestionably his gallery now.

'I suppose you phoned me last night to find out if I'd heard from Lupe?'

He looked a little embarrassed. 'Well, yes, that, too, of course. But the principal reason I called concerned my little Esmeralda.'

He picked the animal up and stroked her. She purred and wriggled languorously in his arms, shedding hairs all over his sleeves. 'I did not like to leave her here alone at night and I certainly did not want to put her in a kennel. It would be like—like putting her in prison.'

Hortense nodded. 'Lady Daphne feels the same about her hounds.'

'I thought I might prevail upon you to take her for a few days. But then Damian and Paul kindly agreed to stay in Roland's apartment; and they said they would be happy to look after her, so it seems I will not have to impose on you after all.'

Not that you would have stood a chance, Susan thought, making a mental note never to accept a free dress from a couturier again—never to accept a free anything from any-one again, or she might wind up with a zoo in her apartment. Not that that would stop people, even those without any real or imagined claim on her gratitude, from asking favours. Hadn't Lupe, a complete stranger, tried to park Rover and Fido on her? However, she had sensed, even at the time, that hadn't been Lupe's real reason for seeking her and Jill out. People didn't come to New York with wolves unless they had already made provision for them.

Had Lupe been asking for some other kind of help, and had Susan been too obtuse to realize it at the time? No reason to feel guilty, Susan told herself; she does have my telephone number. She can get in touch with me if she wants to. And maybe she had tried. Maybe there was a message from Lupe on the tape waiting for her, along with all the other messages she hadn't picked up.

A phone rang somewhere in the back of the gallery. Damian's winsome face appeared between the two halves of the glitter curtain. 'It's for you, Baltasar.'

'Tell whoever it is that I am busy, and I will get back to him later.'

'I know that must seem rude,' he said to his visitors, 'but it has been nothing but one call after the other all morning —the police, the press, the plumbers.' He sighed. 'I suppose life must go on, but must it go on in such niggling detail?'

'It's that detective who was here yesterday,' Damian elucidated. 'He seemed rather anxious to talk to you right away.'

'Again!' Baltasar paled. 'Such a nuisance. I suppose I had better speak to him, though. One must keep in good standing with the police.'

He vanished behind the curtain.

'Such a charming man,' Hortense said. 'Don't you agree?'

Susan agreed.

There was nothing to keep her in the gallery any longer. She made a gesture in the direction of the front door. 'Well, now that I know what he wanted, I must be on my way. I know you two have business to discuss.'

'Nothing private. I'd be happy to have you stick around. In fact, why don't you come look over the place with me, give me your ideas on what should be done with it? Certainly can't be left the way it is. You should see the apartment that man who was killed had upstairs. I hope I'm not a prude, and I know it's all very artistic, but, oh, my dear!' She rolled her eyes.

'Of course I don't mean the room in the basement where the body was found. That's still sealed off and there's a policeman on guard outside. I will have to see it eventually, because it's part of the space the club will occupy. I understand it's quite gruesome, she added with relish, 'all those antique torture instruments. Well, we're going to put in our own instruments of torture.'

She whinnied melodiously. 'On the other hand, you should see Baltasar's own place at the top of the building. Such a contrast, so tasteful, so elegant.'

Susan was surprised. 'I thought it wasn't finished. Why is he staying at the Plaza then?'

'I didn't know he was staying at the Plaza, but it certainly looked as if somebody had been living on the top floor here. Cat hairs all over and whatnot.'

'That doesn't mean anyone's been living there. Esmeralda sheds all over the place.'

'Not just cat hairs. It looked as if a person had been staying there. Of course I only had a glimpse. I'm only supposed to be looking at the gallery floors, but when Baltasar was called to the phone, I couldn't resist dashing upstairs and having a peep.'

She giggled. 'I'm sure you'll think it was very naughty of me.'

Susan did. She also knew she would have been tempted to do the same thing herself. Under normal circumstances, she would have liked to look over the place, even in Hortense's company, but she knew that even at that moment Lieutenant Bracco might be saying to Baltasar, 'I've been trying to get in touch with Susan Melville all morning,' and Baltasar might be saying, 'Why, she's right here. I'll go get her for you.'

'Perhaps I could go over the place with you some other time. Afraid I must dash now. I'm late for an appointment.'

And she practically ran out of the gallery.

The policeman was standing inside the areaway now, leaning over the gate, staring into the street with unfocused belligerence. He paid no attention to her. Just the same, she strode purposefully down the street with the air of someone who has a definite destination.

CHAPTER 24

After she had turned the corner, she slowed down. Why don't I just give up, call Lieutenant Bracco, and make an appointment to see him? she asked herself. All he wants is to ask me a few more questions. Just routine. He isn't suspicious of me; not that there's anything for him to be suspicious of. Might as well get it over with.

That was very sensible advice she had given herself, and she would act on it, she told herself—just as soon as she'd gone to the MAA and spoken to Hal Courtenay. There were several things that needed to be cleared up, and it would be better if they could be taken care of before, rather than after, she spoke to the lieutenant. Why, she didn't even try to explain to herself. It just seemed neater.

She felt a little uneasy about talking to Hal. It wasn't that she feared violence. Even if he were a violent man, he wouldn't be violent in his own museum.

Or would he? Especially since, the way things looked, there was a good chance it was not going to stay his museum much longer. It depended on how much time it would take for the information Andrew had given her about the Turkel Gallery to reach the public.

Hal might try to brazen it out, but what could he say? That he'd been young then? He'd been in his late thirties or early forties, old enough to know better, but that was absurd. No one is ever old enough to know better. He could say he hadn't been a museum curator at the time, so he'd had no responsible position to betray. But he'd been a critic, an art authority, and a teacher—sacred callings all three.

Perhaps he would be able to get away with saying he'd merely tried to bring this neglected artist to the public attention, and had reaped no financial rewards from the arrangement; but that would be difficult to prove and impossible to believe. What a pity Darius Moffatt wasn't Daria Moffatt. Then he could say the artist was his mother and he had done it for her. His father? No, the American public didn't feel the same about fathers. In any case, it wasn't the public he'd have to worry about so much as the Museum's board of trustees. They were a tough bunch, unlikely to be moved by sentiment.

He wasn't likely to be left destitute. As Mimi had pointed out, he couldn't live the way he did on his salary as director of the Museum; he had to have other resources. Even if the settlement he'd received almost thirty years before from Cissy Flicker had been eroded by inflation and attenuated by extravagance, he still had that island of his to which he could always retire. Alternatively, he could sell it. On the other hand, if he had in some way been concerned in the deaths of Roland, Rafael, and/or Darius Moffatt, he might have to worry about more than the prospect of reduced affluence.

She decided it would not be necessary to call for an appointment before she went to the Museum. If his secretary said he was busy, she would simply say, 'Tell him I know his secret.' That should get her into his office without delay. However, if his secret fell among the more sinister of her speculations, she might not find it so easy to get out again. As she recalled, his office and the corridor outside were plentifully endowed with those old wooden chests that always seem to be around in museums, and which seem expressly designed to conceal bodies. She patted her handbag. The gun thumped reassuringly against her side.

The area around the museum was no longer the oasis of peace and quiet she remembered from the days when she was a young art student. Today the noise levels approached the threshold of physical pain. Digging machines were at work in what had once been the museum's parking lot, crunching up rock and spitting it into dumpsters. They were excavating foundations for the Chomsky Addition to the museum. It had turned out the Museum had no choice. The exterior of the building could not be altered. Sometime during the past few years it had been landmarked when nobody was looking. As the only extant work of an architect who had (understandably) never been commissioned to do another public building, it had been designated by the Landmarks Commission as worthy of preservation.

In spite of the excavators' din, street musicians were valiantly playing on their instruments, sidewalk vendors were loudly hawking their wares, and the people whose social life seemed to be spent on the museum's front steps were shouting at each other. The fact that they were failing to communicate did not seem to bother them. They were not there to communicate; only to affirm their existence, apparently through the creation of as much noise as possible.

Not all the vendors were itinerant. A species of flea market had sprung up on either side of the steps. One entrepreneur had been so bold as to set his own (or an associate's) paintings against a wall of the building's projecting side wing. A sudden stop in the excavation process made the words he was bawling audible: 'See the finest in contemporary American art at affordable prices, without an admission charge.'

Susan wondered whether the Museum ever chose to add to its collections from this cheap and convenient source. The pictures seemed to her as good as (at least no worse than) some of the art inside. But she knew that before the Museum would even deign to acknowledge their existence, they would have to receive the cachet of a gallery exhibition. Otherwise they didn't exist.

A car was waiting outside the Museum. For a moment she thought it was a hearse. Then she saw it was a stretch limousine.

As she made her way towards the building through a gaggle of mimes on the sidewalk, Hal Courtenay came down the steps. From a distance he looked the same confident, well-tailored figure as always, but as she drew near, she could see the tense, strained look on his face.

He was about to get into the limousine when he caught sight of her. His smile looked so forced it was painful. 'Susan, have you come to see me or the Appalachian Exhibit?'

Today he was wearing horn-rimmed spectacles. Behind

184

them his eyes weren't nearly as blue as they had been the last time she'd seen him. They were the paler blue she remembered from art school days. Not only contact lenses but tinted contact lenses. Sham clear through.

'I want to talk to you.'

'There is nothing I would enjoy more,' he said. But he didn't look gratified. He looked worried. 'At the moment, though, I'm afraid I have to go see a Lieutenant Bracco at homicide. In connection with DeMarnay's death. He's questioning everyone who knew DeMarnay, even slightly. A nuisance, but one must cooperate.'

He was taking the same tack as Baltasar, but Hal didn't have the excuse of being a foreigner. 'I understand that first they're talking to people who knew Roland fairly well; anyhow, people who'd been associated with him, who'd had business dealings with him.' There was no reason to suppose this was true, but it was a delicate way of making her point without hammering it in.

From the way he changed colour she could see there would be no need to hammer; he took the point. He drew her aside, out of earshot of the driver, away from the kerb. This brought them closer to a balloon seller, who seized the opportunity to try to interest them in a balloon bearing a picture of Whistler's Mother.

Hal turned on the balloon seller with a look of such fury that the man fled, balloons bobbing. Hal almost pushed her against the wall of the building. She could feel the barren ivy stems scratching against her hair. 'How much did Jill tell you?'

'She didn't tell me anything,' Susan said, moving sidewise so she could escape from the ivy's clutches without getting further into Hal's. 'It was the police who told me about you.'

Of course, according to those concerned, Andrew was not actually part of the police force, but there was no point cluttering her implications with technicalities.

'What did they tell you about me?' he demanded.

She was tempted to say 'Everything,' in the best melo-dramatic style. However, that might place her at a decided disadvantage in case there was more that she did not know but that he might think she did—and that might make him feel it necessary to eliminate her on the spot. Not that she was afraid of him. Even though he might possibly, improbably, be armed, she was sure she could outshoot any museum director in the western world. But, although she had not been dismayed by the possibility of having to draw on him in his office, the idea of a shootout in front of the Museum, at—she glanced at her watch—as near as high noon as made no difference, would be ridiculous and undignified.

The events of that morning and the evening preceding must have addled her brain. Why would he kill her to keep her from passing on information that the police had given her in the first place? Unless he then planned to take on the whole police department plus their computers. She couldn't see Hal as Sylvester Stallone. She couldn't see Sylvester Stallone as the director of an art museum.

'I know about the real ownership of the gallery,' she said. 'The Turkel Gallery, I mean, not the DeMarnay Gallery.'

She knew about the real ownership of the DeMarnay Gallery, too, but that was beside the point. It was evident by this time that it had belonged to Baltasar all along, and Roland had been little more than a figurehead. However, as far as she could see, there was no connection between that gallery and Hal or Jill, except through the links of an old animosity.

Hal sighed. 'I'd always been afraid that one day it might come out that I'd owned that gallery,' he said. 'It was a matter of public record. I kept telling myself that there wouldn't be any reason for anyone to look up the record, especially after so much time had passed.'

'You took a big risk.'

'I didn't realize how much of a risk until it was too late; I'd signed the papers. And, of course, I never really expected to become Director of the MAA then. Well, there goes my job, I suppose.' It was no longer a 'position'.

He seemed to have resigned himself to the prospect. But as soon as he learned of Roland's death, he must have known

Roland's past was bound to be investigated and he himself was likely to be found out. Which would seem to argue against his having killed Roland himself. He would hardly have done such a thing, knowing what its inevitable aftermath would be. That is, if he'd killed him in cold blood. If he'd killed Roland in a fit of temper . . . That didn't seem like him, but then she didn't really know what he was like.

'You didn't go to Houston, did you?' she asked, trying to keep any accusatory note from her voice.

'No, there was a change in plans. I had to go up to my farm.'

She didn't believe that he'd ever had any intention of going to Houston. All he'd wanted was to break his date with her and Jill, for some reason that was none of her concern. It was important to make it clear to him that she took no interest in his private life except insofar as it might be connected with Roland's very public death. 'After she heard about Roland, Jill went into a panic. She's afraid somebody's going to kill her.'

'Anybody in particular?'

'It looks as if it would have to be somebody who knew both her and Roland.'

'There are a number of people who fall into that category, but I take it you're alluding to me.' He smiled with what seemed like genuine if bitter amusement. 'Believe me, there have been times when I was tempted to kill both of them, but that was long ago. And I assure you that I didn't break our date just so I could kill Roland, because, as I understand it, it would have been perfectly feasible to do both. Dinner first, murder afterward. However, I was up at Litchfield. I do have an alibi, in case you're interested. There was someone with me at the farm.'

Since his alibi would have to cover the whole night in order to be valid, she presumed that his companion had been a woman. But it was none of her business, she reminded herself.

He looked at his watch. 'Now, more than ever, I don't want to keep the police waiting, but I can see we do need to have a talk as soon as possible. There's something that needs to be straightened out. I'll get in touch with you as soon as the police get through with me.'

'I think Jill should be in on this, too.'

'I agree. If she is seriously afraid of me, tell her we can meet in my office and I can have one or more of the museum guards posted outside to protect her, in case I go berserk.' The idea seemed to amuse him.

Susan just managed to restrain herself from informing him that she could provide all the protection Jill would need, from him at any rate. 'I'd be happy to make the arrangements,' she said, 'but there's just one hitch. I can't find Jill.'

'Oh, she'll turn up,' he said. 'She always does.'

CHAPTER 25

The limousine drove off. She stood there for a moment wondering what to do next. She might even go in and look at the Appalachian Exhibit. But she didn't feel like looking at pictures. She was sick of pictures. Nor did she want to look at statues, curios, architectural models, or period furniture. She'd promised herself to go see the lieutenant as soon as she'd spoken to Hal, but the lieutenant would be busy with Hal now. No sense going over there and having to sit kicking her heels in a waiting-room.

Maybe I'll just go·home, she thought. But before she had a chance to act on that decision, 'Susan, Susan Melville!' a voice called. And Andrew Mackay came out of the Museum and pounded down the steps. Her first impulse was to run, which would be not only unseemly but irrational. Besides, he could probably outrun her.

'I left a message on your phone,' he said reproachfully. 'You never called me back.'

'I haven't had a chance to pick up my messages,' she explained.

'I thought you'd like to know I found Jill.'

He seemed calm, even cheerful, so she gathered that

he had found Jill alive and in reasonably good condition.

'That was quick work. I am impressed.'

'She was registered at the Hilton.'

'Oh, it was that simple.'

'Simple!' he repeated indignantly. 'Do you have any idea of how many hotels there are in the city?'

She had never thought of looking for Jill at a hotel, not even after Hortense had suggested that that might be where Lupe was. Why then hadn't Jill gone to a hotel in the first place and saved her client a lot of grief? Because she'd been afraid to be alone? Because she was cheap? Perhaps cheapness entered into it, but last evening she had been genuinely afraid. And, unless something had happened that Susan didn't know about, she might still be afraid now.

'Did you tell her you knew that Hal had been the backer of her gallery?' she asked. But of course Jill must have realized that he'd known and had told Susan. Otherwise Jill wouldn't have behaved the way she had.

'I didn't get a chance to tell her anything. She hung up on me. But at least she's safe.'

'She was safe when you spoke to her,' Susan reminded him. 'You don't know where she is now.'

'I do know where she is now, and she's safe. I called the lieutenant, and he said he'd send someone to bring her in for questioning. She should be with him now. On her way there, anyhow. Depends on how long it takes her to dress. I don't know very much about her,' he said sadly. 'I know the bare facts, the kind of things you find in dossiers: social security number, birth date, place of birth, parents' names, school records—'

'She'll hate that,' Susan said.

'—But not the important things, like her favourite colour and what kind of music she likes and—'

'Did you look for Lupe Montoya in all the hotels, too?'

'I left that to the police,' he said. 'No reason I should do all their work for them.'

'Did they find her?'

'Not so far, at least not under the name of Montoya or Hoffmann.'

'Why would there be any reason for her to use another name?'

'I don't know why,' he said. 'I don't know anything about the woman except what you told me and Baltasar told the lieutenant. But the people I meet in my line of work use false names as often as not. And the Australian authorities don't seem to have a record of anyone of that name having toured Australia with the kind of act you described.'

'Not act, art. Performance art.'

'Whatever.'

'And I was only repeating what she told Jill and me. I never saw her perform.'

'The Australians say there was an act something like that called Dolores and her Dingoes that was closed down. It's possible she was working under that name, except that she told you she couldn't bring any animals with her, and the name of Dolores's act seems to imply that she was working with animals.'

'Maybe Lupe didn't want Rover and Fido to know she was working with some native animals and get jealous.'

'Well, if we find them we won't tell them. Providing she is—or was—Dolores. And providing they exist.'

They'd checked at the airports to see if they could get a line on Lupe through her wolves, but there was no record of any wolves having arrived at either Kennedy or Newark. 'And that's the only way you could bring wolves in from the Coast unless you brought them in overland.'

Susan thought back. 'She didn't actually say she'd brought them with her. She said they'd been left with friends in San Francisco and she was trying to find a place for them here. They might still be in California.'

'If they are,' he said, 'there'd be no way of tracking them down. In California people have all kinds of animals—lions, tigers, elephants. Nobody would notice a pair of wolves. Another funny thing, there's no record of anybody named either Lupe Montoya or Lupe Hoffmann having entered the United States. I know,' he said, as she opened her mouth,

'Lupe's a short form of something, but the computer's checked out all the possibilities.'

'Maybe her passport is still in one of her former husbands' names,' Susan suggested.

He frowned. 'You didn't say anything about former husbands.'

'For heaven's sake, I couldn't be expected to have total recall of every word the woman said, especially something as trivial as that.'

'Who knows what name she entered the United States under,' he said. 'It could all be a perfectly innocent misunderstanding. And probably the reason we can't find her is that she read about DeMarnay's death in the papers and she's lying low. Foreigners tend to be leery of the law.'

'That's what Baltasar said.'

'He should know. He—' Andrew checked himself. 'He seems to be the only one who knows her at all.'

'What connection do Baltasar and Lupe have with Hal and Jill?'

'None that I know of. Jill is acquainted with Baltasar and, according to you, Lupe, the same way you are. As far as I know Hal Courtenay and Baltasar haven't met. But that doesn't mean there isn't some connection that we don't know about. Anything else you haven't told me?'

There was something on the edge of her mind, something she couldn't quite get hold of, something Lupe had said or done, which probably was of no importance, but that nagged at her. 'Not that I can recall,' she said.

It was beginning to get a little cold standing there. Susan thought she might as well go back to her apartment. Besides, as she informed Andrew, she was getting a little tired of being importuned by vendors to buy their wares. 'Do you think Jill would like one of those?' he asked, indicating one of the Whistler's Mother balloons.

'I'm sure she wouldn't.'

'I was afraid of that,' he said sadly. 'I don't even know her taste in balloons. Well, if you must go, you must go. By the way,' he added, as she turned to leave, 'there's something

I forgot to tell you. I found out something interesting in connection with that first gallery, the one DeMarnay and Courtenay owned.'

'And Jill,' she said.

'And Jill,' he agreed, 'but she was really more of an employee. Her financial interest was minute; not that De-Marnay's was much bigger. The gallery really belonged to your friend Courtenay.'

Had Hal ever really been her friend, she wondered. Was it possible that Jill was still working for him and had been working for him all along, that she had just been a front for him, the same way she had been for the Turkel Gallery? Which would explain why she had seemed so parsimonious; Hal could have been taking the lion's share of the profits from both Melville and Moffatt, and only the IRS would know the truth.

All right, so that first rave review of her work had come before she'd met him and joined Jill, but maybe that had been a promotional venture. He knew he would be bound to meet her because of the Chomsky legacy to the museum and hoped to be in a position to influence her. All those glowing notices afterward, and the museum retrospectives he'd arranged for her, had to be suspect. Even his interest in her might have been merely proprietorial.

No matter that there had been favourable accounts of her work in the press while he had still been in Europe, hot on the trail of those Cassatts, unaware as yet of her existence, or that she might have been just as successful even if he hadn't written a line about her. Whatever he had written about her had all been part of the big hype. She felt like a living Darius Moffatt. *Susan Melville, Woman and Myth*. That wasn't as catchy. *Susan Melville, Woman and Wimp, Susan Melville, Painter and Patsy*—that was more like it.

'That's very interesting,' she said. 'Thank you for telling me, even though I already knew it. And now I really must be—'

'But I told you about that last night,' he said. 'This is about Darius Moffatt, the guy in that book you lent me.'

She waited. 'I'm starving. Care to join me for breakfast

192

or—' he looked at his watch —'an early lunch, while I tell you what I found out?'

More bargains. Maybe that was all detective work consisted of, basically, bargains and deals. Still, all he was bargaining for was her company. At the moment she had nothing better to do.

'I could use a cup of coffee,' she said.

'Great. How about the Museum cafeteria?'

'The food there always tastes as if it had been left over from an exhibit of something prehistoric.'

'Do you have any suggestions? You know the neighbourhood better than I do.'

'There's a coffee shop over on Madison.' They went there and settled on opposite sides of a booth. Suddenly she was very conscious of the weight of the handbag in her lap. I must be sure not to stand up suddenly, she thought; all I need is for it to fall to the ground with a thud.

Andrew ordered a hearty breakfast. 'Got to keep up my strength,' he said.

She ordered coffee and, since she didn't want to seem ungracious and it had been a long time since breakfast, a muffin. He ate as if he were indeed starving, not speaking until he had put away the better part of a plate of bacon and eggs. 'In case you were wondering what I was doing at the Museum, I was there talking to Courtenay. I had to make a phone call and when I came out you were down there talking to him. I didn't like to interrupt, so I waited until you'd finished before I spoke to you. Did he have anything interesting to say?'

'He did say he wasn't the one who killed Roland.'

Andrew looked surprised. 'Had anybody accused him of killing Roland?'

'It occurred to me as a possibility,' she admitted, 'and I think it did to Jill, also. Do I take it the idea hadn't occurred to the police?'

'The police suspect everybody,' he said. 'But, really, Susan, you mustn't go around asking people if they're murderers. It could be dangerous.'

'Why were you questioning him then?' she asked. 'And

why does Lieutenant Bracco want to talk to him now?'

'They're questioning everyone who had any connection with DeMarnay, but I don't think that he's among their prime suspects. As far as that goes the field's wide open. Anyone could have killed DeMarnay.' He grinned. 'You, for instance.'

Susan smiled and buttered her muffin. 'My doorman will tell you I didn't leave my apartment all night.'

'Ah, but would he have noticed if you never came in at all? You could have been lurking in the gallery, waited until everyone had gone, killed DeMarnay; then waited until morning and strolled out. Which anybody could have done. Or somebody could have come late at night and DeMarnay let him in. Nobody on the street would have been likely to notice. We both know that.'

He took a sip of coffee. 'But don't worry. I can assure you the lieutenant doesn't think you did-it. That isn't why he wants to talk to you again, which he told me when I called him from the Museum. I'll take you down there as soon as we've finished eating.'

Trapped! And no way of getting out of it. If only he'd told her before they'd gone to the coffee shop at least she could have seen to it that he went hungry for a good while longer. Of course, that was why he had waited until now to tell her.

But she didn't need to be escorted into the lieutenant's lair, like some sort of malefactor. 'You don't have to come with me,' she said.

'Oh, but I do. You're a very elusive lady. Don't worry, I won't put you in handcuffs, unless you start to get rough.' He laughed merrily.

You wouldn't laugh if you knew I had a gun in my handbag, she thought. 'I was under the impression that you don't have the authority for that,' she said. 'Or have you been lying to me all along?'

'You're right, I don't have the authority. I'll just phone the lieutenant and tell him to send a police car.'

'The way you did with Jill?'

He winced. 'I was afraid she'd get violent if I tried to take her down myself, and I didn't think she could be any madder at me than she is now.' He waited, but she had no reassurance to offer. 'I did suggest to Sergeant Collins that it might be a good idea to interview Courtenay before talking to Jill, if it could be managed. Courtenay's a bigwig at the Museum and the Board of Trustees has a lot of clout. It wouldn't be a good idea to keep him waiting. So we might run into Jill there.'

Oh, we might, might we, she thought furiously. Upholding the law is one thing; using me as a cat's paw is another. I hope Jill never speaks to you again. But she knew Jill would. Young men who looked like toothpaste ads were not to be come by easily.

They had been beating about the bush long enough. 'I suppose you said you'd found out something interesting about Darius Moffatt just so you could hold me here, while you stuff yourself like a pig.'

'I never lie to a taxpayer,' he said, pushing a butter-and-syrup-drenched forkful of pancake into his mouth. That clinched it. Even if he wasn't a policeman, he must have an official position of some kind. No private detective would have a qualm about lying to a taxpayer; and probably no public detective either, but he might have a qualm about saying so.

'Remember you said you thought his death might be tied to this whole thing somehow and I said I'd look into it?'

'You mean you found out something to indicate there was a connection?'

'Have another muffin. I plan to continue to stuff myself and it embarrasses me to have you staring at me. Besides, it might be a while before you get to have lunch. Not that the lieutenant is likely to take all that long with you,' he added quickly, 'but because it may be a while before you get to see him. He's talking to a lot of people today.'

She was hungry, and the muffins were surprisingly good —much better than at far more costly establishments, as is so often the case. She ordered another. Some government agency was probably paying.

'About Darius Moffatt,' she reminded him, as he took

195

another sticky forkful of pancake. All that cholesterol, she thought. He would get fat and his arteries would harden and it would serve him right.

'I searched the records, went back ... oh ... fifteen years. Didn't get any sleep to speak of.'

'You're young,' she said. 'You'll survive. Besides, I expect a computer did most of the work.'

'I suppose it's useless to expect any sympathy from you. Well, here's the interesting part. There's no record during that time of anybody named Darius Moffatt dying of a drug overdose, or of anything else, anywhere in the five boroughs of New York City.'

The revelation became less startling when she considered the facts. 'You must have guessed the biography wasn't ... er ... strictly accurate. Even I guessed that and I'm not a detective.'

'I just glanced through it,' he said. 'I assumed that since there was a whole book about him somebody must have done the appropriate research on his life.'

'Unless that somebody had reason to alter the facts,' she pointed out. 'He could have died long before the date they gave. He could have died in another state, another country. He could have died under another name.'

'I thought of all those possibilities,' he said. 'And none of them has been ruled out, of course. On the other hand, there's one that doesn't seem to have occurred to you, one I like a lot better because it explains a lot of things that none of the others does.'

'What's that?'

'That he never died at all. In other words, that he's still alive.'

CHAPTER 26

After all her tergiversations and equivocations, her hedging, hemming, dodging, pussyfooting, and (she finally admitted to herself) just plain hiding, Susan's interview with Lieutenant Bracco turned out to be almost an anticlimax. He was kind. He understood perfectly, he said, why she hadn't responded right away to the message he had left on her machine. Of course it wasn't reasonable to expect her to pick up her messages from an outside phone. 'I know a lot of ladies have trouble with these mechanical devices,' he said, 'especially if they haven't grown up with them, so to speak.'

Why, you old goat, she thought, I suppose you grew up with them. But then it's only 'ladies' who have trouble with 'these mechanical devices'.

He even forgave her for having neglected to mention Jill's connection with Roland and for not having mentioned Lupe at all. She must have been all shaken up on learning of Roland's grisly death; it was only natural for her to have overlooked such details. How could she, in the stress of the moment, have been expected to realize how important these details might be.

By and large it was the same explanation, rather, extenuation, she had prepared in her mind, but if it had come from her it would have been self-serving; from him it was patronizing, and she did not take kindly to being patronized. If there hadn't been a glass window in his office, through which they were visible to an assortment of police personnel, she wouldn't have put it past him to have patted her hand. And then, in spite of her determination to be amiable and placatory, she would have been arrested for attacking an officer of the law.

Either Andrew had succeeded in getting Jill's interview with the lieutenant postponed until after Hal's, or the fates had ordered it that way, for Susan ran into Jill as she was on her way into, and Jill on her way out of, the lieutenant's office. But that happened only after Susan had been waiting for nearly three-quarters of an hour in an anteroom, along with a number of very odd-looking people and no sign of Hal.

Andrew waited with her, to keep her company, he said, but she knew it was in the hope of getting a chance to speak to Jill. Susan would gladly have done without his company.

There was a lot she wanted to think about. However, there didn't seem to be any civil way of getting rid of him—or uncivil, either, she suspected, though she was incapable of putting that to the test, for she could never bring herself to deliberate rudeness. In any case, she thought, after she'd gotten a good look at the somewhat outré individuals who shared the waiting-room with them, she would probably have had no chance for solitary reflection. All, except the ones who were already carrying on animated conversations with themselves, looked disposed for a chat.

In fact there was one elderly man, garbed in a long black cape and with a bald head that ran up to a peak, who took a warm interest in her from the moment she entered the room. After she had ignored his winks and leers for some minutes, he finally interrupted the conversation she was holding with Andrew on matters of minor meteorological interest with, 'Why don't you run off and play with somebody your own age, sonny? This lady looks like just my type.'

'He can't leave me,' she said, before Andrew was able to stop her. 'He's a plainclothesman assigned to guard me because I'm very dangerous.'

The uniformed policeman standing at the door raised an eyebrow. Andrew shrugged.

'Dangerous, eh? That's the way I like 'em,' the old man cackled, moving his chair closer to hers. 'How about it, baby?'

'Get lost, grandpop,' Andrew snapped, 'before I deck you. And I'm not a policeman, so don't start licking your lips over the idea of a police brutality charge. It'd just be a plain misdemeanour. And worth it.'

'He's a private investigator,' Susan said, not wanting to be publicly branded a liar even before a public such as this. 'Very tough.'

'You're not Magnum, are you?' a woman with chrome green hair and a face that was either masked or so heavily painted that the effect was the same asked.

'Don't be silly,' a woman wearing a nun's habit said. 'He's one of the Simon brothers, of course. The cute blond one.'

They stared at him avidly.

'Ladies,' Andrew said. 'Magnum and the Simons are fictional. I'm real.'

'Of course you are,' the greenhead said. They cackled in unison with the pointy-headed old man.

Andrew got up and went over to the door. 'Isn't there someplace else we could wait?' he asked the man in uniform.

'Are you asking for special privileges?'

'Yes,' Andrew said.

'The answer is no.'

At that point Sergeant Collins came along to escort Susan to the lieutenant's office, from which they met Jill emerging. Although there was an angry expression on her face, she seemed a lot less tense than she had the night before— almost relieved, as if a weight had been lifted from her. She must have unburdened herself to Lieutenant Bracco in some way, Susan deduced, and wondered whether there was any chance she could weasel out of the lieutenant what it was that Jill had told him.

Jill caught sight of her client and looked even angrier. 'You had to go and sic the police on me,' she snarled.

'Not the police,' Susan said, 'just him.'

And she pointed to Andrew, who stood his ground, where a lesser man would have shrunk at the expression of utter loathing on his beloved's face.

'I was worried about you after you walked out like that,' Susan explained.

'Well, he's a policeman.'

'Not a policeman exactly,' Andrew said. 'Or even approximately. Just an *amicus curiae* or whatever it is when there is no actual court.'

'Friend of the family?' Sergeant Collins suggested helpfully.

'And I went looking for you,' Andrew said, 'because I was worried about you, too.'

'Oh, sure! You just wanted to rack up brownie points for fingering me.'

'That's not true. I don't get credit of any kind. It's not my—my job.'

199

'Then why did you tell the police where I was once you knew I was safe?'

'But I didn't know you were safe. Funny things have happened even in the best hotels. And I told the police about you because—well—because I had to,' he admitted.

'In other words, he could not love thee dear so much, loved he not honour more,' Sergeant Collins said. 'Now would you please come this way, Miss Melville? The lieutenant is getting impatient.'

Querulous noises from within appeared to support his claim.

'Just a minute, I'm sure the lieutenant won't mind,' she said, ignoring the expression on the sergeant's face. 'Jill, I have to have a talk with you as soon as possible. Where will I be able to reach you later?'

Jill thrust out her chin pugnaciously. 'What do you want to talk to me about?'

As if she didn't know. 'About you and me and Hal and our various interconnecting relationships.'

Jill turned on Andrew. 'Blabbermouth. All right, go and detect. I suppose you have to; someone has to clean the sewers. But did you have to tell her about Hal and me? It isn't any of her business. Or yours either.'

He opened his mouth as if to deny the allegation; then seemed to think better of it, probably because I'm here to give him the lie, Susan thought. 'I had to tell her,' he said. 'It is her business. She deserved to know.'

'Oh, you're so fucking upright you make me sick.'

'We can't have language like that in a police station, miss,' Sergeant Collins said reproachfully. 'It'll give us a bad name.'

'The whole thing was bound to come out sooner or later once Roland was killed,' Susan told Jill. 'Even Hal admits that. Don't you think it's better that I should hear it from Andrew instead of reading it in the papers?'

It would have been best of all if she could have heard it from Jill herself, but she supposed that would have been too much to expect.

*

The lieutenant appeared in the doorway of his office. He was in shirtsleeves and looked as though he were at the end of his tether. If he'd been dealing with friends and associates of Roland's all morning, Susan could understand it.

'What's going on here? Why is Miss Melville standing out there instead of coming in here?'

'My fault entirely,' Susan said. 'I stopped for a word with my representative.' She indicated Jill.

'I can see how you would want to have a number of words with her,' he said, glaring at Jill. She glared back. Apparently their meeting had not been devoid of acrimony. 'You'll have to wait until later to deal with her, though. And what are *you* doing here?' he demanded, as he caught sight of Andrew. 'Is this a police station or a lonely hearts bureau?'

Andrew paid no attention. 'Look, Jill,' he said, 'please come have a drink with me. In fact, it's lunch-time; let's have lunch.'

After that breakfast he just ate, Susan thought, he's likely to swell up and burst; and she, for one, was not going to feel sorry for him.

'I can explain everything. Well, not everything but a lot. At least hear me out.'

'Seems to me it's she who should do the explaining,' the lieutenant observed. 'Go with him, Jill,' he ordered, 'or I'll have you arrested for loitering.'

Jill looked at Andrew. Andrew looked at Jill. Although she was obviously fighting to hold her stern expression, it softened. He was really a very personable young man.

'Well,' Jill said, 'I don't have anything planned, since you went and busted up my schedule, so I might as well hear what you have to say. Besides, I could use some police protection.'

And, as Andrew opened his mouth, 'Protection from the police, that is.'

'And now, Miss Melville, if you would . . .' The lieutenant indicated the interior of his office.

'Susan,' Jill called, as Susan started to go inside. Susan

turned. The lieutenant emitted a hissing sound, like a kettle about to boil over.

'Gil Stratton didn't really ask you to be his client, did he? That was just a ploy to get my attention, wasn't it?'

'No, it was true. He's been after me to sign up with him for nearly a year.'

'The bastard,' Jill muttered. 'You just can't trust anyone any more.'

After that, Susan's interview with the lieutenant was short and comparatively sweet—except for her thoughts, which she kept to herself. He wouldn't tell her why he seemed so interested in Lupe or what Baltasar had done to make him look so black every time the man's name was mentioned. Was it simply because Baltasar hadn't informed him of Lupe's existence? No. From his expression, it had to be more than that.

He was more forthcoming about Hal and Jill. They had, to his knowledge, done nothing illegal, at least as far as his own area of operations was concerned. 'I'm not even sure they could be accused of product misrepresentation,' he said. 'In any case that would be the concern of some other agency—Department of Consumer Affairs, maybe. Which doesn't mean they're the kind of people a nice lady like you should be associating with. If you'll take the advice of somebody who's maybe got a little more street smarts than you, you'll get yourself another agent. Maybe that girl isn't actually crooked, but she isn't straight either.'

'What makes you think so?' Susan asked. 'Did she tell you anything to give you that idea?'

'If she did I'm afraid it's privileged information,' he said, smiling to show he was not reproaching her for what was, after all, natural female curiosity. 'Now, I have a nephew—'

'I do have a contract with Jill,' Susan pointed out.

'Speaking off the record and as a private citizen rather than a police officer, contracts were made to be broken.'

'I'm going to have to consult a lawyer before I do anything about that.'

'Let me tell you about lawyers. No matter what side they're supposed to be on, they're nothing but—'

He cut himself short. 'I better be careful what I say. Even here the walls have ears.'

Susan visualized a wallpaper patterned with ears of varying size. No, she was a fine artist; she did not do wallpaper. A mural, though, would be another matter—a pattern of ears growing on vines (which turned into telephone wires, perhaps), on which bugs were crawling. And then some designer could turn it into wallpaper and drapery patterns and she would reap royalties. I am developing a business sense, she thought, a little sadly.

As for Darius Moffatt, the lieutenant said, he had no interest in him whatsoever. 'If he's dead and there's no reason to suspect he was murdered, it has nothing to do with me; and if he's alive, it has nothing to do with anybody.'

She made a last desperate effort. 'How about the Bureau of Missing Persons?'

'Nobody's reported him missing.'

'I'm reporting him missing.'

'You don't have the authority to report him missing, Miss Melville. You're not a relative or even a close friend. You've never even met him. Why,' he said, working himself up to oratorical pitch, 'you don't even know that he exists.'

And suddenly she saw the answer. Where Darius Moffatt was and where the mysterious picture had come from and why Jill had kept on lying to her, even when there seemed to be no more need. What a fool she'd been not to see it before. True, the rest of the world had been fooled, too, but they had not had the advantage of her superior and peculiar insights.

'Goodbye, lieutenant,' she said. 'You've given me a lot to think about.'

And he had, indeed.

CHAPTER 27

It was the middle of the afternoon by the time Susan got home; after stopping en route for a quick lunch she found she couldn't eat. She played back the messages on her tape. None from Lupe. She hadn't really expected to hear from Lupe, but it would have been reassuring to hear her voice.

She picked up the phone and dialled the number of the gallery. It was Damian who answered, fortunately. If Baltasar had picked up, she would have had to give an explanation for the request she was about to make. Undoubtedly she would be able to make up a plausible explanation, but it would be increasing the risks.

'Damian,' she began, after identifying herself ('not that you need to tell me who you are, dear Miss Melville, I would recognize your voice anywhere'), 'I don't want to bother Baltasar, but—'

'You couldn't bother him if you wanted to. He left an hour or so after you did, saying he wouldn't be back for a few days and Paul and I would be in full charge until he returned. Such an awesome responsibility.'

'That must have been a sudden decision,' she said. 'He didn't say anything to me about going on a trip.'

'It couldn't have been sudden, because he brought his bags with him already packed when he came in this morning.'

'He did say something the other day about going back to Madrid, to see about replacements for the gowns that were damaged in the fire.' Of course the lieutenant had told him not to leave the state, which would automatically imply that he should not leave the country, either, but perhaps Baltasar hadn't understood that.

'Oh, he couldn't be going to Spain,' Damian said, 'because an official-looking person came by soon after that phone call that came when you were just about to leave and took his passport. He was very angry. Baltasar, I mean, not the official-looking person, who preserved an Olympian calm. The things Baltasar said after the man had gone! He really added to my Spanish vocabulary. And then he told us we should take care of things, and he left.'

He waited, as if inviting her to offer her comments on the situation, but she had nothing to say, at least not to him.

'Damian, I wonder whether you'd do me a favour?'

'Anything at all, Miss M. Your wish is my command.'

'Could you get me the address and phone number of Baltasar's assistant, Mrs Gutierrez? You remember, the lady who fitted my dress? I'd like to get in touch with her.'

'Sanchia? Nothing easier. The police took Rollie's Rolodex—' he started to laugh, then choked a little before he could go on. 'We've always done most of Baltasar's paperwork, though. He didn't have any staff here yet, except Sanchia, of course, and that weird husband of hers. Neither of them speaks much English; in fact, I don't think Diego speaks any. So we do have Baltasar's address file. It's upstairs. If you'll hold on, I'll be back in a jiffy.'

As she waited for him, she found her nervousness increasing, her self-confidence ebbing. Should I be doing this on my own, she asked herself. Wouldn't it be better if I told the police or Andrew what I thought? But her suspicions were so nebulous she couldn't put them into words. If she did she was afraid they might turn out to be ridiculous. She had been able to put up with the lieutenant's attitude of lofty superiority, because she knew he was a male chauvinist fool. She did not want to appear before him as the 'womanly woman'— i.e., the female fool—he took her to be.

She was not going ahead with this on her own, for the sake of her ego, she told herself. She was doing it to keep the possibly innocent from harassment. Not that she believed anyone of those involved was wholly innocent. Even Esmeralda had her secrets.

Damian picked up the phone. He was slightly out of breath. He gave her the address and telephone number, adding helpfully, 'That's in Queens. Over the river, but not through the woods. Terra incognita.'

'I know where Queens is.'

'You're so well informed about such things. I suppose it comes from your . . . er . . . fiancé's being an anthropologist.'

Of course Peter's existence was no secret, and she knew that people did gossip; it was an established form of recreation these days. Just the same she was annoyed. She thought of telling Damian that Peter was not her er . . . fiancé but her lover, and that they had no intention of getting married, but she was afraid she would embarrass the poor boy. Despite his inclinations, he was basically very conventional. Besides, the word *lover* had acquired such squalid connotations through years of misuse that it was not really appropriate.

She knew the safest course would be to approach Sanchia at phone's length. But it would be hard to get the information she wanted without causing alarm. Sanchia's English was, as Damian had pointed out, meagre. It would be hard to convey delicate nuances of suspicion in Basic English. If there was anything to be learned in Jackson Heights, she would have to appear there unannounced and alone.

Perhaps she should tell someone where she was going just in case. But who? Alex? He would tell her to keep out of it, that it was none of her business. If she insisted, he might even insist on accompanying her. The same would hold true for Andrew, even if she could get hold of him. She had no idea where he and Jill might have gotten to.

Maybe I could leave a note with Alex's doorman, she thought, inscribed 'To be opened only in case of my death or disappearance,' but it might cause talk in case she didn't die or disappear. She remembered how embarrassing the results of her suicide note had been when she'd changed her mind and killed her landlord instead of herself.

Her phone rang. She let it deliver its message while she listened on the monitor without acknowledging her presence. The monitor was, she had often thought, the answering machine's one saving grace.

The caller was Mimi, full of news. Eloise Charpentier had

finally gotten her divorce, after a great deal of unpleasantness on the part of her third (or was it her fourth?) husband who'd been trying to get more than his fair share of the Charpentier billions; Ariel Slocum—

Susan turned down the sound without waiting to hear what Ariel Slocum had been up to. She let the tape run on for its two-minute maximum before the caller got cut off. At the end of the two minutes, the phone rang again. Susan turned up the sound. This time it was Hortense Pomeroy. Susan turned down the sound.

The third time the phone rang, she almost didn't bother to turn the sound up. She couldn't resist, however, and she was glad she had, because it was Jill. She wanted to talk to Jill.

She picked up the receiver.

'Oh, you are there,' Jill said. 'Why did you make me listen to all that rigmarole then?'

Wasn't that just like Jill? All Susan's tape gave was her name and an invitation for the caller to leave a message if so inclined. Jill's recording, which included not only her name, but her current hopes, fears, and plans took up so much of the tape there was little time for the caller to do more than give his or her name and telephone number.

'I'm at the MAA,' Jill said. 'In Hal's office, as a matter of fact.'

Susan was surprised. So Hal had gone ahead and made the arrangements by himself. Just as well, it would spare her the necessity of tracking Jill down. But it was Jill who must have approached Hal, because Hal wouldn't have known where to find her.

'I thought you'd still be with Andrew,' she said. 'Or didn't he succeed in getting you to forgive him? Not that there was anything to forgive. He was only doing his duty, whatever that is.'

'I know, I know. Don't you start in on me about that too. We had lunch at Leatherstocking's, and he explained how he couldn't help ratting on me, because it was part of his job.'

'What is his job exactly?'

'He didn't say exactly, but I gather that either it's very hush-hush or he's ashamed of it. I'll get it out of him sooner or later. I don't suppose it pays a lot. He nearly fainted when he saw the prices on the menu. He wouldn't let me pay for the lunch, though; he's very old-fashioned about things like that; don't you love it? So I had them put it on your account. You don't mind, do you?'

'No,' Susan said wearily, 'I don't mind.'

'I told him *everything*. As much as he needs to know, anyway. I explained to him how the things he knew already weren't as bad as they looked.'

And the things he didn't know? Susan had a feeling they might be worse, but who was she to put a blight on young love? Let someone else do it.

'Andy said I ought to get things straightened out with you before I do anything else, and that's why I'm up in Hal's office now. We're going to have a meeting. You and Hal and I, that is. Andy doesn't want any part of it. Just keep things approximately legal, he says.'

Good Lord, Susan thought, he's going to try to make an honest woman out of her. She wished him luck, but didn't think much of his chances.

'You sound a lot different today than you did last night,' Susan told Jill. 'You were practically hysterical then. What's happened to calm you down?'

'I guess I was over-reacting a little,' Jill admitted. 'People I know don't get murdered very often, not even acquaintances. But talking to that pig—' by which Susan presumed she meant Lieutenant Bracco —'helped me get things in perspective.'

'I'm glad to hear it,' Susan said. 'What?'

'So come over right now and we'll get this thing over with.'

'I told you, I'm busy right now. How about tonight? Or would tomorrow be more convenient?'

'It's got to be right now!' Jill wailed. There was a thud on the other end of the wire that sounded as if she were stamping her foot. 'Right away! I have a dinner date with

Andy tonight and I've got to get through with this as soon as possible, so I can go downtown and buy a really smashing dress.'

'He'll think you look lovely no matter what you wear.'

'I do look lovely no matter what I wear. But this is an Occasion and an Occasion calls for a new dress.' There was a dreamy quality in her voice. 'I think this time it's the real thing.'

Susan had heard her say the same thing before, in the same tone of voice. But I mustn't be cynical, she thought. Maybe this time it is real. Maybe the other times it was, too.

'Go buy your dress,' she said. 'I can meet you tomorrow. I have to go to Queens today.'

'To Queens!' Jill shrilled. 'What are you going to Queens for? You don't think you're going to Long Island City to get your paintings out of the warehouse, do you? Because, if you do—'

'I'm going to Jackson Heights. Nothing to do with you.' Eventually, she was going to have to get the pictures out of Jill's clutches, but there was no hurry, especially since as yet she had no idea of whose clutches she was going to deliver them into.

'I'll bet you don't know how to get to Queens.'

'I take a cab.'

'All right, I lose my bet. But couldn't you stop over here before you go out to Queens? It wouldn't take long. Hal wants to talk to you before he writes his letter of resignation to the Board. I think he's crazy myself. I think he ought to hang tough until he's kicked out. It'll take time before the news gets around. Maybe it won't get out at all. After all, who's interested, really?'

The Board of Trustees would be interested, Susan thought, as well as every artist about whom Hal had written unkind things. Even if the general publications didn't pick it up or give it much space—since the masses might not understand what was so wrong in a critic's favourably reviewing the paintings shown in a gallery which he happened to own, or the curator of a museum not only representing an artist but writing glowing articles about him—*Connoisseur* would go for Hal's jugular, and then the art magazines would move in for the kill.

No, there was no way he could avoid scandal, but there was a way he might be able to turn it to his advantage. And, not being ill-disposed towards her old classmate, she did want to talk to him before he burned his bridges in the wrong direction.

'All right,' she said. 'I'll come over right away. But it can't take too long.'

'I told you, I have a date with Andy. We've got to keep it short.'

CHAPTER 28

Hal's office had been designed to impress. Panelled in age-darkened wood, it was furnished with massive eighteenth- and early nineteenth-century pieces that had been not considered quite worthy of the Museum's collections, either because they had been restored by some vandal more interested in utility than in authenticity or because they were a trifle dubious to begin with. Hal was sitting behind his desk as Susan entered. He rose and came to meet her and would have taken her coat, but she refused saying, 'No, thank you, I won't be staying long.'

He was no longer wearing spectacles, but she knew now that the colour of his eyes was not a true blue. 'Susan, I can't tell you how sorry I am,' he began.

'I'm sure you are,' she cut him off. 'We all are. But there's no point going into that now. I don't have much time, but Jill said it was important we meet now.'

'Please sit down.' He indicated a Chippendale wing chair. And, when she hesitated, 'No matter how short a time you're staying you'll be more comfortable sitting down. At least I'll be.'

She looked at him. What made him think she cared whether he was comfortable or not?

'I won't take it as a sign of forgiveness if you sit down,' he said, 'although I hope you will forgive me—a little, anyway—when you hear the whole story.'

'The whole story doesn't concern me,' she said. 'What does concern me is whether Jill was working for you or for me?'

'I was working for both of you,' Jill piped up. 'What's wrong with that? I never said you were my only client.' She was already sitting down, in the most comfortable chair in the room, and looked her old perky self.

'But he's not your client,' Susan pointed out. 'He's your employer.'

'Not any more,' Jill said. But when had their relationship ended?

'If you'll just sit down and listen, Susan,' Hal said, 'I'll explain how it all came about.'

Grudgingly she sat down. He started to sit behind his desk; then thought better of it and took another wing chair across from hers, not so close that he would encroach on her space.

'I started the gallery for a lark really. I'd always thought that if I couldn't be a painter, owning a gallery was what I'd like to do. And I couldn't own one in my own name. Jill and I were living together at the time. I'd met her at a course I was teaching at the New School. I forget its title, but the general idea was how to talk about contemporary art as if you understood it, even if you didn't. It was very popular.'

He smiled reminiscently. He means he was very popular, Susan thought. She was willing to make a small bet that most of his students had been female.

'Jill had just finished college and had some kind of low-level job with a third-rate PR firm—'

'I was a trainee,' Jill said indignantly, 'and the firm might have been small but it was very prestigious. Everybody said I had a great career ahead of me.'

'I thought it would be nice if I could set up something that would give her more meaningful work, and that would belong to both of us.'

Jill snorted. 'Belong to both of us! You needed a magnify-

211

ing glass to see my percentage. Even Roland's was bigger.'

There was good reason for that, Hal explained. Roland had been brought in because Hal had had no expertise as a dealer, and Jill had no expertise at anything at all—at least that related to an art gallery. The gallery had been put in her name only because Roland had to be kept in the background.

Both of them had, according to Hal, received generous salaries (here Jill sniffed) in addition to their percentages.

Since the gallery had been losing money up until the first Moffatt show, everything—salaries, overhead, running expenses—had come out of Hal's pocket.

The plan had been for the gallery to show the work of promising little-known or unknown artists, and for Hal to write enthusiastic reviews for some of their artists. 'Not all,' he said, 'or it would look suspicious. I figured that would make the pictures sell, and in time the gallery would pay for itself, I didn't count on anything more than that.'

'He thought all he had to do was write up an exhibit favourably,' Jill said, 'and buyers would come running, cheque-books in hand.'

'Perhaps I did suffer from an excess of *hubris*,' he acknowledged. 'By the time we broke with Roland, we'd already had three exhibits. I'd written enthusiastic reviews for two of them and—' he smiled sadly —'nobody else paid the least attention. Nobody else wrote a review. Nobody bought the pictures.

Hal's pockets were not all that deep. As things stood, he couldn't afford to keep the gallery going. Then Roland came to him with a proposition. An acquaintance of his knew a Colombian artist who was anxious to have his work shown in New York, and was willing to pay for the privilege. 'Roland showed me some of his work. Decent stuff in the traditional style: nothing to get excited about; nothing to be ashamed of. Something to be going on with until we could find a painter who would sell.'

He swore that they had not known about the drug deal. When Customs found cocaine in the frames of the pictures, he had been genuinely shocked and angry. Jill was still angry. 'Roland went and set up the whole thing without cutting us in on it!'

'That was because he knew we would never go along with such a thing, of course,' Hal said smoothly.

Jill shot a glance at Susan. 'Of course. We wouldn't have dreamed of it. But,' she burst out, 'he was a double-crossing weasel all the same.'

They had gotten rid of Roland immediately. Which left them without a show. 'And just then Old Mother Moffatt happened to turn up with the paintings?' Susan asked.

'Why are you using that tone of voice, Susan?' Hal asked. 'Artists and their relatives were always coming around trying to get us to show their work. She just happened to come around at the right time. You're shaking your head, as if you didn't believe me.'

'I don't believe you. There is no record of Darius Moffatt's ever having died of a drug overdose in the East Village or anywhere else. There's no record of his ever having died at all.'

Hal and Jill looked at one another. 'Uh—oh,' Jill said. 'I told you people would start asking questions about Moffatt once they got to know about your connection with my gallery. I still think of it as my gallery,' she explained, 'because it was in my name and everybody thought of it as mine.'

'Spiritually it was your gallery, and always will be,' he assured her.

'Thanks a lot,' she said.

'I'd been beginning to wonder about Moffatt long before Andrew told me that Hal was the one who actually owned the gallery,' Susan said.

It then had to be explained to Hal who Andrew was.

'That investigator who was up here before!' he said incredulously. 'He's the man you're going out with tonight?'

'Yeah,' Jill said. 'Ain't love wonderful?'

'Well,' Susan demanded, 'is Darius Moffatt dead or alive?'

'He's dead, of course,' Jill said crossly. 'Don't you believe what you see in print? All right, so maybe he didn't die in the East Village, or even in New York. We wanted to hide

213

the truth, that he was a—a sex fiend and murderer, and he died in jail. Under a false name. We didn't reveal the truth because we wanted to spare his family pain.'

'And you made up the whole East Village story to spare the family pain?'

'Yes,' Jill said.

'And his mother went along with that? The drug overdose and all? Didn't she find that painful? Or were you going by degree of pain?'

Jill tossed her head and was silent.

Hal cleared his throat. 'Don't pay any attention to Jill; she's of a melodramatic turn. We kept the true story secret so as not to offend religious sensibilities.'

Both Jill and Susan looked at him.

'Darius—only that wasn't his real name, of course— belonged to a religion which forbade the creation of graven images. His family was very orthodox; consequently he painted under the name of Darius Moffatt, so his relatives would never know what he was doing.'

'So he travelled around the country leaving the paintings with them?' Susan asked.

'That was the reform branch of the family,' Hal said.

Jill snorted.

'And what did he die of?' Susan asked.

'Natural causes,' Hal said. 'A thunderbolt. Oh, what's the use. I can see you don't believe me.'

'How could she?' Jill asked. 'Any religion that forbids graven images wouldn't be the least bit bothered by the things Darius painted.'

Hal looked keenly at Susan. 'You've guessed the truth, haven't you? When I first met you again, after all those years, I was afraid you might. And then I realized I'd been suffering from *hubris* again. You didn't remember anything about me.'

That wasn't strictly true, but the things she had remembered were the things he had probably himself forgotten, or wanted to forget.

'The truth didn't hit me until this afternoon,' she told him, 'while I was in Lieutenant Bracco's office. It was from something he said, but, don't worry, he didn't realize what he was saying. There never was a Darius Moffatt, was there? Except that, since it must have been you who painted the pictures, I suppose it could be said that you are Darius Moffatt.'

'Nonsense,' Hal said weakly.

'I should have known. Somebody who really wants to paint doesn't give up painting that easily. And, you're right, I should have remembered. I'm sorry.'

It was coming back to her now—the student who had driven the teachers crazy by painting like Van Gogh one week, Braque the next, Matisse the third. It had made little impression on her at the time. Technical facility was not something the students at the Hudson were encouraged to set store by. The ability to express one's own personal inner vision was what counted. And Hal, so far as anyone could tell, had had no personal inner visions.

But he'd been so young then. There'd been no reason for him to give up. In time he could have developed a style of his own. And where would he have been then? Perhaps where Susan had been before she killed General Chomsky. Nowhere.

Jill wasn't ready to concede defeat. 'Don't pay any attention to Hal, Susan. You've got it all wrong. Except the part about Darius being alive. He is alive, I admit. He didn't die in prison. He's serving a life sentence for—for unspeakable crimes. And he must have smuggled out that painting somehow and consigned it to Allardyce's—the skunk!' She glared at Hal.

'Give it up, Jill,' Hal said. 'She knows. The thing is, does anyone else know?'

'I haven't told anybody, if that's what you mean. And I don't intend to tell anybody, unless there's something more that I don't know that could make it necessary. But I feel I should mention as a matter of general interest that I have written a full account of my conjectures and deposited it in a safe place, where it will be opened in the event of my death.'

215

'Susan,' Hal said reproachfully, 'you don't really think I . . . Or even Jill . . .?'

'What do you mean "or even Jill"?'

'Of course I don't think you'd . . . er . . . do anything to me. But it's always wise to take precautions.'

'That was the real reason you set up the gallery, wasn't it, Hal?' Susan went on. 'What you really planned to do was exhibit the Moffatt paintings, review them favourably, and clean up on them—at least make some money from them. The other exhibits were just window dressing. You didn't really expect them to go anywhere. They were just to establish the gallery as a legitimate showcase.'

For some reason Jill laughed. Hal shook his head. 'Now, there I can say in all honesty you're wrong. I'd never planned to show the Moffatt pieces. I just did them for fun. I'd always had the knack of being able to paint in any artist's style.'

'I remember now,' she said.

'It took you a long time,' he said bitterly. 'I remembered *you* clearly from the start. But who could forget having been a classmate of Susan Melville, one of *the* Melvilles. Every student in the class was aware of you and determined not to be impressed, or at least to show it.'

She was stunned. 'I never realized. It never even occurred to me to think the other students might feel that I was anybody special.'

'That was the worst part. You were different, and you didn't even have the grace to realize how different you were. When I picked Jill to be a front for the gallery, I tried to teach her a little about modern art. I amused myself by doing a series of paintings that combined all the most egregious elements of contemporary art at once. She and I used to kid around about exhibiting them some day as the work of a real person. We even gave him a name. But we never seriously intended to show them. At least I didn't.'

'Me either,' Jill said. 'My artistic tastes hadn't been refined yet and I thought they were terrible.' She paused to reflect. 'I still do.'

'I know this is a silly question but who were the photographs of?' Susan asked.

'They were of me. After I got divorced from Cissy, I spent a summer working with the Peace Corps—why, I don't know—to prove something to myself, maybe. That was when the pictures were taken. I was sure nobody would recognize them since I'd never looked like that before or since. It was a kind of private joke—not very funny, I suppose, but then private jokes seldom are funny.'

CHAPTER 29

Something occurred to Susan. 'Hal, it didn't by any chance happen to be you who painted those forgeries that Roland sold General Chomsky? And that you then authenticated?'

'Of course not. How could you even suggest such a thing? That would be illegal, as well as most improper.' There was a smile on his lips, not just a smile—a smirk, a self-satisfied smirk.

'Sorry. I'd forgotten you always operate within the bounds of propriety, as well as the strict letter of the law.'

'Incidentally, it was only one forgery that caused the trouble.'

'The one that made the General get rid of Roland, you mean?'

He nodded. 'As I've said, I had nothing to do with it—or with any others still around that haven't been called into question.'

He paused. For some reason he was looking pleased with himself. 'However, it has sometimes occurred to me—in one of the wild flights of fancy to which I am occasionally given—how amusing it would be to think that Hal Courtenay might be represented in some of the major art collections of the world, not merely the Chomsky collection, although under a *nom de brosse*, as it were.'

Using the name of another artist was not precisely a *nom de brosse*, Susan thought, but this was no time to quibble.

'Speaking hypothetically, of course,' she said, 'I can't help wondering why, if Hal Courtenay had been so successful at forging the big names in art, he would have given it up? Of course I know he was doing it for the excitement. He didn't need the money. Still . . .'

'I don't know about Hypothetical Hal, but Real-Life Hal certainly did need the money. And continues to need it. I know people think I'm well off, but I'm not. To begin with, I never got as much money from Cissy Flicker as people thought I had. They always exaggerate. They seem to think the more money you get, the worse you are; and, of course, they always like to think the worst.'

'Only human nature,' Jill said. 'Bad is more fun than good.'

Hal ignored her and addressed himself to Susan. 'I'd already begun to grow accustomed to a life style the earnings of an assistant curator and art critic couldn't support. I made some bad investments that left me worse off than before.'

'But why didn't you—excuse me—Hypothetical Hal go on forging paintings?'

'He got cold feet after the General cut up so rough about that alleged Picasso. The General suspected that Hal had been working with Roland. He couldn't make any charges without some kind of proof, because Real-Life Hal held a respected position in the art world. If the General had been wrong, he could have been sued and taken for everything he had.'

'So that's why Jill's name had to go on the gallery,' Susan said.

'Exactly. The General was out to get me if he could. If he had the faintest suspicion that Roland had any connection with the gallery, he would have his people investigate. They would find out that I owned a majority interest and then . . .' He shook his head. 'I don't know what he might have done.'

Maybe Hal didn't know, but Susan had a pretty good idea. When Hal had said earlier that he hadn't realized the risks he was taking in starting the gallery with Roland, he didn't know the half of it.

'Then the pictures you discarded as forgeries after the MAA inherited the Chomsky collection—or some of them, anyway—were the ones you ... that is, Hypothetical Hal had painted and then authenticated?'

'Isn't it a hoot!' Jill said.

Hal shrugged. 'The merest few.'

Did he mean there had been only a few of his own forgeries in the Chomsky collection, or had he deaccessioned only a few, leaving the rest as part of the permanent collection?

She didn't think she wanted to know the answer. 'But what about Jill? Was she working for you or for me? I know what she said, but I also know Jill.'

Jill made a face at her. Susan tried not to smile.

'As far as the Moffatts went, she was still working for me,' he admitted. 'What did she know about art at the beginning? One course at the New School, which she would have flunked if it had been given for credit.'

'But you said—'

'I said a lot of things I didn't mean then,' he told her. And, to Susan, 'Jill kept on getting her percentage the same as if the gallery had stayed open; and she was getting a very good salary, too—almost as much as I was getting at the Museum, as a matter of fact.'

Susan waited for Jill to deny this, but Jill remained silent. I must ask Mimi how much the director of the MAA makes, Susan thought. But of course he had been only a curator at the time. And, it was none of Susan's business.

'You were something else, though,' he said. 'By the time you signed up with her, she was an experienced rep. You were her entire responsibility. I had nothing to do with you—as Jill's client, that is.'

He caught Jill's eye. 'Well, maybe I did take a small percentage, a sort of finder's fee, for having introduced her to you. That's quite usual in art circles; you know that.'

She did know that. Just as it was usual in medical and legal and financial circles. Just the same, it left a bitter taste in her mouth.

'That's not the whole story,' Jill said. 'For the first year you were with me, he made me split my commissions with him. Then I told him enough was enough. My name was on the contract. I was doing all the work. Since we had already decided Darius Moffatt was finished—we really couldn't keep on finding more pictures—we were each on our own. So he goes and paints another picture and consigns it to Allardyce's.'

'I'm really sorry,' Hal said. 'I know it looks as if I were—'

'Double-crossing me. You bet it does.'

'It so happens that I'm financially strapped.'

'Down to your last yacht, you mean,' Jill snapped. 'Why don't you sell that stupid island of yours?'

'I don't know where the rumour got started that I own that wretched island,' he said querulously. 'Full of snakes and mosquitoes. A friend of mine happens to own it and lets me use it from time to time. When all this comes out, she'll probably never—' he sighed —'well, that's probably the least of my worries.'

'Hal,' Susan said, 'since you did keep on painting, haven't you developed a style of your own by this time? Aren't there pictures you've painted just because you wanted to paint them?'

She took his grunt to be an affirmation. 'Did it ever occur to you to exhibit your own paintings? I mean those that were really your own? Not fakes or jokes.'

He was silent. Jill burst into hysterical laughter.

Hal got up, went to the window, and stood for a minute with his back to them, contemplating the excavating machines as they snarled and spit their way through what had once been the museum's parking lot.

He turned, but, instead of coming back to the armchair, he perched on the edge of his desk, his leg dangling. 'You were right, in a way. The real reason I opened the gallery, even though I didn't admit it to myself, was that it seemed the only way I would be able to get my own paintings shown. Not the Moffatt paintings, the ones I painted . . . the way I wanted to paint. That was the first show we put on. If you thought the write-up I gave Moffatt was enthusiastic, you should have seen the write-up I gave this one. But, as I told you, nothing happened. Nobody else even bothered to review the show.

'I'm really very sorry,' Susan said. And she was.

'I'm not,' Jill said, getting up and starting to gather her things together. 'It's what you deserve. And, now all that's cleared up, I have to go. The shops will be closing soon.'

'You know,' Susan said, 'all this time we've been talking, we haven't once wondered who killed Roland—unless one of you did it after all?'

'If I had been so inclined,' Hal said, 'I would have done it nine years ago, not now. As for Jill, I really don't think she's a killer.'

'Thanks for nothing,' Jill said. She regarded her image in a fret-carved Chippendale mirror. 'The glass is so wavery,' she said, 'I don't know whether my hair needs combing or not. But I guess it wouldn't hurt.'

She started burrowing in her handbag. 'Actually, I think it must have been Baltasar who killed Roland. Drug dealers are always doing each other in, aren't they? And he was the one who bought Rafael's pieces.'

With a triumphant cry she produced a comb. 'I wonder why they bothered to set the place on fire. Maybe as an extra precaution. Roland was always such a fusspot.'

Either Hal was a very good actor, or he really was astounded. As for Susan herself, she was surprised, but not as surprised as she would have been, say, a week ago.

'I expect Roland must have been working for him all these years,' Jill said, getting to work on her red curls. 'He was the one who came into the gallery to see Roland a couple of times. My gallery, I mean.'

'But how come you never said anything about it—to me, anyway?' Hal asked.

'I did tell you at the time that there was a man, a Spanish type, who came to the gallery, and I was pretty sure he was Roland's liaison with the Colombian artist. And you told me not to mention it to the police, that I should keep out of the whole thing as much as I could. Otherwise they'd have me down to headquarters to look at photographs and a lot of stuff like that.'

'Yes,' Hal agreed, 'it seemed best then. What I meant

221

was why didn't you say anything when he turned up this time?'

'At first I didn't recognize him. He's changed a lot, gone way upscale. And I was sure he didn't recognize me. I looked a lot different then.'

'But your name didn't change, Jill,' Susan reminded her. 'And your name was on the gallery.'

'He acted as if he didn't recognize me or my name, so I figured I'd leave it at that. I admit I did start getting a little nervous, after Lupe told us she thought Rafael had been murdered.'

They explained to Hal who Lupe was.

'When Roland got killed I did get panicky,' Jill went on. 'But by that time you and I weren't exactly chummy. Besides, you could have been the killer just as easily as Baltasar. I was too upset to think straight. I should have known you'd never have had the guts.'

For a moment Hal looked as if he would have liked to kill her or at least commit significant mayhem on her person; then he shrugged and turned away.

'Before all that happened, though, I thought live and let live. I mean, what's so wrong with dealing in drugs, anyway? Everybody uses them. It's like prohibition. Everbody drank alcohol in spite of the law. And so they repealed the law. It'll be the same with drugs. Why blame somebody for being in advance of their time?'

'But drugs are destroying people, Jill,' Susan pointed out.

'So is alcohol. So is tobacco. So is candy. I mean, where do you draw the line?'

Susan couldn't think of an answer.

'It's okay now, though,' Jill said. 'I did tell Lieutenant Bracco that I thought I recognized Baltasar as the one who used to come into the gallery, although I was very careful to say that I couldn't stand up in court and swear to it, because I'm not going to. He didn't look surprised. I guess maybe he suspected him already.'

Or Andrew did, Susan thought, and passed the information along. 'Damian—one of the young men at the gallery

—told me they picked up Baltasar's passport early this afternoon.'

'There, you see, I'm safe.' Jill put her comb back into her handbag and snapped it shut.

'They picked up his passport,' Hal reminded her. 'They didn't pick up the man himself.'

Jill thought about this. 'Susan, would you like to come shopping with me? You can go to Queens some other time.'

This piece of information seemed to divert Hal from the question of Baltasar. 'Queens? Why are you going to Queens, Susan?'

Why is everyone so surprised that I'm going to Queens, Susan wondered. What's wrong with Queens? Doesn't anybody ever visit the outer boroughs except under extraordinary circumstances?

'It's getting to be something of an art centre,' Jill observed.

'That's right, I'd forgotten. A number of artists have set up studios in Long Island City and even farther in. Are you thinking of doing something like that, Susan?'

The atmosphere in the office had changed, somehow. If I don't get out of here in a hurry, Susan thought, he's going to have tea sent in. 'No, nothing like that. And I do have to get out there as soon as possible. I think you'd better forget the new dress, Jill.'

'Well, if I must, I must. In fact, I don't think I'll bother to go home and change. I'll call Andy, from one of the phone booths downstairs, because I want some privacy—' here she looked severely at her companions —'and tell him to pick me up in the lobby. Unless you want him to come up, so you can meet him?'

'I've already met him,' Hal said.

'Oh, well in that case, ta,' Jill said.

'Ta?' Hal repeated.

'Surfeit of *Masterpiece Theatre*,' Susan explained.

Jill left. Susan got ready to leave but she was still shaken. Not by the knowledge that Hal had done the Moffatt paintings—that did not touch her personally, except as a matter of non-academic interest—but of how the other students had felt towards her when they were in school. How insensitive she must have been! And, even at that early age, she had prided herself on her sensitivity. She wished she could make up for it somehow.

'Hal, are you absolutely determined to resign from the Museum?'

'It isn't a matter of choice. Unless you mean I should "tough it out", the way Jill suggested? No, leave me with a modicum of dignity. Better to resign now than be kicked out later.'

'Then why don't you at least tell them the whole story? Tell them it was you who did the Darius Moffatt paintings. That way, even the rave review wouldn't look so bad. After all, didn't Walt Whitman write a glowing review of *Leaves of Grass* when he was an anonymous book reviewer? And nobody thinks the worse of him.'

'Nobody thinks the worse of him now, because he's dead. They probably wouldn't have been as tolerant at the time. Besides, he didn't write books and articles about a fake self he'd invented. As far as I know, anyway.'

'But these are different times, Hal. Today people would think it was clever and amusing, a—a very "cool" thing to do. Hard to forgive in a museum director, perhaps, but you know artists are expected to misbehave. It confirms their genius in the public's eyes.'

'I would rather cut off my earlobe,' he muttered.

'That wouldn't do you any good. This will. Admit you're Darius Moffatt. Be Darius Moffatt. Keep on painting—and selling—as Darius Moffatt. Remember that Darius Moffatt is one of the greatest geniuses of the twentieth century; you said so, yourself.'

He laughed and then looked as if he would have liked to cry. 'But the paintings are so goddamn awful.'

'What does that matter? You'll be giving the public not only what it wants, but what it deserves. They say living well is the best revenge. They're wrong. Painting bad pictures and selling them to an undiscriminating public is even better.'

'You make it all sound so easy,' he said.

'Think of the money, Hal. That picture at Allardyce's went for two hundred and fifty thousand dollars. Two hundred and fifty thousand dollars!'

She seemed to have gotten through at last.

'Prices are bound to drop once the word gets out I'm alive,' he mused aloud. 'But they might not drop that far, especially after I appear on talk shows. And then lecture tours ... Maybe I will take your advice. I suppose I do have nothing to lose. If I have to leave in disgrace, I might as well go out in style.'

'That's the spirit,' she said.

My God, she thought, I'm beginning to sound like Hortense Pomeroy!

CHAPTER 30

Outside the Museum she hailed a taxi, but, when she gave the driver her destination, he refused to take her there. 'My shift is almost up, lady, and I live in New Jersey. I'm not going to go all the way out to Jackson Heights.'

She was about to hail another cab, then she changed her mind. Perhaps it would be better to take the subway. Certainly it would be faster and simpler—although, if she had realized what the ride was going to be like, she might have changed her mind again. For the next half hour, she felt as though she had been plunged into one of Breughel's more graphic depictions of hell. Some people do this every day, she told herself, twice a day even. How could they do it and remain human?

The answer was: they couldn't. Going through this ordeal twice a day was bound to deprive them of all humanity. She knew that at the end of this ride she herself would be a little less human.

Maybe she had been wrong about choices, she thought. If these people had a choice, they wouldn't be here. Later, when she emerged from the platform into the chilly evening air—for somewhere along the way the subway had managed to escape from the lower depths and made its way up to ramshackle tracks elevated above the streets—she realized that she had been temporarily bereft of the human gift of reason. Like all the rest of God's creatures, the subway riders did have a choice. They could have taken a bus.

It was almost dark by the time she came down the subway steps (for it was still called a subway even though it was no longer subterranean and had never been much of a way) and descended into a street crowded with people speaking a variety of languages, mostly at the top of their lungs, with Spanish predominant and English virtually non-existent.

As she went from the business section to what appeared to be the residential area, the crowds thinned out, but the noise level did not abate. People were conversing at shriek level both inside and outside the buildings. TV sets and stereos played at full blast, dogs barked; somewhere someone was playing the drums.

Rich cooking odours floated out into the air. They dined at an early hour in Queens. She began to regret the lunch she had rejected earlier.

Because the streets of Queens are arranged more or less in a grid pattern, she found her way to the address Damian had given her without any need to ask for directions. She couldn't explain to herself why, but it seemed important to attract as little attention as possible, to pass through the streets of Queens as though she had never been there.

Her destination turned out to be one of a row of nearly identical two-storey brick houses on a tree-lined street. Each house was separated from its neighbours by a driveway on one side and an alley on the other. Each had a neat little garden in front, some with birdbaths or sundials—impossible to tell one from the other in the growing darkness. Although every house had a light over or next to its front door, the wattage was too low for details to be made out. Those might be gnomes (plastic) she saw in one garden. It might equally well have been a group of short, quiet people.

In only one respect did the house to which she was going differ from its neighbours. The occupants of the others had not bothered to draw their blinds, so that each pair of front windows was like a stage set, with the people inside going about their lives with as little regard for their audience as actors performing before a paper house.

The windows of this one were heavily curtained, so passers-by could not see inside. Only the light, shining through cracks at top and sides, indicated either that someone was at home or electricity was being wasted.

As she walked up the cement pathway to the front door, she began to feel a twinge of unease. Maybe she should have told someone where she was going, giving some explanation —say, that she wanted to talk to Sanchia about having some dresses made—that would sound plausible; yet that would have given a clue as to where to look for her, in case she did not come back.

But if she didn't come back, who would look for her tonight? Or even tomorrow? If anyone called and she did not return their messages, they would simply think she was immersed in her art, avoiding the phone. It would be a long time before they discovered she had never come back. Intellectually she had always realized that she might be walking into danger. Now she was beginning to feel it emotionally as well.

For a weak moment she was tempted to retrace her footsteps, leave the garden, leave the borough, leave the whole thing to somebody else; but she sensed eyes watching her from the upper floor and she could not bring herself to turn her back on them. I am armed; I have a gun, she told herself, without patting the bulk of her handbag, because that might have given too much away to the watchful eyes. The knowledge was not as comforting as it had been before. These people must have guns, too.

She lifted the knocker on the front door and let it fall. It made a soft thud. Nothing happened. Its function must be primarily ornamental.

She rang the doorbell. That made a good loud noise. She could hear it resonate throughout the house. Silence for a moment. Perhaps nobody is home, she thought. Perhaps

227

there is nothing for me to do here after all.

She was about to turn and go when she heard the sound of heavy footsteps descending the stairs. The door opened. A tall man stood there, silhouetted against the dim light inside. For a moment she thought it was Baltasar. Then she saw it was the man whom she had met briefly at Rafael's funeral—Sanchia Gutierrez's husband.

'Is Lupe here?' she asked. 'Lupe Montoya?'

Say no, she asked silently. Say you never even heard of her. That's right; you don't speak English. Just shake your head then. I'll apologize for having disturbed you, and do what I should have done in the first place, tell someone of my suspicions. So what if that did involve the innocent? Let their innocence be their own safeguard.

Without speaking, he gestured her inside and shut the door behind her with a finality that, she told herself, was only in her imagination. She found herself standing in a small vestibule with a staircase to the left and a narrow passage just ahead. There was an archway to her right blocked by a heavy curtain. He held back the curtain and indicated that she was to enter.

Beyond lay the most nondescript room she had ever seen. The colour scheme was a drab monotone. The furniture looked as if it had been chosen, possibly from a catalogue, so that it would neither appeal to—nor offend—any taste. It was very tidy. So that's what they mean by a safe house, she thought. The street noises were hushed in here. The place must be soundproofed.

Reclining on the oatmeal-coloured couch, looking exotic and slightly absurd in those motel-like surroundings, was Lupe. She wore a dull gold trouser suit of some silky stuff that clung to her magnificent body in a way that was wasted on a female audience. Esmeralda reclined on her shoulder, shedding black hairs all over the gold silk. As Susan came into the room, she opened eyes as green as the jewels from which she took her name, and uttered a crooning sound. Lupe stretched up a beringed hand and patted her.

So Baltasar was here, or had been here. Unless he had given Esmeralda to someone else to convey to her mistress. For it was clear from the animal's confident air of possession that it was Lupe to whom she belonged, to whom she had always belonged.

Hortense had been right. Somebody had been living up in Baltasar's apartment. Lupe. Lupe and her cat. And Lupe had left the cat behind when she had gone to Queens.

But when and how long had she been living in Baltasar's apartment? Had she been there before the fire, before the opening of the gallery? Had it been the fire that had caused her to leave? Or had she gone there to live later, after the fire? Had she already been living there when she pretended to have just arrived in the city? And why had she—and Roland and Baltasar—put on that little charade for Susan's benefit? And, of course, Jill's, too, but Susan knew that it had been planned for her.

'Lupe,' Susan said with tinny vivacity, 'I'm so glad to see you're all right. No one seemed to have any idea where you were, and I was worried about you.'

Lupe smiled. 'So kind of you to worry about me, Susan,' she purred, 'and so clever of you to have found me.'

'But you yourself told me where you would be,' Susan said, affecting a wide eyed innocence that, she was well aware, did not suit her and did not fool Lupe. 'When nobody could find you, I remembered your telling us about the house in Jackson Heights.'

Lupe stopped smiling. 'That was very stupid of me. But I did not know then that Roland was going to die.'

Susan thought of saying something like, 'In the midst of life,' but decided against it.

'Please sit down, Susan,' Lupe said. 'The chairs are not attractive but they are not uncomfortable.'

Susan sat, leaning far back in her beige Naugahyde armchair to give an impression of ease and relaxation. Not that she thought she could fool Lupe, but she hoped to fool herself.

'I am sorry I cannot offer you any refreshment,' Lupe said, 'but the place is downside up. We are planning to leave very shortly.'

Leave the house? The city? The country? She didn't like to ask direct questions.

'Is Baltasar leaving with you? I know he must have been here,' Susan explained, 'because of Esmeralda.'

Hearing her name, the cat opened sleepy eyes and gave a meow of acknowledgement.

'Yes, Baltasar was here,' Lupe said, caressing the animal. 'But he has already left. He will not return.'

'You mean he's dead?'

Lupe's laugh seemed genuine, but how can I tell, Susan thought. 'What a vivid imagination you have, Susan. But, of course, you are an artist. It is to be expected. No, he has left the country sooner than . . . he expected. That is all.'

'But they took his passport,' Susan blurted, before she could stop herself.

Lupe's eyes narrowed. 'Ah, I see you are indeed well informed. But he has more than one house, more than one car. Why should he not have more than one passport?'

And more than one name, too, Susan thought, but she didn't say anything.

CHAPTER 31

There were thumping sounds on the stairs. 'Diego is getting things ready,' Lupe explained. 'We are planning to leave within the hour. I know that your government will not be pleased that Baltasar has departed so . . . informally. However, since he is not planning to return to this country, it is not of great significance.'

'Then he's giving up the idea of establishing a salon here?'

'It was a mistake to have tried to establish one here in the first place. I told him so from the start, but he would not listen to me. He does not have the temperament for New York. "If you must have a salon in the United States,

Baltasar," I told him, "why not Miami? All right, Palm Beach." But, no, it had to be New York or nothing. Well, now it is nothing.'

Susan wondered whether this simply meant that Baltasar was never going to have a United States establishment or whether he was never going to have another establishment anywhere, ever; whether his dead body might not at that moment be lying somewhere, perhaps even downstairs in the basement. There wouldn't have been time to dispose of it in a more permanent way.

Lupe had denied that he was dead, but Lupe did not seem to Susan like a woman whose word could be relied upon.

'I am sorry now that I mentioned this place to you,' Lupe admitted, 'but I wanted some way to account for my presence in case I was forced to continue staying here. I invented my wolves and, in a way, myself. I am acquainted with someone who puts on a performance much like the one I described, although not so artistic.'

'Dolores and her Dingoes,' Susan said, before she could stop herself.

'I see you have indeed been working hand in mitt with the police. Yes, Dolores is an employee of ours, a very low-echelon employee.'

Probably travels around Australia distributing drugs, Susan thought. And a good cover, too. The police, arresting Dolores for being herself, would think to look no further. By the time they got to her, there would be no further to look. Everything about Dolores, if Lupe's account had been substantially accurate with regard to the real performer, would be out in the open.

There's no point sitting here, waiting to find out what she's planning as far as I'm concerned, Susan thought. She made a move to get up. 'Well, now that I know you're safe, I'd better be going. I was supposed to meet my brother as soon as I made sure you were all right. He'll be expecting me.'

'Sit down,' Lupe commanded.

Susan was about to protest, caught Lupe's eye, and thought better of it. She sank back in her chair.

'I appreciate the point that you are trying so subtly to make, that there are people who are aware that you are here.'

'I wasn't trying to make any point,' Susan lied. 'It happens to be the truth. A number of people do know that I was planning to come out here.'

'That may be true,' Lupe acknowledged. 'Only a fool would have come out here without telling people where she was going, and I do not think you are a fool.'

How wrong she is, Susan thought.

'However, I do know that you came alone. Diego was watching from the windows. And I do not think you told your brother or anyone else that you suspected you might find me here, or they would not have let you come alone.'

Should I tell her that I've been wired and I have a back-up team waiting around the corner? No, it would be too easy and unpleasant for her to find out the truth. Besides, if I had been wired, the last thing I would do would be to tell her. No, the thing to do is smile enigmatically and let her think I have hidden resources.

'In fact, I would not be surprised to find that, even though you must have told someone where you were going, you did not tell them why.'

Lupe stared hard into Susan's eyes, as if trying to wrest the truth from them. 'You probably made up some excuse about having to see Sanchia, something like that. Which would mean there is plenty of time before anyone will come looking for you, and by then it will not matter any more.'

Her words had an unpleasantly final sound.

'But I told Alex I would be right back.'

'If you do not return as soon as he expects you, he is hardly likely to come rushing out here. Who would come out here, unless it is an absolute necessity?'

Poor woman, Susan couldn't help thinking, how she must have hated having to live out here. But I'll bet she never rode on the subway, she thought, and she hardened her heart.

'No, your brother will wait and then he will telephone, and I will answer the phone and say I am Sanchia and that you have been delayed for some very good reason, which I will think of. We are in the middle of fitting a gown or I have sent my husband out to match some thread or—'

'But why do you want to keep me here?'

Lupe shook her head. 'Do not pretend to be so innocent, Susita; it does not become you.'

Susita, Susan thought indignantly. That's even worse than Susie.

'I cannot let you leave, because you have too many suspicions. Too many accurate suspicions.'

'But I can't prove anything. I don't really know anything, except that you must have been the one who was staying up in Baltasar's penthouse.'

For some reason this seemed to irritate Lupe. 'How did you know somebody had been staying up there?' Lupe demanded. 'Nobody was supposed to know, nobody at all.'

'Hortense Pomeroy ran up to take a look when Baltasar was called to the phone. She is rather nosy, I'm afraid,' Susan said apologetically. 'She's not really a friend of mine, just somebody who used to teach in the same school I did.'

'Hortense who? Oh, yes, that gymnastic woman.'

Lupe shook her head again. 'That Baltasar, he is such a *bobo*. When I said to him—with lightness, mind you—that he might just as well have established a health club as an art gallery in the building, what does he do now that Roland is dead but call in this Pomeroy woman and offer to turn the gallery into health club. *Madre de Dios!*' She rolled her eyes.

'It did seem a little odd,' Susan said.

'Odd!' Lupe said. 'The whole set-out—thank you, set-up —was *loco*. To begin with, he should have known better than to establish Roland in a gallery after what happened with that Turkey Gallery.'

'Turkel Gallery,' Susan said. 'It was named after Jill.'

'Turkel, Turkey, what does it matter? And did he tell me that this Jill was the same Turkel and she might have recognized him? Did Roland? No.'

Luckily for Jill, Susan thought. And she wondered whether the two men had been protecting Jill or themselves.

'I know it is difficult to find good assistants these days. Just the same, he should have known Roland was not a man to depend on. And, worse yet, he established his own atelier in the same building where he established the gallery. It would be more convenient, he said, and it would save money.'

Her voice rose. 'Save a few hundred thousand dollars, when we were spending millions!'

'We?' Susan repeated, knowing the answer, stalling for time.

'Of course we. You must know that neither Baltasar nor Roland had the brains to head an *empresa* like this.'

By this time Susan had realized that it was Lupe who was the narcotics queenpin, but affected ignorance in the hope that this might still save her. Obviously that hope was futile. At least she could have her curiosity satisfied.

'Why did Baltasar kill Rafael and Roland?' she asked.

'Baltasar kill them, pah!' Lupe sneered. 'He has not the *cojones* to kill a flea. Even when it was not a question of killing, merely of having somebody beaten down—an occasional necessity in our business, you understand—he would always delegate it to someone else. But I always say the only way to get something done, is to do it yourself. I was the one who killed Rafael and Roland.'

She stopped. If she's waiting for approval, Susan thought, she's not going to get it from me. Not that she didn't approve of Lupe's method in principle; she didn't like the direction in which she was afraid the practice was taking Lupe.

'You know, Susan,' she said, 'all of this is your fault. None of it would have happened if it hadn't been for you.'

'My fault!' Susan echoed indignantly.

'Roland assured us he would be able to get your work for our opening exhibit. Very impressive, very respectable, very open and over board. But it turned out you thought you were too good for us.'

'It wasn't like that at all. I had other commitments. I told Roland that when he first asked me.'

Lupe shrugged. 'Whatever the reason, we had to use Rafael's work, which we had planned for our second exhibit, one which was supposed to creep quietly into town with no *fanfarria.*'

'I see,' Susan said. That explained several things, not that explanations were going to be of much use to her at that moment.

'If Rafael had not received so much *alabanza* at the opening, to justify our selection of him for that honour, I do not think he would have become so full of himself. He read the press releases and he believed them, poor fool. He said he had decided that he wasn't going to let his "beautiful works of art" be destroyed, no matter how much we had paid him to concoct them. He said if we tried, he would tell the authorities. It did not matter if he got put in prison; it would be good publicity. Naturally, I had to kill him. What else could I have done? We had a good deal of money wrapped up in those things. So you see it was all your fault, Susan.'

Susan decided it was wiser not to debate the point.

'He was already drunk,' Lupe went on, 'so it was simple to give him a shot of heroin.'

'But how could you? I mean, you weren't there; how could you manage to do it? Oh, that must have been while you were living upstairs.'

And Susan realized something else. Even if Rafael had been working for Baltasar, Rafael's wife would hardly have been staying in Baltasar's penthouse. Baltasar would have been living there with his own wife. The exhibition catalogue had not made a mistake in neglecting to mention a wife. Rafael had not had a wife. But Baltasar had. How could I have been so stupid, Susan thought.

'I had been planning to make my entrance into New York society at the opening,' Lupe explained. 'I had been looking forward to it. But I could not, after Rafael's death. I have far too much sensibility.'

Also too much caution, Susan thought.

'*Naturalmente* I could not stay in the apartment after that. Someone might see me and wonder why I had not come to the opening. So I came to stay here. Imagine me, living in a lower-middle-class suburb!'

'It must have offended all your aristocratic instincts, *condesa*,' Susan said.

'So, you have guessed that too! I suppose it was obvious.'

'By this time it is,' Susan said, 'although I really had no idea before.'

Lupe looked happy. 'I have often thought I could have been an actress but, of course, it would not have been suitable for someone of my category.'

Lupe looked sad. 'But after Rafael's death it looked as if I would never be able to make my entrance into New York society. I could not help feeling disappointed, but not very much. New York society is not such a big thing, after all. Not that I wish to offend you, Susan.'

Susan assured her that she was not offended.

'But I did not wish to keep on staying in Queens [she pronounced it 'Quins'] all the time I am in New York. I had a plan. We would arrange that I should arrive at the same time as some very respectable person came to the gallery, to establish the fact that I was Rafael's wife and that I had come because of the money. Then Baltasar—out of kindness towards a poor widow—' she laughed merrily —'was going to offer to permit me to stay in his apartment.'

'Suppose afterwards you ran into someone you knew in the street?' Susan said. 'A lot of Spanish aristocrats seem to spend more time here than in Spain.'

'That is true,' she said. 'However, the kind of people I know do not walk about the streets. They are driven through them in long limousines. But if by misfortune such a thing should happen all I would need to say was that I am not I, but someone else who looks like me.'

'You thought of everything,' Susan said, trying to sound admiring without sliding over in obsequiousness.

'When you telephoned Roland, to tell him you had seen a person prowling outside, he thought this would be a fine opportunity for me to make my appearance. He would ask you to come over and show him exactly where you had seen this person, and I would arrive at a similar time.'

Susan wasn't sure she liked the idea of being classified as a 'very respectable person', but this was no time to quibble.

'However, the whole exercise turned out to be pointless. It became necessary to kill Roland that same evening, before I even had a chance to move my possessions back into the penthouse. After that, I thought it might be advisable for me to return here until I decided what must be done. You will ask me why it became necessary to kill Roland?'

Lupe's smile was apologetic. 'It was almost an accident, can you believe it? If I have a fault, it is that I am too impulsive. All along, I must tell you, Roland had been disturbed because I had killed Rafael. He said he had not bargained on murder when he joined us. But what kind of organization did he think he was joining, *válgame Dios*! The Boy Scouts? Then, when I happened to mention to Baltasar that the man you saw outside the building had a dog with him, Baltasar became agitated. He said the man must be a detective and the place must have been under suspicion.'

'He was a detective and the place had been under suspicion.'

'I know that now, but I did not know it then. I had not been working—what is the expression?—in the field. It did not occur to me that the dog also was a detective, a drug-detective. I do not approve of using animals in such a way, and neither does Esmeralda, do you, *querida*?'

Esmeralda meowed without opening her eyes.

'He's a very nice young man,' Susan said, 'the dog's master, I mean—not that he owns the dog; he just borrowed him—and he seems quite taken with Jill.'

'I am glad to think that perhaps something good will come out of this fiasco,' Lupe said. 'It is a pity that, if they should get married, I cannot come to the wedding. I love weddings. However, I shall send them a very handsome present from Spain, in your memory, Susan.'

Susan didn't ask for an explanation of that last remark. It was, she was afraid, self-explanatory.

*

It seemed important to keep Lupe talking, although there was no logical reason for her to do so. Nobody was going to come save her. If she was going to be saved, she must save herself. 'I still can't understand how you killed Roland by accident.'

'Almost by accident. To begin with, Baltasar started making a scandal. He insisted that now that we were under suspicion we must give up our plans and leave right away. While I was trying to convince him that if we kept firm and behaved innocently, it would all blow away, Roland broke apart. He said that maybe, if he made a clean breast of affairs, the authorities would be lenient with him. After all, he had not killed anybody; he was not even a principal in this *empresa*, just a funky—is that the right word?'

'Flunkey,' Susan told her.

'Thank you. Flunkey. He said he was going to consult with someone about it and perhaps go to a lawyer. I think it was you he was going to consult with, am I not right, Susita?'

Susan swallowed. 'He did say he wanted to talk to me about something, but I hadn't the least idea of what he was going to say.'

'That is as may be,' Lupe said. 'At any rate, he went on talking like that, thinking only of himself; no consideration for others who were also involved and might suffer. He made me very angry, so angry that I hit him with a paperweight —a very nice respectable paperweight cast in the shape of one of the towers of my ancestral castle that I had given to him as a house-heating gift. I had not intended to kill him. Not at least just then, although I am sure that upon reflection I would have killed him sometime. However, he was dead on the instant, so there was no need for reflection.'

At that point, she said, Baltasar had lost his head and gotten hysterical but Lupe was made of sturdier stuff. Came of being born on the right side of the blanket, Susan thought.

'I decided we must make it look like a sex crime. Then nobody would suspect anything out of the ordinary, because such things happen all the time here, especially in artistic circles. I read your newspapers and I know.'

She and Baltasar had carried the body down to 'that obscene place in the basement', where, since Baltasar had apparently been too squeamish, she had 'hit him some more with that disgusting object I found down there, keeping my eyes shut all the time. Such a nasty thing; I could hardly bear to touch it.' And she shuddered.

'I felt *ensuciada*—soiled—afterwards, even though I had put on gloves and an *impermeable* beforehand, so I could keep myself neat and not leave any fingerprints. You see, I know all about fingerprints, from reading the works of Miss Agatha Christie, whom I much admire.'

Subsequently they had thrown the paperweight, along with the gloves, the raincoat, and a small rug which had been somehow involved, into the East River.

'We should also have dropped Roland in the river. Well, it is no use weeping over spilt wine, don't you agree?'

Susan refused to agree.

'After that I decided there was no use trying to carry on at this place, and so I told Baltasar we would do as he wished and terminate our business, at least for the time.'

It seemed to Susan that she was doing the wisest thing possible under the circumstances. But where does that leave me, she wondered. She soon found out.

CHAPTER 32

'And now I am sorry, but I am afraid I am going to have to kill you, Susan.'

'I don't see why,' Susan said, 'since you're closing down anyhow.'

'Because you know too much,' Lupe said simply.

'But I wouldn't have known it if you hadn't told me.'

Lupe looked abashed. 'Well, I had to talk to somebody. You don't know what it is like to be alone in a strange country surrounded by idiots. Besides, you had already unravelled most of it, I am sure. Or you would have, given time. You are a very clever lady, Susan.'

Susan felt the compliment was undeserved. A really clever lady would have kept as far away from this place as possible. 'What use would killing me be?' she asked. 'The authorities are bound to figure out the truth sooner or later. And I did leave a letter to be opened in the event of my death, that outlines all my theories about what I thought might have happened.'

'You are lying,' Lupe said, without conviction.

Susan resisted the temptation to say, 'I am not, either,' and contented herself with an enigmatic smile.

'In any case, you did not know that I was Baltasar's wife. So let them look for Lupe Montoya. They will never find her.'

'But, if you entered the country under your own name,' Susan pointed out, 'which I assume you did, since you were planning to make your entrance into New York society, your arrival and departure will be on record. And, since you were —are—Baltasar's wife, they will eventually suspect that you have some connection with the whole thing.'

'I do not think that your police are as efficient as all that. As I have said, I read your newspapers. But let them suspect me. Once I am back in my own country they cannot touch me, no matter if they do have suspicions, because I am far too well connected.'

'Then why do you feel it's necessary to kill me?' Susan argued. 'All you have to do is make sure that I can't go to the authorities with my story, until you've gone back to Spain.'

Lupe thought this over; then shook her head. 'I am afraid not, Susan. If the police merely had suspicions of their own accord, they would not be likely to try to bother me, but if you told them of your suspicions they would, because you are so very well connected yourself.'

Susan thought of promising never to divulge Lupe's identity, but realized that it would be futile. Lupe would never believe her. In Lupe's position, she wouldn't have believed it either.

'You, of course, I will not hit with a paperweight,' Lupe said. 'First of all, because it is more difficult when the person to be hit is forewarned, but secondly, because I do not wish to cause you unnecessary pain. I am sorry to do this, Susan, because I like you and I am a great *aficionada* of your paintings. You might be interested to know that I have several of them in the collection at my castle. I am very proud of the family art collection, to which I have added many fine pieces, and I am sorry you will never be able to visit my castle and see them, Susan. I find you *muy simpática*. Under other circumstances, I think we could have been friends.'

In a pig's eye, Susan thought inelegantly, but then the situation did not call for elegance.

'On the other hand, as soon as it becomes known that you are dead, the value of your paintings will go up, so at least I will have that to console me for what I am about to do.'

Lupe removed Esmeralda from her shoulder and placed the protesting animal on the back of the couch. Then she took out a gun, a pearl-handled revolver, for heaven's sake, Susan thought in disgust. How corny could you get!

'You will wonder why I am doing this myself, instead of having Diego do it? That is because I seem to have surrounded myself with nothing but weemps.'

Susan had already noted that Lupe had been getting increasingly nervous. Now she was beginning to babble. Good, Susan thought.

'Now, if you will hold absolutely still without moving, Susan, I will kill you with one shot through the head. And you will feel nothing. But if you wriggle it might take more than one shot, and then you will feel pain, and I do not want that. I am a good shootist, you understand, but not an expert.'

'But I am,' Susan said. And, taking the gun out of her bag, she shot Lupe cleanly through the head. Esmeralda meowed and scuttled behind the couch.

Lupe probably did not feel any pain. Susan wouldn't have cared if she had.

And now, Susan thought, getting up, for Diego.

But he did not wait for her. '*Madre de Dios!*' a voice called beyond the curtain. She started towards it but he was ahead of her. Footsteps pelted down the hall. The front door slammed.

She opened the door and saw him running down the pathway and out into the street.

Nobody paid the least attention to him. It wasn't likely that they had heard the shot, but, if they had, no one seemed concerned.

There seemed to be no one else in the house. Susan did not investigate to make sure. She dropped the gun back into her bag. Since she had not taken off her gloves, there wouldn't be any fingerprints on it. Somewhere along the way she would drop it in a litter basket. It would be gone before the sanitation truck came.

Then she quietly left the house and took the subway to Manhattan. The ride back was much less disagreeable.

CHAPTER 33

'They're beautiful children, Alex,' Susan said. 'Beautiful.' In actual fact they looked like blobs to her, but it was not the sort of thing you said to a proud young father. 'And Baldwin is a fine name, but why did you have to call the other one Buckley?'

'The Pattersons expected it,' Alex told her. 'How could we have called one twin after one grandfather and not call the other twin after the other one? But don't worry. His middle name is Alexander. We'll call him by some variant of that.'

'Tinsley is already calling him Bucky,' Susan pointed out.

'Oh, is she? Well, I haven't heard him answer to it.' He laughed. Susan didn't.

'What does it matter, after all, what they're called? If they had been girls, she probably would have insisted on naming one Susan. How would you have liked that?'

'You and Tinsley aren't planning to have any more children, are you?' Susan asked anxiously.

He smiled. 'Too soon to be thinking about anything like that now. Come, you haven't toasted the babies' health yet.'

He steered her through the crowds which had come to celebrate the christening of Baldwin Patterson and Buckley Alexander Tabor. The guests of honour, after a brief public appearance, were no longer on the scene, but, in spite of the fact that the season was over, virtually everyone else in New York seemed to be.

'Where's Peter?' Alex asked, after they had both acquired glasses of champagne and had solemnly toasted the infants. 'I haven't had a real chance to talk to him since he got back. I hear he's no longer with the university.'

'He ran into trouble with some Eskimos on a field trip,' she admitted, 'and the university decided not to renew his contract. He's so excited over his foundation, though, I don't think he even noticed.'

They moved back into the living-room, greeting and being greeted from all directions as they passed. 'My teeth are beginning to stiffen,' Alex said, 'and I wouldn't be surprised to find that my face is permanently stretched. Let's find a quiet corner where I can stop smiling for a while.'

Owing to his superior knowledge of his own premises, they were able to establish themselves behind a screen which partially blocked off an alternative entrance to the kitchen.

'Peter's at the foundation building now, driving all the workmen crazy,' Susan said. 'He says he'll be over later, but I'm sure you'll forgive him if he never makes it. You know how Peter is.'

'I do, indeed,' Alex said, 'and I forgive him in advance. What kind of foundation is it, by the way?'

'We'll think of something,' she said. 'What I mean is that the final details haven't been worked out yet, of course.'

'Of course,' Alex said.

'Hortense Pomeroy isn't here either,' she observed.

'Hortense Pomeroy? Oh, yes, that gym teacher who was planning to set up a health club in what used to be Roland's gallery. Was she invited?'

'I don't know, but that wouldn't have stopped her if she'd wanted to come. She's furious with me, and, by extension, my relatives, because the building went to Peter's foundation instead of to her. She said Baltasar had promised it to her —the two lower floors and the basement, anyway, which I suppose he had.'

'But she must know that the government confiscated it, that the law says a drug dealer's property is forfeit.'

'She does know that, but she says it's quite a coincidence that Peter got the building. She insists that strings were pulled and connections used.' Susan and Alex looked at each other and smiled.

'Doesn't she realize that without Baltasar backing her, she'd never have been able to afford that building, anyway?' Alex asked.

'Apparently she doesn't. Or doesn't want to.' Susan took a sip of champagne. 'I'm sure that, once she's simmered down, she'll find a much more suitable place.'

'You better hope she does,' Alex said. 'I understand that Lady Daphne Merriwether—' of whom he, like everyone else, had heard much of by this time —'has indicated publicly that she's out to get you.' Again Alex laughed and she didn't.

Andrew Mackay came around the screen with a glass of champagne in either hand. Apparently his detecting instincts did not stop with crime. 'Hi, Susan,' he said, 'you're looking great. Great party, Alex. Great-looking kids. Have you seen Jill? She seems to have disappeared while I was getting more champagne.'

'I saw her in the dining-room talking to—rather, yelling at—Gil Stratton. She's never forgiven him for trying to get me as a client.'

'I'd better put a stop to that. Can't have her making scenes at your party.' He went off dining-roomward.

'He seems to have her well in hand,' Alex said. 'I still

can't understand, though, why you kept her on after everything that happened.'

'Well, if Hal thought she was good enough to represent him, I decided she was good enough for me.'

'Quite a surprise, his turning out to be the painter of those Moffatt pictures,' Alex said. 'I must admit I did have suspicions about his . . . er . . . integrity, but I would never have suspected that, and I know you couldn't have either, or you wouldn't have been so surprised to discover he was the real owner of Jill's gallery.'

'No, I never guessed,' Susan said. 'That's one of the reasons I didn't fire Jill. If I had, it would have made me look like a fool—or, even worse, a victim. People would have felt sorry for me. This way—'

'This way, even though you deny it, it'll look as if you might have known about the whole thing all along,' Alex agreed. 'Much more dignified, or should I say "cool"? And what's the other reason—or reasons—you didn't fire Jill?'

'She seems to be doing a perfectly good job,' Susan explained. 'Hal's prices have come down a little, because he's still alive, but his pictures are selling very well. And my prices have gone up. I've broken the six-figure barrier . . . I notice you seem to have acquired a Moffatt,' she said, looking at the adjacent wall, trying to keep a chilly note out of her voice.

Alex looked abashed. 'I like to keep up with current trends,' he said. 'Besides, I got it at a discount because I'm family, so to speak.'

'I'm surprised you didn't hang it in your office to impress your clients.'

'The other one's in my office. Jill gave me not only a family discount but a reduction for quantity.'

Alex looked around. 'Where is Hal? He certainly was invited.'

'He must still be on his honeymoon,' Susan said. 'They're on that Greek island the bride owns—you know, the one everyone always thought belonged to him.'

'I don't envy him the fair Eloise,' Alex said, 'in spite of

245

the Charpentier billions. Not,' he added hastily, 'that I would envy any man his wife when I'm married to the most wonderful woman in the world.'

It appeared that Hal and Eloise had been involved with each other for some time; but, because of the vindictiveness of her most recent ex-husband, they had been forced to keep their affair under wraps until her divorce was final. Had Hal been making up to Susan just as a blind? Obviously it could not have been Susan's modest millions he was after in the light of Eloise's billions. Susan got the idea that, billions or no billions, Hal wasn't altogether happy about having to marry Eloise, but it might have been her fancy. Or her conceit.

'More champagne?' Alex asked.

'I'd better get something to eat first,' she said, 'or I'll get tipsy.'

'And we couldn't have that,' he said, 'not at a christening. It would set a bad example.'

They made their way towards the buffet. 'I wonder what happened to Baltasar after he murdered his wife,' Alex said, as he heaped his plate. 'Such a surprise to find out the woman you knew as Lupe was really the *condesa*. I'm sorry I never had a chance to meet her. I wonder why he killed her.'

'I suppose we'll never know,' Susan said, keeping her eyes on the food as she made her modest selection. 'And nobody knows for sure that he was the one who did it,' she added conscientiously.

'Well, when a drug dealer disappears and his wife is found murdered, it seems a logical assumption that he killed her. It might have been self-defence, though. She did have a gun, although it hadn't been fired.'

'I know,' Susan said.

He looked at her.

'I read about it in the papers,' Susan said quickly. 'And Andy filled me in on some of the details. Apparently, she didn't get a chance to fire it. But it still could have been self-defence, if she drew her gun first.'

'Baltasar beat her to the draw, eh? Well, I don't suppose

we'll ever know. He must have gone to earth in Colombia. He wouldn't dare go back to Spain now.'

'It seems likely,' Susan said. She wondered whether that was true, or whether Baltasar had already been dead when she confronted Lupe. There hadn't been any sign of a body in the Jackson Heights house, Andy'd told her, or any other indication of violence, so there was a good chance he was still alive.

'It's lucky you decided not to go out to Jackson Heights after all,' Alex said, 'or you would have walked right into the middle of things.'

'I didn't actually *decide* not to go. It was just that I couldn't get a cab to take me to Queens. I actually went so far as to go down into the subway, but when I saw what it was like I found I simply couldn't face it.'

Alex nodded sympathetically. 'Andy tells me that if you'd told him about the house as soon as it occurred to you, that Lupe—whatever her name was— might be there, they would have been able to catch the gang red-handed.'

'Of course he'd say that.'

But it wouldn't have been the gang that they would have caught red-handed. Her escape—not from Lupe but from Andrew—had been narrower than she had realized. While Jill and Andrew had been having pre-dinner drinks, Jill had happened to mention that Susan was going to Jackson Heights, of all places! That had alarmed Andrew. He'd called first Alex and then Baltasar to see if either had any idea where Susan might have gone. Damian had answered the phone at the gallery and, after giving him the address, had offered the information that Baltasar had already departed with his luggage and his cat.

Andrew had rushed out to Jackson Heights, doing Jill out of still another dinner. He'd found an empty house and a dead *condesa*. Of course he hadn't known then that she was Baltasar's wife. He had simply assumed that, since she fitted the description, she was Lupe Montoya. It was only later, after her photograph had been published in the papers, that her true identity had been discovered and a scandal of major proportions unleashed.

If the Spanish nobility had been popular in New York's social circles before, now they became the reigning social lions. A tribute to the *condesa*'s memory was being planned at Mimi's Grand Ball and Gala against Drug Abuse.

'But don't they understand she was the one who was behind it all?' Susan asked Alex.

'It wouldn't make any difference,' he said. 'But what makes you think she was the one who was behind it all?'

'She—Andy told me that Baltasar and the rest of the gang seemed to have left the place in such a hurry that they left most of their stuff behind. There was enough there to convict them of drug dealing ten times over. They even left Esmeralda behind. The cat. Andrew took possession of her and gave her to Jill.'

'I wouldn't have taken Jill for an animal lover.'

'She loves Andrew,' Susan said.

Alex put down his empty plate. 'Do you think they'll make a match of it?'

'I don't know,' Susan said. 'It would be nice to think so.'

And Esmeralda's collar could take the place of the wedding present Lupe had been planning to send the couple. Susan wondered whether they knew the emeralds were real. Maybe she ought to point it out to them. No, just to Jill. Andrew was just righteous enough to turn the collar over to the government if he knew its value.

Everything was not necessarily over, she knew. Diego had gotten away and he knew it was Susan who had killed Lupe. But, if he tried to tell anyone, she doubted that he would be believed. Perhaps Baltasar, if he was still alive, would believe, but she did not think he would blame her. Besides, she didn't think he would ever dare come back to the United States.

Actually, Susan thought, I'm in much more danger from Lady Daphne. Of course she wasn't afraid of her, but she felt she owed it to Hortense to make a substantial investment in the health club. After all, she said to herself, it is a worthy cause.

THE END

Miss Melville Rides a Tiger

To Charlotte Sheedy with gratitude
for her patience and understanding

CHAPTER 1

'How come they're givin' a party for us and we wasn't invited?' the red-haired girl demanded. She stood there, legs spread apart, swollen belly thrust forward, as if the baby were not only going to come out at any minute but come out fighting. 'What's the matter? Ain't we good enough?'

'Prob'ly the invitations are in the mail,' said the small, dark girl who carried herself hunched forward, as if to deny her pregnancy. 'Or maybe they just forgot about us. People are always forgettin' about us.' And she heaved a sigh.

The other girls tittered. So the sigh had been intended as mockery, or, at least, taken as such.

Jill Turkel exploded. Although she had been working up to this, the effect was startling all the same. 'Forget about you, you silly little bitches! The party's to raise money for you, so you can have a decent place to stay and proper medical care and the right food to eat until your—' she caught the eyes of the other women and amended the word she was about to use '—until your brats get here.'

Ms Fischetti and Lucinda Rundle were too stunned to speak. Susan Melville didn't speak, because she was too embarrassed. Absurd for Jill to allow herself to be provoked by a fifteen-year-old girl into flying off the handle like that. But Jill frequently flew off the handle—and for even more absurd reasons. And, strictly speaking, the party wasn't for the girls, it was for the building.

Ms Fischetti gathered herself together. 'Now, that will be enough from you, young ladies. As for you, Ms Turkel, I am appalled. Talking to these poor, unfortunate girls like that!'

The 'poor, unfortunate girls' burst into laughter, which did not improve Ms Fischetti's temper. She turned to Lucinda. 'Really, Ms Rundle, if your friends are going to behave like this, I'm afraid I'm going to have to ask them to leave.'

'She's not my friend,' Lucy bleated. 'Susan is my friend. *She's* just Susan's agent.'

'Manager,' Jill corrected.

'I didn't ask her to come up here. I only asked Susan. *She* just came along.'

It was true: Lucy had not asked Jill to visit Rundle House. Jill had taken it upon herself to accompany Susan —'out of duty rather than inclination,' she'd said to Susan when they were alone for a few minutes at the restaurant entrance, Lucy having gone back inside to retrieve the folder of Rundle House literature she had left at the table. 'She would never have asked you to go up there with her, at least not right this minute, if you hadn't started talking about how little of the money that's raised at these charity affairs actually goes to the charities themselves.'

'But you yourself were talking about that just before she showed up.'

'That's right, blame everything on me. I was talking about that in connection with taxes, not morality. I didn't expect you to throw it in the teeth of the next do-gooder who hit you for a contribution.'

'It's a worthy cause,' Susan said feebly. 'Rundle House, I mean.'

'They're all worthy causes to you. But that's not why you let her browbeat you into going up there with her. You're going because you feel guilty about having forgotten what her cause was.'

That was true—in part, at least. Susan *had* felt guilty. But not so guilty that she would have allowed herself to be coerced into a visit to Rundle House, if it hadn't been for something Jill herself had let drop in the course of the conversation, something which made an immediate change of destination seem like a good idea.

Susan and Jill had been having lunch at Leatherstocking's when Lucinda Rundle stopped at their table. For a moment Susan hadn't recognized her. It wasn't that Lucy had changed so radically. In fact, she had changed less than any of the other women Susan had known since their school days, being now simply a faded, crumpled version of the child she had been. It was just that Lucy had always been so dim that no one, except perhaps those close to her, ever recognized her at first glance—far different from her sister Berengaria who, once experienced, was never forgotten.

In spite of Jill's glare, Susan felt she could do no less than invite Lucy to join them. She had already had lunch, Lucy said, gesturing vaguely towards the inner room of the restaurant, but would be happy to have coffee with them. By the time the coffee arrived, she had already handed each of them a handsome brochure heralding the hundredth anniversary of Rundle House, and invited them to buy tickets to a Gala Birthday Ball to benefit the house's building fund, at five hundred dollars each. That was the point at which Susan, instead of simply writing out a cheque for five hundred dollars, found herself saying, 'I'd gladly give you a cheque for a thousand if I knew it would all go directly to—to whatever it is Rundle House is in aid of, instead of having it go to pay for fund-raisers and caterers and the museum.' For the Gala Birthday Ball was to be held in the sculpture court of the American Museum, which, like most public institutions in New York City, was available for party purposes at a price.

Lucy's middle-aged baby face puckered in the way Susan remembered with dread from their early days. 'Oh, Susan, how could you have forgotten what Rundle House is?'

How could she have forgotten, indeed! Rundle House—the Rundle Home for Wayward Girls, as it had been called at its inception, had been the focal point of old Mrs Rundle's life. And the younger Mrs Rundle, Lucy's mother, had been co-opted into serving it as assiduously as her mother-in-law, on pain of having her allowance slashed, for old Mrs Rundle controlled the family purse strings, insofar as they were controllable. Her late husband, irked that his mother, the home's founder, had made over so much of the family's capital for its endowment, had tied up the rest of the still considerable estate in a trust, to make sure that no more of the Rundle capital would go 'to support a bunch of teen-aged tramps', as he'd put it.

He could not stop his wife from devoting as much of her income as she could spare—without depriving herself of such basic necessities as a chauffeured limousine and homes in Palm Beach and Long Island—to the family cause. And the younger Mr Rundle, Lucy's father, the infamous Edmund, Sr., although not otherwise of a charitable disposition, managed to support a number of teen-aged tramps privately on his allowance until he was caught in an involvement with a girl so far below the age of consent that he was forced to flee the country. His wife thankfully divorced him, receiving custody of the two younger children, Lucy and her brother, Edmund, Jr. The older daughter, who was some years older than both Lucy and Susan and had already been thrown out of all of the best schools and most of the second-best, disappeared from the scene at the same time. It was taken for granted that Berengaria had chosen—or possibly had been requested—to accompany her father.

As to where Mr Rundle himself had gone, accounts varied. Most likely he had betaken himself to Paris, where affluent refugees from sex scandals usually headed. But various romantic alternatives were bandied about among Lucy's schoolmates: he had fled to South America; he had entered the service of the Shah of Iran; he had repented of his sins and entered a religious order; he had not repented of his sins and had founded a religious order.

A few years later, Susan's own father had undeniably fled to South America, taking with him the family millions and some millions belonging to other people. Susan and her mother had gradually lost contact with the Rundles and most of the other people they knew. Not that they were cast out socially—a Melville would retain her social standing even if she sank into the gutter—but that they could no longer afford to keep to the same style of living as their former friends.

Still, there was no excuse for Susan to have forgotten the nature of her mother's favourite charity. The younger Mrs

Rundle had been Mrs Melville's best friend, so Susan had been aware of the Rundle Home for Wayward Girls even before she knew what a wayward girl was. By the time she was six or so, its name had been changed to the Rundle Home for Unwed Teen-Aged Mothers, which, although more explicit, was not entirely accurate. The home's concern was, as it had always been, with the months that preceded their actual parturition. When Susan had inquired, with youthful naïveté, what happened to the babies afterwards, her mother said she had no idea. 'Probably they're adopted and get nice homes.'

'As nice as ours, Mummy?' Susan had asked.

'Well, not quite that nice, dear. You could hardly expect that.'

'And their mummies? Their real mummies? What happens to them?'

'They probably go back on the streets,' her father had said, to which her mother said, 'Buckley!' in such a tone that neither he nor his daughter had pursued the matter.

Now, Susan noted, the place was called simply Rundle House, in keeping, she supposed, with contemporary mores; for being a wayward girl or an unwed teen-aged mother no longer set a girl apart from the moral mainstream. 'Of course I haven't forgotten what Rundle House is, Lucy,' Susan said. 'I was just trying to be—er—discreet.'

Jill snorted. Jill was a notable snorter. Hers were not subtle snorts. They had been known to wound far less sensitive souls than Lucy's. Her pale blue eyes filled with tears. 'It may seem to you that Rundle House has no place in today's world, but our work is more important than ever. The rate of pregnancy among adolescents is higher than it's ever been. In New York City it's fifteen per cent—over thirteen thousand babies each year. It's such a tragedy —children giving birth to children, babies having more babies . . .'

'Why don't they get abortions if they're too young to be mothers?' Jill demanded.

255

'Jill!' Susan said. Reasonable though the question might be, it was hardly tactful to query the very basis on which the foundation rested.

But Lucy seemed unperturbed. Obviously she had heard this before. 'The girls who come to Rundle House want to have their babies. And they don't know how to—or they can't afford to—take proper care of themselves. They don't eat right. They don't get the proper medical care. They—'

'I'm sure you're doing wonderful work there,' Susan interrupted before Lucy could recite the entire contents of the brochure from memory. 'I'll send you a cheque for a thousand dollars—and Jill will do the same,' she added, frowning at Jill to indicate that Jill had better kick in if she valued her association with a client who brought her a very comfortable annual income.

Lucy intercepted the glance and misunderstood. 'You don't believe me. You think we're a—an anachronism.' And, when Susan tried to protest, 'All right, then, promise me you'll come up to Rundle House and see for yourself.'

'I'll come up there, Lucy,' Susan said. 'Very soon, I promise.' And, when Lucy looked sceptical, 'Call me later this week, and we'll make a definite appointment. Here, I'll give you my number.' She wrote it on the margin of the brochure Lucy had thrust upon her, and pushed it across the table.

Lucy pushed it back. 'I already have your number. And I can see you don't have the least intention of coming; otherwise you wouldn't treat the brochure like a bunch of scrap paper.'

'I knew I could always get another one,' Susan said, taking back the brochure and stuffing it into her handbag. 'And Jill has her brochure'—Jill held it up—'which she is going to file as soon as she gets back to her office.' Jill nodded vigorously.

But Lucy would not be satisfied. 'Why don't you come up there with me right now? That way you won't be able to say we did anything special to prepare for your visit.'

'No Potemkin villages at Rundle House, eh?' Jill said.

Lucy looked bewildered. 'What do Cadillacs have to do

with Rundle House? Unless you're talking about that man who sits across the street in his Cadillac all the time. He has nothing to do with Rundle House. Nothing.'

Susan tried to explain the difference between Grigori Potemkin, Catherine the Great's trusted field marshal, and Victor Potamkin, Manhattan's well-known automobile merchant, but Lucy could not or would not understand. 'I don't see what Catherine the Great has to do with it,' she said. 'After all, this isn't Russia.'

That had been a favourite phrase of old Mrs Rundle's; she had considered it the unassailable answer to any argument, the absolute last word. Apparently her granddaughter felt the same way, because she began to gather her things together. 'Let's get started. It's getting late.'

'Lucy, I do wish I could come with you now, but I'm busy.'

'Whatever you have to do couldn't be as important as this,' Lucy persisted with the single-mindedness that had made her the hardest of her family to deal with, say what you might about Berry. 'What do you have to do that makes you too busy to help the poor and suffering?'

Her voice grew louder and louder as she got more excited. Some of the nearby lunchers looked at them reproachfully.

Jill spoke slowly and clearly, as if to a foreigner or an idiot. 'We are going to the Fothergill Gallery to look at an exhibition of pictures.'

'Pictures! You think pictures are more important than Rundle House?' And, when it was obvious that Jill, who was only minimally less single-minded than Lucy, did, 'You can see pictures any time!' Lucy's voice started to take on the shrillness that in the old days had heralded a tantrum.

'But we're expected,' Susan said, conscious as she spoke that she was adopting Jill's tone. 'People will be waiting for us there—the man who owns the gallery and the artist who painted the pictures. They would be very disappointed if we didn't come.'

'And Andy—he's my husband—said he might join us there. He'd be disappointed, too,'

Oh, he would, would he? Susan thought. And how is it

you didn't happen to mention before that Andy was thinking of joining us? Suddenly the prospect of an immediate visit to Rundle House began to look less unattractive. 'If I don't go up there with her now, she'll make a scene,' she whispered to Jill. 'It won't take long, and we can go to the Fothergill later. It isn't as if we'd promised to be there at a definite time.' And aloud, to Lucy, 'Oh, very well, I'll go up with you now, since you insist.'

She had not, she told Jill while they were waiting for Lucy at the entrance to the restaurant, said, *'We'll* go up there with you.'

'Oh, didn't you? Well, maybe I misheard you. Anyhow, if you're set on going, I'm going with you.'

So, after Lucy had reappeared and Jill had gone to make a phone call to Freddy Fothergill, during which time Lucy handed out Rundle House brochures to those sitting at the bar until M. Bumppo, as the proprietor, a James Fenimore Cooper fan, liked to call himself, politely but firmly ushered her into the street, the three ladies piled into a cab. Lucy gave the driver the address and they headed west and uptown, via a somewhat devious route, because of a water main break, which, as the driver explained, rendered a direct approach impossible. That was probably why the streets through which they passed seemed a strange conglomeration, even for New York, some elegant, some middle-class, some seedy, all mixed together higgledy-piggledy, instead of breaking down into well-defined neighbourhoods.

The people they passed were a strange conglomeration, too, in all types of dress, ranging from clothes that would not have been out of place on Madison Avenue to clothes that would not have been out of place on the streets of Calcutta. What was surprising was the number of people in ethnic costume—men wearing turbans, and women in what seemed to be Islamic attire.

Susan sat between Lucy and Jill and tried to make small talk that would provoke neither of her companions. 'How are your father and mother?' she asked Lucy.

'They're both dead. And yours?'

'They're dead too. What about your brother. Where is he?'

'Edmund's in Peru, been living there for years. He's in the export business.'

'What does he export?' Jill asked.

'Oh, this and that. Whatever it is they usually export from Peru. He doesn't get up here very often. Too busy with his business and his family.'

'I gather he's married,' Susan said. 'Any children?'

'Three times,' Lucy said. 'I mean he's been married three times. And there are children from each marriage. I've lost count, there are so many. Are you married, Susan?'

Susan started to say no, then thought better of it. Lucy's mother had tried to 'fix Susan up' with Edmund when they were young. If Edmund happened not to be married at the moment, Lucy might try the same thing. 'I'm engaged,' she said firmly. No point trying to explain her relationship with Peter. Lucy wouldn't understand. Sometimes she didn't, herself. Jill looked out of the window and smiled.

'You haven't asked about Berry,' Lucy said.

'Oh, somehow I had the impression she was dead.'

Lucy gave a girlish laugh. 'No, it was her husband who died. She's been a widow for almost three years now. But she still lives abroad. She's more at home there by this time.'

'Good,' Susan said. 'What I mean is, she always said she wanted to live abroad, that Americans were so—so American.'

'She has come to New York a few times on business. And she's been sorry she didn't have time to look you up.'

'Really,' Susan said.

'She keeps saying how nice it would be to see you again. You two were always such great friends. We must make a point of all getting together the next time she comes to town.'

'That would be lovely,' Susan said. 'Just give me advance notice of when she's expected.' So she could leave town. New York City was too small to hold both her and Berengaria Rundle at the same time.

CHAPTER 2

'Want me to wait?' the taxi driver asked, as the three ladies got out of the cab on one of the side streets between Amsterdam and Columbus Avenues.

'No, thank you,' Lucy said. 'We're going to be here quite a while.'

Jill groaned. Lucy misunderstood. 'You won't have any trouble getting a cab back downtown, although you might have to go over to Broadway. Cabs don't cruise here too much.'

Susan could believe that. She remembered Rundle House as having been on a pleasant, tree-lined, slightly shabby street, filled with brownstone row houses and a couple of small apartment buildings. The street could no longer be described as pleasant, nor could you call it 'slightly' shabby. It had run all the way down to squalid. The buildings were the same, but most of them were boarded up; and those that weren't looked as if they should have been, as much to keep whoever or whatever was inside from getting out as whatever or whoever was outside from getting in. Garbage, some spilling out of plastic bags, some completely uncontained, was strewn over the sidewalks and stoops, and cats and rats were nosing in it together—an extreme example of the West Side's vaunted cultural diversity. West Side rats, she noticed, were larger and fatter than their East Side counterparts (which she had observed disporting themselves on Park Avenue in the wee hours of the morning). The trees were dead and some were gone, leaving only squares of barren earth and dog pats in the sidewalk to mark where they had been.

Yet both sides of the street were lined with prosperous-looking cars, many of them late models, though none the equal of the big silver Cadillac parked directly across the street from Rundle House. There was a man sitting in it and no wonder. You'd have to be crazy to leave a car like that unguarded on a street like this. But what a price to have to pay for parking space.

At first he seemed to be the only human being in sight. Then she saw that there were other people around; in the shadow of a doorway, three men engaged in furtive transaction; in an alley, a glimmer of movement; on a stoop a heap of rags that stirred and became a man. Or a woman. Somewhere a radio was playing rock. In the distance the rat-tat-tat of a jackhammer could be heard. Otherwise, it was very quiet. Strange for a street in New York City to be so quiet.

'The neighbourhood certainly has changed,' Susan observed. 'I can see why Rundle House is anxious to move.'

'Move?' Lucy repeated. 'Who said anything about moving?'

'The brochure said the party was for the benefit of the Rundle House building fund.'

'Rundle House couldn't possibly afford to move anywhere else in the city, no matter how much money we raised. We're planning to expand. If we pay cash, we can get the building next door cheap—cheap, all things considered, that is. If we wait, they'll start gentrifying the street and prices will go even higher.'

The street seemed an unlikely candidate for gentrification, but Susan had seen even more unsavoury places transformed into pricey real estate. At least this street had originally been residential. No zoning changes would be needed, and the West Side of Manhattan was currently fashionable. Probably Rundle House knew what it was doing.

'It isn't as bad as it looks,' Lucy said.

'Maybe so,' Jill said, 'but I'd hate to walk along it alone after dark.'

'No street in New York is safe after dark. Only last year a man was gunned down right in front of my house, somebody from the United Nations, I believe, a foreigner, but still it was on Park Avenue, in the Seventies, and, if you're not safe there, where can you be safe?'

*

For a moment Susan's breath seemed to stop. She was very conscious of the weight of the gun in her handbag. Then she relaxed. Of course Lucy hadn't meant anything personal. It was just the kind of remark anyone might make in the course of a casual conversation about crime. And Jill didn't mean anything personal when she said, 'There seems to have been a lot of killings of UN people during the last few years. Did you happen to read that article about it in *Time*?'

No, she hadn't, Lucy said, seeming surprised that anyone should ask her if she had read anything. And Susan, affecting calm, said Lucy was right; there was crime all over New York, as well as drugs and corruption and something really should be done about it. 'I see you've managed to keep Rundle House in good shape,' she said. It was grimier than she remembered but, aside from the metal plate over the front door that bore the legend 'Rundle House' in large letters that covered, she knew, the smaller letters of the original name incised in the stone, the place didn't seem to have changed since she'd last seen it some-thirty-odd years before. Then it had struck her as grim and fortresslike. Today, now that fortresses had become the architectural style of necessity in the city, it seemed an attractive, old-fashioned building. If there were bars on the ground-floor windows, there were bars on most ground-floor windows these days. Rundle House stood out like a healthy thumb on that sore street, save for the brownstone on its left which also appeared to be well-kept.

Was that the building they were planning to buy or was it the boarded-up apartment house on the other side? That was in a state of advanced decay and would certainly need to be rebuilt; however, for any kind of expansion pro-gramme it would obviously be the more sensible buy, since it was at least six times the size of the brownstone. Yet, no matter how much they raised from their anniversary festivities, how could they hope to make enough to cover an outlay of that size? Land in Manhattan, even in such a rundown area as this, cost the earth. Inflation must have shrunk Rundle House's original endowment over the years, yet Susan had never, since she returned to affluence, received a solicitation from Rundle House, although it seemed to her that her name was on all the mailing lists.

Lucy led the way up the three steps that fronted the entrance. She rang a bell next to the door. A rather tough-looking young woman admitted them to a spacious lobby that was pleasant in an airy, institutional kind of way. A little too colourful, perhaps. It was a bit like being inside a kaleidoscope. On the other hand, it was preferable to the heavy dark furniture and dun draperies that Susan remembered from the old days. The only thing that she recognized was the graceful curving staircase that led up to the second floor. Otherwise, everything was different. Even the reception desk was of light-hued wood with a dark-hued receptionist behind it, the very opposite of what it had been.

Behind the reception desk were several doors presumably leading to offices. Susan could hear the clack of word processors from behind one of them. It all looked very efficient. The youngish middle-aged woman who emerged from the office marked 'Director' also looked efficient, a far cry from Miss Henderson, who had reigned in the old days. Ms Fischetti, as Lucy introduced her, and as she seemed to expect to be called—no bureaucratic informality here—smiled as she greeted them. She showed no sign of resentment at having been interrupted in her work to welcome Miss Rundle and her guests. True, this was one of the administrator's duties, but that had never stopped Miss Henderson from being brusque with visitors who arrived without forewarning.

Ms Fischetti took them into a pleasant, almost luxurious office overlooking the street. It was decorated with a formidable array of certificates, attesting to the fact that Diane Fischetti possessed advanced degrees in sociology, psychology, business administration, and similar sciences. Miss Henderson's only qualification had been that she was a Rundle on her mother's side.

Ms Fischetti told them about Rundle House, past, present, and future, while Lucy, who must have sat through this many times before, gazed at her with the rapt attention of someone hearing it for the first time. Jill's eyes glazed over. Finally she got up, and, muttering something about 'needing to go to the bathroom', wandered out. Ms Fischetti's voice never faltered, but her eyes followed Jill, and she cut short her speech before, Susan thought, it had come to its appointed end. 'Sorry to be so boring, Ms Melville,' Ms Fischetti said, as she got up, 'but one does tend to get caught up in one's enthusiasms.'

'But you haven't been boring at all. And there were a couple of questions—'

'You can ask them while I take you around the place. I know you're a busy woman, and I don't want to impose on you unduly.' And she herded Susan and Lucy out into the reception area, where Jill was wandering about, poking her nose into things. 'Why didn't you show Ms Turkel where the visitors' rest rooms were?' Ms Fischetti asked the receptionist.

'Because she didn't ask me.'

'The urge left me, as soon as I got up. It sometimes works that way. How come none of the girls are around? Aren't they allowed downstairs?'

'The mothers are free to go wherever they want. There simply isn't any reason for them to come down here. Those who aren't in their rooms are probably in the lounges. We'll see them when we go upstairs.'

Jill was not as curious as all that. 'You're not going to give us the grand tour?' she groaned.

'We really couldn't ask you to take so much time off from your duties,' Susan said. 'Besides, as a matter of fact, I am rather busy. We're both rather busy.'

'Taking visitors around is one of my duties,' Ms Fischetti said, showing her teeth. 'Miss Rundle might report me to the trustees if I failed to give you the grand tour, as Ms Turkel puts it.'

Lucy gave a nervous laugh. 'Oh, Ms Fischetti, you know I'd never do any such thing. But I hope you don't mind if I don't go around with you. I do want to get caught up on my mailing.' And she plumped herself down in an easy chair covered in a cheerful Mondrian-like print, took out a pile of brochures and a bunch of envelopes from her tote bag, and deposited them on a small table, which she drew up before her.

Ms Fischetti looked as if she did mind, but undoubtedly Lucy had been on the tour many times before. It made good sense for her to stay downstairs and occupy herself usefully. Or what seemed to be usefully. Susan wondered to whom Lucy would be sending the brochures. She hoped she wouldn't be asking her for the current addresses of all their old friends.

Ms Fischetti showed them all over Rundle House, from top to bottom. She showed them the kitchens and dining-rooms, the medical offices, the therapy room, the lounges, and the classrooms. That's right, Susan thought, the girls would be of school age. In the old days pregnancy usually meant the end of a girl's education. Now, often, it meant the beginning.

Ms Fischetti introduced them to the housekeeper. She also introduced them to the resident nurse and the visiting doctor, the porters, the cooks, the clerks, and the cleaners. Rundle House appeared to be very well staffed, indeed.

'They must have some endowment!' Jill observed. Susan had been thinking the same thing.

The higher they got in the building, the more mothers they saw. There were girls in the bedrooms, girls in the corridors, girls in the lounges. There were white girls, black girls, Asian girls, and indeterminate girls, all looking sleek and well-fed and well, if not always appropriately, dressed. Ms Fischetti did not introduce Susan to any of the girls, and she did not seem pleased when some of them left off whatever it was they were doing or planning to do to follow the visitors around, apparently seeing better entertainment in them than from the television sets and radios that had been providing a rap and rock accompaniment to their tour.

Susan was surprised when she saw the mothers-to-be. 'Children giving birth to children,' indeed! These girls weren't children; they were fully mature women despite their tender years. If their years were as tender as purported, Jill suggested to Susan when they and their guide were alone in the library—their followers having halted on the threshold, as if a step further would plunge them into some abyss. In contrast to the other public rooms, the library looked unused, the magazines symmetrically arranged on the tables, the books in perfect formation on the shelves. Apparently the girls were not great readers.

'Oh, I think they really are teen-agers,' Susan whispered. 'Girls like that—girls tend to mature early these days.'

Ms Fischetti's back froze. 'Well, you've seen everything,' she said, hustling them out of the library. She entered the elevator, obviously expecting Jill and Susan to follow. However, several of the girls crowded in behind her, whispering and giggling. 'Now, mothers,' Ms Fischetti said, 'you haven't left any room for our visitors.'

'They can wait and take it on the next trip,' the red-haired girl who seemed to be the ringleader said. at the same time as Susan said, 'We can easily take the stairs.'

Ms Fischetti emerged from the elevator, pushing the girls out ahead of her. 'We will all take the stairs,' she announced, and started to lead the way down.

But none of the others followed. Jill positioned herself in front of the red-haired girl. Susan stopped to see what Jill was up to, and the rest of the girls halted, sensing sport.

'How old are you?' Jill demanded.

'Fifteen,' the red-haired girl replied in a what's-it-to-you? voice. The smaller, dark girl at her elbow said she was the same. The others gave ages ranging from thirteen to sixteen. Only one—the one who looked most like a child—admitted to being as old as eighteen, the cutoff age for admission to Rundle House. That didn't mean they had to be lying, Susan thought. Wash the thick makeup off their faces, change the weird hair styles, and they probably would look like young girls—but still biologically mature, not children by any manner of means.

'Don't you think you're too young to—to take on the responsibilities of motherhood?' Jill demanded of the red-haired girl. Jill was red-haired, too. There was something of kinship between them, Susan thought, if only in their

266

belligerent attitudes. Only, where the red-haired girl looked older than her years, Jill looked younger than hers. She was somewhere in her thirties, but she seemed no more mature than these overripe adolescents.

'If you can get pregnant, you're old enough to be a mother,' the red-haired girl said. The other girls laughed as if she had said something witty.

'Didn't anybody suggest that at your age it would be better for you to have an abortion?'

'Ms Turkel, please! I don't know what Miss Rundle would think if she heard you talk like that.' Ms Fischetti looked at Susan.

'Really, Jill,' Susan said.

The red-haired girl seemed undisturbed. 'Lotsa people told me I oughta have an abortion, but I don't want one. I wanna have my baby. I love babies. I'm gonna have lots of them.'

'Abortions are murder,' the eighteen-year-old declared. The other girls snickered.

Jill swelled with wrath. It was obvious she was about to make a speech. 'We must go back down,' Ms Fischetti said, desperation in her voice.

Susan placed her hand against Jill's back and applied pressure—not quite a shove but enough to remind Jill that she was there in her capacity as Susan's employee. Jill started down. The girls trailed after, Ms Fischetti vainly trying to get them to go back by talking to them in quiet, reasonable undertones. Susan had a feeling that if she and Jill hadn't been there, Ms Fischetti would have shrieked.

At every landing a window looked out on the street, each framed in colourful draperies rather than veiled by an ecru lace curtain as in Miss Henderson's day. As they passed each window, the girls would wave at the young man sitting in the silver Cadillac, and he would smile and wave back. Once he even broke off from a conversation—or was it a dispute?—he was having with someone on the other side of the car to smile and wave at the girls.

'Who is that man?' Susan asked.

'I have no idea,' Ms Fischetti said.

'He's my boyfriend,' the red-haired girl said.

'He's *my* boyfriend,' the dark-haired girl said.

Half a dozen of the other girls also claimed him as their boyfriend. They were very jolly about it. It seemed to be some kind of inside joke. And singularly free from prejudice, because, while the young man was black, at least half of the girls were white.

Jill continued to interrogate the girls as the procession wended its way down the stairs. 'But how will you be able to take care of your babies after they're born? A lot of you aren't old enough to have jobs. Are you planning to give them up for adoption?'

They shook their heads. To a mother, they were planning to keep their babies. It made sense, Susan thought. Why nurture a being in your body for nine months at considerable personal discomfort only to have to give it up at the end? But this was neither the time nor the place to bring that up.

'How can you afford to take care of them?' Jill persisted.

'The Lord will provide' the red-haired girl said. The other girls laughed. There were nuances here, Susan realized, that she failed to grasp.

They reached the head of the flight of stairs leading down to the lobby. Ms Fischetti paused. 'Well, you mothers will want to go back to your rooms now. This has been rather an exhausting afternoon.'

But the girls showed no signs of leaving, although only the red-haired girl and her dark-haired sidekick actually followed them down into the lobby, where Lucy was busily stuffing brochures into envelopes and humming to herself. A few girls came halfway down; the others hovered at the head of the stairs. I'll bet Jill was right, Susan thought; I'll bet they aren't supposed to come down into the lobby.

Ms Fischetti forced a smile. 'I'm afraid there are a number of things I must do before the office closes for the day. And I'm sure you'll want to leave before it gets dark. It was so nice of you to come visit us—'

She was interrupted by a cry of outrage from the red-haired girl, who had picked up one of Lucy's brochures and started to read it before anyone could make a move to stop her. At least she can read, Susan thought.

Apparently the girls had not been informed of the festivities that had been planned to mark the hundredth birthday of Rundle House. There was outrage; there was explosion. Both Ms Fischetti and the receptionist moved towards the front door. Susan and Jill were about to be thrown out. Lucy looked distressed, but did not attempt to intervene. Susan had an unworthy thought. Lucy could hardly ask her for addresses if she allowed Ms Fischetti to throw them out.

Susan spoke quickly before the same thought could occur to Lucy. 'Thank you so much for an interesting and informative afternoon.' She grabbed Jill's arm and pulled her to the front door.

Ms Fischetti held it open for them. She closed it behind them. It opened again, and the upper part of Lucy emerged. 'I hope you won't let Ms Fischetti bother you,' she said in a low voice. 'She's so devoted to her work that sometimes she gets carried away, and we can't afford to have her upset.'

'Of course not,' Susan said soothingly. 'I'm sure good administrators are hard to find these days.'

'I suppose they are, but her godfather is a trustee, which—'

An arm came through the doorway and hauled Lucy inside, cutting her off in midsentence. The door closed again, this time with a bang.

CHAPTER 3

Outside it was even quieter than before, perhaps because the jackhammer had stopped. Only the radio was still playing thinly in the distance. It was growing dark. Jill shivered. 'It's getting cold,' she said. 'I'm surprised they don't have a security guard,' she went on. 'Seems a place like that in a neighbourhood like this ought to have one.'

'Perhaps they do. A security guard doesn't have to be male, you know.'

'You could be right. That receptionist looked like a pretty tough cookie. In fact, they all looked like pretty tough cookies. Except your friend Lucy, of course.'

But in her own way, Susan thought, Lucy could be a very tough cookie, indeed. Like all the Rundles.

They went down the steps and into the street. 'Somehow, I have a feeling you're mad at me.'

'I'm certainly not pleased with you. There was no reason for you to behave like that.'

'There was every reason. You know what those girls are —whores! And that's their pimp, sitting across the street, protecting his investment.'

'I got the impression that he was a drug dealer.'

'The two occupations aren't necessarily mutually exclusive. Anyhow, with a lot of his girls off the street, he probably makes money any way he can.'

'But what makes you so sure he's a pimp?'

'I recognized him. His pictures were in the papers a while back. Not the kind of papers you read. The tabloids.'

She overestimated her client. Or underestimated her. Susan did read the tabloids, but her interests were very specific. She ignored everything that lay outside her area of operations. Perhaps she had drawn her parameters too rigidly. 'Why was his picture in the papers?'

'He used to go to the bus and train stations, picking up teenage runaways; then seducing them. Raping them, actually, because that's what it is when it comes to a twelve-year-old, no matter how willing. And then he'd send them out on the streets.'

'Some of the girls at Rundle House couldn't have been much more than twelve when they got pregnant,' Susan observed.

'Some of them might have been less than that when he got them started. He was in the papers because an eleven-year-old girl's parents came looking for her. Most of them don't.'

'And he's still running around loose?'

'That was a couple of years ago. Maybe he served some time. You know what the law in New York is like. It isn't as if he were a stock manipulator or an insider trader. Or if the girl's parents had been middle class or of the right ethnic persuasion.'

'You mean that all the girls in Rundle House are prostitutes?'

'Couldn't you tell just by looking at them?'

'Hard to tell with today's fashions. Streetwalker seems to be the current role model.'

'I don't suppose all of the girls are hookers,' Jill conceded. 'Or even that all of those who are hookers are his girls. But I'm sure most of the gang that followed us are.'

Both of them had continued to stare at the man in the Cadillac while they were speaking. He rolled down the window and smiled at them, the smile widening to a leer as he took in Jill from head to toe. He leaned out of the car. 'Hey, Momma,' he called, 'you're a little over the hill for my customers, but I'm the sophisticated type. I could go for you myself. Whaddya say you ditch auntie and let me take you for a ride?'

Jill spat at him. Susan wished she would find some other way of expressing her displeasure. She dragged her away. They walked towards Broadway, followed by the sound of his mocking laughter. 'People like that should be killed,' Jill said. She stared defiantly at Susan. Susan shrugged.

Broadway was a relief. It was wide and crowded and cheerful, with bright lights, stores, and street vendors selling books, fruit, and other wholesome things. The beggars—or homeless people, as they were now called—smiled as they asked for money to buy soup and bread and vitamins. Even the garbage seemed neater. There was plenty of noise, street musicians combining with boom boxes and the ever-present workmen tearing up the streets to create a cacophony that seemed to bother no one. Cabs, buses, cars, and the occasional police cruiser went up one side of the avenue and came down the other. Ambulances and fire trucks clanged and shrilled merrily. Susan felt as if she had come back to civilization. She gave generously to the alms-seekers, to Jill's obvious disapproval. Jill did not believe in nondeductible charity.

'Let's not get a cab right away,' Jill said. 'I need a drink.'

'I could use one, too.' Actually, Susan felt no particular desire for a drink, but it fitted in with the plan she was beginning to formulate. They went into a restaurant of respectable aspect, sat down at a booth in the bar, and ordered.

'I wonder which building they're planning to buy,' Susan said, 'the apartment house or the brownstone?'

'The apartment house. They already own the brownstone.'

'What makes you think so?'

'Because there was a door in the reception room that didn't seem to lead anywhere. First I thought it was a fire door, but the fire doors were marked "Exit", and it was locked.'

'You mean you tried it?'

'How else would I know it was locked? Then I remembered that the brownstone was built smack against Rundle House, so the door would have to go there or lead into an airwell inside the brownstone's property line. So, either way, it's got to belong to them.'

'Now that I think of it,' Susan said, 'there used to be a trustees' room on the ground floor and that space seems to have been turned into offices. And there was an apartment for the director on the top floor, but that's all bedrooms now. Maybe they put the trustees' room next door and Ms Fischetti has an apartment there.'

'I'd hate to live in that neighbourhood myself, but it isn't easy to find an affordable apartment in Manhattan these days, even if your godfather is one of the trustees. Maybe that's one of the attractions of the job.'

'Salary could be another. The Rundles were always generous with their employees.'

The waitress placed glasses before them. Jill drank her bourbon and soda in thirsty gulps. Susan sipped her vodka martini. She wanted nothing to affect the clarity of her thought. Or her actions.

'What's between you and this Berry—Berengaria, God what a name—Rundle, anyway?' Jill asked.

Susan was startled. Whatever had possessed Jill to come up with that question?

'I saw your face when Lucy suggested you all get together.'

Susan hadn't realized she'd been so immoderate as to let her emotions show, but Berry Rundle was a special case. 'Oh, we just didn't get along. You know how it is with teen-aged girls.'

'I thought you got along with everyone, Susan.'

'I try to, but sometimes it's difficult.' She gave Jill a meaning look.

Jill laughed and patted her client's arm. 'Oh, come on, Susan, you know you get along with me better than anyone else.'

Susan was not going to allow herself to be baited. There were far more important things on her agenda. She had formulated her plan; now it was time to put it into action. She gave a muffled exclamation and started to rummage in her handbag. 'Oh, bother, I must have left my address book over at Rundle House.'

Jill looked at her inquiringly.

'Lucy wanted the addresses of some people we both knew. I gave them to her while we were in Ms Fischetti's office and you were snooping around outside.'

'I was not snooping. I never snoop. I was just taking an intelligent interest.'

Susan refused to dignify that statement with a reply. 'I'm afraid you're no longer *persona grata* there,' she said. 'In fact, I'm not entirely sure that I am. So I think it might be a good idea if you stay here and have another drink while I run back and get the address book. It shouldn't take more than a few minutes.

Jill half rose, then subsided in her seat. 'Sure you don't mind? I feel guilty about letting you go back there alone, especially at night.'

'I'd rather face the potential dangers of the street than the actual wrath of Ms Fischetti if I come back bringing you with me. Anyhow, it isn't dark yet.'

Actually it was almost dark by the time she got back to Rundle House; but that was all to the good, as long as the onset of darkness didn't bring out the local wildlife. And, if it did, there was the heft of the gun in her handbag to reassure her, although she would have felt even more confident if it had silver bullets in it. It was that kind of neighbourhood.

There seemed to be no one around except the young man in the silver Cadillac. No sign of movement in the alley-ways. Even the bundle of rags had vanished from the stoop. Nothing appeared to have changed except that draperies had been drawn across the ground-floor windows of Rundle House. Through the cracks where they did not quite meet, she could see a light in the lobby. Somewhere, not too far away, she heard the thin strains of vaguely Oriental-sounding music. It seemed to come from the brownstone next door, but the windows were all dark.

She rang the bell of Rundle House. After a pause, Ms Fischetti herself opened the door. She appeared to be alone in the reception room. Lucy must have gone home, unless she was elsewhere on the premises.

Ms Fischetti did not look pleased to see Susan again. 'I'm sorry to disturb you,' Susan apologized, 'but I felt I had to come back and apologize for Jill. I'm afraid she can be quite outspoken sometimes, but—' Susan could not bring herself to say 'she means well'—'but she has many good qualities.'

'I'm sure she's a very good manager, at any rate. It was thoughtful of you to come back, but really there was no need . . .'

'And I didn't get a chance to tell you that I'd like to buy a whole table at the benefit. You'll get my cheque for five thousand dollars in the mail. Unless you'd like me to come in and make it out now.'

If this had been any of the charitable institutions Susan

was familiar with, she would have been hauled inside and held there, by force if need be, until the cheque was signed, sealed, and delivered. But by this time Susan had already come to realize that Rundle House was not like any other charitable institution she knew.

Still, Ms Fischetti did unbend a little. 'It's very kind of you, Ms Melville, but all the secretaries have gone, and it really wouldn't be convenient. If you'd just mail the cheque, that would be fine.'

'Of course,' Susan said. 'I wouldn't want to cause you any further inconvenience. I'll get the cheque out first thing in the morning.'

She walked down to the corner in case Ms Fischetti happened to be watching from the windows; then crossed to the other side of the street and came back, keeping in the shadows of the parked cars, so that it would be difficult for anyone on the Rundle House side to see her.

She paused next to the silver Cadillac. The young man inside rolled down the window and grinned at her. 'Hey, auntie, has your girlfriend changed her mind and sent you to negotiate?'

She took out her gun and shot him between the eyes. A neat little hole appeared in the middle of his smooth brown forehead. He slumped sidewise. The sound of the shot had seemed very loud, but no one came out from any of the buildings to investigate.

She put the gun in her bag and walked back to Broadway. An old line of verse that she had learned in her childhood, when she and Lucinda Rundle had been at school together, came into her head. 'Something attempted, something done, has earned a night's repose.'

She had, she felt, earned her night's repose.

CHAPTER 4

When Susan got back to Broadway, she found Jill hovering anxiously about the entrance to the restaurant. As soon as Susan came into view, she leaped forward and clutched her arm. 'I thought you were never coming back. I called home: Andy left a message on the machine. He says I've got to come home right away. Some kind of emergency. He must be hurt! Maybe he's dying!'

No such luck, Susan thought. Although she liked Andy, it was undoubtedly true that life would be much easier for her if he were no longer on the scene. 'Was the message in his own voice?' she asked Jill.

Jill gave a grudging nod.

'It doesn't seem likely that he's dying then, does it? And if he were seriously hurt, he'd ask you to come to the hospital, not the apartment.'

'But you know how brave Andy is.'

Since tactfulness was bred in her bones. Susan refrained from pointing out that if Andrew Mackay had been the sort of man too brave to acknowledge that he felt pain, he would not have left a message for his wife; he would simply have expired heroically on the rug. But Susan did not blame Jill for her anxiety. Andy's line of work justified a certain amount of apprehension. He was engaged in covert operations, working for an agency that, he had assured her, had no connection with the United States Government.

No official connection, perhaps; otherwise he would—or should—have felt obliged to report her peccadillos to the authorities. But his organization certainly seemed to have a working relationship with various branches of the government; she had seen for herself the cooperative terms he was on with the New York City Police Department, reluctant though its cooperation seemed to be.

Although Susan wished Andy reasonably well, all things considered, she was relieved that something had arisen to compel Jill to forsake her and rush to his side. It was obvious to her now that Andy had schemed to 'drop in' at the art gallery, so that he could join Jill in persuading Susan to have dinner with them at their apartment. That way he'd have a chance to get Susan alone while Jill was wrestling with the dinner, for Jill fancied herself—erroneously, as far as Susan was concerned—to be a gourmet cook, and, like all true artists, she needed to be alone while she was in the throes of creativity.

Jill had been aware that Susan would be available that evening, because she knew that Susan had been scheduled to go with Peter Franklin to a dinner meeting of the Neanderthal Society. Then, the day before, Peter had suddenly announced that he'd decided to go on an expedition to one of the more obscure areas of the Amazon Basin to visit a newly discovered tribe of Indians, saying he couldn't pass up the opportunity to investigate them before they underwent either civilization or extinction, whichever came first.

Susan knew the true reason for his leaving was that he'd become fed up with the noise and confusion of the renovations that were going on at the Melville Foundation building. So off he'd gone, and Susan had not been sorry to see him leave as, like most men, he tended to get cranky when inconvenienced. She couldn't help wondering, however, whether Dr Katherine Froehlich, his former assistant, who had left the foundation after the unpleasantness there the previous Christmas, was also going to be a member of the expedition, but she would rather die than ask him. Besides, he wouldn't have told her the truth, anyway.

No doubt Jill had mentioned Peter's abrupt departure to Andy, and he had seized the opportunity to attempt to get Susan alone and offer her still another of those 'assignments' he was always dangling in front of her. As if I couldn't pick my own kills, Susan thought crossly. 'Of course you must go to Andy right away,' she told Jill. 'After all, one never knows. And don't worry about me. I can find my own way home.'

Jill hesitated. Although she loved her husband, she treasured her clients, especially this one. 'You're sure? This is a pretty rough neighbourhood.'

'Come on, Jill. This is Upper Broadway, not Beirut.'

So she had seen Jill off in a cab, and, after looking over the wares of a surprisingly well stocked sidewalk bookseller and marvelling over the window display of a shop devoted entirely to fearful and wonderful embellishments for the feet, she secured a cab of her own. On her way home, she passed several police cars, sirens shrieking, rushing in the opposite direction. She couldn't help wondering whether they were the result of her own modest effort or whether there were other perpetrators abroad that evening.

When she got home, she was sorry she hadn't lingered longer among the delights of upper Broadway, for, sitting in the lobby of her apartment house, his handsome all-American-boy face aglow with the smiles of one sure of his welcome, sat Andrew Mackay, undying, unwounded, unperturbed. She had known him to be a devious young man, but never had she deemed him capable of so despicable a trick as this—or herself capable of falling for it.

He looked pleased with himself. 'I knew the only sure way to detach my loving spouse from your side was to send her off on a false trail. And I did want to have a word with you alone. Sometimes I have the feeling that you're avoiding me.'

She would have liked to forbid him the house, at least the apartment, for he was already in the house; but that would have aroused comment among the building personnel, particularly since she could not pretend he was a stranger. He had been her guest too many times before. Lucky that he was as unwilling to attract attention as she was. Otherwise, she was sure, he would have been waiting for her up in her apartment. Little things like locks did not hinder someone in his profession.

That was one of the reasons she had fewer regrets than she might otherwise have had that in a few months (the gods willing) she would be leaving the apartment to take up residence on the top floors of the building that housed the

Melville Foundation on its lower storeys. For a long time, Jill had been urging Susan either to rent out those floors or to move up there herself. Susan might be well-off now, but not so well-off that she could afford to let such expensive real estate lie fallow. For a long time Susan had resisted, but the old loft building where she did her painting had been sold to a developer. Soon it would be torn down and replaced by high-rise condominiums. There was no longer any place in the neighbourhood where she could rent suitable studio space. On the other hand, there was a vacant penthouse at the top of the Melville Building that could easily be converted into a studio.

She finally gave in but without grace. 'It's going to mean that I've come this far in life only to find myself living over the shop,' she told Jill.

'Think of it as being mistress of your own castle. There's even that cute little balcony on the top you can use to pour boiling oil down on unwelcome visitors. Come on, be practical, Susan.'

The more she thought about it, the more Susan began to see the advantages of such a move. It was time she left the apartment which she had fought so hard to keep. Spacious as it had seemed in her poverty-stricken days, it was beginning to cramp her now. It was time to make a break, especially since the type of people who were beginning to buy into the building were not the type of people who would have been welcome in the past. These newcomers were boors who seemed to have no idea of the niceties of civilized behaviour. Downstairs there were doormen to protect her from people trying to gain entry to the house, but nobody to protect her from neighbours trying to gain entry to her apartment. They would ring her doorbell attempting to 'drop in' on her, making it impossible for her to spend a quiet evening at home, unless she sat there, letting the doorbell ring, pretending she was not at home. She could, of course, afford live-in help to repel evening intruders, but that would mean she would have to sacrifice her privacy in another way.

Worse yet, when Peter was around and not off giving a

lecture or attending a seminar or spending the evening at the Foundation catching up on his work, or so he said, he would encourage these intrusions. Dropping in on people without notice or invitation was a characteristic of many primitive peoples, he told her. He was delighted to have the opportunity to study them in their native habitat without the inconvenience of field research. And she was too conscious of the fact that it was she who was paying the bills to reprove him for his lack of consideration. If she bought another apartment in another building, she could still be at the mercy of invading neighbours. Standards were dropping all over the place.

In the Foundation Building she would, as Jill had pointed out, be mistress of her own domain, and Peter could always entertain uninvited guests in his offices—far more suitable for anthropological research, being equipped with tape recorders, devices for measuring the sizes of people's heads, and other appropriate equipment. Moreover it would be far more difficult for Andy to obtain entrance to a building that was her own property, protected by state-of-the-art locks and alarms, with a caretaker in the basement and, if need be, a brace of Dobermans in the foyer.

Unfortunately, such a setup would throw her and Peter together far too much. Even though he would be working on another floor, she would always be conscious of his presence below; and, for all she knew, he might feel the same way about her above.

That was no reason for her to feel trapped. She could—she would—take Jill's advice in yet another respect and buy a house in the country. Jill's idea of a house in the country was a place in the Hamptons. Peter's idea was an igloo—or whatever they lived in—in Patagonia. Susan's was to get something in-between, preferably in another country but one more comfortably situated than Patagonia, where Andy would have neither unofficial authority nor clout. She might not even welcome him as a visitor. Which meant Jill would have to be unwelcome as well. I could live with that, Susan thought. Although she had grown used to Jill by this time, and was even fond of her, in a way, an occasional respite from her constant nagging would not be unwelcome.

CHAPTER 5

She was still very angry with Andy. She tried to make him feel guilty. 'Poor Jill was so worried about you,' she told him as she unlocked the door to her apartment. 'She rushed back home to see what was wrong.'

'As is only proper in a dutiful and loving wife. Think how happy she will be when she gets there and finds another message from me telling her it was a mistake and all is well.'

He followed Susan into her study. How heartless he was, she thought. How well he and Jill deserved each other. Sitting down without invitation, he opened his attaché case, exposing a row of coloured knobs and buttons and dials. He pressed a couple of buttons; then he twisted a knob, consulted a dial, and pressed another button.

There was a pretty display of coloured lights, followed by a series of beeps. Since she'd seen him do this whenever he came to her apartment and also when he came back to his own apartment, she knew he was testing for listening devices. Someday, she told him, he was going to forget himself and run a security cheque on the apartment of someone who was unaware of his true activities. 'And you're going to find it hard to explain why the deputy director of the National Resource for the Homeless'—for that was his cover post—'should be afraid of eaves-droppers.'

'Oh, I don't know. There's a powerful landlord group that would stop at nothing to convert all the residential real estate in New York into cooperatives or condominiums—not to speak of citizens who're afraid we're going to build shelters for the homeless in their neighbourhoods—and all of them anxious to know our every move.'

He sighed. 'If we'd known how much attention we were

going to attract, we would have chosen another cover. But it's too late now; we're stuck with the Resource. Pity the mayor had to go and give us a Golden Apple for having done more to provide homes for the homeless in New York City than any other organization. Now everyone's expecting even more from us.'

'That's what comes of being superefficient.'

He nodded sadly. 'How true, how true. We've got to learn how to hold back.'

Since the social graces were too inbred in her for her to forgo the traditional rites of hospitality, she offered him a drink. 'Scotch,' he said, 'with just a splash of soda. You know how I like it.' He lifted his glass in a silent toast. She would have liked to throw her wine in his face, but that would have been descending to his wife's level. That was the trouble with good breeding; it discouraged spontaneity.

The phone rang. 'That will be Jill,' Andy said. 'Don't answer. Let the machine take it.'

'But she'll worry about me, if she thinks I haven't gotten home yet.'

'Let her worry,' Andy said. 'Do her good. You can call her back later.'

Although she wouldn't have admitted it to him, he was right. It would be difficult to listen to Jill's plaints, knowing that Andy was right there with her. But she resented his behaviour, the more so because she knew why he had gone to all this trouble to speak to her alone. He wanted her to kill someone.

Ever since he had discovered her other career, he had been anxious to have her go to work for his agency on a free-lance basis; although why his agency, with all its resources, couldn't take care of such matters itself was a mystery to her. She'd asked him about that the first time he had proposed a candidate for her attentions. 'There are certain difficulties for us,' he admitted.

'That apply to you and not to me?'

'But you're outside the law,' he'd said with a smile to show that he was joking, which was the way they usually conducted these conversations, although she knew he was serious. Dead serious. Ha ha.

What he said was true. She *was* outside the law, and she intended to stay that way. When she'd been a paid hit woman, she'd had no choice except that of refusal. Now that she was independently wealthy, she could pick and choose. She dealt only with those lawbreakers whom the law could not touch, like United Nations personnel who committed crimes for which they could not be prosecuted because of their diplomatic immunity. She was not a policewoman, she kept explaining to Andy; the only time she took the law into her own hands was when there were no other hands to receive it.

And she had her limitations. She lacked the expertise of the trained assassin, who could function with the same efficiency (or inefficiency) in any part of the world. She could not follow a criminal out of the country and confront him on his own turf. Even in Washington she was not at her best. Only last year she had botched her killing of the Romanian *chargé d'affaires*, leaving a bloody mess of which she was thoroughly ashamed outside the Lincoln Memorial. The only reason she had taken him on in the first place was that ever since it had become obvious that there was a serial killer at work gunning down diplomatic malefactors, the diplomatic community in New York had become so well behaved as to qualify for near sainthood.

Perhaps she had placed too many limitations on herself. Wouldn't someone like, say, Carlo (the Bat) Battaglia be an appropriate candidate for her gun? The Bat was said to be the current head of the Puzzone 'family', the nation's first family of crime in the opinion of many, although there were other contenders for the title. He had achieved this eminence through killing—or, as he climbed in the hierarchy, having had killed—everyone who stood in his way, including all the Puzzones. He was also said to be behind most of the organized crime in the city—drugs, loan sharking, illegal gambling, white slavery, bribery of public officials, and toxic waste dumping; and, except for a couple of minor episodes early in his career, he had never been convicted of so much as a traffic offence.

She could not fault the police in this regard, for they seemed to be doing their best to get him behind bars. Yet, every time he was brought to trial, which happened at regular intervals, he was acquitted for lack of evidence. Witnesses vanished before they could testify, after which their bodies—sometimes dismembered—would appear in secluded spots in the metropolitan area. Jurors turned mysteriously reluctant to vote for his conviction. Evidence disappeared from the district attorney's office. Once the district attorney himself disappeared from his office.

Surely the Bat was worthy of her gun. But how would she get at him? She was not likely to meet him in her own social circles, nor could she march into Federigo's Fish House in Little Italy and gun him down. She would be too conspicuous there. If only he would frequent places like La Caravelle or the Four Seasons it would be a cinch to kill him.

She did not regret having killed the man outside Rundle House. Certainly he was no loss to the community. But she was not going to make a habit of killing pimps. Pimps were simply not up to her standards.

'Now, who is it you want me to do away with this time?' she asked Andy. 'Don't tell me; let me guess. You want me to kill Salman Rushdie on behalf of the Ayatollah Khomeini.'

'More likely the Ayatollah Khomeini on behalf of Salman Rushdie—and a lot of other people,' Andy said. He looked thoughtful. 'No, you'd never be able to get near him.'

'I was afraid you were going to suggest that I put on a veil and shoot him through it.'

'Speaking of veils, have you ever heard of the Begum of Gandistan?'

'There must be a number of begums in Gandistan.'

'But only one who's known outside of Gandistan. You must know who I mean.'

She did, indeed, as did everyone who read the news-

284

papers and magazines. For such a retiring lady, the Begum had gotten a lot of press in recent years. She had been the principal wife of the late Sultan of Gandistan, having worked her way to the top through a combination of intrigue and attrition. Over the more than fifty years of his reign, the sultan had had dozens of wives, both simultaneously and sequentially. She was the only one who had lasted. Most of the others had died—some of sudden ailments, some by the executioner's axe. A half-dozen (those with the most powerful connections) had managed to escape through divorce. Three had simply disappeared.

During the final years of his life the sultan apparently became monogamous, with the Begum as his only queen —a sop to Western sensibilities, according to some, an acknowledgment of his failing powers, according to others. Whenever he appeared in public, she was always at his side, mute, veiled, but unmistakably a presence. When he passed away, she was reported to have been at his side. Enemies of the regime claimed she had poisoned him.

Her son, Prince Serwar, was the sultan's only legitimate male heir; for, of the two hundred or more children the sultan was said to have sired, no other male survived. The sons who had been young men when the Begum first made her appearance as a junior member of the harem had died, one after the other, in a succession of hunting accidents. Since then, all other male children had died in infancy. Prince Serwar had plenty of sisters but no brothers. His claim to the throne was undisputed. Perhaps old King Serwar had been genuinely interested in forging ties with the West, for Prince Serwar had been educated at Harvard, the first member of the Gandistani royal family to be educated outside the country. Frogface, as he had been affectionately known at Harvard, had been a popular figure, with a warm interest in sports, the opposite sex, and liberal causes, in that order.

It had been expected that once he ascended the throne things would change. The culture of the opium poppy would be prohibited in Gandistan, along with the manufacture and export of its derivatives. Convicted criminals would not be deprived of bodily parts. There would be no more torture of prisoners and summary executions without trial. Prisons would be brought up to at least subhuman standards. Schools and hospitals would be built. Censorship of the press would be ended. Child labour would be abolished. There would be universal suffrage, guided tours, and indoor plumbing.

So far, none of these things had come to pass. In fact, although this might have been only because expectations were so high, conditions in Gandistan seemed to become even worse than before. Even the carpets—their only export outside of opium—seemed to have deteriorated. And now the begum was at her son's elbow, mute, veiled, omnipresent. Rumour said that she was, as she had been for the past decade or more, the real ruler of Gandistan.

The Begum was . . . how old now? No one knew. Considerably younger than her late husband, for he'd married her some thirty-five years before, when he was in his fifties. He was not likely to have taken unto himself a bride of more than eighteen years old tops, for in Gandistan there was no Western nonsense about children bearing children. A girl of childbearing age was a woman and that was that.

So the Begum would be in her early fifties at most. She was good—or, rather, if rumour was correct, bad—for years to come.

'I know whom you mean when you say "the Begum of Gandistan",' Susan admitted, 'although, strictly speaking, the title of "begum" is applied to women of rank, rather than royalty.'

'I'll bear that in mind,' Andy said. 'What do you think about taking her on? All expenses paid plus a handsome fee to you or the charity of your choice.'

Susan laughed. 'You can't seriously expect me to go to Gandistan and kill her?'

'Well, no. There would be logistical difficulties in getting you into the country. Tourists are admitted, but not exactly encouraged. And they're always followed.'

'Then why bring her up in the first place?'

'Because I understand that King Serwar is going to be coming to the United States within the next few months in order to establish a chair in Islamic studies at Harvard and get an honorary degree, and you can bet that wherever he goes Mama's going too.'

Susan was shocked. 'You mean you want me to go up to Cambridge and shoot his mother at the commencement ceremonies?' If it had been Princeton or even Yale, it wouldn't have been so bad, but *Harvard*!

Andy laughed and shook his head. 'No, I wouldn't expect you to do that, but he'll be spending time in New York, and he'll probably go to parties and things. He used to be a great party-goer, I hear, though with Mama along I doubt he's going to have much fun.'

'Not everyone feels that way about their parents, Andy,' Susan said.

She had managed to sting him. 'Come on, Susan, you know I love my folks. But I wouldn't invite them to a party unless it was—uh—a very quiet party.'

'I know,' Susan said coldly. She had been invited to meet his parents at a quiet party. They had seemed to feel she was in some way responsible for Andy's marrying Jill, and they had treated her accordingly. Which was unfair, since Susan had met Andy only because he was investigating Jill and her former shady artistic associates. However, they'd proved to have no connection with drugs, which seemed to be his chief area of concern, and their other peccadilloes were of no concern to him.

Susan had been a little shaken to discover that Hal Courtenay, esteemed director of the American Museum, had at one time been one of those shady associates. It was he who had recommended Jill Turkel to Susan as an agent. 'She's an excellent woman of business,' he'd told Susan.

And that, at least, had turned out to be true, so, even though Jill had rubbed Susan the wrong way from the start —and occasionally irritated her even now—Susan kept her on as an agent and even allowed her to promote herself to manager. Much could be forgiven someone who, rather than shrinking from verbal confrontations, like Susan, actually seemed to enjoy them. Susan had hoped that falling in love with Andy might mellow Jill, but, although it might have softened her head, it had not softened her heart. As for Andy, nothing, Susan thought, would ever change him.

'Just for the sake of argument,' she asked him now, 'how would you expect me to get at the Begum? Even if she does accompany the King, she might not go out in public at all. If she does, she's going to sit or stand behind him, along with several other veiled ladies, the way we saw her on "Sixty Minutes". How would I know for sure which one she was? It isn't likely I'd be introduced. It isn't even likely I'd be invited. Even if they have a private all-female party, there'd be no way I could get an invitation.'

That wasn't entirely true. Susan felt sure she could get an invitation to any party in New York City, if she set her mind to it. And, in the remote event that she was unable to secure an invitation, she could always crash the party.

But she didn't tell Andy that, because she had no intention of killing the Begum. If Andy's employers wanted the lady dead, he would have to find another agent. 'Perhaps you could smuggle one of your men into the harem disguised as a eunuch,' she suggested helpfully.

'They don't have them any more.' It wasn't clear whether he meant harems or eunuchs. 'Anyhow, you're underestimating your abilities. If anyone could assassinate the begum, it would be you. You have special qualifications.'

'And what are these special qualifications? Beyond my being a woman?'

'Well, only a woman would be able to find out what she looks like.'

'You mean you don't know what she looks like?'

'Not—' he began, then stopped. 'No, we don't know,' he said.

'That does make it difficult, but surely you have female operatives who could do the job.'

'We don't have any female operatives at the moment,' he said.

'Well, you do have a problem, don't you?'

She got up to show that the conversation was at an end. He remained in his seat. 'You're absolutely right. We should have some female operatives, and I'm going to get started on a training programme right away, but that's going to take time. Like most bureaucracies, we move slowly.'

He held out his glass for a refill. She ignored it. He got up and refilled it himself.

'Even if I could kill this begum or would kill this begum,' Susan said, 'I don't see why I should kill her. She hasn't done anything wrong in this country. As far as I know, she hasn't done anything wrong at all.'

'Don't you believe anything you read?' Andy asked.

'Very little of it,' Susan said.

'Take my word for it. Everything you've read about the Begum of Gandistan is true.'

She remained silent.

'How about the people of Gandistan. Wouldn't you want to see them liberated?'

'Of course I would, but I don't see why I should be the one to liberate them. Let them get their own champion, one of their own people. What about the King's sisters? Or, if they're squeamish about knocking off their mother, one of his half-sisters?'

'All of them are in purdah, or so I understand. It's hard to break the habits of a lifetime.'

I did, Susan thought, why can't they? But there was no point arguing. It wasn't her problem. She told Andy, as she had told him a number of times before, that she categorically refused to kill whomever he had suggested for her consideration. And he asked her, as he always did, at least to think it over.

'It's useless. I'm not going to change my mind,' she said, as she had said all those other times. Those other times she had been right. But this time she was wrong.

CHAPTER 6

After Andy had gone, Susan found herself wondering why his group wanted the Begum done away with. It had been obvious why he had wanted most of the other people whose names he had brought up in the past disposed of, but Susan couldn't see how the Begum, no matter what her short-comings, posed any threat to the well-being of the United States.

It was true that Gandistan was a drug-producing country. However, it was a very small country. Surely it couldn't grow enough opium poppies to make it merit such particular attention. Besides, what good would it do to remove the Begum? It wasn't likely that she cultivated the poppies or processed them with her own hands. If she died, the business would continue under new management.

Perhaps this had nothing at all to do with drugs. Perhaps somebody in a position of power in Washington simply didn't like the Begum and had given orders that she was to be disposed of. Regrettable, but such things often happened in political circles, she knew. What puzzled her was how anyone in the United States or, indeed, anywhere outside Gandistan, could have gotten to know a lady who had spent all her adult life behind the veil well enough to have reason to want her killed? It was, as another Oriental potentate had observed, 'a puzzlement'.

Possibly the Begum's life had not been quite as seques-tered as the American public had been led to believe by the mass media. If Susan consulted some more authoritative sources, serious intellectual publications that dealt with the Near East in depth, she might be able to get a handle on the Begum. But she was loath to go to the library and look the lady up. She knew that whenever you consulted a book or a magazine in the library, the very act of filling out a call slip put your choice of reading matter into the computers of the world. She didn't want to go on record as having shown any interest in the Begum, particularly as she was not interested in the Begum, only mildly curious about Andy's interest.

So she put the Begum out of her mind. She would have liked to put the Rundles out of her mind as well, but she was too conscious of her obligations to Rundle House, especially after she looked at the *Times* the morning after her visit there, and saw, buried in the second section (Metropolitan News) a paragraph to the effect that one Philip Lord, many-times convicted pimp and drug dealer, had been found shot to death in his car on the Upper West Side. It was a very small paragraph. Even the tabloids had little more to say. Pimps and drug dealers were found shot to death in that part of town with such regularity that it barely qualified as news.

No notice was taken of the fact that the killing had taken place across the street from Rundle House. But, then, why should it have occurred to anyone on any of the newspapers to make the connection—or even to be aware of Rundle House's existence? It wasn't as if it had been a well-known institution like Covenant House, where even a run-of-the-mill chain snatching would have gotten headlines.

The murder didn't even rate a mention on the broadcast morning news, but then one would hardly have expected it to, what with all the shootings and stabbings that had taken place that same evening, not to speak of the suspicious fires in Brooklyn and Queens, the dismembered body on the Hutchinson River Parkway and the oil spill in the Kill Van Kull. Then there were the less routine crimes, like the bicycle messenger who sprayed affluent-looking women with purple paint, while yelling, 'Down with imperialist whores!' as he whizzed past.

Susan wondered what Lord's girls would do, now that he was no longer there to offer them protection. It would be nice if they would go on to acquire skills that would enable them to earn their livings in a more socially acceptable way, but common sense told her the likelihood was that either they would find a new protector or go on welfare.

Or both. However, she couldn't help feeling a little guilty, so she wrote out a cheque to Rundle House for double the amount she'd originally promised.

And, a couple of days later, as she and Jill were having lunch at Leatherstocking's, she reminded Jill of the cheque she had promised Rundle House, or, rather, that Susan had promised Rundle House on Jill's behalf. 'Don't you think it would be hypocritical of me to contribute money to a cause I don't believe in?' Jill asked.

'As long as I believe in it,' Susan said, 'that's what counts.'

'Yes, boss,' Jill said.

'Besides, it's a worthy cause, if that cuts any ice with you.'

'Worthy, shmirthy,' Jill said. 'Did you read the brochure all the way through? Did you notice who was on the board of directors?'

Jill couldn't be referring to any of the Rundles, Susan reasoned, because she would have expected to find Rundles on the board of directors. Probably she had spotted some indicted investment banker or peculating stockbroker. She still didn't seem to realize that these were the stuff of which boards of trustees were made these days. As long as they succeeded in evading conviction or served their sentences, they were socially acceptable, providing they had kept enough of their ill-gotten gains to make them worth cultivating. But Jill had aroused her curiosity and she made a mental note to find the brochure when she got home and see what Jill was talking about.

'A worthy cause doesn't have to have worthy trustees,' she told Jill. 'Write the cheque or I'll fire you.'

'You're very persuasive,' Jill said. She took out her chequebook and wrote a cheque for a thousand dollars, which she handed to Susan. 'Here, you mail it so you can be sure I've sent it.'

Susan had been wondering how she could suggest that Jill do just that. Jill was being unusually cooperative. I'm going to have to pay for this later, Susan thought.

'Mind you,' Jill said, as she put her chequebook away,

'I doubt that they're going to have much success with their gala. They should have had it sooner. People aren't going to these charity affairs the way they used to. Money's beginning to get tight. Besides, too many party-goers are getting mugged on the way home. The crooks read the papers and lurk outside. A lot of people are hiring bodyguards, but then they have to buy tickets for them too. The whole thing gets to be too expensive.'

'They could save themselves even more money by just contributing without attending the event. I know I'm not planning to go to the Rundle House Gala. Not that I'm frightened, but I'm obliged to go to too many things already.'

Jill laughed. 'We've been through this a thousand times. You know as well as I do that if the contributors were willing to do that there wouldn't be any need for these bashes in the first place. People don't want to contribute major sums to charity unless they can get something in return—either have something named after them or wear fancy clothes and get their pictures in the paper, and maybe even have some fun.'

'Are you planning to go?' Susan asked.

'I haven't made up my mind yet.' But she would go, Susan knew. Jill hated not getting anything she'd paid for, even if it meant she would spend a rotten evening. 'Who knows,' she'd explained to Susan in connection with the Alopecia Foundation's Masked Ball, 'I might get to sell a painting or two. Besides, Andy likes to go to benefits. "You get to meet a lot of upscale drug abusers that way," he always says.'

The fact that Jill had allowed herself to be persuaded into writing a cheque so easily didn't fool Susan into thinking that her manager had mellowed. Jill wanted something out of Susan and she was prepared to make minor (tax deductible) concessions as a basis for what Susan knew were going to be major demands.

A show of Susan's paintings was scheduled to open at the Fothergill Gallery in September, and Jill was determined to make a gaudy international event out of it, with a full-time public relations staff working feverishly to get Susan's name in all the right places—and, inevitably, a few of the wrong ones as well. There would be interviews, press breakfasts, press luncheons, and gala openings (one for insiders, one for outsiders, and, possibly, if the demand was great enough, one for those in-between). Thank the gods, Susan thought, that artists—serious artists, that was—were not in the habit of advertising on TV or she wouldn't have put it past Jill to have a video made. Money—Susan's money —would be spent like water. Although she could afford it, she felt that there were better uses to which it could be put.

Susan knew protest would be futile, but she protested anyway. 'All the pictures are already spoken for, so it isn't as if I needed the publicity.'

Jill gave her the tolerant smile managers reserve for their clients. 'Oh, Susan, Susan, we want to keep your prices up, don't we, especially now that there's this talk of a recession coming. And the way to keep your prices up is to keep your name before the public. Do you think the Sultan of Gandistan would have bought one of your paintings for the royal collection if he hadn't seen your name somewhere?'

'Jill, I've told you before, I resent being marketed as if I —the sultan of what, did you say?'

'Gandistan. I never heard of the place either until this little man wearing a turban turned up waving a cheque-book. But what the hell, it's a real country—I looked it up —and the sultan is a genuine ruler and the cheque is a genuine cheque. It gives an artist enormous cachet to be bought by royalty, even small-time royalty. We really must invite the sultan to the opening. He could be the guest of honour.'

The Sultan of Gandistan had bought one of her pictures! Could this be some ploy of Andy's to arouse her interest? But she couldn't see Andy parting with so hefty a chunk of the taxpayers' money in order to induce her to assassinate the sultan's mother. And why would she want to assassinate the mother of one of her patrons? No, she was looking at the whole thing from the wrong angle. She was a distinguished artist. Why shouldn't the Sultan of Gandistan want to buy one of her pictures to dress up his palace? This was just a coincidence—no more.

'It's time we were going,' Jill said, 'if we want to check on Iverson before we go to the gallery.'

Mr Iverson was the architect working on the Melville Building and, like most architects, he had to be watched carefully lest he go off on some mad flight of fancy. Jill always insisted on accompanying Susan whenever she went to inspect progress on her building. 'You're too soft on the man,' she would say. 'He'll restore the place to its original condition and have it landmarked before you know it if you don't watch out.'

So Susan was surprised when, just as they reached the restaurant door, Jill suddenly said, 'Sorry, forgot—matter of life and death—must run. Meet you at the gallery.' And, jumping into a cab, she was off, leaving Susan staring after her.

CHAPTER 7

All was explained when, a moment later, Susan saw Dodo Pangborn loom on the horizon. Jill must have spotted her lurking outside the restaurant and taken evasive action. The least she could have done was drag me into the cab with her, Susan thought. She's always telling me one of a manager's duties is to protect her clients, and here she deserts me in my hour of need.

Dodo looked after the departing taxi. 'You know, I have a suspicion that she's avoiding me.'

The rules of civilized behaviour being what they are, Susan gave the deprecating murmur suitable under the circumstances.

'It's guilt that makes her act like that. She knows that if she'd only let you show some of your pictures in my gallery, it wouldn't have had to close down.'

Actually, Dodo's gallery had been closed down for showing pornographic exhibits—which takes some doing in New York. Perhaps, if she'd been able to get anything else that would attract the public's interest, she wouldn't have had to resort to the notorious Parenti photographs. On the other hand, nothing she could possibly have exhibited—not even Susan's paintings—could have attracted as much public interest as the Parenti photographs.

'Jill has good contacts. She could help me find work,' Dodo went on. 'But she won't even let me talk to her. Every time she sees me, she runs away. And don't tell me I'm just imagining it.'

I wouldn't dream of it, Susan thought. If I had seen you in good time, I would have run away myself. Everybody ran from poor Dodo these days. Susan had been among the numerous victims of Dodo's next project after the gallery fiasco, but prudence and the fact that her contract with Jill had kept her from making any sizable financial investments without Jill's knowledge had kept her from being taken for very much, so she could afford to forgive, unlike a number of her old schoolmates who were very bitter about their losses. Luckily for Dodo, all of them had agreed not to press charges, not because of old-school solidarity but because they hated to look like fools.

Not that they didn't anyway. 'Who but a fool would have taken the idea of a fashion magazine for older women seriously?' Jill had observed, not being aware of Susan's modest investment in the venture.

'Oh, I don't know,' Susan had replied. 'It seemed—seems like a perfectly feasible idea to me. Of course I don't suppose Dodo knows anything about publishing a magazine.'

'Dodo doesn't know anything about anything,' Jill said, 'except fucking up anything she has anything to do with.'

Dodo's opinion of Jill was no higher than Jill's of her. 'I don't know what that nice husband of hers sees in her,' she concluded, after a highly unflattering sketch of Jill's character, appearance, and abilities. 'I'm sure he could've done much better than that vulgar little tramp.'

'I didn't know you knew him.'

'Oh, well, I introduced myself. Told him I was a friend of yours. He was very sympathetic. He said he was afraid there were no openings at the Resource for the Homeless —I've done a lot of charity work, you know—but he'd keep an eye out in case anything came up. And he bought me lunch.' She eyed Susan hopefully.

'How nice of him,' Susan said, wondering what had gotten into Andy. 'I do wish I could ask you to lunch now, but I've already eaten,' she added mentally, kicking herself for sounding apologetic. 'We ate early because we—I— had an early appointment . . .'

'Couldn't you put your appointment off for a few minutes and have a cup of coffee with me?' Dodo pleaded. 'It's so long since I've had a chance to talk to you, and you've always been one of my very favourite people.'

What could you say to something like that? 'Stop trying to butter me up, you disgusting little sycophant?' That's what Jill would have said, except that her choice of words would probably have been different. What Susan said was, 'But really I'm afraid I'm so late.' Weakly.

'Can't you be just a little later? I'm sure whoever it is won't mind waiting, especially when it's you. It's so good to have a chance to talk to an old friend.'

'Well, just a quick cup of coffee,' Susan said, even more weakly.

M. Bumppo looked ill-pleased to see Susan return in Dodo's company. 'But you have already eaten,' he protested, as if the meal had somehow slipped her mind.

'I've come back for another cup of your delicious coffee, while Ms Pangborn has lunch.'

Being French, M. Bumppo had not been trained to conceal his feelings. Horror, shock, and dismay all manifested themselves upon his distinguished countenance. 'But there is no more room. Every table is occupied . . . except for those that are reserved,' he added, as Dodo started to point out the obvious empties.

Susan appreciated his position. Even though Dodo's

meal was going to be paid for, he was reluctant to have her hang about his establishment. It lowered the tone.

'I had hoped you would stretch a point for an old and, I had hoped, valued customer. However, we can go to Le Cirque. They always have a table for me.'

He groaned. 'Oh, I suppose it is possible to squeeze you in somewhere.' And he gave them a table in a dark corner, close to the kitchen.

'He has some nerve putting us here,' Dodo said. 'Surely you're not going to sit still for it. Why don't we just get up and go to Le Cirque and teach him a lesson?' She looked at Susan hopefully.

'Dodo, I have no time to spend going from restaurant to restaurant.'

'Oh, all right. It was for your sake I made the suggestion. It doesn't matter where I sit. He can put me in the kitchen if he likes. I don't care.' But M. Bumppo's chef certainly would, Susan thought.

Dodo studied the menu. 'I'm glad to see M. Bumppo has given up trying to offer his own versions of early American food. Pity he doesn't give up calling himself Natty Bumppo, too. Of all the ridiculous pretensions!'

Susan had often felt the restaurateur had gone a little overboard in his enthusiasm for James Fenimore Cooper, but she wasn't going to let Dodo Pangborn put him down. 'He's done very well with those "pretensions" of his. Leatherstocking's is one of the most successful restaurants around.'

'He has a good PR man. Or woman. I expect, since he's French, it would have to be a man. You know, I was going to open a restaurant, but my backers backed out at the last minute. Something to do with me having been in jail. But that had nothing to do with the restaurant business.'

It was true that Dodo's conviction had not been food-related. She had done time for having run a brothel—under the guise of a religious institution, but a brothel all the same. The fact that she had been in prison was not likely to inspire investor confidence, especially since it would stand in the way of her getting a liquor licence.

Dodo gave her order to the waiter and returned to Susan. 'I see you've taken my advice and touched up your hair. You look so much better. Blondes always fade so fast. Now, if you'd only do something about the way you dress. You can take it from me, understated elegance is passé.'

Dodo's food arrived with a speed uncharacteristic of the normal stately pace of M. Bumppo's establishment. Clearly he wanted to get rid of her as fast as he could. So did Susan. But how could she get up and go while Dodo was weeping into her oysters *en croûte* with truffles.

'Somehow, whatever I try, I always get into trouble,' she moaned through a full mouth. 'I'm jinxed, it's the only explanation. Sure you won't have some wine, Susan?'

'No, thanks,' Susan said. 'Do you think that perhaps your troubles with the law stem from—have you ever thought of going to a psychiatrist?' She didn't think much of psychiatrists, but she didn't think much of Dodo, either.

Dodo looked offended. 'It isn't as if I was the only one who got into trouble with the law. I hear your brother had to leave the country a step ahead of the SEC. Insider trading, wasn't it, or something like that?'

'Alex and Tinsley sold their brokerage and are travelling around the world with their family. Obviously if there had been any question of—er—hanky-panky, the sale couldn't have gone through.'

This was accurate in fact if not in spirit. For it was from a spirit that Alex and Tinsley had received the stock market tips that had led to their amassing a fortune—the spirit of Nicolas Fouquet speaking through a psychic, or channeler, as they were called these days. The law, so far, did not classify psychic tips as insider information, so Alex and Tinsley were legally in the clear. However, if they continued to operate their brokerage, they would forever be feeling the hot breath of the SEC on their necks.

Since it would be difficult to conduct business under such conditions and since they didn't need the money, being rich now—not beyond the dreams of avarice for in today's greedy world no one can be—but rich enough so they could live in luxury to the ends of their lives without having to lift a finger except to summon the help, they disposed of the brokerage and set forth on their travels. Since neither Alex nor Tinsley was the type to sit around idly, they were planning to go into some other line of work when they returned. 'Probably something to do with the environment,' Tinsley had declared, 'for or against, depending which one's in by the time we get back.'

Dodo looked disappointed. 'I'm glad to know everything's all right with them. Amy must miss them a lot.'

'I miss them too,' Susan said.

She hadn't realized how much she would miss Alex. He was the only person she could talk to, the closest thing she had to a confidant.

But Dodo was not interested in Susan's sufferings, only in her own ends. 'I suppose you see a lot of Amy, now that you're part of the family, so to speak. I'm dying to see her again.'

'She's so busy with her committees and—and things, she hardly has a chance to see her old friends. I haven't spoken to her in—oh—ages.' Amy Patterson was Tinsley's mother and an old schoolmate of Susan and Dodo. She had told Susan she never wanted to see or hear from Dodo Pangborn again. Susan deduced that Amy had been another of Dodo's victims.

'Speaking of old friends,' Dodo continued, 'do you know whom I heard from the other day? Remember the Rundles? Well, of course you do, your family was always so thick with them. I got a brochure celebrating the hundredth or some such anniversary of Rundle House and inviting me to attend their gala. Who would have thought the old place was still going after all these years?'

'Everybody's been getting their brochures,' Susan said. Apparently Lucy had had no need for her as a source of addresses, she seemed to have very good sources of her own. Susan's phone had been ringing with calls from old friends who were similarly surprised to receive brochures from Rundle House after all these years.

'Did you notice the board of trustees? Such strange

people on it. And the Rundles—I would've sworn at least half of those listed were dead.'

Susan made a mental note to have a look at the brochure. If even Dodo Pangborn thought the board members were strange, then they must be strange, indeed.

'I was surprised to see Berry Rundle on the board. Listed as Berengaria Rundle. Hard to believe she never got married. Now you, I can understand. Oh, I know all about Peter Franklin, but that doesn't count. Still, I would have thought that he would have wanted to marry you now that you're making so much money.'

Susan counted to five, which was the most a Melville allowed herself in order to gain control of her temper. 'You still keep your maiden name and you've been married,' she pointed out. She knew that at least one of Dodo's divorce settlements had been predicated on the stipulation that Dodo cease using her former husband's name.

'With me it's different,' Dodo said, shovelling paillard of salmon into her mouth. 'I'm a career woman.'

'Which career were you referring to?'

'All of them,' she said, attacking the crusty rolls.

'As a matter of fact, Lucy Rundle told me Berry was a widow, so she must have been married at least once.'

'So you've been in touch with Lucy and not with Berry? That's funny, when you and Berry were so close, even though she was four years older.'

'Three. And we weren't really close, while Lucy and I were schoolmates.'

'Remember those camping trips your father was always taking the two of you on? You and Berry, I mean.'

Susan was filled with an emotion stronger than any she'd felt in years. She kept her voice calm. 'Father took me on lots of camping trips, and we often took one or two of my friends along, since Mother didn't care for camping. I believe we even took you once.'

Dodo laughed. 'That was a disaster, wasn't it? I was never the outdoor type. But Berry Rundle was at home everywhere, inside, outside, and in-between. The world was

301

her bedroom. I've often wondered, Susan, whether your mother was as blind as she made herself out to be.'

Susan looked Dodo in the eye. 'I haven't the faintest idea what you're talking about.'

Dodo wagged an arch finger. 'Oh yes you do. You can't fool me. Don't tell me it still bothers you after all these years.'

'My goodness, I didn't realize how late it was,' Susan said, without bothering to look at her watch. She got up. 'If I don't leave this instant, I'll miss Mr Iverson; he's the architect who's working on my place.'

'He's the architect who's working on everybody's place this year. Maybe I should have taken up architecture. Interior design, anyway. I always had a flair—'

'Goodbye, Dodo, enjoy your lunch.' And may you choke on your mousse. 'Don't worry, I'll sign for your cheque on the way out,' she said loudly.

But, if Dodo felt humiliated, it didn't show. 'Don't forget to send me a ticket to the opening of your show,' she called after her departing hostess. 'At least that won't cost you anything.'

Susan left the restaurant, conscious of the fact that M. Bumppo was giving her back reproachful glances. So let Dodo badger his other customers, Susan thought; into each life some rain must fall. She must watch herself. She was developing antisocial tendencies.

She remembered those camping trips all right. At the beginning she had wondered why Berry Rundle, who was not only older than she was but mature and sophisticated beyond her years, had wanted to go camping with her. All the same, she couldn't help feeling flattered that Berry would want her as a friend. Even when, as time went on, it was only Berry who was asked to join them on their camping trips and none of her other friends, it seemed perfectly natural. Most of the other girls didn't care for guns, didn't even know how to shoot.

Shooting was her father's favourite sport. He had turned Susan into an expert shot. However, she liked to shoot at targets. She did not like to kill innocent animals. He liked to kill animals, regardless of their innocence or guilt.

Berry was also a killer, and also, as Susan recalled, a pretty fair shot. Both she and Susan's father teased Susan for being so 'squeamish'. She had good-naturedly put up with their teasing, glad she no longer needed to feel guilty about spoiling her father's sport. She kept herself busy by sketching the local wildflowers and taking long walks to observe the beauties of nature. She hadn't realized how much Berry had contributed to her father's sport until, early one morning in the course of one of those long nature walks, she had caught the two of them *in flagrante* in a duck blind.

She should have been suspicious long before, she realized, because she had not been so innocent as to be unaware of Berry's sexual proclivities. The chauffeur, the gardener, the music teacher—that was to be expected. But a father—her father—that went beyond the pale. Even Berry's father —the infamous Edmund—never messed around with his daughter's friends.

There was a scene. Her father blustered. Berry wept. Susan raised her voice.

Later, when her father was off stowing their gear in the station wagon, Berry's tears vanished. 'If you breathe a word to anybody—anybody at all—about this, Susan Melville, I'm going to break every bone in your body, bone by bone!'

Remembering what Berry had done to the gym teacher at her last school, Susan knew this was no idle threat. But that wasn't the reason she never told anybody what had happened. It was because she could not bear to think about it.

She never spoke to Berry again. And, by the time both Berry and Berry's father vanished from the scene a couple of years later, she had almost forgotten that episode in her life. It must have been festering away in her subconscious, though, for, now that Dodo had brought it out, she found she felt angrier at Berry than ever.

CHAPTER 8

She did not, after all, go to the Melville Foundation Building to confer with the architect, nor did she go to the Fothergill Gallery to confer with Jill and Freddy Fothergill. She was in no mood for conferences. What she wanted was to go home and brood. She went home, but there was an impediment to her brooding. Michelle, her housekeeper, was there.

Michelle did not attempt to conceal her displeasure at her employer's unexpected appearance. 'I thought you was gonna be out for the afternoon. You said you was gonna be out for the afternoon.'

'I changed my mind. Please bring me a vodka martini, turn off the television, and try to work as quietly as possible.'

'Maybe I should take the rest of the day off. That way I won't bother you in case you got a headache or somethin'.'

'I don't have a headache. I feel fine. I just have some paperwork that needs to be done in a hurry,' she said, to forestall any conversational attempts.

She went to her study. Presently Michelle came in, bearing a glass on a tray that also held a bottle of aspirin. 'Thank you, Michelle,' she said. Michelle opened her mouth. 'That will be all.' Michelle withdrew, tiptoeing ostentatiously.

Susan sipped her drink and tried to focus on the current issue of *Today*, while Michelle rattled and rumbled in the other rooms. She tried to forget about Berengaria Rundle, about all the Rundles. As a result, she found she couldn't think about anything else. She remembered the Rundle House brochure. This was a good time to have a look at it. Where could she have put it? She rummaged around, opening and shutting drawers, finding all sorts of interesting things she had forgotten about.

Michelle stuck her head in the doorway. 'You lookin' for somethin'? Maybe I can help you find it.'

'No, thank you, Michelle. It's just a brochure, nothing important. I might have thrown it away.'

'If you threw more stuff away, I wooden have so much work.'

'If you have so much work to do, why aren't you doing it?'

'I was jus' tryin' to be helpful, okay? Some folks jus' don't 'preciate helpfulness.'

Michelle left with a sniff. Presently Susan heard the distant—but not distant enough—strains of rap from a radio. She would have liked to let it go, but that would be setting a precedent. It was dangerous to set any kind of precedent with Michelle. Susan tracked her and the radio down to the kitchen. 'Would you mind turning that off?'

'You mean you can hear that all the way out there? My, you must have ears like a bat.'

A bat! I'm getting hypersensitive, Susan thought. I've got to watch it. She returned to her quest, and finally she found the missing brochure, pushed to the back of a drawer crammed with invitations and announcements for events she had no intention of answering or attending. Most of them should, indeed, have been thrown away.

She looked at it. The first thing that struck her about the Rundle House board of trustees was its length. Set in eight-point type, it occupied a whole page of the brochure. Most of the trustees listed were, as they had always been, members of the Rundle family. To her surprise, Lucy was listed as chairman. It was true that most of the other Rundles on the list were of so advanced an age it wasn't likely they'd be able to function. She remembered that Malvina Rundle had been placed in a home for the mentally disturbed some twenty-five years before, and, although madness did not necessarily disqualify you for membership on the board of trustees of a charitable institution, it was generally held advisable that the chairman should be *compos mentis*. However, since Berengaria and Edmund, Jr. were, according to Lucy, living out of the country, which would make them ineligible to head the board, perhaps it was not so surprising after all that Lucy was chairman.

What was really surprising was the other names, non-Rundle names that she had never seen before on any board of trustees of any organization she knew—names that, at first sight, seemed unfamiliar, like Douglas Chiang, Philip Lord, C. Montague Battaglia, Desmond Schwartzberg, Gianfranco Molinelli, Antonio Savarese . . . At the same time, she knew she had heard—or at least read of—most of those names. In the society pages? No. Not in the financial pages either. Now, where had she seen them?

Philip Lord . . . Wasn't that the name of the pimp she had killed? Of course. Quite a coincidence that a member of the board had exactly the same name as a pimp who was killed across the street. Or was it a coincidence?

Then a name on the list sprang out at her. C. Montague Battaglia. Battaglia was, of course, a common name in New York. The telephone directory was loaded with Battaglias. And the C did not necessarily stand for Carlo. Lots of other men's names began with 'C'—Clarence, Cedric, Chauncey —all names you would expect to find on a board of trustees. Ridiculous to think the Bat could be on the board of Rundle House. On the other hand, if a pimp could be on the board, why not a mobster? At least he would be in the right financial bracket. Nonsense, she told herself, they're both coincidences.

Michelle stuck her head in the door. 'I know you're itchin' to have me go but you're too polite to say so,' she announced, 'so I figgered I'd leave early, okay? Have a good night, Miss Susan, an' don' worry if I'm a little late tomorrow on account of family troubles.'

'I won't worry,' Susan said, 'but you might have to.'

'Are you threatenin' me?'

'Yes.'

'Oh. Well, just as long as we know where we're at. See you tomorrow.'

If she comes late tomorrow, Susan thought, this time I definitely will fire her. Should fire her. But good help was so hard to find, might as well stick with the old bad, as break in a new one.

She looked at her watch. Time for the early news. She always watched the news on television. It had become a habit. She so often happened upon candidates for her gun on the news or had the opportunity to observe those already chosen—so much better than the still photographs with which she'd been supplied when she was an employee, and which she had to supply for herself after she had gone out on her own.

The news followed the usual pattern. Yet another trial of Carlo Battaglia had ended in a mistrial, the only remaining witness against him having suddenly recanted his testimony after the others had disappeared. Six people had been killed in the past twenty-four hours, one over the daily New York quota, two accidentally, the rest deliberately; one was what the media liked to describe as an 'execution-style' murder. All the murders were thought to be 'drug-related'. A welfare mother in the Bronx had gone berserk and thrown her three infants out of a fifth-floor window. An abortion clinic had been bombed. A church dignitary, after deploring the bombing, had threatened to excommunicate all pro-choice public officials who were of his own faith and to put a curse on those who were not. The bicycle messenger who had been spray painting rich-looking women had been apprehended and claimed it was a political act to protest female liberation. Tonga had fired off a second manned rocket to Mars. The usual routine.

The rest of the hour dealt with nonviolent, hence less newsworthy, events. A number of celebrities had arrived in the city that day, including several entertainment personalities, a pair of royals, and an ex-dictator who was coming to the United States for medical treatment. For a moment, Susan thought of killing him for his past sins, but decided that he wasn't worth the effort. She'd had enough trouble with the ex-dictator of Mazigaziland, though in the end, it had been an act of God and not of hers that had done him in.

Still looking at the screen, she found herself watching a

stocky young man in a turban and sunglasses descend from a plane at Kennedy Airport. Something familiar about him, but he must be a notable of some kind or the cameras wouldn't be focusing on him. She must have seen his picture somewhere. He was followed by a group of burly men similarly accoutred in turbans and sunglasses, though moustached rather than bearded. A few paces after them came several shapeless black forms that looked like sinister bundles of laundry; and proved, as the camera closed in, to be veiled women.

'Among today's arrivals is Serwar II, Sultan of Gandistan, accompanied by his—er—entourage,' the reporter said.

Gandistan, Gandistan, everything seemed to be coming up Gandistan. First Andy had brought up the Begum, then the sultan had bought one of Susan's pictures, and now here he was in the United States. But Andy had told her the sultan was coming to get an honorary degree at Harvard, as the reporter was now informing viewers, so that was no surprise. If it was true that the sultan never went anywhere without his mother, one of the shapeless bundles must be the Begum.

'Who are the ladies with the sultan, Ralph?' the anchorman back in the studio asked.

Ralph admitted that he had no idea who the ladies were. 'And I couldn't ask because you know how touchy they are about their women.'

The anchorwoman made a face. The anchorman glared at her before she said something that might offend their Muslim viewers. 'None of them could be his wife—or wives —because the sultan isn't married,' he said.

'Rumour has it,' the anchorwoman added, 'that he left his heart at Harvard when he was an undergraduate there. He was unable to marry the young lady, because she was not of his faith.'

The anchorman bared perfect teeth. 'Trust you to find romance everywhere.'

'But I feel so sorry for the poor young couple. To think that a thing like that could still happen in this day and age!'

Susan did not feel sorry for the young man. A sultan should have more gumption. As for the young woman, if a quarter of what Susan had heard about the Begum was true, she'd had a narrow escape from acquiring the mother-in-law to end all mothers-in-law.

Andy phoned that evening. 'Did you see who arrived in town today?'

'The Duke and Duchess of York. Gerard Depardieu. The Portuguese ambassador.'

'They did, indeed. And also, in case you hadn't noticed, the Sultan of Gandistan. And his mother. I thought perhaps you might have changed your mind and would like to have a pop at the Begum. They're staying at the Waldorf,' he added, as if he thought that of itself would tempt her.

'What reason could I possibly have to change my mind?'

'Oh, I don't know. Everything changes—the weather, pace, women's minds. Scratch that,' he added hastily, 'What I meant was people's minds, without reference to gender.'

'Well, I'm still of the same mind. Look, Andy, this joke has been going on long enough. I'm just an artist with a hobby. I'm not a professional assassin.'

'Just sleep on it,' he said.

That night Susan had a dream. The Sultan of Gandistan stood at the foot of her bed. He was wearing a turban but the sunglasses were gone. His eyes were large and sad and, improbably, blue. He stretched out his hands towards her. 'Help me, Miss Melville,' he implored. 'Help me. I have nowhere else to turn.'

'I'm afraid all requests for aid must be directed to my manager, Jill Turkel,' she said. She awoke, feeling vaguely guilty.

The next day Jill phoned to apologize for having deserted her client in the face of Dodo Pangborn. 'I'm sorry but I just can't abide that woman. You don't know what a pest she is.'

'Don't tell me what a pest she is. I've known her since I

was a child, while you've only known her since I became your client.'

'I'm glad to see you admit responsibility.'

'I don't admit any such thing. All I'm saying is that I've suffered longer from her.'

'Well, I've suffered more. As if it wasn't enough that she kept trying to get my other clients to exhibit in that gallery of hers, after it was clear she couldn't get you; and that she tried to get me to invest—either your money or my money; I was never sure—in that silly magazine idea of hers'—Susan blushed inwardly—'she actually goes and asks Andy to find her a job at the Resource. Can you imagine such chutzpah? When she knows what I think of her. And he encouraged her, damn him. He even took her to lunch. I can't seem to make him understand that if he keeps on acting like that he'll never get rid of her.'

'Maybe he doesn't want to get rid of her.'

'Dodo Pangborn! You've got to be kidding. Why, she must be over a hundred years old.'

'We went to school together,' Susan said coldly. 'She's the same age I am.'

'Don't be like that, Susan. You know that wasn't what I meant. Are you suggesting that he's cultivating her for professional reasons, that she's mixed up in a drug ring—something like that? I wouldn't put it past her, but then there wouldn't be any reason for him to bother about it. With her on board, whatever it was would be bound to self-destruct.'

'I know,' Susan said. So, she was sure, did Andy. Maybe whatever it was he was up to with Dodo had nothing to do with her. Maybe he simply was being kind, although surely he could find worthier objects of charity than Dodo.

'Let's eat before we go to the Foundation Building,' Jill said. 'I can't deal with an architect on an empty stomach.'

They breakfasted together at an obscure coffee shop where nobody they knew was likely to run into them, after which they went to the Foundation building, where Jill reduced the architect to a quivering jelly. Susan wondered whether she could get Jill to do something similar to the

310

landlord of the building where she still had her studio. He was giving her trouble.

Before proceeding to the Fothergill Gallery they stopped at Susan's house to pick up her mail, which was delivered late in the residential sections of the city to keep even the most well-heeled citizens from getting too uppity. There, among the invitations and advertisements and letters from friends —none from Peter, but mail service from the Amazon Basin was very poor—was a square off-white envelope with the Rundle House logo embossed on its flap. Inside was a chilly little thank-you note acknowledging Susan's contribution and stating that her tickets would arrive in due course. It was signed 'Diane Fischetti'.

'I got one at my office this morning,' Jill commented. 'You'd think your friend Lucy would have signed the notes herself, since she's the chairman, even if Fischetti is actually running the place. I'll bet they aren't even having the tickets printed until they see what kind of a response they get.'

'That would seem like the sensible thing to do.'

'I can't see how they could possibly expect to raise enough money from a gala to buy the building. Probably they expect the trustees to kick in with the difference.'

'That's what trustees are for, isn't it? Although in this case, I can't see why they bother with the gala at all. Unless it's some kind of money laundering.'

Jill hailed a cab. 'I see you have taken a look at the board of directors,' she said, as they got in. 'I showed it to Andy. He said it was interesting.'

'Did you ask him whether he thought C. Montague Battaglia could possibly be Carlo Battaglia, the one they call the Bat?' Susan asked hopefully.

'Well, actually, I asked him about Douglas Chiang. There's a Hong Kong art collector of that name, Sir Douglas, if I'm not mistaken, and I wondered if it could be the same man.'

'What's so odd about an art collector's being on the Board of Rundle House?'

'Ah, but he's supposed to be a big wheel in one of the Triad Societies. And they deal in drugs, among other things, which is right up his alley. Do you suppose Chinese gangsters and American gangsters pal around with each other? Like Masons or Elks?'

'I have no idea. What did Andy think?'

'I didn't ask him about that. It hadn't occurred to me then.'

Susan felt an unladylike desire to beat Jill over the head with her handbag. 'Did he think that your Douglas Chiang and the Douglas Chiang on the board could be the same man?'

'He just said that Chiang was a very common Chinese name. Then he asked me if you were going to join the Rundle House board.'

'Where on earth did he get that idea?'

'From me. It's perfectly obvious that they're going to try to get you on the board. Over my dead body, remember.'

'Don't tempt me. You know I haven't allowed myself to be persuaded to join any other boards. Why should you think they could persuade me to join this one?'

'Oh, they can probably be very persuasive. Make you an offer you can't refuse.'

Both of them laughed as they got out of the cab and entered the Fothergill Gallery. Although Susan made the appropriate responses, she wasn't really attending to the colloquy between Jill and Freddy Fothergill. Wouldn't it be wonderful, she was thinking, if C. Montague Battaglia did turn out to be the Bat? Rundle House was far more accessible than Federigo's Fish House—at least as far as she was concerned.

Of course trustees weren't generally kept on the premises of the institutions they served, but they occasionally came there and certainly were open to being lured there. How could she get to meet the trustees without offering herself up as a sacrifice to the board?

Cultivating Lucy seemed to be her best bet. She would call Lucy up and invite her to lunch, express her interest in Rundle House, tell her how much she would like to visit

312

the place again, perhaps offer some volunteer help. No, that might involve her in something she wouldn't be able to get out of gracefully afterwards and she always liked to make her exits graceful. Besides, it might give them the impression she actually wanted to be a trustee. The best thing to do, she decided, was simply to have lunch with Lucy and wing it from there.

The days passed, and she still hadn't brought herself to the point of calling Lucy, when Lucy herself called to thank Susan for her contribution and to invite her to a trustees' tea. It was as if the gods had granted Susan's wish in the perverse way that gods have of granting you your heart's desire in such a way as to spoil your enjoyment of it. Susan's mother had dragged her to the Rundle House trustees' teas, and Susan always had nightmares afterwards. In fact, she sometimes had nightmares during the teas. Nobody in her age group had ever done anything but suffer through them, except Lucy, she remembered. Lucy had enjoyed them.

'Lucy enjoys pain,' she remembered Berry saying.

'So you still have those teas,' Susan said. 'Keeping up the old traditions.'

'Actually, we haven't had the teas for some time. I was really sad about it. But, now that we're undergoing a sort of . . . well . . . renaissance, I suppose, we thought it would be nice to get started again. And our trustees are anxious to meet you. There are some of them who haven't seen you since you were a little girl.'

Susan hesitated. She didn't want to go to the tea and meet anyone who had known her when she was a little girl. She was afraid they would pinch her cheek and tell her how much she resembled her mother or her grandmother or, in the case of at least one Rundle still listed as on the board, her great-grandmother. On the other hand, this was the only way she could find out for sure whether or not C. Montague Battaglia was the Bat.

She temporized. 'I'm really very busy with my upcoming show. And Jill is even busier, since she's handling the details.' After all, if they were going to start having the teas on a regular basis, she could always go to a later one. Cowardly custard, she told herself.

Lucy sounded embarrassed. 'We aren't—uh—exactly inviting Miss Turkel. After all, she only bought a pair of tickets. And her mother was never associated with Rundle House the way your mother was—which is why we're so anxious to have you come to our very first new tea. Please say you'll come, Susan.'

'Jill's feelings will be hurt. You might not think so to look at her, but she's very sensitive.'

'Oh, I can tell,' Lucy said, 'and I wouldn't for the world want to hurt her feelings. But, to tell you the truth, she does seem to rub Ms Fischetti the wrong way, and we're very anxious to keep Ms Fischetti happy.'

Ms Fischetti's godfather must be a very generous contributor to Rundle House, Susan supposed.

'You don't have to tell Miss Turkel about everything you do, do you?'

'She seems to expect it.' She had no intention of telling Jill about the tea, in any case, because, if she did decide to go, Jill would insist on accompanying her. The fact that Jill had not been invited, that she would in fact, not be welcome, would cut no ice with her. I'll tell Jill about it afterwards, she said to herself. That is, if I do decide to go. But she knew she was going to go.

As she hung up there was a click on the line. It sounded as if someone might be bugging her phone. Andy? He hadn't seemed interested in Rundle House activities. But, if the makeup of the board was what she hoped it might be, there were other law enforcement agencies which might be interested in anybody who had anything to do with that institution. Looks as if I might be getting into something, she thought, and her pulse quickened with anticipation.

CHAPTER 9

'Sure this is where you want to go, lady?' the driver asked as the taxi drew up in front of Rundle House. If he thinks the place looks bad now, Susan thought, he should have seen it the way it was the last time I was here. There had been a vast improvement. Although the block still could not be described as clean in the absolute sense of the word, there was no more loose garbage lying about. The road no longer seemed to be in use as a parking lot. In fact, across the street where once the silver Cadillac had stood, there were only three cars, a Mercedes, a Lincoln Continental, and a Rolls-Royce, each with a dark-haired young man sitting on the front seat, each with his car radio tuned to a different station.

The boards had been removed from the windows and doors of the apartment house to the right of Rundle House, and scaffolding was being erected around it in what Susan hoped was not an excess of optimism. On the other side of Rundle House, the brownstone showed definite signs of life. The windows on the first floor were unshaded and, between the draperies, she could see the soft glow of silk-shaded lamps and figures moving about. It seemed to her also that she could hear music from inside, although she could not be sure; there was too much noise from the radios in the parked cars. Jill seemed to have been right about the brownstone. It did belong to Rundle House, and that was where the trustees' tea was being held.

She smiled at the cabdriver. So nice of him to be concerned. 'Yes, this is where I want to go,' she told him.

'Well, it's your funeral, lady.'

Someone's funeral, perhaps, she thought, but not mine.

Since Lucy had said nothing about her coming in via the brownstone, she mounted the steps of Rundle House and rang the bell. It took some little time before the door was

315

opened, by a dark-haired young man who looked more like a gangster than the kind of person you'd expect to see at a trustees' tea. That was wishful thinking, she knew. She wanted gangsters; therefore, she saw gangsters.

Behind him she could see that the lobby was dark and empty. The offices of Rundle House must have closed early today, as, she remembered, they always did on trustees' tea days. The young man made no move to let her inside. He stood there waiting.

'My name is Susan Melville,' she told him. 'I've come to the trustees' tea.'

He frowned. 'Are you a trustee?'

'No, I'm a guest. Miss Rundle's guest. Miss Lucinda Rundle,' she added, because there would be other female Rundles around, and she wanted to make her provenance clear.

He still seemed undecided.

'Susan!' a voice called, and Lucy appeared in the lobby. She was wearing a calf-length gauzy garment in a mauve print that was the very epitome of a tea gown, but had probably been offered under the category of cocktail dress, since tea gowns were no longer part of the fashion repertory, unless they had sneaked back when Susan wasn't looking. It had ruffles at neck and sleeve, and there was a lavender velvet bow in Lucy's hair. Ms Fischetti followed, clad in a dark green wool and brocade suit that was obviously a designer original. They must pay their help very well here, Susan thought.

'I'm so happy to see you!' Lucy cried, pushing the young man aside and embracing Susan more warmly than, Susan thought, the renewed relationship justified; but the Rundles had always been an effusive lot. 'I was so afraid you might change your mind and not come!'

'Glad you could make it, Ms Melville,' said Ms Fischetti, with a chilly smile and an even chillier handshake. Clearly, Ms Fischetti had not wanted Susan to come to the trustees' tea. Even more clearly, she had been overruled. But who had overruled her? Lucy? Not likely.

Despite the two ladies' welcome as testimony to her bona

fides, the young man did not seem satisfied. 'All guests are supposed to come through next door,' he said. 'There's a maid to answer the door there. She's wearing one of those uniforms like in the movies and she's got a list of people to let in. Also she's got a metal detector because Mr Schwartzberg says it's not polite to frisk people coming to a tea.'

Susan remembered Desmond Schwartzberg's name. He was one of the trustees of Rundle House; apparently he was their social arbiter as well. She had read or heard something about him, too, recently, but she couldn't remember where or what.

Ms Fischetti looked at the young man coldly. 'I can assure you that Ms Melville is not only an invited guest but the guest of honour. She does not need to be—ah—frisked.'

That shows how much you know, sister, Susan thought, glad to have escaped embarrassment, if nothing more. But what was this about her being the guest of honour? Probably a ploy to put the young man even further in his place.

He looked cowed. Ms Fischetti turned to Susan. 'I must apologize, Ms Melville, but these days everyone's got to take precautions.'

Against outsiders, perhaps, but that didn't explain why they were having their invited guests searched or why, if guests were supposed to arrive at the brownstone, there was a guard at the door of Rundle House. Ms Fischetti looked as if she knew what was going through Susan's mind, but she offered no further explanation.

Lucy looked penitent. 'It's my fault. I forgot to tell you the party was going to be held next door.'

'I didn't know the house next door belonged to Rundle House.'

'Oh, Rundle House has owned it for years,' Ms Fischetti informed her. 'We bought it years ago when real estate around here was going for a song, and it's used for most of our administrative functions. That way we can use the whole of this building for the mothers.'

But the director's office was on the ground floor of this building, Susan thought, and she had seen other offices

317

upstairs, when she had been given the grand tour. How many administrative offices did they need? The trustees' room would be next door, of course. Perhaps an apartment for Ms Fischetti. But that would leave three floors unaccounted for.

'The tea's this way,' Lucy said. Slipping her arm though Susan's, she led her towards the door that had been the object of Jill's inquisitiveness on their previous visit. Susan looked back over her shoulder. The young man had moved into the back of the lobby and taken up a post at the foot of the stairs. Under his tight-fitting jacket, she could see the outline of a gun. He was not guarding the door at all; he was guarding the stairs. But against what?

Then she saw the glitter of eyes in the darkness at the top of the stairs and heard the muffled giggles. He must have been posted there to keep the unwed mothers from trying to crash the tea.

Poor things, Susan thought, they never get invited to the Rundle House festivities, not even those being held next door. She hoped they had parties of their own. Baby showers, perhaps. Did unwed teen-aged mothers get to have baby showers? She must ask Ms Fischetti later. It would give them something to chat about.

The door opened directly into a large room which occupied the whole of the brownstone's main floor except for an anteroom at the front and an archway that led into what appeared to be an annex in the back. The room was furnished in traditional trustee style—panelled wooden walls, solid mahogany furniture, Oriental rugs, portraits of past Rundles glaring down from the walls. None of the modernistic frivolity of the lobby. This was serious decor, meant to impress.

Advancing over the threshold, she felt as if she had stepped back in time. There was the long table covered with a gleaming white cloth and upon it the huge silver urn she remembered so well. The Crown Derby looked like the very same china they used to bring out at every tea, and the muffins, petits fours, finger sandwiches, and other small comestibles piled upon them the same refreshments—at least the same kind of refreshments—they used to serve. A pianist was playing the same old show tunes on what looked like the same old Bechstein. There even was the same smell of furniture polish.

One obvious change had been made. A bar had been set up in one corner, with a white- jacketed barman presiding over it. There had been a bar in the old days, too, but discreetly hidden in an adjoining room, so that old Mrs Rundle could pretend to be unaware of its existence. 'We have to have it; otherwise we'd never get any of the gentlemen to come,' Susan could hear the younger Mrs Rundle whisper to Susan's mother. Not that, even with this inducement, very many of the men put in an appearance at the teas. The atmosphere alone would put a dampener on their spirits, her father had been heard to observe.

Today there were a lot more men present than there had been in the old days. At first sight most of the people there seemed unfamiliar; then she picked out a few aged and bewildered-looking Rundles who had apparently been hauled out of their retreats, dusted off, and propped up here and there among the furniture, holding teacups in their shaky hands and smiling vacantly.

And of course she recognized the chunky, middle-aged man in the custom-made Italian silk suit who was talking to the imposing-looking lady behind the tea urn. He was, as she had come to expect by this time, Carlo Battaglia, C. Montague Battaglia, the Bat himself, the man she had so often seen and hissed in her mind on TV, the man for whose sake she had come here. If she needed further confirmation of his identity, the small weasel-faced man in English tweeds at his elbow was the small weasel-faced man who had been at the Bat's elbow every time she saw him entering or leaving a courtroom, the man who kept smiling at reporters with perfectly capped teeth and saying, 'Mr Battaglia has nothing to say at this time.'

Name and face came together. His lawyer. Desmond Schwartzberg. Mouthpiece for the mob. *New York* magazine had done a feature on him. He sounded like a slimebag. He also sounded like the lawyer she'd want to hire if ever she should happen to get caught in her avocational activities. His clients always seemed to get off, although the judge and jury weren't always so lucky.

She was, of course, gratified to see the Bat. It meant that she had not inflicted this ghastly fête on herself in vain. At the same time, she found herself even more stirred by the sight of the woman sitting behind the urn, the woman who rose to her feet upon catching sight of Susan and cried, in a stentorian voice that boomed back over the years, 'Susan Melville! Long time no see!'

Susan halted in her tracks. 'Hello, Berry,' she said. 'It has been a long time, hasn't it? My, you have grown a lot.' Berengaria Rundle seemed to be over six feet tall, but who knew how high the heels might be under the shimmering caftan of heavy green silk that swept the floor, as, abandoning the Bat and his lawyer, she swept across the room and enfolded Susan in an embrace even warmer than her sister's.

Really, Susan thought, if she's going to go around hugging people, she shouldn't douse herself in cheap (though probably pricey) Oriental perfume. Through the thick makeup and the extra chins, Berry was barely recognizable. If only Daddy could see her now, Susan thought, but her father was dead; and, if he had still been alive, probably he wouldn't even have remembered who Berry was.

Berry seemed to have done well for herself financially, either through marriage or other means, for the outsize emeralds and diamonds clustering around her neck and wrists and dripping from her ears were all vulgarly real without a doubt. There was even a diamond fillet threaded through the black braid that crowned her head, creating a tiara effect that was most unsuitable for a tea. Evidently she didn't worry about getting mugged on the way home, Susan thought.

The caftan obscured the lines of Berry's figure, but couldn't hide the fact that she had increased in girth far more than she had in height. Fat, fat, the water rat, Susan thought, regressing.

She looked at Berry and a wave of hatred engulfed her. She didn't want to kill the Bat—yes, she did want to kill the Bat, but even more did she want to kill Berry Rundle. Now, now, she chided herself, a Melville must let herself be controlled by reason, not desire, but she did not feel at all reasonable.

Berry kneaded her arm. 'When they told me you were coming to the tea, I was so excited I could hardly wait.'

'She was like a little girl,' Lucy said, 'so full of questions, asking me what you looked like now and what you were doing and whether you ever spoke of her.'

She took her sister's other arm and stroked it fondly. Could she really have forgotten the things Berry used to do to her, Susan wondered.

'I suppose you must be wondering why I never got in touch with you all these years,' Berry said.

Susan counted to five. 'I've lost touch with so many people over the years. And a lot of people have lost touch with me. It's to be expected.'

'Life marches on,' Lucy observed.

Berry made a small hissing sound between her teeth. She'd always done that when exasperated, Susan recalled. 'I've been living abroad ever since my marriage. While my husband was alive, I never could manage to get away to come back home for a visit. He depended on me so much, especially in his last years.'

'I'm sorry to hear your husband is dead,' Susan said.

'He was a lot older than me, so it wasn't unexpected. He died a couple of years ago, but I've been so busy getting his affairs in order I've only had time for a few flying trips back to the States. I hope you'll forgive me for not looking you up.'

'Think nothing of it,' Susan said. 'I'm surprised you even remember me.'

'Oh, I remember you, all right.'

'Where were you and your husband living abroad?'

Susan asked. Not that she cared, but it seemed a safe topic of conversation.

Apparently Berry had become a little hard of hearing, because she seemed to misunderstand the question. 'He died at home, in his sleep. It was very peaceful.'

'I'm so glad to hear that,' Lucy said. 'I hate to hear of anyone suffering.'

Her sister gave her a baleful glance.

'What country—?' Susan began.

'But at least I have a son left to console me,' Berry went on, as if Susan hadn't spoken. 'That makes up for a lot.'

For a lot of what, Susan wondered. Could Berry's marriage have been less than idyllic? She hoped so.

'He's a wonderful boy. Everything a mother's heart could desire, except that he hasn't given me any grandchildren.'

'That's because he isn't married,' Lucy pointed out. She looked guiltily at Ms Fischetti. 'Of course people can have children without being married or there wouldn't be any reason for Rundle House. But not people like us.'

'I look forward to meeting your son, Berry,' Susan said, looking around to see which of the young thugs present might be Berry's offspring.

Lucy giggled. 'Oh, he isn't here. He said he wouldn't come within a mile of the place again after what happened the time he came to look around. I told him the mothers weren't going to be at the tea, but he said he wasn't going to chance it. He—'

'Come, dear,' Ms Fischetti said, taking Lucy's arm, 'you'll feel better after you've had some more tea.'

'But I feel fine. And I don't want any more tea. I want to see Susan meet Mr Battaglia again. It's so romantic.'

Again? What on earth was Lucy talking about? However, Carlo Battaglia certainly seemed interested in meeting Susan. He was advancing on her, breathing heavily, or perhaps that was the way he always breathed. 'Aincha gonna interduce me, Di?' he demanded of Ms Fischetti. 'Ya know I came here specially to meet this lovely lady.' And he indicated Susan with a wave of his arm which would have been a pat if she hadn't moved away.

'I was just going to, Uncle Charles,' Ms Fischetti said.

'I thought he was your godfather!'

'He's my uncle,' Ms Fischetti said coldly.

'It's my fault,' Lucy said. 'I'm always making that same mistake.'

Somehow Ms Fischetti was the last person Susan would have taken for a Mafia princess, but sociology degrees did funny things to people.

Ms Fischetti turned to her uncle. 'I was waiting for Ms Melville to finish saying hello to—to her old friend before I brought her over to meet you.'

'No, I'm the one who oughta be brung over to meet her, ain't that right, Queenie?' And the Bat dug his elbow in Berry's caftan at the approximate point where her ribs should be. Berry did not look amused.

I wonder if everybody calls her Queenie or whether that's just his name for her? And how does she come to know her well enough to call her by a nickname? Had she been the wife of a Mafia—what did they call them?—don, and was that why she had been lying low all these years? It figured.

'Susan Melville, may I present my uncle, Charles Montague Battaglia,' Ms Fischetti said formally.

The Bat bowed low over Susan's hand. She had often wondered why the media referred to him as 'the handsome don'. Seeing him in the flesh now, she conceded that he had a certain crude animal attractiveness.

'It is a honour and a privilege to meetcha, Miss Melville. I seen your paintings—Di took me to the museem specially —and I reely like 'em, because you can tell what they're about, not like mosta the stuff they call art nowadays.'

Desmond Schwartzberg winced and shot a glance at Susan that was supposed to establish a communality of spirit. She pretended not to notice.

'Acksherly I metcha a long time ago. When Johnny del Vecchio married that bubble-headed broad—what was her name? Mimi something.'

'Mimi Fitzhorn,' Susan said.

'For heaven's sake!' Berry cried. 'I never knew Mimi married a—a friend of yours, Carlo.'

'He was my second cousin,' the Bat said. 'It was a terrible tragedy, him being shot down like that. You don't remember me,' he said to Susan, 'How couldja? I was a skinny kid—and look at me now!'

He gave a hearty laugh. Everyone else gave a wary smile. 'But I never forgotcha. I thought ya were the classiest lady I ever seen.' He breathed even more heavily. 'And ya still are, even classier, if that's possible.'

The pianist launched into 'Some Enchanted Evening'. Ms Fischetti gave him a dirty look.

This has to be some kind of joke, Susan thought. Mob humour.

'Uncle Charles—' Ms Fischetti began.

His voice overrode hers. 'I can't tell ya what a thrill it is for me to be on the same board of trusties as a classy lady like you. Not that you two aren't classy,' he assured Berry and Lucy, 'but you're Rundles. People expeckcha to be on the board. But she's no relation, which makes the whole thing a lot classier.' He beamed all round.

'Uncle Charles—' Ms Fischetti began again.

This time it was Susan's voice that overrode hers. 'Mr Battaglia, I'm afraid you're under a misapprehension.'

'Call me Carlo, Susie.'

'I am not a member of the Rundle House board of trustees.'

He looked arch. 'Not yet. But a little bird told me ya were gonna join and'—he laughed jovially—'I wooden be surprised if ya were gonna be ast to be chairlady of the big bash, which I understand is quite a honour. They don't ast just anybody to be chairlady of a classy party like this one's gonna be; ya gotta be somebody special. Which ya are.'

And now it was Susan whom he dug in the ribs.

CHAPTER 10

Susan was outraged. The idea! Taking her for granted like that. Even a gangster should know better. Ms Fischetti certainly did. She looked dismayed. Even Berry looked uncomfortable. Only Lucy seemed unperturbed, smiling away in her own little world.

I've got to be careful, Susan thought. I don't want to provoke a scene with the Bat. He might go off into one of those screaming rages I've heard of. And I might forget myself and shoot him in front of all these people, which would be not only suicidal but gauche.

She picked her words carefully. 'Mr Battaglia—'

'Carlo.'

'Carlo, I know it's a great honour to be asked to be chairman of the Rundle House gala, but, if the chairmanship should be offered me—and really I've done nothing to deserve it—I couldn't accept. I haven't the time to serve on a board of trustees, let alone chair a benefit. They're both very great responsibilities, and I take my responsibilities very seriously.'

The Bat looked accusingly at his niece. 'Ya promised me she was gonna join the board. I want her on the board. And I want her to be chairlady of the gala.' He thrust out his lower lip and looked ready to stamp his foot. On someone else it would have been funny.

Desmond Schwartzberg placed a restraining hand on his arm. 'Now, now, Mr Battaglia, you must restrain your enthusiasm. Remember your blood pressure.'

'Mr Battaglia has a tendency to let his enthusiasm for a worthy cause run away with him,' he said to Susan. 'I'm Desmond Schwartzberg, by the way, Mr Battaglia's attorney, and also a trustee.'

'Mr Schwartzberg,' Susan murmured. They shook hands in an incongruously civilized way.

'Sorry I didn't get a chance to introduce you two before,'

Ms Fischetti said, 'but things started getting so—so out of hand.' She turned to the Bat. 'Uncle Charles, didn't we agree that we were only going to talk to Ms Melville about joining the board, that we were going to tell her how much we'd like to have her as a trustee . . .'

'Yeah, yeah,' the Bat muttered, 'but—'

'We can't just rush at her the instant she comes in the door and tell her she's going to be a trustee.' Ms Fischetti's tone was admonitory.

Susan held her breath, but apparently the Bat would take this kind of thing from a relative. He smote his forehead. 'I guess I just don't understand how things work in society. But what can ya expect from a simple guy in the removal business?'

Susan was startled. She hadn't expected him to be so candid about his activities.

'Furniture removal,' Ms Fischetti elucidated. 'Uncle Charles owns a moving and trucking corporation. Battaglia and Sons. You may have heard of them; they have an international reputation.'

'Estimates cheerfully given without charge,' the Bat added. 'also extensive storage facilities, both hot and cold.' His mind appeared to be elsewhere. 'I got it all figgered out,' he announced. 'It's like in the old days. A girl would always say no a couple times before she said yes.'

'Uncle Charles!'

He flushed, to Susan's amazement. Could gangsters actually blush? It didn't seem right somehow. 'What I meanter-say is it's the same with askin'' a lady to be a trusty. She's got to be coaxed. I like that. I'm an old-fashioned guy. Sorry I jumped the gun, Susie—'

'But the guns are all in the cloakroom,' Lucy said. 'I saw them there myself. In the old days people never took guns to tea. To weddings sometimes, but—'

'Shut up, Lucy,' Berry said, quite as if it were the old days.

'I'm sorry I was maybe too anxious to getcha to say yes right away,' the Bat told Susan. 'About joinin' the board,

I meantersay, but, like Schwartzberg says, it's such a good cause I was sure ya'd wanna support us.'

'Of course it's a good cause,' Susan said, 'that's why I bought two tables for the gala.'

'And most generous of you,' Ms Fischetti said. 'That's what made us think of you as a possible member of the board.'

Susan could hear Jill saying, 'I told you so,' but no, they'd been planning this long before Susan made her contribution. Lucy's having waylaid her in Leatherstocking's was no accident. I am never going to eat there again, Susan thought. No more fashionable restaurants for me. From now on it's exclusively coffee shops, diners, lunch counters, places where no one could possibly look for me. 'But there are so many worthy causes—the homeless, abused children, AIDS—' here the Bat frowned and she changed that to 'incurable diseases'. 'I can't give my time to all of them.'

'Nobody's astin' you to. Just this one. This one is special because—'

'Because your mother was on the board of trustees and it was her favourite charity,' Berry interrupted. 'Because your mother was my mother's best friend. Because . . .' She stopped there, but Susan in her mind could hear the fifteen-year-old Berry saying, 'Because, if you don't, I'll break every bone in your body.'

'Of course we can't force you to become a trustee,' Ms Fischetti said.

Her uncle gave her a look. 'We wooden wanna force you to become a trusty,' he said to Susan.

Lucy put her hand on Susan's arm. 'All we're asking you to do is think about it. That isn't too much to ask for old times' sake, is it?'

It was a great deal too much to ask, but Susan made the noncommittal noise that serves instead of speech on such social occasions.

It seemed to satisfy Lucy. 'Come, have some tea and then we'll circulate and you can meet the other trustees.'

'What a good idea!' Ms Fischetti cried, more enthusiastically than the suggestion seemed to warrant. 'Circulate, by all means. That way, Ms Melville will get some idea of—get some idea.'

Teacup in hand, Susan dutifully circulated with Lucy, glad to get out of the line of fire for the moment. It turned out that only a handful of those present were actual trustees, as listed in the brochure. There were three aged Rundles who smiled vacantly and said of course they remembered her and one who just smiled vacantly. The elegant middle-aged Chinese gentleman who spoke with a British accent told her he was from Hong Kong and how much he admired her paintings and hoped one day to have some in his collection, so he was probably Jill's Douglas Chiang. Not that she'd doubted it once she'd seen the company he was keeping. Nor was she in any doubt about the occupations of the three Italian men who kissed her hand and smiled and appeared to speak little or no English.

Edmund Rundle, Jr.—although she supposed he was no longer a junior now that his father was dead—was not present. 'He was sorry he couldn't make it,' Lucy said. 'There's always so much to do in Peru.'

'I understand it's a very busy country,' Susan agreed.

'And we'd hoped Cousin Malvina could come, but this turned out to be one of her bad days.'

None of the other people present was introduced. 'You can meet the volunteers another time,' Lucy said.

They didn't look like volunteers; they looked like hoods. Susan had no desire to meet them at any time.

As Susan and Lucy started back towards the tea table, the door to the building next door burst open and the gangsterish-looking young man burst over the threshold, shut the door behind him, and stood with his back to it. His eyes were wild, his clothes in disarray; there were red streaks all over his face and shirt. From behind him came the sound of shrill screams, fists beating on the door, and gunshots.

'It's a raid!' someone cried. Several of the 'volunteers' stepped forward, guns in their hands. Apparently they had not been required to pass through the metal detector.

The young man put up his hand. 'It's not a raid. It's those girls. They'—he turned red—'I can't say what they tried to do to me, but I'm not gonna go out there again.'

The screams were girlish laughter, Susan realized, the red streaks, lipstick. There was a ripple of laughter.

The young man looked sullen. 'When I went to work for you, Uncle Carlo, I never expected nuttin' like this.'

'Now, Nicky,' the Bat said, 'you meantersay you can't handle a bunch of high-spirited teen-aged girls in the family way?' There were more shots from the lobby. 'And you let 'em get your gun too, dincha?' He shook his head sadly.

This time the laughter was louder.

Ms Fischetti looked grim. 'Don't blame Nicky. You don't know those girls. I'll take care of them. Get out of the way, Nicky.' Opening the connecting door, she strode through.

Everybody watched her admiringly. 'Now there,' said Mr Schwartzberg, 'is a very capable woman. You should be proud to have a niece like her.'

'I yam, I yam,' the Bat said. 'As for you, Nicky, I'm ashamed of you. Go clean yourself up. I'll deal with you later.'

Nicky paled. Surely, Susan thought, they wouldn't do anything drastic to him. He hadn't been derelict in his duty, merely overwhelmed by *force majeure*. 'You're not—' he almost whimpered '—you're not gonna tell Mama . . . ?'

'I haven't made up my mind yet,' the Bat said. He took Susan's arm.

'Is Nicky Ms Fischetti's brother?'

'Cousin. Come have some more tea.' He guided her back to the table where Berry was presiding over the urn.

'Some fun, eh?' Berry said. 'Trustees' teas were never like this in the old days.'

She began to pour.

'No more tea for me, thanks,' Susan said. 'I've had a wonderful time and I hope to see you all again soon. But I must leave now. Pressing engagement.'

She would find some way to kill the Bat at a time when he was not surrounded by relatives and henchpersons. Now that she had been formally introduced to him, it should be easier to get at him. Not easy but easier. Maybe she could hint to him that she might be willing to chair the gala if . . . If what? She would think of something. There was no hurry about killing him. There was a hurry about getting out of there. She didn't know how much longer she would be able to keep control of the situation. If she was in control of the situation.

The Bat gave her arm a gentle squeeze. 'I know what you're thinkin'.'

She gave a guilty start.

'You're wonderin' what somebody like me and them'—he waved a hand towards the non-Rundle trustees and their associates—'are doin' here, why we're spendin' so much time and money on this.'

Susan hadn't been wondering at all. Rundle House activities were being used to cover other activities of a nature she could only guess at. The only thing of which she was sure was that they were nefarious. That should have been plain to the meanest intelligence.

Apparently it wasn't. 'I don't see why anyone should wonder,' Lucy said. 'It's a splendid cause.'

'Right you are, cookie,' the Bat agreed. 'None splendider.' He turned to Susan. 'Ya see, what we all got in common is that we all believe in life and Rundle House'—he took a breath—'Rundle House represents the affirmation of life.'

Is he joking, Susan wondered. More mob humour? Am I expected to laugh? Better not.

Lucky she didn't, because the Bat didn't so much as crack a smile as he went on, 'Somebody gotta pertect the lives of the innercent unborn. It ain't enough to bomb abortion clinics—'

Mr Schwartzberg coughed.

The Bat paused and chewed his lip. 'What I meantersay is we gotta supply a alternative to those murder mills without bombin' 'em or even'—he looked wistful—'settin' 'em on fire. We gotta act positive.'

He glanced at the lawyer, who nodded.

'We gotta take care of those poor teen-age girls so they

330

shunt feel there's nuttin' they can do but kill their own innercent unborn babies.' His voice rose. 'If I could only get my hands on those murderin' medicos—'

'Mr Battaglia, Mr Battaglia, as you yourself said, we must take a positive approach,' Mr Schwartzberg interrupted. 'And you know you mustn't let yourself get excited . . .'

'Yeah, yeah, yeah, I know I gotta watch my blood pressure, but I get so darned emotional when I really care about sumpin. I'm a very emotional guy. Comes of bein' Italian.'

He looked at Susan. 'You like Italian food, Susie?'

'I'm very fond of it,' she said, startled by the sudden transition.

'What kind do you like best?'

'Perhaps we could discuss Italian cuisine another time, Mr Battaglia—Carlo. Right now I really must rush. I've enjoyed meeting you—all of you—so much, but I do have a dinner engagement.'

'With a handsome high-class fellow, I'll bet. I'm jealous,' the Bat declared with a twinkle.

Hard enough for her to accept a gangster who blushed. Now here was a gangster who twinkled. My heavens, she thought, he's flirting with me. It was the last thing she had expected when she had come there to meet him, but then she'd had a number of surprises that evening, and she had a feeling that if she didn't leave right away she was going to have even more. Unpleasant ones, as most surprises are.

'I will forgive you only if you promise to have dinner with me,' the Bat went on, 'very soon. I'll call you and we'll make the arrangements.'

Looks as if I'm going to have access to Federigo's Fish House after all, she thought.

CHAPTER 11

'I want to talk to you,' Berry said to Susan.

'We must have lunch together one day,' Susan said, starting towards the front of the brownstone, where she assumed the exit must be . . . and the metal detector. She hoped it wasn't retroactive. 'Then we can have a nice long talk and catch up on—on things.'

'I want to talk to you now.' Berry clamped a firm hand on Susan's arm, bringing her to a halt. Berry's rings, great gobs of rock and mineral, bit cruelly into Susan's flesh through the thin material of her sleeve. Susan didn't let herself wince. She would not give Berry the satisfaction.

The Bat beamed at the two ladies, 'So nice to see old friends getting together after so many years.'

'It warms the heart; it really does,' Mr Schwartzberg agreed.

Ms Fischetti came back into the room looking dishevelled but triumphant. Berry caught her eye. 'Let's have some more tea,' Ms Fischetti said, without looking at Susan.

She took her uncle by the arm and led him back to the tea table. Mr Schwartzberg and Lucy followed. Lucy settled herself behind the tea urn. 'Let's all have lunch together,' she called out to Susan.

The Bat looked over his shoulder. 'Remember, you and me are gonna have dinner together real soon, Susie. I'll give ya a ring.' He didn't ask for her number, which didn't mean anything, of course. If he really meant to call her, he could get it from Lucy.

'I'm so glad you and Carlo hit it off,' Berry told Susan, as she urged her, virtually pushed her, towards the archway in the back of the room. 'It makes things simpler.'

Susan had almost forgotten her original purpose in coming to this place. She recollected it now. Yes, it did make things simpler for her. But what did it do for Berry? Surely she wasn't trying to 'fix Susan up' with the Bat? The idea was ridiculous!

'We'll go upstairs where we can be private. I have a little place up here that I've been using—that I'm planning to use as a pied-à-terre when I'm in town,' Berry explained. 'I expect to be here a lot now.'

It seemed an odd place for a Rundle to pick for a pied-à-terre, but one could hardly expect reasonable behaviour from Berry Rundle. And why did she 'expect to be here a lot now'? Was it simply that having wound up her late husband's affairs she was free to spend more time in her own country? Or did she have some other reason for being 'here a lot'—something connected with whatever it was that was going on?

'I've told you I've got to leave now. I have a dinner date.' She tried to pull away from Berry, but Berry had a grip of iron. 'This won't take more than a few minutes. And it's only a little after six. Even an American wouldn't think of having dinner before eight.'

So Berry didn't think of America as her country any more. No loss for America, but what country did she think of as her own then?

Susan tried to protest. 'I have to meet my friends for cocktails at seven.'

'Nobody ever arrived on time for cocktails in my day, and I'm sure things couldn't have changed that much. Anyhow, there's plenty of time. I won't keep you long, and afterwards my driver will take you wherever you want to go, so you won't have to worry about getting a taxi.'

'If I can't get a taxi, I can always take a bus.'

'A bus! Public transportation! Don't be silly, Susan.'

'I could even take the subway!'

'Now I know you're kidding!'

There didn't seem to be much chance of avoiding a tête à tête with Berry. Even if she resisted, she had a feeling that Berry would simply drag her bodily across the room. And no one would blink an eye. The Bat would simply assume that this was the way middle-aged upper-class ladies disported themselves on festive occasions. Ms Fischetti and Mr Schwartzberg would pretend not to notice. The others—oh, who knew what foreigners would think?

So Susan allowed Berry to lead her through the archway. Beyond was a narrow flight of stairs, an open door through which came catering noises, and a closed door, which Berry opened. She pushed Susan inside and thrust herself in afterwards. The door shut behind them, cutting off all sound from the party.

Susan found herself in a very small elevator, barely large enough for two average-sized people. Although Susan was slim, there was enough of Berry beneath that flowing caftan to make at least two average-sized people. In so confined an area, the scent of Berry's perfume was overpowering. I'm going to be sick, Susan thought; still, if I have to throw up on anyone, I would rather it was on Berry Rundle than anyone else in the world.

But she managed to retain both her dignity and her lunch, and they emerged on the top floor into a small square foyer without any untoward incident en route. Ahead of them was a blank wall. On the other two sides patterned silk curtains hung from floor to ceiling. What light there was came from the dim bulbs in two metal wall sconces. Except for the faint strains of a recording playing what sounded like oriental rock, it was quiet.

Berry parted one set of curtains, put her head through, and said something in a language Susan didn't recognize. The music stopped and a woman wearing a plum-coloured patterned silk tunic and trousers came out, wrapping a scarf around her head. She bowed to both ladies and held the other set of curtains aside so they could go through. As the curtains closed behind them, Susan heard the sound of the elevator descending.

She and Berry came into a room which seemed almost bright after the murkiness of the foyer, even though it was lit only by fast-fading daylight. The room was good-sized by New York standards, but it seemed small because it was so full of things—Oriental carpets and hangings, silken cushions, ornate screens, carved furniture, gold and ivory and jade figurines, pierced metal lamps, and the like. It was like a room in an expensive Oriental bazaar, rather, an office in an expensive bazaar, for there was a small desk of some wood she could not identify, inlaid with other woods equally unidentifiable by her, all probably rare and expensive. On a carved wooden stand stood a computer, with a paisley shawl thrown over it. Susan wondered whether Berry had decorated the place herself.

There was a reek of sandalwood that Susan soon identified as emanating from a metal bowl on a side table. An incense burner. Susan was sure Berry was not burning incense to conceal the smell of pot, which was what incense burners had been used for in her younger days. She was burning incense because she liked it. Heaven knew what kind of country she had been living in.

I would ask her to open a window, Susan thought, but through the thin gauze curtains and the grille beyond—a common feature of New York windows that led to fire escapes, as this one did—she could see that the room overlooked a rundown, possibly abandoned apartment house, its backyard filled with trash. All that opening the window would achieve would be to add the odour of decaying garbage to the sandalwood.

Berry seated herself behind the desk, and indicated that Susan was to sit in the chair opposite, a carved teakwood affair with clawed feet and ferocious heads on the tips of both backposts. The desk was crowded with a clutter of artifacts, all silkbound, gold-inlaid, jewelled, and otherwise ornamented to the fullest extent that their various functions would accommodate. Who would ever have believed that the owner of that desk had attended Miss Pinckney's School for Young Ladies, however briefly? Even Dodo Pangborn had better taste, and she had been expelled.

A carved ivory frame held the photograph of a dark, clean-shaven young man in his mid or late twenties, good-looking in a batrachian sort of way. Berry followed the direction of Susan's gaze. 'My son,' she said, turning the picture so Susan could see it better. 'Isn't he handsome?'

'Very handsome,' Susan agreed. Where had she seen that face before? Did he resemble one of the senior Rundles? She dismissed the thought. It wasn't a Rundle face. It was a foreign face, an alien face. 'Is he staying up here with you?'

'He's here in town, but not here in this building. It's no place for a young man. Or a man of any age. Those mothers! You saw what they tried to do to poor Nicky. Little bitches.' But she chuckled all the same.

'I'm surprised you have anything to do with them yourself. As I recall, you were never the altruistic type.'

'But I'm grown-up now, Susan,' Berry said. 'I've changed. There are a lot of things about me that would surprise you.'

Suddenly Susan remembered where she had seen Berry's son before. A lot of things fell into place. I doubt that there's anything about you, Berry, that could surprise me now, she thought. But she didn't want to disclose her new-found enlightenment. It would not, she felt, be prudent. She kept her face and voice impassive. 'I suppose all of us have hidden depths, Berry.'

Berry gave her a suspicious look. 'Don't try to be enigmatic, Susan. It doesn't suit you.'

'I wasn't trying to be enigmatic, Berry. I was just asking you where your son is staying. Of course, if you don't want to tell me—'

'He's staying at a hotel downtown, and I'm staying there with him while he's here, except when I have to be away on business, like now. I hated to leave him even for a few hours, but he wouldn't come up here with me.'

'I suppose you can't bear to let him out of your sight.'

The intent was ironic, but Berry took her literally, 'You can bet I can't. I know he'll go running off to see that girlfriend of his. But how did you know about her? Did Lucy tell you? She's such a blabbermouth.'

'Lucy didn't tell me anything. She didn't even tell me you had a son. How old is he?'

'Twenty-eight.'

'Surely he's old enough to pick his own friends. And see them whenever and wherever he pleases.'

'That's not the way we do it in our country,' Berry said. 'There, children respect their parents' wishes.'

Her son must be a wimp to put up with this, Susan thought. If he does, indeed, put up with it.

'But it isn't just that he goes off like that,' Berry said. 'He goes off alone. He keeps ditching his—his attendants.'

'Attendants! Oh, I'm so sorry. I didn't realize. I remember what used to happen when your cousin Malvina got away from her attendants. And your Uncle Hubert—'

'There's nothing wrong with my son!' Berry snapped. 'They're more like bodyguards. It just isn't safe for a foreigner, particularly a young, well-dressed man, to wander about New York alone. Not that, from what I hear, it's safe for anyone to wander about New York alone.'

'Things aren't as bad as the media make them out to be,' Susan told her. At least the mayhem here wasn't officially sanctioned the way it was in some other countries. But she couldn't tell Berry that until she had told her a lot of other things first. 'What's your son's name?'

'I call him Sonny,' Berry fitted a cigarette into a long jade holder, the likes of which Susan hadn't seen since her schooldays. 'They won't let me smoke anywhere any more here,' she complained. 'Some nonsense about it being unhealthy. Unhealthy, tcha! Every time I come back here, they're off on some health kick—fitness, pollution, vegetarianism, no smoking, no drugs, no nuclear power, no nothing. And they call this a free country!'

She puffed furiously. 'Do you smoke? The last time I saw you you were too young. Of course, I started smoking when I was eleven, but then, I was always precocious.'

'No, I don't smoke. I did smoke for a while when I was in college, but I gave it up. Not for health reasons; I . . . just gave it up.'

'Good for you!'

Berry waved a dismissive hand. 'Enough of the small talk. Let's get down to business. Susan, we need you on the board of Rundle House.'

'It's very flattering of you to ask—'

'I'm not asking, I'm telling.' There was an imperious note in her voice, born of years of command, but this was the United States of America, for heaven's sake. Berry had no authority here, no authority whatsoever.

Berry leaned across the desk. 'There's a vacancy on the board of trustees and, since you're the one who caused it, you're the one who's going to have to fill it.'

CHAPTER 12

The room did not go dark around Susan. Instead, it seemed to splinter into a multitude of bright, flickering colours. She felt dizzy, as if she had been sucked into a paisley-patterned whirlpool. She struggled for control. I must not give Berry Rundle the satisfaction of seeing me hyperventilate, she thought.

What seemed to be someone else's voice uttered the words appropriate to the occasion: 'I haven't the least idea what you're talking about.'

Berry made that hissing sound. 'Don't give me that, Susan; you know perfectly well what I'm talking about. I don't know why you shot Phil Lord and, to tell you the truth, I don't care. I always said it was a mistake to put him on the board in the first place.'

Susan took an unobtrusive breath. 'Am I to understand that you're accusing me of having shot someone named— what was it?—Lord?' She would have laughed, except that she was afraid she would be unable to achieve the correct note of merriment. 'Me! You're mad, absolutely mad!'

Berry smiled and shook her head. 'I know it sounds crazy, but the fact remains that you did shoot him and you were seen doing it.'

'If I had done such a thing—absurd as the idea is—and I had been seen, surely the police would have been called.'

'Not necessarily. People around here don't care much for the police, as you might imagine.'

'Is that why you live here, Berry?' Susan couldn't help asking.

Berry glared at her. 'You want to know why I live up here? All right, I'll tell you. It's because I'm cheap. Don't try to sidetrack me. You killed Phil Lord and you can't get out of it.'

'Has it occurred to you that this alleged person who allegedly saw me shoot this alleged other person might be lying through his or her alleged teeth?'

'They wouldn't dare lie to me! Besides, who could make up a story like that?' She laughed uproariously.

Susan counted to five. 'Tell me, who was this Mr Lord and why am I supposed to have killed him? Revenge? Jealousy? Lovers' quarrel?' And she laughed, too, though in a far more decorous manner.

'I already told you; I don't know why you killed him. As far as I know, you never set eyes on him before in your life. He was a drug dealer and a pimp. He was sitting in a car across the street from Rundle House when you came up to him, poked a gun in the window, and shot him. Maybe he said something you didn't like. Maybe you had a fit. Maybe it's your time of life. Some women do strange things when they get to be your age.'

I'm three years younger than you are, Susan seethed inwardly. Not that you haven't been doing even stranger things than I have, and starting to do them a lot earlier. But then, as you yourself pointed out, you were always precocious. Aloud she said, 'I assure you, your informant, whoever he—or she—may be, is quite mistaken. Unless you're making up the whole thing just to annoy me.'

'Now, why would I want to do a thing like that?'

Susan couldn't answer that without getting down to personalities, so she contented herself with a shrug.

'What beats me is how you happened to be carrying a gun in the first place,' Berry went on. 'I'm told, though, that in New York today lots of people you wouldn't expect to be carrying guns are packing them. In fact, I wouldn't be surprised if it turned out you were carrying one at this moment, since I understand you didn't get to go through the metal detector because Lucy is such a goop.'

'What beats me is how a pimp and a drug dealer got to be on the board of trustees of Rundle House.'

'I told you I thought it was a lousy idea myself. Beggars

can't be choosers, the Fish told me, but I always say choosers don't have to be beggars.'

'The Fish? Oh, Ms Fischetti.'

'That's what the girls call her. I understand. And it fits. She is a cold fish. Not the kind of gal you can warm up to.'

'She seems very efficient,' Susan said, moved by an obscure desire to praise anyone of whom Berry expressed disapproval.

There was a rap on the doorframe. Berry called out what Susan assumed was an invitation to enter. The woman in plum-coloured silk came through the curtains carrying a tray on which was a tea set and plates stacked high with what looked like refreshments from the party. In response to a command from Berry, the woman cleared away most of the bric-à-brac from the top of the desk and arranged the contents of the tray on it. Berry spoke to her again. The woman lit several of the lamps—it had grown quite dark outside—and withdrew.

'You didn't get a chance to have much tea,' Berry said, 'and I could use another cup myself.' She poured tea for both. She took milk in hers and lots of sugar. Susan took hers straight. She would have liked lemon but there seemed to be none available.

'Sandwich?' Berry asked. 'Tea cake? Muffin?'

'No, thanks, I'll have just tea.'

Berry put her cigarette holder down in an onyx ashtray and, after some deliberation, selected a petit four. 'As I was saying,' she said, through a full mouth, 'if you play ball with us, nobody has to know what happened to Phil, except you, me, and, of course, the lamppost.'

'And if I refuse to play ball, whom are you and the lamppost threatening to tell? Mr Battaglia? Or does he know already?'

'Not on your life, and I do mean your life! It would destroy all his illusions, and it's important for men to have illusions. They're not hardheaded and practical like us gals. And I didn't tell the Fish either, in case you're worrying about that, because I wasn't sure how she'd take it. She tends to get stuffy about unauthorized operations.' Berry contemplated the plates, took a finger sandwich, and bit into it.

'Then whom are you threatening to tell?'

'Watercress! I told that idiot not to bring any watercress! I hate watercress! Just wait until I get my hands on her!' She caught Susan's eye. 'Oh, well, I suppose one couldn't expect her to understand.'

She picked up the half-eaten sandwich. For a moment Susan thought she was going to put it back in the plate; instead, she put it in the ashtray. Then she opened sandwich after sandwich until she found something she fancied.

'Oh, I'm not threatening to tell anybody,' she went on, through a full mouth, 'and the lamppost is out of the country, so he couldn't tell anybody even if he was so inclined. Anyhow, even if he had called the police when it happened, they wouldn't have believed you killed Phil unless they caught you with the smoking gun in your hand. Little Goody Two Shoes; that's what you always were as a kid, and now you're Big Goody Two Shoes.'

That was one of the things that had made Susan so successful as an assassin; she was so improbable. At the same time, it would have been embarrassing to have to explain matters to the police. From now on, she must watch these lethal impulses of hers. Any killing she did must be carried out with care and forethought. Mere dislike for someone, she told herself, as she eyed Berry wistfully, was not sufficient cause for eliminating her. Or him.

Berry picked up a cookie. 'I just want you to realize I know you're not as pure as you make yourself out to be, and you have no right to turn up your nose at the Rundle House board.'

'But I'm not turning up my nose at the board, and I've certainly never made myself out to be pure. I just make it a rule not to belong to boards of trustees. If you don't believe me, just check my bio in *Who's Who*.'

'Oh, believe you me, I have checked your bio. That's what convinced me you'd be perfect for our purposes. One of the things that convinced me, anyway.'

Susan didn't ask her what the other things were. She didn't want to know. 'I can't understand why you feel you need me. There must be lots of people who'd be glad to serve on your board.'

'Nobody with your "class", dear,' Berry sneered. 'And I promised Carlo I was going to get him—us, that is—a classy board of trustees. Sure, the Rundles still have a position in society, but the rest of the board of trustees—well, you've seen 'em.'

'It wasn't class that they seemed to lack,' Susan said. 'What I mean is, Mr Chiang seemed classy enough for all reasonable purposes to me. And those Italian gentlemen—well, standards in Sicily probably are different from what they are here. No doubt in their own country they rank high on the social scale.'

Berry gave her a long, cold look. 'What we want to do is bring in other trustees who have class according to local New York standards. We want to make this gala a big success. Your name alone would sell dozens of tickets.'

Which was true enough, and one of the reasons Susan didn't join any boards. It wouldn't be fair to the boards she didn't join and would lead to hard feelings among her friends. 'I would think that with Mr Battaglia and his—er —associates on board, you'd be able to get all the money you needed. You wouldn't have to sell tickets at all.'

'When did any charity get all the money it needed just from trustees' contributions?'

'It depends on the kind of trustees you have.'

Berry took a muffin. 'Sure you won't have something, Susan? You didn't eat anything downstairs.'

Susan shook her head.

'Well, if you want to starve to death, it's your funeral.'

And if you want to eat till you burst, it's yours. For heaven's sake, hadn't the woman ever heard of cholesterol?

'I gather you recognized Carlo even if you didn't remember him from Mimi's wedding. So she was married to Johnny del Vecchio.' Berry shook her head. 'My, my, who would have believed it!'

'Mimi's been married to a lot of people since then, includ-

342

ing a count and a rock singer. Her present husband is a baron.'

Berry looked resentful. 'My late husband was . . . very well placed, well placed, indeed. You'd be surprised at how high a position he held.'

'I'm sure I would.' Susan smiled graciously to show Berry that she understood and sympathized with Berry's desire to give the deceased due honour, perhaps more honour than was his due.

Berry picked up her cigarette and puffed furiously at it. 'I was hoping Carlo would manage to win his way into your heart before you found out who he was.'

'Surely you must have realized that I'd be bound to have recognized him from television.'

'I didn't think you'd be a television watcher, or at least that you'd watch any news programme but *MacNeil/Lehrer* and I don't believe Carlo was ever on that though I could be wrong. I watch Cable News Network myself, because that's what we get in my country.'

She got up and began to walk up and down the room. As she turned her head to keep her hostess in sight—you wouldn't want to turn your back on Berry Rundle—Susan kept meeting the stare of the animals on the back of her chair, which seemed to have moved slightly in her direction, so that they could keep her under observation. Their eyes were black and white enamel, their protruding tongues blood red, and their teeth very sharp and white.

'It's like this: Carlo has been very generous in his support for Rundle House but he does expect something in return.'

'I thought he was committed to the cause of those poor, unwed teen-aged mothers-to-be. Surely the knowledge that he's helping them should be enough; that is, if he's really sincere about his commitment to the sanctity of human life.'

'Oh, he is, he is. If he wasn't sincere, would he bomb abortion clinics? No profit out of that. He does it because he believes in it.'

'And you—are you committed to the sanctity of human life?'

Berry made an impatient gesture. 'I can take it or I can leave it.' She sat down again, to Susan's relief; she was getting a crick in her neck.

'What I'm committed to is carrying on the work my family began. Understand?'

Susan was too well-bred to give Berry what in their youth would have been called the raspberry, and perhaps still was.

'Like a lot of people who've made money, Carlo has a yen to make it on the social scene. He knows one way to do it is to get on the board of trustees of a prestigious nonprofit organization. He's even thinking of buying some high-prestige business, like Bloomingdale's, for example. Did you know it was for sale? I was really surprised when I found out. The things that have happened to New York since I last lived here . . . it boggles the imagination.' She shook her head sadly. 'Altman's and Gimbel's gone, Bloomingdale's bankrupt, Saks fifth Avenue in the hands of Arabs!'

'I know, I know.'

They shared a moment of nostalgic silence.

'What the city needs is a firm hand on the rein, but then the power of the mayor is so limited that even an effective one couldn't do much. Now, if I were running the show, I could clean it up in no time.' Berry's eyes shone with administrative fervour. 'Let me tell you what needs to be done.'

Her ideas were sound, Susan had to admit, but carrying them out would require a total suspension of civil liberties, which would be impractical. Although the individual New Yorker was not unduly respectful of other people's rights, he (or she) set great store by his (or her) own.

Anyhow, the reorganization of the city was not her primary concern at the moment. Did Berry really think Susan was so stupid as to accept the idea of Carlo Battaglia as a social climber, or, even more improbably, of Berry herself a do-gooder?

Apparently she thought Susan was even stupider than that. 'Don't get me wrong. It isn't because you're way up in the stratosphere societywise that Carlo wants you. He has a yen for you. He's a widower—natural causes; his wife choked on a fishbone—and he's on the lookout for a new one. I know you'd think a fellow like him would naturally go for some teenaged bimbo and, all things being equal, he probably would. But he's a family man and he has three grown sons who wouldn't like the idea of him getting hitched to a girl who might produce more sons to compete with them. This way he gets their blessing. More tea?'

'No, thanks.'

'Muffin? Sandwich? Tea cake? Brownie?'

Susan shook her head. Almost absent-mindedly, Berry helped herself to one of each. 'Mind you, I'm not insisting that you get involved with Carlo, if you really don't want to; all I want from you is that you join the board of trustees. Or trusties, as Carlo would say.'

'I still can't understand why Rundle House has come to mean so much to you now, Berry,' Susan said, 'why it means anything. Lucy, yes, she would do anything for Rundle House, but you never cared about it. In fact, as I remember, you used to spike the trustees' tea with marijuana, long before it became pot, and you sneaked boys into the unwed mothers' rooms until Miss Henderson said, Rundle or no Rundle, she was going to have you committed to a home for delinquent juveniles unless your mother kept you away from Rundle House forever.'

Berry smiled reminiscently. 'I was quite the little cutup wasn't I? I remember—' she stopped, and the smile left her face. 'I was a child then. I'm not a child any more. I've become aware of my social responsibilities.'

'I'm glad to hear it, but please don't try to involve me with either Rundle House or Mr Battaglia. I have my own responsibilities.'

She started to get up.

'Sit down!' Susan stood still. She wasn't going to walk out, because that would necessitate turning her back on Berry. Neither was she going to obey her commands.

Berry assumed a placatory tone. 'All right, *please* sit down, Susan. Surely you owe me the courtesy of letting me finish what I have to say.'

She didn't owe Berry anything, but an appeal to courtesy could not be denied. She sat down again. The heads on the back of her chair seemed to have grown closer together. Was this one of those trick pieces of furniture you read about in old-fashioned horror stories, the kind that squeezed the unwary sitter's head flat? But what good would a flat-headed Susan do Rundle House?

Berry's eyes were very bright. 'What can I offer you to persuade you to become a trustee? Money—I suppose you have enough for your simple needs. Position—you've already got that; it's why we want you. Power? I'm not sure I'd want to give power to you, Susan. So what's left? Your life. You shot one of our trustees. You'll take his place on the board or I'll shoot you.'

And she'd enjoy doing it, Susan thought. She hates me just as much as I do her. But why? I have a reason to hate her. But she has no reason to hate me. She's up to her old tricks—trying to scare people into doing what she wants. Trying to scare people for the sake of scaring them. She can't be serious.

'You're joking.'

'No, I'm not.'

'You wouldn't dare.'

'I would, too.'

'Somebody might see you.'

'It's a chance I have to take. You took it.'

'No, I didn't.'

'Yes, you did. Don't argue with me, Susan.'

'I'll argue with anybody I want to.'

True, as Berry had observed, she wasn't a child any more, and neither was Susan, but no one who overheard the two of them at that moment would have agreed to that.

Susan decided she would have to take the offensive if she was ever to get out of that stifling, overcrowded, claustrophobic room. 'What makes you think you could shoot me, especially now that you've warned me? Remember, I'm a crack shot.'

Berry laughed. 'Sure, you were pretty good at target

shooting, but you've never gone after live game. Oh, I'll grant you Phil Lord, but he was a sitting duck.'

Was she deliberately, maliciously referring to that long-ago episode at the duck blind? Could even Berry be that crass and insensitive? Yes, she could. She made that clear when she went on, 'Even when we were kids you were never as good a shot as I was. Buck himself said so. And I've had a lot of practice since then.'

So have I, Susan thought, so have I. And you were never as good a shot as I was. Daddy (Buck, indeed!) told you you were, for reasons which I would rather not think about. I could shoot you right now. Even if you're holding a gun in one of those pudgy overringed hands you're so ostentatiously keeping behind the desk, I could outdraw you. I have been watching too much television, she thought, I might as well ask her to step outside and settle it there.

'You think I'm just talking through my turban? You know how many people I've killed, Susan? Dozens.'

You have no idea of how many people I've killed, Susan thought. Hundreds. What a pity she couldn't tell Berry that, wipe that smug look off her face.

'And, now that we're letting down our hair, let me tell you, my husband didn't die a natural death. I killed him.'

'But you didn't shoot him. You poisoned him, which takes no skill whatsoever. Any harem girl—' She cut herself short, but it was too late.

CHAPTER 13

There was silence. Then Berry's voice came, very softly: 'So, you know who I am?'

'You're the Begum of Gandistan, and that's why the Bat —Mr Battaglia—called you "Queenie". You are a queen, in a manner of speaking.'

'Not "in a manner of speaking". I *am* a queen. I was never a harem girl, and you'd better remember that if you want to go on living.'

Susan's hand firmly gripped the gun in her lap. She knew that, although she could kill Berry easily enough, she didn't have a chance of shooting her way out of a building packed with gangsters, thugs, and Heaven knew what other kinds of lowlife. 'Yes, Queenie,' she said.

Berry glared. Then she laughed. 'I keep forgetting I'm not in Gandistan. Actually my proper title is sultana, but I don't use it because it makes me sound like a raisin or something. I don't know why the media insist on calling me "the Begum"—some kind of putdown, I don't doubt. The foreign press have had a grudge against me ever since —well, never mind that. But you can keep on calling me "Berry". No need for formality among old friends.'

'Thanks,' Susan said.

'Who told you I was the so-called begum? It was supposed to be a secret. If Lucy—'

'I keep telling you Lucy didn't tell me anything.' Although why Susan should defend Lucy, when Lucy was the one who had gotten her into this, she didn't know. 'Nobody told me. I didn't even know you were the Begum or Queen or whatever until you showed me your son's picture. Then I recognized him. Not right away, though, because in the picture he didn't have the beard and the turban—and, of course, the dark glasses.'

'What are you babbling about?'

Susan counted to five. 'He was wearing them the other day when he arrived at Kennedy. I saw him on TV. I suppose you were there, too, lurking behind one of those black burnooses. You were always fond of fancy dress, Berry, but, really, don't you think—?'

'They're not burnooses, they're *burquas*, and all proper Islamic women in Gandistan wear them to cover their faces.'

'So you converted to Islam?'

Berry looked angry. 'Of course I converted to Islam. Otherwise the sultan wouldn't have been able to marry me.'

A Mohammedan Rundle! Old Mrs Rundle must be spinning in her grave. But then a Jewish or a Catholic Rundle would have caused a similar revolution, and even a Methodist would have made her coffin rock.

'There ought to be a law against TV. Against all cameras. Nowadays, if you're anybody at all, you can't go anywhere without being followed by them. In this country, I mean. In Gandistan there is a law against them.' And she laughed. Clearly it was not safe to be a TV cameraman in Gandistan.

'At least you can hide behind your veil, or whatever you call it.'

'And I'm thankful for that. My life wouldn't be worth living if people knew what I looked like.'

'Oh, it isn't as bad as all that. I know you've put on weight, but I understand that in some countries plumpness is considered attractive. Just the same, if you keep stuffing yourself with fatty foods like that, you're heading for a coronary.'

Berry put the muffin she was about to lift to her mouth back on to the plate. 'I meant my life wouldn't be worth living if people could recognize me,' she snarled, 'and I don't need you to lecture me about my health.'

She put another cigarette into her holder, lit it, and puffed furiously.

Andy had expected Susan to recognize Berry. He had known Berengaria Rundle was the Begum of Gandistan and that Susan had known her as a child so she would be likely to have access to her. But that still didn't explain how he knew Susan would have had reason to dislike Berry.

Dodo Pangborn, of course. No wonder he had wined and dined her; probably put it on his expense account, too. Right then Susan didn't feel any better disposed towards Andy than she did towards Dodo.

'What I don't understand,' Berry said, 'is how come you paid any attention to Serwar's arrival. With all those British royals and movie actors flocking into the city, I wouldn't have thought you'd even notice the king of a small, obscure country like Gandistan.'

'Small, but not obscure. There was a lot about it—and

about the royal family—in the media a couple of years ago, just after the sultan died. It all sounded very . . . colourful.'

'All lies,' Berry said. 'Well, maybe not all of it, but highly slanted. I finally had the foreign press thrown out of the country, but that didn't stop them from spreading stories. I thought they'd died down, though.'

'They had,' Susan said, 'but naturally your son's arrival would start things up again.'

'I asked him not to come this time, but he said it would look very odd if he didn't come to get his honorary degree after everything had been fixed up—as if there were some kind of trouble in Gandistan—and I couldn't afford any rumours like that right now. Of course he set the whole thing up so he could get to see Audrey.' And she muttered something in Gandistani which sounded decidedly uncomplimentary to the absent Audrey.

Susan wondered why a king had to go to the length of establishing a chair of Islamic studies in order to be able to see his girlfriend, but decided, in the interests of peace, not to ask. 'The main reason I took an interest in your son was that he bought one of my paintings. Did you know that?'

'Of course I know, you goop. I was the one who bought it. He doesn't know a painting from a poster.'

'My manager said something about inviting him to the opening of my show at the Fothergill this fall.' Might as well put in a word for Jill and her projects.

'He'll be delighted to come, whether he wants to or not, and, what's more, I'll come too—as the Queen of Gandistan, not Berry Rundle. We'll knock 'em all dead with our pomp and circumstance. You just cooperate with us, Susie, and we'll cooperate with you.'

Susan was dying to ask whether the Bat was going to come along too, as part of the pomp and circumstance. Again she decided to leave well enough alone.

Berry leaned forward across the desk. 'Play your cards right, Susie, and we'll buy a lot more of your pictures.'

Susan couldn't help laughing. 'Oh, Berry, Berry, did you really think you were doing me a favour by buying one of my pictures? You've made a very good investment. My pictures have been going up in price every year.'

Berry blew a cloud of smoke into Susan's face. 'Remember this, though. They'll go up even faster after you're dead.'

She's threatening me, Susan thought happily. That settles it. I've got to kill her, no way out of it. Self-preservation, the best reason in the world. Then, after I've finished her off, I'll take care of the Bat, if I have the chance. But first things first.

CHAPTER 14

Susan had dreaded going back downstairs and out through the trustees' room, smiling and saying good night and shaking hands, as if these had been ordinary guests at an ordinary social occasion. But the big room on the main floor was quiet and empty and, except for a couple of low-wattage lamps, dark. Everyone had gone; the food had vanished; the furniture was back in place. Hard to believe that only a little while before a party had been in full swing. It was as if the play had ended, the set been struck, and the cast dismissed.

She glanced at her watch. Almost eight. She and Berry had been talking for longer than she had realized. Berry seemed to have an almost compulsive need to talk ('You have no idea how good it is to have someone to talk to!'), especially after she'd produced a bottle and a couple of glasses from a locked cabinet. 'Afraid it has to be vodka, because a Muslim isn't supposed to touch alcohol, and I wouldn't want any of my people to smell liquor on my breath.'

Susan had accepted a glass. She could hardly refuse to join Berry in her toast: 'Success to all our ventures.' However, she felt sure that she wouldn't want to wish Berry success in any of her ventures, and she felt even more sure that Berry wouldn't wish her success in at least one of hers.

She made only a pretence of sipping her drink, while Berry tossed hers off at a gulp and poured herself another, which she drank as she told Susan the story of her life; how her father had sold her to the Sultan of Gandistan to pay his debts, and how she had suffered as the most junior member of the sultan's harem. 'But not a harem girl. I was his wife, which is a totally different job category. After all, I was a Rundle. Dad wouldn't have settled for less than marriage, even if they had applied lighted matches to the soles of his feet, which the sultan was quite prepared to do, until I talked him out of it.'

'Didn't it bother your father that you had to convert to Mohammedanism?'

Berry hesitated for a moment. 'Oh, that didn't worry him,' she said. 'It wasn't as if he were a regular church-goer or anything.'

'Of course,' Susan said, 'stupid question.'

'I wasn't the sultan's only wife, you understand. He's allowed four at a time, and he already had the full quota, so he had to dispose of one of them so's he could marry me.'

Susan opened her mouth.

'Don't ask,' Berry said.

Susan didn't.

'She'd been very popular with the other gals, so there was a certain amount of resentment towards me. For years I had to be careful not to eat anything unless somebody else tasted it first. Lost a lot of eunuchs that way.'

Apparently she doesn't worry about that any more, at least not here, Susan thought, or she wouldn't have been pigging out like that. All the same, she was glad she herself hadn't eaten any of the refreshments served to Berry. Unless the tea . . . better not think about that.

'But a Rundle never gives in. I hung on, not that I had much choice, and eventually I got to be senior wife and I could call the shots.' Her shoulders shook with mirth. 'Little private joke,' she explained. Harem humour, Susan thought.

*

To Susan's surprise, the media had been more accurate than she'd given them credit for. Berry's story was, allowing for a natural difference in viewpoint, much the same as the accounts Susan had read: how, through intimidation, manipulation, and, she admitted, the occasional annihilation, she had achieved that seniority. 'But some of those hags were so stubborn there was nothing else I could do. You do understand, don't you, Susan?'

What Susan understood was that Berry was trying to scare her. You, too, could die if you don't do as I say, she was implying. Susan wished she could emit sinister implications in her turn, but both modesty and dignity forbade it. Besides, as she had already pointed out, it was foolhardy to threaten someone whom you intended to kill and thereby put her on her guard. Berry has made the mistake of underestimating me, she told herself; I must not make the mistake of underestimating her.

She was a bit surprised that Ms Fischetti had not waited in the trustees' room to speed them on their way. After all, even though Lucy was the titular chairman of Rundle House, Berry was clearly the operating head and thus, one would think, entitled to a ceremonial farewell. Perhaps she had waited and given up. Perhaps Berry had indicated that she did not want a farewell committee. Perhaps the niece of Carlo Battaglia waited for no one.

In any case, there didn't seem to be anyone around downstairs except for the swarthy man in a dark business suit and a turban who was standing in the anteroom. He bowed to both ladies; then said something in Gandistani to Berry.

'My car's outside,' Berry informed Susan. 'I'm going back to the hotel and I'll drop you off on the way. No trouble at all.'

As if Susan had been likely to worry about inconveniencing her. But she did not accept right away. Enough that she had let herself be talked into having dinner with Berry and her son on the following night.

She'd been reluctant to accept. She was not anxious to meet a young man whom she expected to make into an orphan. On the other hand, she must not let sentiment interfere with moral imperative. The more she knew about Berry and her habits, the easier it would be to kill her.

Still, she did not like the idea of being penned up in such close quarters now with a tipsy, irascible overscented monarch who could not seem to get it through her thick head that her rule was not absolute here.

'No need for you to bother,' Susan said. 'I'll get a cab. They're not as hard to get up here as you think.'

'We've been through all that already. Don't argue with me. I have a car; I'm taking you home; and that's that. And, in case you're worried about me finding out where you live, I already know where you live. Same old place you used to live in when we were kids, right? Be it never so humble and all that jazz.'

'It was our Manhattan pied-à-terre then. My only place now. But it's still considered one of the better parts of the city.' Be it never so humble, indeed! Berry might live in a palace, but Gandistan was not generally considered one of the better parts of the world.

Odd that Berry should remember her address after all these years. She didn't remember Berry's ever having visited the apartment. Lucy, yes, but Berry no. Of course, Berry could simply have asked Lucy for Susan's address. Just the same, Susan couldn't help wondering whether, at any time when she and her mother had been staying up at the Pound Ridge house, her father had brought Berry to the apartment. He was a man who liked to take risks, but would even he have dared?

'Why should you think I'd worry about your finding out where I live? I'm sure you wouldn't drop in on me without an invitation.' Which was true. Berry might have been guilty of all kinds of crimes, speakable and unspeakable, but even she would not sink that low.

'Oh, I don't know, I thought it might make you nervous for some reason. But how come you're still living in that apartment after all these years? I would have thought you'd have gotten a more up-to-date place, although I suppose you must have had it renovated at some time. Of course you really have to have lived in a seven-hundred-year-old palace to appreciate modern conveniences.'

'Surely you have modern conveniences there now?'

'We have indoor plumbing, and there's some talk of air-conditioning once we get a reliable source of electricity, but there's no chance of redoing the whole place. Some kind of sacred tradition. Like landmarking here, you know.'

'I'm sure it must be very interesting and historic.'

'It's like living in a museum. Matter of fact, once things get going, I think I will turn it into a museum and build myself something on the order of the Taj Mahal. Atlantic City, not Agra,' she explained. 'That Donald Trump knows how to do things right.'

She didn't explain what the things that were supposed to get going were.

'You don't have to feel too sorry for me, though. I do have a summer place up in the hills which is quite comfortable. You must come there for a visit; I promise to give you a good time. Not all of the young men are eunuchs. In fact, none of 'em are, now Sonny's abolished the harem. Where's your summer place, Susan? Newport? Or have you fallen back on the Hamptons?'

'I don't have a summer place at the moment, but I'm looking around,' Susan said, trying not to sound defensive. 'As a matter of fact, I'm going to leave my apartment soon. I bought a building further downtown a few years ago, and I'm having the upper floors converted into an apartment,'

'Oh, yes, that foundation of yours for scatological research or some such.'

'Anthropological research.'

'Whatever it is that boyfriend of yours is supposed to do.'

'You seem very well-informed about my private affairs,' Susan said coldly.

'Well, you're a celebrity in your own small way. Celebrities aren't allowed to have private lives. Especially in this country. And now that you've brought the subject up, I must tell you that Carlo doesn't know about your boyfriend

—he doesn't read much—so you'd better not mention it. He's an old-fashioned guy. He wouldn't like it,'

'Mr Battaglia's approval does not concern me. And I wouldn't dream of discussing my private affairs with him.'

'Good enough,' Berry said.

Susan could have killed her. But I *am* going to kill her, she reminded herself, so I mustn't let her get under my skin.

Berry began to swathe herself in the black garment in which Susan had seen her arrive at Kennedy—or one very similar. 'I wear my burqua when I go into the hotel officially, so no one knows what the Queen of Gandistan looks like,' she explained. 'Then, if I want to go shopping, I just put on regular clothes and take a back elevator. I come out in the lobby as plain old Berry Rundle, and no one gives me a second glance. The doorman calls me a taxi and I go wherever I want. I come back the same way, and no one's the wiser. I've even kept my charge accounts in my maiden name so I can shop in peace.'

Susan repressed a smile. The Waldorf was accustomed to potentates and their peculiarities. She'd bet every member of the staff was familiar with the begum's face. Otherwise, she might be able to leave the hotel unobserved, but she'd never make it back to her suite unchallenged.

'But what do you do about bodyguards, then?'

'Bodyguards! Don't be a simp, Susan. How unobtrusive would I be if I went out with a flock of bodyguards baying at my heels?'

'If you're afraid of letting your son go out without bodyguards, how come you're not afraid of going out without them yourself?'

'For Pete's sake, Susan, what's there to be afraid of on Fifth Avenue or Madison or even Lexington?'

She hasn't been reading the papers, Susan thought. Otherwise she would realize that nowadays Fifth Avenue and Madison and even Lexington were hardly the safe havens she fancied them to be. Or that plenty of people with no other distinction than their wealth went around with bodyguards these days.

'I did have a rather unnerving experience when I was here last year—very briefly—doing a spot of shopping incognito,' Berry confided. 'As I was coming out of Saks, a photographer took my picture, just like that, without asking permission. My first impulse was to smash his camera, but I was afraid that would make me too conspicuous. So all I did was give him a good smack on the head with my handbag, and he ran away.'

If she had hit him with anything like the large crocodile bag she was carrying at the moment, Susan thought, she had probably given the man a concussion.

'I figured he couldn't possibly know who I was. He must just be one of those pests who take your picture in the street and then hand you a little card telling you where you send money so you can buy a copy. Still, I was a little surprised to see one of them working Fifth Avenue.'

'Fifth Avenue has degenerated,' Susan agreed, 'but not that much.'

'Then, a week or so later, I happened to be looking at the *Sunday Times*—they get it up at Rundle House—and, you'll never believe it, there was my picture. *My* picture! On the woman's page—woman's pages, rather, because they go on and on.'

'The *Times* doesn't have a woman's page—or pages—any more. They call it "Style" now.'

'I don't care what they call it; it's the same old guff. This was in a piece called "On the Street"—"On the Street," can you beat that? As if I were a hooker or something. There wasn't just a picture of me but of half a dozen other well-dressed, good-looking nonanorexic women. The subhead was "Queen-Sized Chic". Oh my God, I thought. My cover's blown. The *Times* knows who I am. I'll never be able to go out without my veil any more. Then I read the article. Guess what it was about.'

Susan tried not to smile. 'I'm afraid I have a pretty good idea.'

'By "queen-sized" they meant fat. *Fat!* Can you imagine!

I got so mad I wanted to sue the paper—start a class action on behalf of female rulers everywhere. But the fish talked me out of it. "Your picture got in the paper," she said, "which was unfortunate. Still, nobody knows who the woman in the picture is. If you sue, you'll have to come out in the open. If you want to stay anonymous, you have to keep quiet."'

'Sensible woman,' Susan said, a little regretfully. She would have enjoyed seeing the media coverage of the lawsuit.

'What's become of this constitutional right to privacy I hear so much about, not to speak of human rights, if anybody can just walk up to you and take your picture and print it anywhere?'

There might be an answer to that, but Susan couldn't think of one.

The turbaned man opened the front door of the brownstone. The street outside was empty of cars now, except for the silver stretch limousine waiting in front. The lower floor of Rundle House was dark, but upstairs she could see lights and hear the sound of music (if you could call it music) and girlish voices. The mothers seemed to be having a good time. Perhaps they were feasting off the leftovers from the party, if there were any leftovers after Berry's predations.

The man opened the door to the car. Berry went inside, tripping over the skirts of her burqua. The man continued to hold the door open. After a considered pause, Susan followed Berry inside. The man closed the door and got into the front of the car, next to another turbaned man seated at the wheel. My, we are travelling in style, Susan thought, but she's the Begum now, not plain old Berry Rundle; no need to be unobtrusive.

Berry gave what Susan assumed to be her address to the driver. At least she said something in Gandistani to him. It could have been, 'Wrap her in the spare burqua and throw her in the river.'

'Where is this Foundation Building of yours, anyway?' Berry asked. 'You said it was further downtown than your apartment. How much further? Not down in that grungy old manufacturing district they tell me's become so fashionable—what do they call it?—So What? What Ho?'

'Soho. No, it's uptown.'

'You don't mean to tell me that you own that creepy old building your studio's in?'

She seems to know a lot about me, Susan thought uneasily; she must really have been investigating me. But not too thoroughly, or she wouldn't have dismissed my killing of that man outside Rundle House as an aberration.

'No, the Foundation Building's in the East Seventies and it's between Fifth and Madison.'

'Now that used to be a really great address, unless things have changed even more than I imagined.'

'It's still quite good,' Susan acknowledged. 'I'm planning to have my studio in the building, too.'

'That will be nice and convenient.' The burqua billowed impatiently. 'God, I wish I could smoke behind this thing, but I've already set myself on fire three times.'

There was a glugging sound behind the burqua. Good heavens, Susan thought, she's got the vodka bottle in there. How come she hadn't noticed Berry's putting the bottle in her bag? Maybe she hadn't. Maybe there had been a bottle in the bag already. One thing about the Begum of Gandistan the press hadn't caught on to. She was a lush.

'To tell the truth, I'd like to have myself a place in a better part of town. I lied to you when I said I was staying up there because I'm cheap, but you knew that. I stay there because up in that neighbourhood nobody asks questions.'

Another glugging sound. 'Nobody knows who comes in, or goes out up there, and nobody cares. Nobody cares about me at all, not even Sonny.'

There was a snuffling sound behind the black veil.

A response was obviously expected. Susan was damned if she would say she cared, even in the interests of hypocrisy. 'Lucy cares.'

'Goosey Lucy; that's what I always used to call her, and it still fits. I suspect her of being the one who got me a subscription to *Big Beautiful Woman* anonymously.'

'No doubt she meant well.'

'Lucy always means well. That's her trouble. Anyhow, I was telling you why I keep that apartment in Rundle House. Security reasons. Uneasy lies the head that wears a crown and so forth.'

'I thought that applied to ruling monarchs, not dowager queens.'

Berry sat bolt upright. Susan could sense her glare, even through the veil. 'You will not call me a dowager queen, if you know what's good for you. I'm in charge.'

'I thought your son was in charge. He's the king. Yours is only a courtesy title. That's what I read, anyway.'

'He's king in name only. He isn't fit to rule. He doesn't have the necessary killer instinct. In fact, though I hate to say this about my own son, Serwar is a wimp.'

Here again the media seemed to have been right. The Begum was, indeed, the power behind the throne, and not very far behind, either, judging from the way she was acting.

But why had her son allowed her to usurp his power? Was young Serwar mentally disturbed, after all? He had, it was true, obtained a degree—two degrees, if she remembered correctly—from Harvard, but that didn't prove anything.

CHAPTER 15

Berry patted Susan's knee. Susan pulled away before she could stop herself. 'Oh, come on, Susie, you haven't been taking me seriously, have you? I'm a great little kidder, as Carlo would tell you.'

Yes, and Carlo was a great little kidder himself. Wrap you up in cement and drop you in the East River for a laugh. Mob humour. Though he wouldn't do that to me, Susan thought. You don't drop someone with class in cement, especially someone for whom you're supposed to have cherished a secret admiration over the years.

Could it possibly be true that he was interested in her as a woman? No, a gangster wasn't likely to have such good taste. It had to be part of their scheme to lure her on to the Rundle House board, though it wasn't clear whether they thought that the idea of Carlo Battaglia's devotion would attract her or frighten her.

But why were they going to all this trouble to get her on the board in the first place? No use asking Berry; she wasn't likely to get an honest answer from her.

Susan picked her words carefully. 'I knew you must be —well—exaggerating when you said you'd killed dozens of people. After all, people like us—the Rundles, the Melvilles —don't go around doing things like that, do they?'

'No, we don't. At least not very often.' Berry chuckled.

Susan chuckled, too, but inwardly. 'But you do come on so—so strong.'

'Comes of having been a queen all these years. I can't help throwing my weight around . . . And no cracks,' she added sternly. 'I'm comfortable with the way I look.'

'I wouldn't dream of making any cracks,' Susan said. 'And what does it matter what you look like as long as you're healthy?'

There was silence behind the burqua. 'I'm like the Queen of Hearts, you know,' Berry finally said. 'I never really killed nobody. For the most part, anyhow. My husband, of course, but that was really a mercy killing. I'd been poisoning him slowly so he wouldn't even think of getting rid of me now that I was getting on a bit, so he could bump up the wives next in line and marry some young chick. I finally decided to put the old goat out of his misery.'

'That was very thoughtful of you. And those dozens of people you were telling me about whom you said you'd killed? Before you changed your mind about that.'

'Haven't you been paying attention? I said I was just putting you on. Trying to get a rise out of you. Sure, the other wives died, but they killed each other. Or the harem girls killed them, hoping to be promoted. Common practice behind the veil. Besides, they used to torture the younger girls a lot. Really sickening. You must have read about it in those supermarket tabloids that seem to have sprung up all over the place.'

'I don't read supermarket tabloids.'

'No, I don't suppose you would. Or admit to it, if you did. You were always such a snot, even when you were a kid, and people don't change that much.'

In some cases they don't change at all, Susan thought. And I never read supermarket tabloids. I even try not to look at the headlines at the checkout counter.

'Maybe they do go overboard now and then, but there's a lot more truth in them than in the establishment papers, and they're a lot peppier.'

Susan wondered whether Berry subscribed to the supermarket tabloids or just caught them on her trips to the United States; and, if so, whether she actually went shopping in supermarkets herself. Oh, if only she did. A supermarket would be such a splendid place to assassinate someone. The body could lie in the aisle for hours and people would just walk around it. Only when someone tripped over it and threatened to sue would the store manager finally deign to take notice.

'Now, what were we talking about? Oh, yes, the death rate in Gandistan. Naturally it's high. Primitive country—poor sanitation, rampant witchcraft, no industrial safety regulations—what can you expect?'

'I didn't know Gandistan had any industry.'

'Cottage industry, mostly. But we're going to change all that. Yes, siree, things are going to be a lot different from now on.' There was a glugging sound behind the burqua. She'll be lucky if she gets across the Waldorf lobby without falling flat on her face, Susan thought.

Berry's voice grew loud. 'Oh, sure, there's the occasional execution. Every well-regulated country has executions. Criminals and people with the wrong politics are beheaded or garrotted from time to time. Publicly. No theatre in Gandistan to speak of, and we discourage the importation of movies, so we've got to give the people some kind of entertainment. Then, of course, there are always a lot of accidents—highway, hunting, horseplay—you name it.'

She gave a royal hiccup. 'Why do you keep looking over your shoulder like that, Susan? It makes me nervous.'

'Maybe it's my imagination, but there seems to be a car —or cars—following us.'

'It's not your imagination. Cars follow me all the time. Don't worry about it.'

She offered no further explanation. Maybe it was her own people in the light grey Dodge sedan that Susan had noticed behind them and the dark green Mercury hatchback that seemed to be following the Dodge (and what of the tan car that was too far away to be identified and might simply be going in the same direction?). Or it could be the FBI, the CIA, local law, Andy's group, terrorists, anybody. And did whoever it was follow the Begum only when she was in her limousine or did they also follow plain old Berry Rundle in her cab?

It is also possible that they're following me, she thought. Andy and his merry men to keep an eye on me or to see what I'm up to. Or maybe I have enemies. But why would any enemies of mine follow me? What would they hope to gain by keeping track of my movements?

Berry flung back her veil. 'This thing is stifling me. Funny how it never felt stifling in Gandistan, and it's a lot hotter there.'

Because you'd never dare let yourself get drunk in public in Gandistan, Susan thought.

Berry leaned forward and slid open a small panel in the partition that separated them from the driver. She said something in Gandistani into the opening this disclosed. A moment later a blast of icy air rushed into the passenger compartment.

Susan shivered.

Berry took no notice. 'What were we talking about? Oh, yes, the deaths in Gandistan. I guess maybe I lied to you a little there, too. You get into the habit of lying when you spend most of your life in a harem. Necessary survival technique.'

Whom did she think she was fooling? Berry had been an

accomplished liar from the moment she first drew breath. More likely she'd given lessons in deceit to the rest of the harem.

'Okay, so maybe I did shoot a few of my stepsons. But they were awful boys, always trying to kill each other, always trying to kill anyone they felt could get in their way —the prime minister, Sonny, me! I had to kill them, Susan, for Sonny's sake, if not my own, especially after they potted the prime minister. You do understand, don't you?'

Wearily, Susan said once more that she understood. Berry patted her knee again, and this time Susan didn't pull away.

'I knew you would. After all, you are Buck's daughter.'

You're going to pay for that, Susan thought between her teeth. She had never thought between her teeth before, but desperate times require desperate measures.

Berry seemed to pull herself together a little, though it was hard to know what was going on behind that burqua. 'By the way, I'd appreciate it if you didn't tell any of the gals that I'm the Queen of Gandistan. If your old schoolmates find out you're a queen it makes for strained relations.'

She gave another hiccup. 'Just ask Queen Noor of Jordan if you don't believe me. I've never met her, but I know how she must feel, being an American gal like me.'

'But won't you want to get in touch with all your old friends?' Susan asked, thinking: friends, indeed, they hated your guts. 'Since they've all been getting the Rundle House brochures, I took it for granted that meant you were anxious to see them again.'

'Of course I'm anxious to see the old gang again. Champing at the bit, in fact. But I'm going to the gala as Berry Rundle. You're the only one who knows my secret, Susan, and the only one who's going to know it. That's because there's a very special relationship between us.' And she chuckled drunkenly to herself.

The limousine drew up in front of Susan's house. The first turbaned man got out and opened the door. 'Remember,' the Begum said, 'you're having dinner with Sonny and me tomorrow night.'

The conventional phrase sprang automatically to Susan's lips: 'I'm looking forward to it.'

'I hope you weren't thinking of bringing that boyfriend of yours along, because he isn't invited.'

Susan's voice was as frosty as she could make it. 'He wouldn't be able to come in any case, because he isn't in town. He's down in South America.'

'For a good long time, I hope. We wouldn't want him to interfere with our plans.'

Susan made a noncommittal noise. Peter hadn't given any indication in his last letter of when he planned to return. In fact, now that she thought of it, she hadn't heard from him in weeks. But that often happened when he was in a remote area with poor mail service; silence for a while, then a bunch of letters arriving all at once.

She must remember to get in touch with the young man who was looking after the foundation's affairs in Peter's absence and ask if he'd had any word. What was his name again? She had it written down somewhere.

'I'll call you and we'll work out the details,' Berry said. 'We'll eat up in my suite. Can't eat in a restaurant because Serwar might be recognized, so I'd have to wear my burqua and it's no fun trying to eat with that on. Don't bother to dress; it'll be quite casual. You won't even need to carry a gun. I promise not to kill you tomorrow night.' She laughed heartily.

And I promise not to kill you tomorrow night, Susan thought. She knew through bitter experience that it was not easy to assassinate anyone in the Waldorf and get away with it. Besides, call her sentimental, but she didn't like the idea of assassinating Berry while her son was around, even though, in the long run, she would probably be doing the young man a favour.

'You must remember to tell me when your building is going to be finished,' Berry called after her as she got out, 'and I'll send you a couple of carpets.'

*

The turbaned man shut the door of the car and rushed to the entrance of Susan's house in order to open that door as well, but the doorman was before him. No one, he seemed to say, is going to open the door of this house but me.

He glared at the man in the turban. The man in the turban glared at him.

'Ali!' the Begum called.

After a black look at the doorman, Ali re-entered the limousine. It drove off.

The doorman continued to hold the door open, but Susan didn't go inside right away. She wanted to see how many cars had been following the limousine. The only vehicles that came by were a small van and two yellow cabs. None of the cars that she thought had been following.

Perhaps the cars that had been following had turned off just before the limousine entered Susan's street, and would pick it up once it started down the avenue. Or they could have been camouflage to cover the van and the cabs which had been the actual followers. Or it was just possible that nobody had been following them at all.

Several of the neighbours had been watching Susan's impressive arrival, mouths agape. Not native New Yorkers; native New Yorkers took such things in their stride. She shouldn't allow the neighbours to get on her nerves like that, Susan told herself.

'My goodness, Susan,' said Mrs Halloran from the fifth floor, a provincial pest who was under the impression that mere residential proximity entitled you to use a person's first name, 'who was that interesting lady who brought you home?'

'Mother Teresa,' Susan said, and pressed the elevator button.

CHAPTER 16

'What makes you so sure that if Berry—the Begum—were out of the picture her son wouldn't just go ahead with the same plan?' Susan asked.

Andy shook his head. 'He's not the kind of fellow to do anything like that.'

'How can you be so sure?'

'Remember we talked about this before, when I was trying to—er—interest you in the Begum? And I haven't given up hope on that.'

She shook her head. 'Even if I were an assassin, I'd never kill an old classmate.'

'Is that a fact?' Andy said. 'Now, if I were going to kill someone, some of my old classmates would be among my top choices. But, then, I went to a public school.'

Susan was surprised. It was the first time she had seen any evidence of class consciousness from him. Probably he had picked it up from Jill, who had been born and brought up in the Bronx and had never gotten over it.

Susan and Andy were having a late supper in the spacious dining-room of her apartment. At first, when the buzzer rang and the doorman's voice informed her that Mr Mackay was downstairs, she was tempted to tell him to tell Mr Mackay that she was not at home. She was annoyed with Andy. How could he have put her in this position without telling her what the score was?

Yet she must be fair. He hadn't put her in this position. She had put herself in it. He hadn't suggested that she go to Rundle House; she had gone there of her own volition, without any inkling that Berry Rundle was the Begum of Gandistan, his designated victim.

Andy had undoubtedly known, through Jill if not his own private sources, that Susan would be invited to participate in the Rundle House festivities. What he could not have known was that Berry was going to try to involve her directly in the other, less innocent activities that were going on there.

In any case, it would be stupid to let her annoyance with him keep her from trying to find out as much as she could about what was going on there. 'Tell Mr Mackay he can come up,' she said.

Andy arrived smiling, bearing an enormous pizza and a bottle of Chianti. 'I know the kind of food they serve at trustees' teas. I figured you might be hungry.'

She wondered whether his choice of food were a not-so-subtle allusion to the membership of the board of trustees. Or whether it was simply that he knew she liked pizza.

What did it matter? The pizza smelled good, and she was, indeed, hungry. So she threw together a salad and put out the china and silver and crystal—one must keep up civilized practices—and they sat down at the long mahogany table that Michelle had polished only that morning.

She would have a fit when she discovered that its shining splendour had been dulled by place mats. She always had a fit whenever Susan used the dining-room for any but formal occasions. 'Don't see why you can't eat in the kitchen like regular folks,' she would grumble, 'specially when you're eatin' alone, which you're doin' an awful lot of these days.'

Susan could not point out to Michelle that she was not 'regular folks', because it wasn't the kind of thing you said, even to an employee. According to myth, there were no class distinctions in America.

There were no such myths in Gandistan apparently, although, if the accounts were true, Serwar would have liked to initiate them. 'Maybe the king's politics have changed,' Susan suggested. 'People's ideas do change as they get older. Some people's, anyway,' she added, thinking of the king's mother.

'His haven't.'

'How do you know?'

'I have information from a reliable source,'

'Who is that?' she asked. 'Whom do you have access to who's close enough to him to know what he thinks?'

368

'I never reveal my sources. You should know better than to ask, Susan.'

There was a note of patronage in his voice. She resented it.

'Did your reliable source tell you why he seems to have let his mother take over the country? Surely that would be carrying filial devotion too far.'

'That isn't the answer,' Andy admitted. 'Only thing we've been able to think of is that she must have something on him and she's holding it over his head.'

'You mean she might be blackmailing him? Her own son?'

'Such things have been known to happen, especially in royal families.'

'But how can you blackmail an absolute monarch? In Gandistan there's nothing he can't do legally—in theory, anyway; and in practice there's nothing he can do that can't be covered up. Unless there's something he did outside of Gandistan . . . ?'

'Not likely that he'd have done something blackmailable here that we wouldn't know about. Besides that, he seems to be a well-conducted young man.'

'Then what do you suppose she has on him, if you're right about that?'

'That's what we'd like to know.' He looked at her hopefully.

She smiled and helped herself to another piece of pizza. 'You hardly think Berry'd be likely to confide in me?' Or that I'd tell you if she had, she thought.

'No, but something might have slipped out in the course of the long chat you two ladies had earlier this evening.'

She counted to five. No use getting angry. She'd taken for granted that he and his colleagues had been watching Rundle House. What more likely than that they should have someone on the inside as well, someone who'd reported to him on how long she'd been upstairs with Berry.

'She didn't say anything that could account for it,' she told him.

But was that entirely true? She went back over the

conversation in her mind. Had Berry let drop anything that could give a clue to the hold she might have over her son? There was the glimmer of . . . something on the edge of Susan's recollection. If only she could pin it down.

'He has a girlfriend somewhere in this area,' she offered. 'Her name's Audrey. Maybe you could look into her.'

'We've already checked her out.'

His tone was dismissive. Could Audrey be the informant whose identity he was protecting?

Obviously it would be no use asking him. But Audrey's existence seemed to be no secret. The TV anchorwoman, for instance, seemed to have known about her.

As soon as Susan had a chance, she told herself, she would go to the library and delve into the subject of Gandistan and its ruling family. No need to conceal her interest in the Begum now; it must be already a matter of record. Although it wasn't the Begum she was interested in at the moment. And it might not be necessary to make a trip to the library. She was going to meet Serwar tomorrow night. If he was anything like most young lovers, he was likely to tell her more about Audrey than she wanted to know.

'I suppose you're aware that Berry's keeping her married name a secret. She says she doesn't want anyone to know that she's the Begum of Gandistan, because it would destroy her privacy.'

'And she's right. If the media knew that the Begum of Gandistan was an American, they'd be all over her. And it would also attract a lot of attention to Rundle House, which, as you must have gathered by now, the mob is planning to use as a cover.'

She knew that whatever was being covered must have something to do with drugs, because of Andy's concern, but she pretended innocence. 'A cover for what? Prostitution? White slavery?'

He looked surprised. 'Wherever did you get an idea like that? Oh, of course, those girls. No, that would be too obvious. If they wanted a front for a white-slave operation, they'd choose a drug rehabilitation centre, something like that. Are you going to eat that last piece of pizza?'

'No, you go ahead and eat it. Meanwhile, I'll make some coffee and see what I can rustle up by way of dessert.'

Over cheese and crackers and fruit, he gave her a sketchy outline of what was going on, although she felt sure he held back more than he divulged. Since the South American drug cartel seemed to have effectively cornered the cocaine market, he told her, the Mafia, both Sicilian and American, as well as some of the Hong Kong Triads and crime organizations from other countries—'We think even the Turkish Mafia might be involved'—had decided to concentrate their efforts on heroin.

'And heroin is derived from opium, which is Gandistan's chief crop.' She was puzzled. 'But it's such a small country. Surely their entire opium crop wouldn't be enough to make anything as elaborate as this worthwhile.'

'No, it wouldn't. The idea seems to be that the organizers of this thing would centralize their entire heroin manufacturing process in Gandistan—import opium and raw heroin from all over East Asia, and manufacture it with the state-of-the-art technology, like any legitimate big business—which, of course, it would be in Gandistan. They're planning to call it the Gandistan Development Corporation and there'll be a Gandistani national nominally in charge. They've already picked their man. A member of the royal family, of course, someone named Prince Abdul Fuzla. Naturally the Mafia would do the actual running of it.'

'I thought there weren't any male members of the royal family left,' she said.

'No close ones. He's a cousin of some kind, and a pretty shady character, I understand.'

'Where does Rundle House come in?'

'That's going to be their international headquarters.'

'But how could they run things from Rundle House? Berry says nobody pays attention to what anyone does in that part of town, and that's probably true when it comes to the neighbours. But it wouldn't apply to law enforcement agencies. They're bound to know about the place, if only by following people like Carlo Battaglia up here.'

'So what if they do? Rundle House itself would be used exclusively for administration. All records coded and kept in the computers. They'll be able to hold conferences there without fear of being bugged because they'll own the buildings. And, of course, by getting themselves put on the board of trustees, people like the Bat and Chiang and their associates will have a perfectly legitimate reason to go in and out. And there's nothing the law will be able to do about it. How would it look if law enforcement officials kept getting search warrants and raiding the rooms of underprivileged teen-aged expectant mothers? Imagine what a field day the media would have with it, especially when they don't find a trace of drugs on the premises. And they won't, unless some of the mothers happen to have stashes for their own use, which isn't likely. The Fischetti woman is very strict about things like that. No drugs, no cigarettes, no alcohol.'

'You mean she's legitimate?'

'If by legitimate you mean does she really care about unwed teen-aged mothers and their babies, it seems she does. Done a lot of good work in that area, I understand. Very dedicated.'

'Don't tell me she doesn't know about this whole drug thing?'

Andy looked exasperated, as if Susan were being deliberately obtuse. 'Of course she knows. She's Battaglia's niece, or didn't you know that? But under the new setup, Rundle House will be able to take care of nearly three times as many mothers as they're able to handle now, and they're also planning to open a nursery for the babies. That's all that matters to her.'

'Your informant seems to have been working overtime.'

'I know all that through the Resource. Our representative on the Metropolitan Charity Council is acquainted with Ms Fischetti and speaks very highly of her. As a matter of fact, he tells me our outfit has placed quite a few homeless pregnant teen-agers with her, and he was very impressed with the care they got.'

It all seemed very well thought out, except for one thing.

'Why are they calling attention to Rundle House by holding this big gala?'

'Don't you see? It's to account for the sudden influx of money. Otherwise, how could they explain how Rundle House could suddenly afford to expand like this? The Rundles are rich but not that rich. Actually, they're not attracting all that much attention. Once an organization starts organizing events and sending out press releases and trying to sell tickets, people tend to run when they see them coming.'

'Sort of overt covert activities,' she said.

'That's one way of looking at it. Did they tell you they were planning to set up branches of Rundle House all over the world?'

'No, they didn't get around to it.' She wondered how many charities all over the world were fronts for illegal activities, as well as covert legal ones, like Andy's. It would be a perfect setup for laundering money, if nothing else. From now on, she decided, she would scrutinize the boards of trustees of every organization to which she contributed with an eagle eye.

One thing still puzzled her. 'Why do they want me on the board of trustees? Why should they take the risk of having an outsider who might find out what they're up to?'

'They probably didn't think there was much of a risk that you'd catch on,' he said, in what she felt was an offensive manner. 'And I imagine that they're trying to recruit everyone they can think of who's trustee material, so the board can look more . . . plausible. Not that it would with them on it, but everyone has his blind spots.'

Should she tell him that Berry claimed the Bat had joined the board because he had social aspirations? No, he would only laugh. Should she tell him the Bat was supposed to have romantic ideas about Susan herself? No, Andy might have the grace not to laugh, but he would certainly snicker behind his hand. In any case, why should she tell him anything? It was his job to find out things for himself.

CHAPTER 17

When Andy asked her when she expected to see the Begum again, she said, 'Oh, I don't know. Sometime soon, probably.' She didn't tell him she'd already agreed to have dinner with the royal family the following evening. If he was so smart, let him find that out for himself—which he probably would.

She spent a restless night being pursued by Berry, who had developed into an Oriental deity with six arms and six hands, each with a gun in it. She woke up with an urge to make a painting of this six-gun goddess, so she got dressed and went over to her studio. These days she had been going there less and less often, as working there was getting to be an unpleasant experience, rather than the uplifting one it should be; but today she was determined to put in at least a few hours' work.

The front door to the loft building where her studio was located stood open, instead of being locked as it should have been when there was no one on duty downstairs—which there hadn't been ever since the new landlord took over and announced that the building was scheduled to be demolished and all the tenants had better get out if they knew what was good for them; although, not being an absolute monarch like Berry, he had couched this threat in less actionable terms.

The downstairs lobby was lit only by a dim bulb, which was sufficient to show that the place was crowded with a miscellany of objects—a couple of discoloured sinks, several doors, some worm-eaten lumber, and a number of crushed and mangled cartons, all covered with the grime of ages. Even though it was a warm spring day outside, inside it was chilly and damp; and there was a strong odour of mould and decay and other unpleasant things.

A man was lurking in the shadows near the elevator. She

hesitated. He came towards her and she saw that it was only the landlord.

Only the landlord! What mythical monster could compare with the reality of this man! Miss Winkler of Bonnie Buttons had told Susan shortly before she moved to Florida ('I'm too old and too tired to deal with anything but mail order') that she'd heard he had hired thugs to menace the tenants of a building he wanted cleared for demolition. 'Of course that was in Queens. I don't think he'd dare try anything like that in Manhattan—at least not on the upper East Side, but one can never be sure.'

'Good morning, Mr Bloodstone,' Susan said, coming all the way into the lobby. 'It seems to me that service here has been allowed to slip below the limits of acceptability. I'm sure that all this junk—' she prodded a pile of what seemed to be filthy old rags with the toe of her shoe '—is in violation of the fire laws.'

'Bonnie and the Frame Master have moved out. That leaves you and Pegasus as the only tenants. Am I expected to keep up full services for only two tenants?'

'Yes, you are.'

'If it weren't for you two, I could have the wrecking crew here tomorrow.'

'I don't know how long Mr Pegasus's lease has to run, but mine still has three months to go.'

'I offered to buy you out, but I don't suppose money means anything to people like you. And nothing seems to mean anything to Mr Pegasus.'

Mr Pegasus was a little old Englishman who dealt in objects of an unspecified nature to the antiques trade. In the past, Susan had seen him flitting wraithlike about the halls. From time to time he had leered at her and made what might have been improper suggestions; she couldn't be sure, because the combination of an upper-class British accent and ill-fitting dentures made him almost impossible to understand.

She was not thrilled to discover she would be alone in the building with him for the next three months. She was even less thrilled when Mr Bloodstone went on, 'I'm warning you, the security system isn't as effective as it ought to be because Pegasus turns it off when he comes in and forgets to turn it on again when he leaves.'

'The responsibility for keeping the alarm on at all times is yours.'

'What am I supposed to do—follow him around? I haven't seen him for days. And he doesn't answer his phone. Maybe he's dead. Though not on the premises,' he added hastily. 'I checked.'

'You're supposed to hire a guard to watch the place while there are still tenants here.'

He appeared to think this was intended as a witticism. 'You slay me, Miss M, reely you do.' He laughed heartily. Then he gave a dramatic start. 'Did you see that!' He pointed to the shadows at the back of the hall. 'A rat!'

'I didn't see any rat,' she said. Except you, she thought. He did look very like a rat with his small beady eyes and his quivering pointed nose. Even his sandy moustache bristled like a rat's whiskers.

'They move very fast. That was a good big one.'

'I'm not afraid of rats.'

'Very strong-minded of you. Most ladies are terrified of rats. 'Course, there's no reason to be. You leave 'em alone; they leave you alone. Unless, of course, they're very hungry.' He grinned. He had pointed teeth like a rat's, too. 'Not like people. There are degenerates running around who would do . . . things without any reason. Especially to a woman.' He licked his lips. 'I hate to think of you alone in a deserted place like this, on the top floor, too. Somebody, anybody, could be lurking in the hallways and on the stairs.'

'If the alarm system were on, nobody who didn't belong here would be able to get in.'

'Oh, they have their ways. These homeless people are very cunning about getting into abandoned buildings—nearly abandoned buildings—alarm system or not.'

'I thought you said it was degenerates who got in.'

'Homeless degenerates.'

'It's your responsibility to keep them out. My lawyer—

'Or you could get sick or have an accident up there, and nobody would know for days.'

'People know where I am, and I do have a telephone.'

'Good, good, I don't want to have to worry about you. Didja hear about the building in Brooklyn that the landlord couldn't start demolishing because there was one tenant who wouldn't leave, and how when somebody from the buildings department came on Monday to inspect the premises, he found a dead body lying in the hall? Looked as if it had been there all weekend; it was already discomposed.'

'I heard something about it on the radio. I thought it was the landlord's body they found.'

'I understood it was the tenant's.'

They smiled at each other with hatred in their hearts —the normal landlord-tenant relationship in New York; perhaps the normal landlord-tenant relationship anywhere.

She pressed the elevator button. There was the usual sound of creaking and groaning as the ancient car, roused from its torpor, started bumping its way down the shaft from floor to floor.

'One day the elevator's gonna stop running,' Mr Bloodstone's voice said in her ear. 'Maybe it'll even stop between floors, and it'll be hours before anyone finds anyone who happens to be stuck in it. Days maybe. Oh, the elevator alarm's working . . . but there won't be anybody to hear it.'

The elevator door opened. She went inside.

'The building could catch on fire!' he yelled after her. 'Burn to the ground. With all your beautiful paintings inside.'

'They're fully insured,' she told him, as she pulled the elevator door shut.

No need to mention that only the paintings she was currently working on were in the studio. The bulk of her output was safely stored in a fireproof warehouse in Long Island City. That had been Jill's idea. Susan could see now it was a good one.

This building might be a good place to dispose of Berry, she thought, as the elevator wobbled its way up to the top floor. No one to see her go in; no one to see her not go out, as long as Susan chose her time carefully. Mr Bloodstone never appeared except in the morning. Afternoons he went out to persecute tenants in Brooklyn and Queens before going home to his palatial estate on Long Island.

There should be no difficulty in luring Berry here on the pretext of showing her Susan's paintings. Although it might be difficult to persuade her to come alone. This was near First Avenue, well beyond what Berry seemed to consider the safety zone, although it was still a high-rent area.

Suppose she did manage to get Berry up to the studio alone and killed her? What was she going to do with the body? Even if she could get her out of the studio and into the elevator—and, with a heavyweight like Berry, that was no small task—what then? She couldn't leave it in the lobby; it would be too easy to establish a connection between Susan Melville and Berengaria Rundle. The thought crossed her mind that in a pinch she could call on Andy for removal—but, no, he might expect a reciprocal courtesy. She didn't want to put herself under any obligation to him.

Then, of course, there was the possibility—the very remote possibility—that, if she tried to shoot Berry, Berry would shoot her first. Berry would have no trouble getting rid of the body. She'd just have her attendants bring a carpet, roll the corpse in it, and carry it to the limousine; then up to Rundle House, where there would be complete removal facilities, courtesy of the Bat and his henchmen. Would he reproach Berry for having killed her? Would he shed a silent—or noisy—tear on her behalf?

What does it matter, she told herself sternly. Besides, Berry could never outshoot me. She's too fat.

She unlocked the door to her studio and went inside. Andy had told her the night before that Jill wanted to get in touch with her. She'd call her now. She picked up the phone. The line was dead. No dial tone, no humming sound, no tiny distant voices. Nothing.

Suddenly she was no longer in a mood to paint. She would go out, do something else. Shop, perhaps. She did need a new handbag. Her bags wore out quickly. The weight of a gun, no matter how light, tended to take a toll on their seams, especially dress bags, and most of her assassinations were dressy affairs.

She could, of course, have a bag specially made. But how could she explain her needs to the bag maker?

On the other hand, as Berry had pointed out, today women in all walks of life carried guns for self-protection. Perhaps handbags especially designed for gun-toters were already on the market. She remembered having seen an ad for a catalogue of such merchandise when she'd turned out her drawers looking for the Rundle House brochure. She'd always meant to send away for it and had never gotten around to it. She would make a point of sending for it as soon as she got back home.

She locked the studio door behind her; then paused, reluctant to take the elevator. The building was only seven storeys high. Walking downstairs would be no problem. But she had a feeling that she would meet Mr Bloodstone on the way and he would smirk at her and say, 'I hope I didn't frighten you into using the stairs, Miss M. Or were you just walking down for the exercise?'

Why should she let him get to her? She opened the door marked 'Exit', and looked down the stairwell. Pitch black. All the light bulbs had been allowed to go out. Or had been removed. Something rustled on the stairs.

She took the elevator. It rattled and clanked, but it arrived at the ground floor. Mr Bloodstone was still in the lobby, bending over the corpse of a large grey rat.

He jumped when he saw her. 'I got it right after you went up. I was just about to get rid of it.'

Oh, sure, she thought. You didn't expect me back down so soon, did you? You were going to leave it there, hoping it would scare me.

Probably he hadn't seen a rat at all before, she thought.

Probably he had brought this one along with him. Very likely it had died of natural causes.

'I hope you're going to give it a decent burial,' she said, resisting the temptation to add, 'in your family plot.'

Now, if she wanted to kill Mr Bloodstone—if she were *planning* to kill Mr Bloodstone; she wanted to kill him all right—there wouldn't be any problem. No one would question the appearance of a landlord's body on his own premises. Moreover, the death wasn't likely to be associated with her any more than with any of his other tenants, past and present. The field would be wide open.

But she had promised herself that from now on, she would keep from giving in to her lethal impulses. She had already killed one landlord on impulse. And it was true that his demise had brought her out of poverty and eventually opened the way to fame and fortune. But the second time, she told herself, she might not be as lucky.

There was no reason for her to keep on suffering. She would go to one of the many real estate offices in the neighbourhood and see if she could rent studio space for a few months. She knew it would make Mr Bloodstone happy, but she couldn't sacrifice her comfort for his pain.

She needn't have worried. It turned out to be impossible to find anything in the neighbourhood to suit her needs. 'You might be able to find something in the financial district or in Soho,' the agent suggested. 'Maybe even the Twenties or Thirties. But, even so, for just a few months . . .'

'I'd be willing to sign a lease for a year.' Even if the work on the Melville building got done in the three months that had been promised, it probably would be several months more before she'd actually be able to move in. 'But I want space in this neighbourhood. I like to walk to work. Aren't there any subleases available?'

The agent would have sneered if Susan hadn't been such an important person. She shrugged instead. 'Well, we'll keep an eye out. But frankly I can't hold out much hope. Now, if you'd like a nice condominium . . . ?'

CHAPTER 18

Susan could try other agents, but she knew they would say the same thing. She could go back to painting in her apartment, the way she'd done before she became affluent again. But now that she'd had the place renovated (and that had taken more than twice as long as promised) she would hate to have it all stained and smeared with paint. And Michelle would have fits.

Susan didn't need to paint for a livelihood. She could easily stop painting until the Melville Building was ready for occupancy. She could easily stop painting for the rest of her life. The warehouse was crammed with enough paintings, which Jill was letting out one by one for fear of depressing the market, so that she would never need to lift a brush again. Moreover, Jill had made a number of excellent investments for Susan. So, if the art market crashed, if the threatened recession materialized, Susan would still be a wealthy woman.

But she needed to keep on painting because it was what defined her, made her Susan Melville, not only in the eyes of the world but, more important, in her own eyes. And she supposed that she kept on disposing of evil-doers for much the same reason, even though that defined her only in her own eyes (and perhaps in Andy's eyes, too, although she supposed he did not see it as a matter of definition).

She went over to the Melville Foundation to see how matters were progressing. They did not seem to have progressed at all. Mr Iverson had suffered a nervous breakdown, the foreman told her. There was a distinct suggestion of cause and effect. She wasn't sure whether he was joking or not. Construction humour? Maybe she should call Mr Pilokis, the contractor. No, she'd call Jill. Ask her to call Mr Pilokis. Give him a nervous breakdown, too, if that was what was necessary to get things done.

She had lunch by herself at a little place over on Second Avenue that she had discovered on one of her outings with Jill. Then she went to Bloomingdale's, since it was handy, to check out their bags. She couldn't bring herself to ask whether they had any bags specially designed for gun-carrying. Maybe at Macy's, but not Bloomingdale's. So she bought herself an ordinary but sturdy one.

Since she had time on her hands, she took a little of it to explore Bloomingdale's. Each time she went there it seemed to have changed. Now it was more of a sound and light show than a department store. Nothing seemed to be left of the original façade, except for a rather sinister bit on the north side that had been relegated to entrances for employees and deliveries. All the rest of the building had been given a false face.

Bloomingdale's had always been a regular rabbit warren of a place, with numerous entrances on all four sides, elevators and escalators and mezzanines and basements and sub-basements. She was surprised to see that there were still entrances to the subway in the sub-basements. She wouldn't have thought that Bloomingdale's catered to the subway crowd any more. But, then, they did hold sales, as the little banks of TV screens at the head of every esca-lator were constantly reminding you.

The customers seemed divided among young women who looked like hookers (yuppies) and middle-aged women who looked like bag ladies (old money), with a sprinkling of overly well-dressed young men and men trying to look young, plus people who would blend into any crowd but this one.

Although there were still aisles on the main floor, much of the rest of the store had been divided up into clusters and 'boutiques', so that it was more of a rabbit warren then before—a warren for trendy, well-heeled rabbits. What an ideal spot for an assassination it was! She wouldn't even need to use a silencer. There was so much noise from the music that was continually being played that the sound of a shot was not likely to be heard, or, if it was heard, to be noticed.

It shouldn't be hard to lure Berry there. By her own admission, she was an ardent shopper. And she had mentioned Lexington Avenue as one of her stamping grounds. What else was there on Lexington Avenue but Bloomingdale's? Yes, it was definitely the place for her to get Berry. She would come back tomorrow and reconnoitre the ground carefully, study the little maps posted on each floor for the benefit of hapless shoppers who had lost their way in the maze. She didn't think she could take any more of it today. Bloomingdale's was an experience you had to prepare for, if not with fasting at least with prayer.

As Susan opened the door to her apartment, a wave of perfume engulfed her. The place was filled with flowers, masses of them in baskets and bowls and vases, even one arrangement that looked like a wreath, spilling out of the living-room into the foyer in a riot of colour. And, in the midst of all this floral abundance, Michelle's grinning face. 'Looks like somebody's got herself a new beau.'

'Don't be silly, Michelle, they must have come from Mr Peter.'

But Peter was not accustomed to express his affection with botanic displays. Even in the early days, when they had been more ardently involved, his love tokens had taken the form of a shrunken head here, a bunch of poisoned arrows there. He had never said it with flowers.

'Mr Peter!' Michelle made a rude noise with her tongue. She had never approved of Peter. 'These're from some fellow named Carlo. "Your devoted Carlo," he signs hisself. Such a romantic name, Carlo.'

'Michelle, you had no right to read the card.'

'The public has a right to know and I'm the public!' And Michelle stomped off before Susan could say anything further.

If only Michelle knew what Carlo's last name was, who Carlo himself was, Susan thought, she wouldn't think his name was so romantic. Or maybe she would. Maybe it would give her new respect for her employer.

Susan supposed she would have to call the Bat and thank

him for the flowers. Or would a thank-you-note be more appropriate? She would decide later. Meanwhile what was she going to do with all this botanical extravagance?

She'd take them to her studio, use them as models. Then she remembered how little the atmosphere of her studio was conducive to painting now. Maybe she'd ask Jill to find out from Mr Pilokis whether it might be possible to finish the studio on the top floor first. Then she could work there while they were doing the rest of the building. It might be noisy but it wouldn't be creepy.

At around four, a male voice with a foreign accent called and said the Begum's limousine would pick her up at seven-thirty, if that would be convenient. Susan said that would be quite convenient.

What to wear? She contemplated her wardrobe. It was important to dress in such a way as to show she did not regard the occasion as anything special without compromising her own sense of what was fitting. Finally she decided on basic black with . . . pearls? No, pearls—even fake pearls— were too corny.

A simple gold chain and earrings? Of course, the first rule of living in New York is never to go out in the city wearing visible gold jewellery. But she wouldn't be going out in the litreal sense. She would be stepping out of a well-staffed apartment house and into a well-guarded limousine. From that limousine, she would be stepping into the Waldorf Astoria. If, to paraphrase the words of the song, you were not safe from chain-snatchers there, you were not safe anywhere.

Michelle came in to inform Susan that she was leaving and to ask whether she could take some of the flowers home with her. 'Otherwise, you're likely to get sfixiated, you got so many of 'em.' It wasn't until she'd reached the door that she remembered to tell Susan that there had been a number of calls for her while she was out. 'This time I left a list by the phone like you tole me to,' she said virtuously. 'Have a nice time.'

'Nice time?'

'Thought you said sumpin' 'bout goin' out to dinner tonight when you give me that dress to press. And, if you ask me, it's more fitten for a funeral. Anyways, give him my love.'

'Give whom your love?'

'This Carlo. Ain't he the one you're going out to dinner with?'

'I'm going out to dinner with an old school friend.'

'And you went to an all-girls' school, right? In that case, the dress is perfeck.'

There was, indeed, a list by the phone, but, as far as Susan could tell from Michelle's scrawl, it was a laundry list. Unless Susan's callers had consisted of individuals variously named Sheets, Towels, Pillowcases, and something she could not decipher at all. There were figures that looked like telephone numbers but seemed to bear no relationship to anything else. Michelle must have gotten the two lists mixed up. Or figured her employer would be able to tell from the phone numbers who her callers had been. But none of the numbers was familiar. Oh, well, Susan thought, if any of the calls were important, they'll call again.

The limousine arrived precisely at seven twenty-nine. 'Good evening,' the turbaned man said, as he opened the car door for her. So he spoke English. But, of course, some of Berry's entourage must speak English. The man on the phone, for example. Unless he'd been someone from the Waldorf.

Susan entered the car, observed by a small group of neighbours who seemed to have sprung up out of nowhere. If only the contractor would get a move on and finish the whole building, so she could get out of this place. Maybe if she dropped a word in Carlo Battaglia's ear, he would be able to rush things. She'd heard he had influence in the construction industry.

But you couldn't ask a man a favour and then kill him. Did she really want to kill him? Was he really that much worse than Mr Bloodstone?

CHAPTER 19

A woman in Gandistani garb admitted Susan to the royal suite, where the Begum and the king awaited her. The suite was standard Waldorf luxury, plus a few Oriental touches which the Gandistanis had presumably brought along with them to give the place a homey touch. There was the same spicy odour of incense she had smelled up in Berry's boudoir, although she saw no signs of an actual incense burner. Perhaps it was against fire department regulations.

Berry was resplendent in a crimson and gold garment, adorned with rubies and diamonds in all probable places plus a few improbable ones. This time there was an out-and-out tiara on her head. 'It'll be quite casual,' she'd said. Perhaps this was casual for Gandistan.

The young king wore a business suit. No turban. No beard or moustache, either. He looked much as he had in the photograph, except thinner and older, and what hadn't been evident in the picture was obvious now. His eyes were blue. As they had been in Susan's dream.

Susan looked at Berry to see if she had developed two additional pairs of arms to match Susan's other dream. She seemed to have only one pair, but there could easily be several more concealed beneath her voluminous dress.

Stop being fanciful, Susan told herself. She's not some mysterious Oriental. She's only Berry Rundle.

Both Serwar and his mother looked flushed and angry, as if Susan's arrival had interrupted a heated argument. Even royal families had their differences, Susan supposed, but she hoped they wouldn't continue their quarrel while she was there. Always so difficult for a guest to feel comfortable while a family quarrel raged around her.

The king shook hands with her. His grip was firm. 'Delighted to meet you, Miss Melville,' he said in a pleasant baritone.

He didn't look delighted. Does he have something against

me? Susan wondered. Could Berry have told him something to prejudice him? Or was he simply sulky about having to spend an evening entertaining one of his mother's friends?

On the other hand, he was a king. Kings ought to be accustomed to spending a large part of their time entertaining people who bored them.

No, Susan thought, he disapproves of me specifically.

She was intrigued. No one had ever disapproved of her before.

'Would you like a drink, Susan?' the Begum asked. 'Sonny and I are prohibited by Islamic law from touching alcohol, so we're sticking to fruit juice, but there's no reason why you shouldn't have a regular drink.'

'Oh, come off it, Mother. Everyone in Gandistan knows you drink like a fish.'

'You're just saying that to hurt me. I may take a little drink from time to time, but I've always taken great care to be discreet.'

Serwar gave a short, sharp laugh. His mother puffed angrily at her cigarette. Her holder this time was of carved white jade.

Before Susan had a chance to say she would be perfectly happy with fruit juice, another Gandistani woman glided in bearing a tray that held a bottle of sherry—apparently considered an appropriate preprandial beverage for a genteel infidel—with one glass and a plate of canapés. She was followed by the first woman carrying another tray with a glass pitcher containing a rather noxious-looking orange liquid and two glasses, as well as another plate of canapés.

Both set down their burdens and left with choreographic precision. There should have been music, Susan thought. At least a gong.

Serwar sipped at his sherry with obvious distaste. 'Don't you have something stronger secreted on the premises, Mother?'

'Not now, Sonny,' she said.

'Mother is always so concerned with appearances,' he said to Susan. 'Do you, too, worry about appearances, Miss Melville?'

'Don't call her Miss Melville,' Berry interposed. 'Call her—um—call her Aunt Susan.'

Susan gave her a dirty look.

Serwar laughed. 'I'm curious about you, Miss Melville,' he went on, 'because you're the only friend—the only American friend—of Mother's I've ever met, and I wondered what her friends were like. Did she have a lot of friends when she was growing up here in New York?'

Susan refused to be drawn into the royal differences. 'She was very popular,' she lied.

'You'll meet a lot of my friends at the Rundle House gala,' Berry told her son. 'Then you can see what they're like for yourself.'

'I told you I was not going to that gala. And I don't see how you can possibly expect me to. My face, even without whiskers, is known to some of the media. If you introduce me as your son, everybody will know who you are.'

A wave of Berry's cigarette holder sent ashes all over her rubies and diamonds. She brushed them off with a jewelled hand. 'But I'm not going to introduce you as my son. Think I'm a fool? You are going to go with Susan, and she's going to introduce you as her royal patron. What's more, you are going to go to the opening of her show in the fall—'

'Only if you want to,' Susan interrupted.

'Oh, I don't mind,' he sighed. 'I go to so many of those things, one more . . .' And he shrugged. 'I suppose I'll have to be the guest of honour, unless,' he added hopefully, 'you're also inviting the king of a large country or a president or prime minister.'

'I'm afraid Jill will expect you to be the guest of honour,' Susan apologized. 'Jill is my manager and very concerned with what she fancies to be my best interests.'

She is also, she thought, the wife of a secret agent who is taking a very unfriendly interest in your mother, and who will also be at the opening. But by that time, she told herself, it shouldn't make any difference.

Berry chuckled. 'I've heard about this Jill. Really rubbed

the Fish the wrong way, didn't she? Better not let her come near Carlo, though, if you value her health.'

Berry finished the sherry in her glass, as well as the contents of one of the plates of canapés, on which she had been nibbling ever since they arrived. 'I've been telling Sonny how much New York has changed since I used to live here.'

'I've been here before, Mother. I know that it's changed.'

'You never set eyes on New York until ten years ago. I was born here!'

She turned to Susan. 'I hadn't seen it since I left the country until about six years or so ago, when the old man started to fail and I was able to get away from time to time. Believe you me, it was a shock. Double-decker buses gone, Penn Station gone, the Astor gone. Remember how we used to meet our friends under the clock at the Astor, Susie? No, you were too young.'

So should you have been, Susan thought. One did not meet people of the same sex under the clock at the Astor.

'Before that, for over thirty years I was practically a prisoner. I could get magazines and newspapers from abroad. I could order anything I wanted from abroad. I lived in a marble palace with—with—'

'Vassals and serfs at your side,' Susan suggested.

'That was the trouble. I couldn't get them to leave my side. I couldn't get away from Gandistan.'

'Why should you have wanted to get away?' Serwar asked. 'Gandistan's an earthly paradise; isn't that what you've been telling those new business associates of yours?'

'For their purposes it is. They won't find a better place in the world to do business.'

'To do their kind of business. Oh, I agree to that. Don't you, Miss Melville?'

She didn't know what to say. Fortunately, the question seemed to be rhetorical, because, without waiting for an answer, he picked up the sherry bottle and looked at her. When she shook her head, he poured more sherry in his own glass.

Berry took the bottle from his hand and filled her own

now-empty glass to the brim again. Apparently she didn't worry about her attendants smelling her breath in the Waldorf.

Susan tried to shift to a neutral topic. 'What's the climate of Gandistan like?'

'Terrible,' Berry answered. 'Hot and sticky most of the time, with nasty little black flies that go after you in a very purposeful way.'

She seemed to recollect that she was supposed to be a Gandistan booster. 'Up in the hills it's quite cool, though. A lot of people go there in summer to escape the heat and, of course, the floods. But it's all absolutely unspoiled. No overdevelopment, no pollution.'

'Not yet,' Serwar said.

Once again Susan tried to change the subject. 'You speak remarkably good English, your majesty. I know you went to university here, but—'

'Still, I should have some sort of accent, eh? Well, don't forget I am half American. And all my tutors were either American or English. Please don't call me your majesty; it makes me uncomfortable.'

'Yes, your—er—Serwar.' If he'd had an English royal name, like Charles or Philip, it would have been easier. She couldn't bring herself to call him Sonny.

'Besides that, my grandfather didn't speak any language but English. My maternal grandfather, that is. My paternal grandfather died—of unnatural causes, like most of the rulers of Gandistan—long before I was born.' He sighed, as if he were wondering what his own chances of dying a natural death would be.

'My father lived in Gandistan till the end of his life,' Berry explained. 'He was great pals with my husband. They used to . . . engage in all kinds of sports together.'

'What happened to him? Susan asked.

Serwar opened his mouth.

'He died of a fever,' Berry said, a little too quickly. 'It must've been—um—around fifteen years ago. You were thirteen, weren't you, Sonny?'

He nodded.

'Yes, fifteen years. We gave him a lovely funeral. Remember his funeral, Sonny, wasn't it lovely? I will say this for my late husband, he really knew how to throw a funeral.'

'I would have thought you'd have had your father's body shipped back to the United States to be put in the family vault.'

'The family didn't want him alive; they didn't get him dead,' Berry said. 'Besides, he expressed a desire to be buried in Gandistan.' But she avoided Susan's eye, as she spoke.

'Your Majesty—' Susan began, after a moment of respectful silence.

'I told you, call me Serwar. Otherwise, I'll call you Aunt Susan.'

'Serwar, I happened to see you get off the plane the other day.'

He looked surprised. 'You were there? At the airport?'

'No, no, I mean I saw you on television that evening.'

'Ah, yes, the ubiquitous TV cameras. I noticed them but I hadn't realized I'd gotten on the evening news.'

'You were wearing a beard and moustache. And you're clean-shaven now . . . ?' She stopped, wondering whether the question had been too personal.

He laughed. 'No, I did not come here in disguise. Nor am I in disguise now. I shaved my beard and moustache off as soon as I got here. Audrey doesn't like them. Audrey, as I suppose my mother has told you, is my fiancée.'

'Audrey's your girlfriend. You don't have a fiancée.' His mother poured a little more sherry into her son's glass and a lot more into hers, which emptied the bottle. If the staff of the Waldorf thinks I'm the only one who drank the sherry, Susan thought, then they're going to think I'm a souse.

'You're probably thinking that Sonny doesn't need my permission to get married; he's the sultan. And you're right. As long as his bride is a Moslem—or converts to Islam, the way I did—' here she gave her son a peculiar smile '—nobody can interfere. After all, nobody stopped Sonny's dad from marrying me, did they?'

Serwar looked furious. 'Mother, must you wash our dirty linen in public?'

'I'm sure Audrey would be gratified to hear herself referred to as "dirty linen". Not that it isn't an appropriate description for—'

'*Mother!*' Serwar said warningly. Apparently he would stick up for the woman he loved, even if he wouldn't stick up for his country.

'And Susan isn't public,' she went on, waving her cigarette holder. A shower of sparks fell on her ample bosom.

'Be careful, Mother,' Serwar said, as he helped her brush them off. 'If you set fire to the place once more, royalty or not, we're never going to be allowed into the Waldorf again.'

She ignored him. 'Susan is my oldest and dearest . . . friend. We were practically brought up together. We even think alike in many ways.'

Now what does she mean by that? Susan wondered. Is it an insult? A threat? A warning?

Berry wiped away a tear that was ploughing a furrow in her makeup. 'Her father was the only man I ever loved. Your father was a good man, Sonny, but I never loved him. Oh, who's kidding who? He was a monster and I hated him. But I loved Buck Melville.'

Serwar looked from Susan to Berry and then back again. 'I knew there had been some romance in your life before you married my father. Heaven knows, you've talked about it often enough. But . . . Miss Melville's *father?*'

'Your mother had a crush on my father when she was fifteen,' Susan said quickly. 'You know how schoolgirls are. It didn't mean anything.'

'It meant a lot,' Berry said hotly, 'to him as well as me. You knew it then, Susan Melville, and you know it now. You just won't—'

The woman who had let them in appeared in the doorway and said something in Gandistani.

'Dinner seems to be ready,' Serwar said. 'And high time, too.'

CHAPTER 20

Berry rose and, waving her cigarette holder like a baton, led the way into an adjacent dining-room, where there was a table set for three. Here there was music, but it was Mozart, nothing Oriental. Susan wondered whether this was Berry's or her son's choice? Most likely it was the Waldorf's.

The Gandistani woman bowed and left.

'We're going to dine *en famille*,' Berry said. 'Serve ourselves. That way we'll be able to talk. You never know how much English they understand.'

The food, which had been laid out on a side table, appeared to have come from the Waldorf's kitchens, so it was standard *haute cuisine*, with no exotic Gandistani touches. Susan was thankful. During her previous sorties into United Nations circles, she had had enough experience with the various cuisines of Southeast Asia to last her a lifetime. The table settings were obviously the Waldorf's, except for a huge bulbous decoration of gilded (or, possibly, gold) metal, which was too hideous to be part of the hotel's service. It had to belong to Berry.

There was wine, too, presumably for Susan's exclusive consumption, since her place setting was the only one that held a wine glass. Was Berry under the impression that the servants would think Susan had been able to get through three bottles of Bordeaux all by herself?

'Why do you go on with this charade, Mother?' the young king asked, as he poured water into his and his mother's water goblets. 'Nobody thinks you're strictly observant. Our people all know you wear Western clothes when you go shopping.'

'Wearing Western clothes is one thing. Drinking alcohol is another.'

He made a little hissing sound between his teeth, just like his mother, Susan thought. Pity he wasn't more like her in strength of character, but she wouldn't wish any other of his mother's character traits upon him.

'Speaking of going out shopping,' Berry said to Susan, 'I'm planning to go to Bloomingdale's again with Lucy tomorrow. Not that she's the companion I'd choose if I had my druthers. She got sick when we were there this morning, and I had to send for someone to take her home. But I don't know anyone else in these parts any more. I guess the Fish would go if I asked her, but she's not the kind of gal you'd want to go shopping with.'

'I thought you liked to go shopping alone, as plain old Berry Rundle,' Susan said.

'Well, I do, but it's always more fun when you're with someone.'

She took a second generous helping of pâté. 'Now, Bloomingdale's is one of the few places in New York that's changed for the better. Remember what a dowdy old place it used to be? And look at it now. World famous for its sh-chic.'

She had trouble pronouncing the word. The wine was beginning to get to her. Not that, Susan suspected, the sherry had been her first drink of the evening.

Berry hiccuped. 'I must say I was really impressed by the place. It's like no other store in the world, their slogan says, and I believe it. As soon as things really get going in Gandistan, I'm going to see if we can't arrange to get a department store like that for Sultanabad.'

Serwar appeared to choke on his wine. He wasn't eating much, Susan noticed. She didn't feel much like eating herself, but she made an effort to put up a good show in order to demonstrate to Berry that she was entirely at ease.

'Maybe you would like to come to Bloomingdale's with me tomorrow, Susan?'

That thing in the middle of the table must be a magic lamp, Susan thought—even more magical than the one in *The Arabian Nights* because she hadn't even had to rub it to get her wish. Hadn't she been thinking only that afternoon what a perfect place Bloomingdale's would be in which t despatch Berry and wondering how she would lure her there. And now—presto!—Berry was inviting her to go shopping with her.

It couldn't simply be a coincidence. The genie of the bulbous thing must be on Susan's side. Perfectly understandable if he was a Gandistani genie.

All the same, Susan wished she could have another day or two in which to explore the terrain and plan her strategy. She had been thinking of getting a camera and photographing the maps on each floor so she could work out her campaign at home. Pity to give up her plans.

She tried stalling. 'I'd love to go with you. Trouble is, I promised myself I was going to spend the whole day tomorrow painting. I find it's very important to structure your life when you work on your own. Otherwise it tends to get—uh—unstructured. Couldn't we make it later in the week? Or, better yet, next week?'

'I'm afraid it has to be tomorrow. There are some things I need that I didn't have a chance to pick up today, because of Lucy. I know I could have tradesmen come up here and show me their wares, but then I might just as well be back in Gandistan.'

Sometimes overplanning could wreck a campaign. Many of Susan's best killings had been played by ear. 'Oh, I suppose I could take tomorrow off and go with you. After all, we haven't seen each other for so many years.'

'That's big of you,' Berry said. 'I promise I'll make it up to you.'

'I'm sure you will,' Susan said.

Serwar looked bewildered. 'Is there something here I'm missing?'

'Just girl talk,' his mother said. 'Maybe you'd like to come with us, Sonny?'

'I'd rather be dead.'

'Men always hate to go shopping,' his mother told Susan. Susan wondered on what life experience Berry based this observation. Had she been unable to drag her late husband, the supreme ruler of Gandistan, to the bazaar? Had the eunuchs turned petulant when asked to pick up a few things at the market?

Berry pushed a cigarette into her holder, and lit it, after several tries. Her son made no attempt to light it for her. 'Mother, I wish you wouldn't smoke while we're eating.'

'If wishes were watches, they would be fried,' Berry said thickly, and hiccuped.

Serwar said something in Gandistani that sounded distinctly unfilial.

There followed one of those awkward silences that so often fall in the middle of a social gathering. Susan felt it was up to her, as the representative of Western civilization, to break it. 'Since you seem to have been so favourably impressed by Bloomingdale's, Berry, are you going to recommend it to Mr Battaglia as a good buy?'

Berry looked uncomprehending. So did her son. 'Your mother was talking to me yesterday about his buying it,' Susan explained. 'She says it's for sale.'

'That's right,' Berry nodded. 'He's looking to buy into some upscale enterprise.'

'But Bloomingdale's! The Bat's thinking of buying Bloomingdale's! I don't believe it!'

'No doubt it's Audrey's favourite store,' Berry said.

'Audrey does all her shopping at discount stores. She says it's the politically correct thing to do.'

'A fine queen she'd make, I don't think,' his mother sneered.

Even though there were probably no discount stores in Gandistan, it did seem an unregal attitude. 'What does Audrey do?' Susan asked. Obviously a young woman who shopped only in discount stores and was politically correct was not likely to be a lily of the field.

'She works for the Coalition of Oppressed Minorities Everywhere. As a paid employee, not a volunteer,' he added. There was a distinct note of smugness in his voice. He had spent at least five years in the United States, Susan reminded herself. Plenty of time to pick up these activist attitudes.

'Big deal,' his mother observed, shaking ashes all over the table. She took a second helping of braised duck and all the rest of the herbed potatoes.

'Why, I know COME,' Susan said. 'I spoke at their auction of art by displaced Transylvanians last year, and I met a number of their people. I wonder if Miss—?'

'Skeat, Audrey Skeat. She says she met you.'

'The name doesn't ring a bell,' Susan apologized.

'Tall, thin girl who looks like a horse and brays like a donkey,' Berry said helpfully.

Serwar started to say something; then thought better of it.

Susan gave up representing Western civilization, and was silent.

'Since this is a special occasion, I have something very special here.' Berry lifted off the top of the bulbous thing and pulled out a bottle of Courvoisier with the air of a magician pulling a rabbit out of a hat. 'Oh, drat, we've already used the water glasses!'

'I'm sure there must be other glasses in the serving pantry,' her son said. 'If you're worried about the staff, you can always wash the glasses and put them back afterwards.'

'I am a queen,' Berry said. 'I do not do washing up.'

Serwar made the little family hissing sound between his teeth; then got up and came back with three glasses. He set one at each place. He was very obliging for a king, Susan thought. Too obliging, in fact. Audrey's influence, no doubt.

'No brandy for me, thank you,' Susan said. 'I've drunk too much wine as it is, and I'm beginning to feel a trifle sleepy.'

'No brandy for me, either,' Serwar said. 'I'll probably be going out for a drive after dinner.'

'To see Audrey, I suppose,' his mother said.

'Perhaps.'

'Then why did you get three glasses if you weren't going to drink?'

'I don't know. I suppose I didn't think.'

'You never think,' she said. 'That's your trouble. One of your troubles. Very well, then, I shall drink alone.' And, lifting her glass in the air in pantomime salute, she tossed off her brandy. She set down her glass. 'I wonder what your cousin Abdul would think of Audrey.'

'I don't give a damn what Cousin Abdul would think of Audrey,' Serwar said.

Abdul . . . the man who was going to be the titular head of the operation in Gandistan was called Abdul something or other; probably the same man, since Andy had said he was a cousin. But why should his opinion of Audrey matter?

'Aren't you going to eat your dessert, Susan?' Berry asked.

'I'm too full to eat anything more.'

So should Berry have been. In addition to eating most of the canapés before they even sat down, she'd cleared everything on her plate and finished what was left in the serving platters. Now she lifted Susan's dessert dish to her place. 'Build a better moussetrap and the world will beat a mousse to your door. And don't look at me like that. I'm not worried about my cholesterol. In fact. I don't believe there is such a thing as cholesterol. Just something those food fascists made up. And I'm not going to an exercise saloon—salon, either.'

Serwar looked surprised. 'Did Miss Melville suggest that you go to an exercise salon?'

'No, my beloved little shishter—sister, Lucy did.'

'You know you never pay any attention to what Aunt Lucy says. Why pay attention to her now?'

'It hurts when your own kith—whatever that means— and kin think you're too fat, even when they're an idiot. You don't think I'm too fat, do you, Sonny?'

'No, Mother, I think you're perfect.'

'You're being sus-sarcastic. You don't'preshiate all I've done for you, and I'm going to do for you. Hospitals, schools, libraries, everything you've always said you wanted.'

'Not everything,' he said. 'Not by a long shot.'

CHAPTER 21

He turned to Susan. 'Did you meet your fellow board members yesterday? And I don't mean my mother's relatives. I suppose you must have known them from before.'

'They're your relatives, too, Sonny. Your own kin and kith. Kith me, kith me again,' Berry sang to herself in an undertone.

'That's unfortunately true.' He shook his head. 'Maybe Audrey's right in refusing to marry me. My genes are nothing to write home about.'

'But I thought . . . ?'

'Oh, it's Audrey who won't marry me. If she'd say yes, I wouldn't care what Mother or anyone said; I'd marry her right away.'

'Oh, you would, would you!' Berry said. 'Jush you try and shee how far it gets you.' She hiccuped.

She's really disgusting, Susan thought.

'What I meant, of course,' Serwar said, 'is that I'd marry her if she'd agree to convert.'

'That's ri',' Berry said. 'If she won't convert, you can't marry her. Royal resh—reshponsibility. When the time comes, I will pick you a nishe wife. In Gandistan,' she explained to Susan, 'marriages are always arranged. Mush the bes' way.'

Serwwar pretended to ignore her. 'When I said "fellow board members" I was referring to the non-Rundle members of the board.'

'You mean those gangsters?'

'That's just what I do mean. Are they the kind of people you'd feel comfortable associating with?'

Berry frowned. Apparently her son was committing something that in anyone other than the king would be *lèse-majesté*. 'Have you heard about Carlo and Susan?' she asked him. 'Quite a little romansh there. Like you and Audrey. But with a happier ending, I trusht.'

'The Bat and Miss Melville! You said something about that before, but I thought you were joking.'

'She is joking,' Susan said. 'She's a great little kidder; she said so herself.'

Berry shook her head. 'I kid you not. He met her years ago at a wedding, and he's carried her image in his heart ever since.' She heaved a sigh which might not have been mock. She was so drunk she could have been sincerely maudlin.

'Your mother is exaggerating. I was at that wedding and I suppose I must have met him, although I don't remember it. He apparently remembers me. And that's all there is to it.'

'You're too modesht,' Berry said. 'How could anyone forget you? I certainly never did.'

She got to her feet unsteadily. ' 'Scuse me, mus' go to the little girls' room. Too much fruit juice.' She staggered out of the room.

'Poor mother,' Serwar said. 'I suppose in some ways she's led a difficult life. Gandistan is no place for a Western woman.'

'And an Eastern woman?'

'Eastern women are at least used to it, although conditions are changing for them in most countries, and I hope they will in Gandistan, too.'

'It's up to you, isn't it?' Susan asked.

'Ah, but even a king must answer to a higher power,' he said. She wasn't sure whether he was referring to his God or his mother.

'Maybe I will have some brandy, after all,' Serwar said. 'Sure you won't change your mind?'

She shook her head.

He poured brandy into his glass, but, instead of drinking, he looked into the depths of the liquid as if he saw some kind of vision of the future there. If he did, it was not a happy one.

'I'm glad to have the chance to speak to you alone, Miss

Melville,' he said at last. 'Tell me, why are you going along with all this?'

'I'm not going along with all this. I'm trying to keep out of it.'

'Then why didn't you just tell Mother that flat out? Why did you come here tonight?'

She couldn't tell him she was preparing the ground for his mother's demise. 'I hadn't seen her for forty years—I wanted to catch up on old times.'

He eyed her sceptically.

'And I was curious to meet you.'

He smiled. It was an attractive smile. 'Oh, and what do you think of me?'

'You're not what I expected.'

'And what did you expect? More of a wimp?'

'Something like that,' she admitted.

'I know it's hard for you to understand the way I've been acting—or not acting,' he said. 'Believe me, I have my reasons. But I can't tell anyone what they are, not even Audrey.'

There was nothing she could say in reply to that, not even that she understood, because she didn't understand.

'But then I can't figure you out either. Mother said you were definitely going to join the board of trustees. Was she lying again?'

'Not exactly,' Susan admitted. 'I didn't tell her I would join the board. On the other hand, I didn't tell her I wouldn't.'

'Why not?'

She shrugged. 'Oh, like you, I have my reasons.'

'I thought perhaps'—he hesitated—'she might be black-mailing you, too. It's an ugly little habit of hers, blackmail.'

Too? So Andy had been right. The Begum did have something she was holding over her son's head. But then Andy was almost always right. It was an ugly little habit of his.

'Was it something you did as a child?' Serwar persisted. 'But surely after all these years it must be long since forgotten, and probably it wasn't anything so terrible to begin with.'

She smiled and shook her head.

'Believe me, I'm not trying to pry into your affairs. It just occurred to me that she might be trying to blackmail you because of that fellow you killed outside Rundle House. I'm sure you must have had a very good reason,' he added hastily.

Oh, Lord, Susan thought, I seem to have been playing to a larger audience than I imagined. Should she pull out the stock phrase: I have absolutely no idea what you're talking about?

No, he deserved better than that. 'Were you the one who saw me?'

'No, if it had been I, I'm afraid that, not knowing who you were, and not knowing who the—er—object of your attention was, I would have called the police.'

'Yes, you would, wouldn't you,' his mother said from the doorway. 'Self-righteous little pig—prig—whatever. You could have gummed up the whole operation.'

'Then I wish I had been there,' Serwar said. 'Even if it meant turning you in, Miss Melville. You do understand, don't you?'

'I'm glad you didn't see me,' she said.

'The only one who saw you was an attaché from the Gandistani Mission who happened to be there on business. He's back in Gandistan now. You don't have to worry about him.'

'I already told her that,' Berry said, holding on to the back of a chair to steady herself. She seemed to have sobered up a little, but she was still by no means sober. 'I always play fair.'

He shook his head. 'No, Mother, you never play fair.'

'What I also told her was that I'd kill her if she didn't join the board. That was when she caved in.'

'I didn't cave in. I merely said I'd think about it, and I'm still thinking.'

'What was it with the girls of your generation?' Serwar

asked. 'Did they teach you to become killers in those exclusive private schools of yours?'

'You're a fine one to talk about exclusive private schools,' his mother said. 'You were tooted by tauters. Taught by tutors. What could be more exclusive than that?'

He laughed. 'I suppose that did sound funny, coming from me. I must have got it from Audrey. She's against privilege.'

'She's a Commie,' Berry said. 'A rose red Commie. "The King and the Communist." What a title for a romantic novel. Or how about "the Sultan and the Socialist?"'

'Don't you think you'd better go to bed, Mother?'

'I'm not in the leasht sleepy. Maybe I'll kill Audrey, too,' she said musingly. 'Solve everything.' She appeared to think. 'Well, not everything, but a lot.'

Susan looked at Serwar. He seemed unimpressed by the threat. 'Go to bed, Mother. I told Jumaan and Azra they could take the rest of the evening off after dinner, so it's the Waldorf staff that are going to come clear away the dinner things. We don't want to run the risk of having any of them see you in that state. It's not the impiety I'm worried about,' he explained to Susan, 'it's the embarrassment.'

CHAPTER 22

'I'll call you in the morning,' Berry said, 'an' we'll fish it up about Bloomingdale's.'

'Do you think you'll feel up to shopping tomorrow?'

Berry looked indignant. 'Shertainly. Why shouldn't I be?'

Well, if she wanted to go shopping—or shooting—with a hangover, far be it from Susan to dissuade her. At the same time, she couldn't just sit around waiting for Berry to call her. 'I have an early morning appointment, so I might leave before you get up. Why don't we arrange when and where we're going to meet now?'

'Good idea. Shave a lot of trouble. Ten o'clock? No,

maybe 'leven would be better, jus' in case I sleep late.'

'Which of the front doors shall we meet by?'

Berry shook her head for a somewhat longer time than a simple negative required. 'No, I hate waiting by doors. It makes me feel ekshpozhed. How about Intimate Attire—Intimashies—whatever they call it? You know, underwear. Tha'sh where we were heading when Lucy started carrying on.'

'Mother, Aunt Lucy got sick. She couldn't help it.'

'She could, too, if she put her mind to it.' Berry gripped the chair so hard she canted to one side. Her son took her by the arm and righted her. 'An' I wanna go to the Main Dish,' Berry said. 'Get glashes of my own. Drink whenever I like.'

'Main Dish?' Serwar asked.

'They call the floor where they sell housewares and dishes something like that,' Susan explained.

'Oh,' he said.

'So you'll take a cab downtown,' Berry crooned, 'an' I'll take a cab uptown.'

And, with any luck, Susan thought, I'll be in Bloomingdale's afore you.

'We'll meet on the third floor at 'leven. How does that sound to you? Or would you prefer to meet on the 'leventh floor at three?'

'The third floor at eleven will be fine,' Susan said. 'Bloomingdale's doesn't have eleven floors.'

'That wouldn't sh-shtop me.'

'But where shall we meet? The place is a maze.'

'Why don't we meet by the eshkalators? I love eshkalators. We don't have 'em in Gandistan and very few lellelevators.'

'And very few buildings more than two storeys high,' her son pointed out.

'That will all change. I have plans that will ashton-ashton-shurprise you.' She pointed a finger at Susan. 'The limou-limou-car will take you back now. That is, if you're going home. I don't want to rush you.'

'I am going home, but really it isn't necessary to get the limousine out for me.'

'It is neshesary. Gandistanis do not let their guests go home by themselves. There might be tigers. It'sh a jungle out there. S-sonny will make the arrangements. Nighty-night.' She held out her cheek for her guest to kiss; then, with a valedictory hiccup, she staggered off in an aura of alcohol and sandalwood.

Serwar sighed. 'She gets worse and worse, and there's nothing I can do. Anyhow, I'll drive you home myself. There are some things I want to say that I don't want anyone to hear.'

'But surely we're private enough here.'

'We'll be more private in a car. Just because Mother has gone to bed doesn't mean she'll stay there.'

'I hope she'll feel well enough to go shopping tomorrow,' Susan said, trying to sound concerned without sounding anxious.

'Mother has a pretty hard head. But I doubt that it will stop her from going shopping. I doubt that anything would stop her from going shopping.'

And if it does, Susan thought, I'll just have to postpone her killing to another day. But I will be disappointed.

'I'll call the garage,' he said. He left.

Susan was not happy at the prospect of being driven home by him. She knew that his blood alcohol level had to be way above the legal limit, even though it didn't show. The Rundle men had always been able to hold their liquor. Up to a point. And you never knew when that point had been passed. She visualized the headlines: POTENTATE AND PAINTER DIE IN FIERY CRASH. Or: PAINTER AND POTENTATE DIE IN FIERY CRASH. Depending on which paper you read.

She could offer to drive, but she didn't know how he would take such a suggestion. Even American men hated having their sobriety questioned. She could propose that they both leave in the limousine; then he could come up to her apartment and they could talk there. But that would mean the limousine with the two turbaned men would be waiting downstairs all the while, attracting nosy neighbours like a lodestone.

Serwar was off telephoning for what seemed like a long time, although according to her watch it took only ten minutes. 'The car's waiting. You didn't have a coat or anything, did you? All right, let's go.'

Downstairs, a dark blue Mercedes was waiting for them. Also waiting was the silver stretch limousine, complete with the two turbaned men. There was a short discussion in Gandistani, accompanied by a pantomime so expressive that Susan had no trouble understanding what they were saying. The two turbans were telling the king his mother wouldn't like him to be chauffeuring their guest himself, to which he was replying, 'Who's the king here, anyway?'

Finally they bowed, got into the limousine, and drove off.

'They'll follow us, of course,' he said, as he and Susan got into the Mercedes, 'but I'm accustomed to being followed. Usually less obtrusively, but they're stuck with the limo. If they stop to get another car, they'll lose us. Not that we'd be alone even if they did lose us,' he added, as the car swung out into Park Avenue. 'You'll notice that there'll be another car behind the limo and maybe another car after that.'

'I noticed when I was driving with your mother that there did seem to be some cars following us. Who were they?'

He shrugged. 'Local enforcement agencies, perhaps, anxious to protect us or to see what Mother and I are up to. Possibly some Gandistani organization, for the same reason.'

'The—er—board of trustees?' Susan ventured.

'The Mafiosi, you mean?' He laughed. 'Maybe they'd follow Mother; I doubt that they'd follow me. They wouldn't think I was worth following.'

There was a bitter note in his voice. Susan could not sympathize. She did not feel that the fact that the Mafia did not consider you worth following was an occasion for bitterness.

*

Serwar made a right turn and headed east. Stopping the car next to a little park overlooking the East River Drive, he opened the door for her. 'Let's get out here. We can't talk in the car. Someone might have bugged it—planted a listening device.'

'I know what "bugged" means,' Susan said.

The park was very dark and quiet. At first it seemed empty. Then she could make out the shadowy forms of bodies stretched out on the benches, perhaps sleeping, perhaps not. 'Do you think it's entirely safe here?' she asked. 'Some of those homeless people can be dangerous.'

'Audrey says we shouldn't call them homeless,' he observed. '"Residentially disadvantaged" is what we're supposed to say.'

Susan had some very unkind thoughts about Audrey. 'Whatever you call them, it doesn't make them less dangerous.'

'No, I should say it would probably make them more dangerous. At least if they heard it,' he added with a smile. He seemed to know what was passing through her mind. 'Audrey does get a little excessive in her zeal. But you must agree that it's a fault on the right side.'

Susan didn't agree at all. She changed the subject. 'Does Gandistan have a lot of homeless people?'

'No, we're too small and poor to be able to afford such luxuries.'

He took her arm, and urged her towards the park. 'There's no need to worry about this lot. Look, Ali and Samir are keeping an eye on us.'

He pointed with his free hand. Half a block away she could see the limousine parked in the shadows, glimmering like a ghostly chariot. 'They're licensed bodyguards, so they're armed,' he told her.

He looked at her with a faint smile. 'And, come to think of it, I wouldn't be surprised to discover you were carrying a gun, too.'

She gave the deprecating murmur that had, in the past,

usually stood her in good stead when the conversation took an awkward turn.

'Mother said it was quite customary for a woman in New York to carry a gun when she's going to a neighbourhood like the one Rundle House is in, but Audrey goes into even rougher neighbourhoods in the course of her work, and she never carries a gun.'

'Then Audrey's braver than I am,' Susan said, mentally crossing her fingers. A dismaying thought struck her. 'You didn't tell Audrey about that Lord man . . . ?'

'Of course not. She wouldn't understand. What's more, she wouldn't believe me. She thinks a lot of you.'

Under the circumstances, Susan was not unduly gratified by the compliment. I hope she isn't under the impression that I'm politically correct, she thought.

Serwar and Susan leaned over the rail and looked at the river down below. It was a beautiful spring night. The air was soft and warm and a faint breeze rippled the reflection of the moon in the water. You could hardly smell the garbage floating past. It was very quiet except for the occasional faraway scream across the river, from Queens.

For a moment Susan wished it had been someone other than Serwar standing beside her. Not that he wasn't an attractive young man, but he was the son of her childhood friend (loosely speaking). He had been gracious enough not to call her 'Aunt Susan' at his Mother's behest, but, if she asked him not to call her Miss Melville, then Aunt Susan was what he probably would call her. Hadn't he threatened as much? How could she have romantic ideas about anyone who called her Aunt Susan?

If only it could have been Gil Frias standing beside her, or possibly that nice young artist who had been so attentive to her at the Von Schwabes' dinner party the week before · last. But Gil was having trouble in his own country with a group of dissidents so incoherent in their manifestos that no one, including, many felt, the dissidents themselves, was sure whether they belonged to the radical right or the radical left. As for the young artist, she couldn't remember

408

his name, and, if he remembered hers, she told herself, it would be only because it was a celebrated one.

However, there were advantages to celebrity. After she had taken care of Berry tomorrow, she would, if she were still in a position to do so, call Mimi von Schwabe and see if she could weasel the young man's name out of her without Mimi's realizing what her friend was up to. Mimi tended to be very protective of her protégés.

Peter . . . ? Did Susan wish he were standing beside her? She would be glad to see him again, of course, but it was a long time since she had thought of him in connection with romance. If he were there now, they would probably be discussing the foundation's expenses, which had been increasingly over budget of late. She wondered whether he ever spoke to Dr Froehlich about romance? She wondered again whether Dr Froehlich had gone down to South America with the expedition? Dr Froehlich had been asked to resign from the Foundation back in January, but the expedition had not been Foundation-sponsored.

She really must call that young man from the foundation. Towers, that was his name, Ralph Towers, to ask if he'd heard anything from Peter. And, while she was talking to him, she might ask casually what Dr Froehlich was doing now.

'Audrey said she was planning to get in touch with you,' Serwar said.

'Audrey? With me? I hope she doesn't want me to serve on a committee because I'm already in over my head . . .'

'Nothing like that. I think she wants to talk about our situation. Hers and mine, I mean. She can't talk to anyone she knows. It's not that her friends don't know about her and me; it was no secret while I was going to school here. But she didn't know about the Rundle connection then. Now that she's met Mother and does know, I've asked her not to tell anyone.'

'And, since I already do know, she feels she can talk to me?'

He nodded.

'Did Audrey meet your mother here or in Gandistan?'

'Here. I've been here a few times since I left school. I arrived much less conspicuously since these weren't state visits, which getting an honorary degree at Harvard is, more or less. And once all three of us got together in Paris.'

'Has Audrey ever been to Gandistan?'

He shook his head. 'No, Mother invited her to come for a visit, but I advised against it. You never know what Mother might do.'

Susan could imagine. 'Audrey sounds like a determined young lady. Supposing she decided to go, anyway.'

He smiled. 'Gandistan doesn't exactly encourage tourism. And I've given instructions that if Audrey applies for a visa she isn't to get one.'

Susan and Serwar watched the water for a few minutes without speaking. A sightseeing boat glided past. Apparently some kind of party was being held on board because suddenly the comparative peace of the night was broken by raucous laughter and the sound of what passed for music in these degenerate days.

Several of the recumbent figures on the benches stirred restlessly. One sat up and waved his fist, before subsiding into his previous position.

'I know it sounds crazy,' Serwar said, 'but I think you should watch out for Mother. Sometimes I get the feeling that she doesn't like you as much as she says she does.'

'Sometimes I get the same feeling, especially when she threatened to kill me if I didn't became a member of the board of trustees.'

'Oh, I'm sure she was only joking about that. The board of trustees can't be that important, even to her.' But he spoke the words without conviction.

My joining the board of trustees isn't that important, Susan realized. It's my *not* joining that's important. She wants an excuse to kill me, something that would make sense to her twisted mind—or maybe something that would mean the Bat would be less upset if I were dead (although I don't suppose she'd let him know she was my killer, just to be on the safe side). She invited me to go shopping with her at Bloomingdale's because she realized as soon as she saw it that it was the perfect place in which to shoot me. She doesn't know I thought it would be the perfect place to shoot her. Or does she?

'I'm surprised Audrey hasn't called you yet,' Serwar said. 'When I told her yesterday that you were going to have dinner tonight with Mother and me, she said she was going to call you up before you left. And, when Audrey says she's going do so something, she always does it.'

'Maybe she did call and Michelle forgot to tell me. Michelle's my housekeeper,' she explained. 'Taking messages is not one of her strong points. Of course, I'd be happy to talk to Audrey, but I don't see what good I could do. From what you say, it isn't your mother who's standing in the way of your marriage, it's Audrey herself.'

'Oh, you mean because she won't convert? That's the official story. The truth is that Audrey's perfectly willing to embrace Islam. She says all religions are equal in the sight of God. Or the gods, depending. As long as you lead a'—he looked embarrassed; after all, he had been to Harvard— 'moral life.'

'Sort of the Abou Ben Adhem approach?'

Serwar looked defiant. 'Audrey may not be perfect, but I love her.'

Susan wondered if she were expected to say something supportive, like 'Good for you!' She didn't. 'Maybe she changed her mind about calling me—' she began. Then she remembered Michelle's laundry list. Sheets could have been Skeat. And, yes, pillowcases might be Pilokis, the contractor. And towels? Towers, of course. When she got back home, she would call Ralph Towers right away. Pilokis she would leave to Jill. And Audrey? Susan would wait and see what the morrow would bring.

'The truth of the matter is,' Serwar said, 'Audrey says she won't marry me unless I get rid of Mother.'

*

Susan was startled. There seemed to be more to Audrey than she had imagined. But she was disappointed in Serwar. Getting rid of one's enemies was one thing, but even the ancient Greeks, who were by no means squeamish, had frowned at matricide. And Serwar seemed like such a nice boy, too.

She felt relieved when he went on, 'Audrey wants me to pension Mother off and exile her from Gandistan. It isn't as if she would be alone in a strange land. She was born here and she has family here. So it shouldn't be a real hardship, especially as Mother kept telling Audrey how she was never happy in Gandistan. Actually, I think she was very happy there, particularly after my father became senile and she took over, which wasn't as long after their marriage as she would have people think, because otherwise it would make her responsible for a lot of things even she doesn't want to be held responsible for.'

'Well, why don't you do that? Pension your mother off. I mean. It sounds to me like the ideal solution to your problems. And, if you do it fast enough, you'd still have a chance of stopping the—ah—Rundle House gang from taking over your country. I gather the whole thing is still in the planning stage, that they haven't established a presence there.'

He nodded. 'No, none of the bigwigs have ever even been there. However, Mother won't take kindly to the idea of being pensioned off.'

'But what can she do if you put your foot down? After all, you're the king.'

There was a very long pause. 'Not really,' he said.

CHAPTER 23

For a moment she thought she'd misunderstood him. Then, from the expression on his face, she saw she had not. 'You mean you're not Berry's son? Or your father's son?' Hanky-panky in the harem; that would explain a lot.

'Oh, I'm her son, all right. And I'm the sultan's son,

too. I'm legitimate here in the United States, but not in Gandistan. You see, Mother never did convert to Islam. She and my father were married outside Gandistan, in an Episcopalian ceremony, she tells me. Her father, my grandfather, insisted on it. He said Rundles always had Episcopalian weddings, no matter whom they married.'

'I did wonder about that,' Susan said, 'but she told me your grandfather didn't mind her converting to Islam. Of course, she would have had to say that, wouldn't she, if she didn't want me to know the truth?'

Serwar nodded glumly.

'What I can't understand is why, under those circumstances, your father gave in and married her at all?'

'I suppose he was crazy to have her. His mind must have been going even then.'

Children never seemed to realize, Susan thought ruefully, that their parents had once been comely and desirable.

'And they were outside Gandistan when they got married, so he couldn't just have taken her by force, the way he could have at home. Anyhow, according to Islamic law, I'm illegitimate. So now you know why she can make me do anything she wants—almost anything, anyhow.'

After a pause, he said, 'I've never told anyone about this before, not even Audrey, and I'm sure Mother's never told anyone; she'd probably have signed her own death warrant if she had. But I don't know what to do, and I've got to do something. Before, when Mother was simply running Gandistan, I could say to myself: Well, things aren't any worse than they were before. I can just let them go on the way they are until—well—it isn't that I want anything to happen to Mother, of course, but she isn't a young woman . . .' His voice trailed off, as he met Susan's eye.

'She isn't all that old,' Susan said coldly. 'She could last for years.'

He looked abashed. 'Oh, I am sorry, Miss Melville. I didn't think. But you seem so much younger than Mother. Probably because you keep yourself in such good shape.'

He went off on a tactful tangent. 'When Audrey becomes queen—if she becomes queen, I should say—she's plan-

413

ning to institute a system of universal physical education, she says. Make Gandistan the fittest nation in the world.'

Susan had begun to suspect it before; now she was sure of it. Audrey was not the right girl for Serwar. There must be someone I know who would make him a more suitable wife, she thought, and she ran through all the princesses of her acquaintance in her mind. None of them seemed right.

'But how can your mother get away with it?' Susan asked. 'I know you said she never told anyone, but there must be other people who know you're not exactly legitimate.'

He shook his head. 'There's no one who could possibly know. No one who's alive, anyway. Mother's never had any confidantes. And, as I've said she was married outside of Gandistan—where, I don't know; she would never tell me. Maybe there are records, but nobody would know where to look for them.'

'You said no one who's alive,' she said. 'You mean your grandfather, I suppose.'

'At the time she was married, I think the current prime minister might have known, too, but he died soon after. Rumour said he was poisoned, but they always say that whenever anyone dies of natural causes in Gandistan. Besides, even if he was poisoned, he had lots of enemies before she ever got there. Prime ministers always do. It goes with the job.'

'Your mother said something about your step-brothers' having killed him.'

'That was his successor. I was too young to remember exactly what did happen to him. And the prime minister I do remember was openly beheaded; no mystery there. Since then there hasn't been a prime minister. And'—he laughed a little—'no great rush of applicants for the position.'

Susan was not interested in Gandistani's politics. 'If your mother is the only one who can prove you're not legitimate, I don't see why it should worry you.'

'Don't you see? That's what she's blackmailing me with. If I don't go along with what she wants, she says, she'll tell everyone I have no claim to the throne.'

414

Susan didn't see. She didn't see at all. 'But if you lose your power, she'll lose her power. Why don't you call her bluff? Tell her to publish and be damned.'

'It's more like publish and perish. You don't know Mother. Or, rather, you do know Mother. You should know she'd cut off her nose to spite her face any day.'

'But she'd have to be crazy to—' Susan broke off in midsentence. Berry *was* crazy.

'There wouldn't be any financial incentive for her to keep her mouth shut either,' he continued. 'She's been siphoning money from the treasury over the years, so I know she has a healthy account tucked away in a bank in some other country—which is one of the reasons Gandistan is so poor. Any pension I could afford to give her would be ridiculous. If she told the people of Gandistan the truth about me, she'd be quite comfortably off, provided she got away in time, and she'd be sure to do that. And, unless she gave me a chance to do the same thing, I'd be dead.'

'They wouldn't just kick you out?'

'No, they wouldn't.' He ran his hand through his thick, dark hair. 'The worst part of it is that I'm not sure the whole thing isn't a ploy of Mother's to get me to do what she wants, and she converted to Islam and married my father in a perfectly legal Muslim ceremony.'

'Does it mean so much to you to be king?' Susan asked.

'Are you suggesting that I just walk out while I'm here in this country, marry Audrey, settle down here, and get a job?'

'Well, yes, more or less.'

He sighed, and leaned with his back to the rail. 'Don't think I haven't thought about it. I wouldn't have any trouble getting a job; there's always a modest demand in this country for ex-kings. I could be a car salesman, professor, lobbyist, lots of things. And, even if I couldn't find a job, I wouldn't starve. I'm entitled to my share of the Rundle trust.'

'I'm sure Audrey would be pleased,' Susan said.

She was by no means sure that this would be true and

neither, it seemed, was Serwar. 'I'm afraid she might be disappointed. She's set her heart on being queen and establishing a new order, which is difficult when you're trying to bring in democracy, because people don't always want a new order. But Audrey wouldn't want me to be king if she knew I wasn't legally entitled to the throne,' he finished confidently.

'Don't you think the best thing for you to do would be simply to abdicate while you're here? You wouldn't even have to say that you think you might be illegitimate. Just do a reprise of Edward VIII.'

It was a while before his answer came. 'I suppose this is hard for you to believe, Miss Melville, but my roots are in Gandistan. I love my country. If I thought it would be good for Gandistan, I'd abdicate like a shot and live in exile for the rest of my life. But, if I do, my cousin Abdul would become king. He's next in line. If something should happen to me.'

'Abdul is the one whom the Mafia—or was it your Mother?—picked to head their—er—operations?'

He nodded. 'He's the largest opium grower in Gandistan, but that's not enough for him; he wants to make it internationally, and he doesn't care how he does it.'

'He doesn't sound like a nice man.'

'He isn't, but he isn't nearly as bad as my cousin Karim, who's the second largest poppy grower. Karim also could assert a claim to the throne if something should happen to me. If he does, there could be a bloody civil war.'

'Don't you have any nice relatives?'

'Princes don't stay in power by being nice,' he observed. 'Whichever of them succeeds in the end, Gandistan will be turned into a major international drug processing centre, just the way they've planned it, only without Mother, and they don't really need Mother.'

'So you're the only one who could save your country?'

He winced. 'I know it sounds conceited, but it's true. If I become king in fact as well as name I can put an end to their plans before they start. As it stands now, the army would be loyal to me. But once the Mafia have established themselves and their people in the country it would be too late.'

It was clear now why Andy wanted to get rid of Berry, though why the people in his own agency didn't handle the matter themselves, now that she was in the country and an easy target, was beyond Susan. Perhaps they always subcontracted assassinations so they could claim that their hands were clean. She hated to play into their hands by disposing of Berry, but she would be doing it for her own sake, and perhaps for King Serwar's, but not for theirs. And she could always console herself with the knowledge that this way she was saving the taxpayers money. They wouldn't even have to pay for the bullet.

'I suppose the first thing you'd do if you got your power is to destroy the opium fields,' she suggested.

He looked startled. 'I couldn't do that. The economy would collapse. Opium is our major industry as well as our only cash crop.'

'How do you think Audrey would feel about your continuing to grow opium?'

He looked thoughtful. 'We've never discussed it,' he said.

I'll bet you haven't, Susan thought.

'But that's a bridge I'll cross when I come to it. Right now the thing to do is put a crimp in Mother's plans. I don't suppose you have any ideas?'

None that I'm going to divulge to you, she thought. 'Maybe she could be declared *non compos mentis* as Berengaria Rundle while she's here. There's a very nice place where she could stay. I believe there are several members of your family living there already. But, of course, she can claim Gandistani citizenship. All they'd be able to do is deport her.'

'And in Gandistan she's as sane as any member of the royal family ever has been,' he said sadly.

CHAPTER 24

Suddenly there came a screech. A man had leaped up, either from a bench or out of the bushes, and was waving a knife at the two Gandistani attendants. 'Alien invaders!' he shrieked. 'Come to take over the earth. Begone! Take your spaceship and return to the stars, or I'll rip out your gizzards!'

His words made a crazy kind of sense. The stretch limousine looked as much like a spaceship as it did a regular car. In the moonlight, the two turbans, with a stretch of the imagination, could resemble space helmets. But neither Ali nor Samir looked like birds, and only birds, Susan believed, had gizzards. Oh, well, one couldn't expect biological accuracy from a madman.

One of the two bodyguards drew a gun. 'Don't shoot, Ali!' Serwar cried. 'He's crazy. He doesn't know what he's doing.'

Ali said something in his own language. He didn't lower his gun. Probably in Gandistan Serwar's words wouldn't make a whole lot of sense. Like most backward peoples, the Gandistanis would think, in their simplicity, that the only way to deal with a homicidal maniac was to kill him before he started carving up the community.

Serwar ran towards the man who was brandishing the knife. The man continued to advance. As he came into the pool of light cast by a street lamp, Susan saw him more clearly. He didn't look like a homeless person. His clothing, though casual, seemed to hail from Ralph Lauren rather than Canal Street. Probably he shopped at one of the better thrift shops. Susan had gotten some nice buys there in her preaffluent days, she recalled.

Before Serwar could reach the maniac, two men in business suits came up, one on either side of him. Each gripped him by an arm. The knife clattered to the ground.

'Police officers,' one of the business-suited men said,

showing a badge. The other one said nothing. He was Andrew Mackay. He carefully did not look in her direction. Let him tell me that he has no official connection with the government after this, she thought, keeping her own face a studied blank.

A police car rolled up. Two uniformed policemen emerged and took the man into custody. He didn't resist while they handcuffed them; in fact, he seemed to recognize them as old acquaintances. 'Hello, Joe,' he said. 'Hello, Bert. It's been a while since I've seen you. You're looking good.'

'You're looking pretty good yourself,' one of the policemen replied.

Several cars drove past in almost ceremonial procession, each with two men (or, in one case, a man and a woman) in it, all aggressively minding their own business. These, too, must have been watching them, Susan gathered. Such a lot of attention devoted to one minor monarch and one important but innocuous artist. Probably some of the people in some of the cars had been watching other people in the other cars.

'We've had trouble with this gentleman before,' Bert or Joe explained. She wasn't sure whether he was addressing Serwar and herself or Andy and his companion, but, as the only unofficial representative of the American people present, she took it upon herself to reply.

'So sad about the homeless. If only they had access to proper psychiatric treatment . . .'

'Oh, Mr Frobisher's not homeless.'

Mr Frobisher bowed, seeming to take this as an introduction. Susan, not to be outdone in courtesy, gave him a gracious inclination of her head.

'And he's under constant psychiatric care. He's a retired stockbroker. Lives on Beekman Place. Overdosed on *Star Trek* when he was young, or so they say. Every now and then when the moon's full he gets away from his attendants and comes out here to watch for invaders from space. First time I've seen him with a weapon, though.'

'First time I ever caught any invaders,' Mr Frobisher pointed out. 'Of course, if I'd known you were watching, I would never have taken it on myself to repel them. I have the utmost faith in New York's finest, no matter what people say.'

'So nice to have met you,' he called to Susan, as he was stuffed into the police car. 'You know all about me. Perhaps we could do lunch one of these days, and you can tell me all about yourself.'

The police car departed, Andy and his associate vanished into the shadows. Ali and Samir got back into the limousine. All was as before. 'I feel as though I'd been part of a show,' Susan said.

'In a way, I suppose, you have. Well, now I've got my secret off my chest, you know what? I don't feel any better. In fact, I feel worse.'

'I'm sorry I couldn't have been of more help,' Susan said.

'No need to blame yourself. Probably there's no one who could help me. Maybe you're right. Maybe abdication is the only answer. If I can't save my people, at least I can save myself. There are worse things than exile, I suppose.'

'Don't be in a hurry to abdicate. Maybe we can think of something less drastic.' Or more drastic, she thought; only he wasn't to know that.

'It's getting late. I think I'd better drive you home.'

Both of them were silent on the way back. He escorted her to her front door and bade her good night. The neighbours who hung out in the lobby at all hours paid no attention. If only they knew he was a king, Susan thought, they would be all over him.

When she got upstairs, she looked up Ralph Towers' number and called him. Only an answering machine responded. She left a message, then started to check her tape to see if anyone else had tried to reach her.

Before she could finish, the phone rang. 'Susie! 'Bout time you got home. I tried to reach you before, but a machine answered. I don't talk to no machines.'

'Why, Mr Battaglia—'

'Carlo.'

'Why, Carlo, how—how nice to hear from you. I was planning to write you and thank you for the beautiful flowers.'

'Glad you liked 'em,' he said. 'And you don't hafta write. That's too formal for old friends like us. So, tell me, how'd the dinner with Queenie go? Did she tell ya about the great things we're gonna do for Rundle House? Did she make you see you gotta be a member of the board of trusties? We need ya, Susie, we need ya.'

How did he know about her dinner with Berry? Had Berry told him about it? Or had he been having either Berry or Susan herself watched? More likely Berry. For which she could hardly blame him. If she'd been about to go into a business venture with Berry Rundle, she would watch her like a hawk.

'We didn't talk about Rundle House at all. We were too busy reminiscing about old times. And this was the first time I'd met her son.'

'Yeah, Serwar, Sonny, whatever his name is. Snotty kid. Although, of course, bein' a king, I guess he can't help bein' snotty.'

'He seems to me like a pleasant, unaffected young man.'

'Well, people like that—kings, princes, even dooks, I shunt be surprised—are brought up not to show their feelin's, so you can't expect him to be affectionate. His mom said somethin' about him wantin' to marry an American girl. And not a society girl, either. You'd think he'd marry a princess, somebody like that, keep the royal blood blue.'

'Times have changed. Look at the British royal family.'

'Yeah, just look at 'em.'

It had been narrow-minded of her, Susan thought, to restrict her attention to princesses in connection with Serwar's prospective bride. There were plenty of red-blooded American girls who might make him a good wife. Amy Patterson's youngest, whatever her name was. And didn't Mimi have some nieces who might be eligible? She would have to look into them.

*

421

'Well, I din't call ya to gossip about the love life of royal folks; I called to ast if you could have dinner with me tomorrow night.'

She didn't want to accept any invitations until she had completed her task at Bloomingdale's. Even if all turned out well, she wasn't sure he wanted to have dinner with Carlo Battaglia on the evening of the day he lost a business associate. In fact, she wasn't sure she wanted to have dinner with Carlo Battaglia at all. It wasn't that she was image conscious, but it wouldn't look well for a serious artist to be seen having dinner with a notorious gangster, even if she had Jill spread it around that he was thinking of starting an art collection.

'I'm afraid I'm not free tomorrow night,' she said, wondering whether declining a dinner invitation from a Mafia don was the mob equivalent of *lèse-majesté*.

'What about Friday?'

She couldn't keep putting him off. 'Friday will be fine,' she said. Would he take her to Federigo's Fish House? At least Federigo's was not likely to attract gossip columnists.

'Good. I'll make reservations in some classy place. You got any preferences? Four Seasons? Lutèce? Palm? You name it.'

She couldn't say she would prefer Federigo's Fish House. 'They're all fine with me.' She tried to console herself with the thought that it wasn't likely that he'd be able to get reservations at a 'classy place' on such short notice. On the other hand, maybe *he* could.

'Then I'll pick ya up at—say—seven?'

'I'll be looking forward to it,' she said, trying not to strangle on the words.

He started to bid her good night; then interrupted himself. 'Oh, by the way, when're ya gonna see Queenie again?'

'I'm going to see her tomorrow.'

'You two havin' lunch?'

'We're going shopping at Bloomingdale's. I suppose we will have lunch afterwards.' Why was he quizzing her like this?

'Bloomingdale's,' he repeated. 'Fine store, fine store. My

late wife, God rest her soul, would never shop anywhere else. Always kept astin' me to go there with her, but I never had the time.'

He sighed, as if the late Mrs Battaglia would be alive today if he had agreed to accompany her to Bloomingdale's. 'Did Queenie tell you I'm thinkin' of maybe buyin' the place? I meantersay if the price is right.'

'She did say something about it.'

'Mind ya don't say nuttin' about it to nobody,' he cautioned her. 'Once people know you're interested, the price goes up.'

'I wouldn't think of it.'

''Course not. But it never hurts to make sure. Well, I'll be countin' the minutes till Friday. Sweet dreams. Susie. and I hope I'm in 'em.'

He was, but not in any way he would have appreciated.

CHAPTER 25

The next morning Susan got up and searched through her wardrobe for an outfit suitable for stalking a human quarry through a department store. A tweed suit would seem most fitting and would probably be a fashion editor's selection, but the sleeves of a tailored jacket would almost certainly be a hindrance, unless it had been specially designed for shooting. In the end, she opted for a short-sleeved slate blue linen dress with a matching long-sleeved jacket which she would later take off and carry draped over her arm to conceal her gun until such time as she was ready to use it. She hoped she wouldn't be forced to shoot through the jacket. The ensemble was a favourite of hers. She'd been told that it matched her eyes.

She loaded her best Beretta and put it into the handbag she had bought at Bloomingdale's the day before—only right that a Bloomingdale's kill should be accessorized with a Bloomingdale's bag. Did Bloomingdale's sell guns? To use a Bloomingdale's gun would add to the symmetry of the occasion, but it was too late to do anything about that now.

She didn't feel hungry; however, she knew it would be a mistake to go on a hunting expedition on an empty stomach, so she forced herself to swallow a cup of coffee and eat a slightly stale croissant, which was all she could find in the kitchen.

Michelle arrived as she was finishing the croissant. 'I was savin' that for myself,' she complained.

'You can buy some more when you go shopping this morning,' Susan said as she rose, 'along with whatever else we need—which is practically everything. I've made you a list, but that's just for starters. Feel free to add to it if I've left out anything.'

'Don't look like you lef' nothin' out,' Michelle said, looking at the lengthy screed her employer had prepared. 'Folks who run the supermarket are gonna be eatin' high off the hog for a long time after an order like this 'un. Does this mean you're gonna be back for lunch?'

'I'm not sure.'

'I wish you'd make up your mind. How can I make any plans if you don't make any plans?'

Susan counted to five. 'Just plan to go shopping this morning so there'll be food in the house.'

Michelle sighed. 'Okay, okay. You're the boss.'

As if there had been any doubt about it, Susan thought. She really must do something about Michelle. But there was time for that. Which is what I always keep telling myself, she thought.

'Whaddya want me to say if somebody calls? I 'spose you want me to lie for you again?'

'Just tell them the truth, that I'm out and you don't know where I am or when I'll be coming back.'

' 'Sposin' that Mr Towels starts callin' again? He was mighty anxious to reach you yestiddy. Lessen you got to talk to him las' evenin' . . . ?'

It was none of Michelle's business, but Susan didn't want her to think her employer had neglected any of the norma obligations of courtesy. 'I did call him, but he wasn't in, so I left a message on his machine.'

'Great. Now he's gonna call and drag me away from my work. How can you expeck me to get any work done if I hafta keep answerin' the phone?'

'I've told you over and over to leave the answering machine on. Then you won't have to answer any calls. In fact, I would prefer—'

'But some of the calls might be for me,' Michelle objected. 'I wooden wanna miss any of my calls. By the way, I meant to tell you. Mr Pillowcase said he insisted on talkin' to you personably; said he'd rather deal with Tilly the Hon than that there Miz Turkey.'

Susan had planned to call Ralph Towers that morning, but she didn't want anything to distract her for her immediate project. Besides, she wanted to get to Bloomingdale's at least an hour before her appointment, so she could spy out the lay of the store, and it was almost ten o'clock now.

'I'll call Mr Towers again from outside,' she said, picking up her bag and gloves. 'As for Mr Pilokis, if he calls again, tell him he's going to have to deal with Miss Turkel. That's what I pay both of them for.'

'What about Tilly the Hon?'

'Tilly . . . ? Oh, he'll have to take his chances.'

'He! I thought he was a she!'

'You learn something new every day,' Susan told her.

When she got to the lobby, Susan asked the doorman to hail her a cab. Hailing a cab was easy. Not so getting one. 'Always a shortage of cabs at this hour,' the doorman apologized as cab after cab sailed past with its light off. 'People going to work, stuff like that.'

He made it sound as if it were all part of some kind of plot. Perhaps it was, Susan thought. Why should everybody go to work at the same time or approximately the same time? It made sense in the dark ages but, now that artificial illumination had been invented, how much more efficiently the city's resources could be utilized—how much safer the city would be—if working hours were extended around the clock.

*

She could always make the journey downtown on foot. Bloomingdale's was less than thirty blocks away—a mile and a half—no great distance for someone who lived in Manhattan, where feet were the only reliable method of transport. Under normal circumstances, she would have walked to the store and enjoyed it. But it would take her at least twenty minutes to get there, what with stopping for traffic lights and circling to avoid street solicitors. She couldn't afford to spend twenty minutes.

An unoccupied taxi appeared. With a cry of triumph, the doorman flung himself in front of it, at considerable risk to life and limb, but desperate measures were needed. A bankerly type was hailing that same cab from across the street, and bankers would stop at nothing to achieve their ends, especially now that chivalry had long since died in financial circles.

Susan rewarded the doorman with appropriate lavishness and got inside the cab, twisting herself so she could look out of the rear window as she rode. Was anyone following her? Not that she could see, but a skilful tail would probably be able to conceal himself from her nonprofessional eye. No reason why anyone should follow her, she assured herself. It had been the king and the queen who were being followed on the previous days.

She arrived at Bloomingdale's. There was a demonstration going on outside for or against something or other. Ignoring the demonstrators, she entered the store, and, after evading the ladies who lurked in the aisles poised to spray shoppers with the latest scent, she got into an elevator. A young man who had obviously been less lucky in dodging the spritzers squeezed in through the doors just before they closed, filling the elevator with oppressive aromas.

Even though this was the classic behaviour of a follower, at least in the movies, she might not have paid any attention to him had his face not been somehow familiar. Where had she seen him before? Not an acquaintance or the son of an acquaintance; his tailoring was too sharp for a member of her own circle.

There was a leather case slung over his shoulder—a squat case, too large to contain binoculars, and the wrong shape. A camera? No opening for a lens. A tape recorder, perhaps, or a radio. If she figured out what it was, perhaps she could figure out who he was.

She gave him a half smile in case he turned out to be someone she had encountered without noticing, like a delivery man or a supermarket clerk. He avoided her eye in a manner that was so furtive it increased her suspicions. So, instead of getting off at 'Intimacies' on the third floor, she continued up to the fourth, where, according to the store directory, a ladies' room might be found.

On the fourth floor the store seemed as she had noticed before, to have departed from the traditional concept of aisle and counter almost entirely. Almost everything seemed to be arranged in clusters and boutiques, so that it was impossible to proceed on one's way in a straight line. As she zigged and zagged her way through to the rear of the store where, a map on the wall indicated, the ladies' room lay, she kept catching glimpses of the young man behind her in one of the many mirrors set all over at such angles that often the shopper found herself (or himself) walking into a reflection instead of his (or her) intended destination. Music kept playing, not loudly but insistently, while banks of television screens showed what she feared must be the latest fashions.

She went into the ladies' room. Let him try to follow me in here, she thought! However, her victory was only a moral one—and a transient one at that. There was no other exit, at least not for shoppers. There might have been some secret means of egress known only to store employees, but a fat lot of good that would do her.

She spent several minutes in the seclusion of a cubicle, practising the art of taking off her jacket and draping it gracefully over her right arm, while, at the same time, she held her gun in her hand. She put the gun back in her handbag, since—she checked her watch—there were still twenty-nine minutes to go before her rendezvous with Berry; and she didn't want to run the risk of dropping the weapon absent-mindedly, in case she should happen to come across a really good buy. Putting the gun back, however, she was soon to find out, was a grave mistake.

When she came out of the ladies' room, the young man was not only standing outside, he had extracted a portable telephone from the case he carried—so that mystery was solved—and was talking into it. 'But I can't follow her into the ladies' room, Uncle Carlo—' he was saying, when he caught her eye and broke off. His face flushed a bright red. Squawking noises came from the instrument.

Another mystery solved. She recognized him now. 'You're Nicky—whatever your last name is. Mr Battaglia's nephew.'

'Lady, I don't know what you're talking about,' he said without conviction.

'If you don't stop following me, I shall complain to the management. Or I might not need to. There are store detectives all over the place.'

Which was probably true. She'd better watch her own step.

The young man turned even brighter red. 'I was not following you,' he said. 'I—'

'It's my belief you're some kind of pervert. Loitering outside the ladies' room with a cellular phone and making suggestive remarks as people come out.' Her voice was not loud, but clear and carrying.

'He must be sick,' a young woman dressed in the height of fashionable bad taste said to her similarly attired companion as they emerged from the ladies' room. 'Imagine making suggestive remarks to *her*!'

Both of them giggled. Nicky's face was like a sunset. He tried to stuff the phone back in its case. 'I was not making suggestive remarks to her,' he gulped. 'Or anybody. I—I was just standing here, minding my own business. I—I—'

And he turned and fled, plunging into a rack of garments which collapsed, taking him down with them in a tangle of wildly patterned organzas from which, Susan thought with satisfaction, he would not be able to extricate himself in time to avoid the stern-looking young man, obviously a Bloomingdale employee, bearing down on him.

The two young women burst into girlish laughter. Susan could almost feel sorry for the unfortunate Nicky.

What was Nicky doing in the store? Clearly he had been dispatched by his uncle to keep an eye on her. But why? Was the Bat aware of Berry's plan to terminate Susan? Even less likely, did he suspect Susan's plans to terminate Berry? No, it was impossible that he could have known what was in Susan's mind, only minimally less likely that Berry would have confided her intentions to him. What did it matter? She had twenty-five minutes left to check out the third floor, pick her vantage point, and get out her gun, so she had better get cracking.

She reached the top of the escalator leading down to the third floor. There seemed to be some sort of disturbance at the bottom. A stout lady dressed in a purple silk suit topped by a sable stole and a floppy cream-coloured hat was hitting a young man over the head with a large stiff leather hand bag. 'Get away from me, you sex fiend!' she was shrieking.

The young man was whimpering. Could Nicky have gotten downstairs that quickly? No, this was another young man who looked very much like Nicky, and dressed very much like him, even to the leather case banging against his side which, Susan presumed, held another cellular telephone.

Shoppers smiled as they passed, clearly thinking that this was a piece of performance art devised by Bloomingdale's in its constant effort to keep the tourists entertained. Under other circumstances, Susan would have thought the same.

As the escalator started moving downward, bearing Susan inexorably towards 'Intimacies', the lady in purple gave the young man's head a final thump. He ran off, howling.

The stout lady looked up and met Susan's eyes. Susan should have realized that, if she planned to come early, the same idea might have occurred to Berry. Hadn't Berry herself pointed out that they thought the same way? A result of their upbringing, of course, rather than any similarities of character, Susan assured herself.

For the first time a dreadful thought occurred to her. Her father had taught her to shoot. Her father had also taught Berry to shoot. Although she had denied it before—to Berry, to her self—was it possible that Berry was as good as a shot as Susan was? Was it possible that Berry was an even better shot than Susan?

CHAPTER 26

Whether she was as good a shot as Susan or not, she certainly had the drop on her. Susan's gun was still in her handbag. Berry's gun—it had a jewelled handle; wouldn't you know it—was out.

Slowly Susan moved her hand towards her handbag. Berry lifted her gun. A smile slowly spread over her face— an evil gloating smile. This is it, Susan thought. Curtains for Susan Melville. NOTED ARTIST SLAIN ON DEPARTMENT STORE ESCALATOR. What a way to die.

There was a cough. 'Pardon me.' An elderly man in tweeds popped up at Berry's elbow. 'Could you tell me where the sporting goods are?'

Berry's mouth worked but no sound came out. The elderly man brought his mouth close to her ear. 'I said, "Do you know where the sporting goods are?"' he bellowed, in a voice calculated to penetrate even the most obdurate eardrum.

Berry regained a measure of control. 'No need to yell. I'm not deaf. And I have no idea where the sporting goods are.'

'Then why are you standing there waving a gun about?'

Berry looked down at the gun in her hand as if she didn't know how it had gotten there. 'Oh, this isn't a gun. It's a —a cigarette lighter.'

Those seemed to be the magic words. Suddenly the area in front of the escalator was filled with store personnel.

'Smoking is not allowed in the store,' said an authoritative young woman.

'It's against the law,' said an equally authoritative young man. 'On the other hand, it is permitted in all of our restaurants.'

'Sorry, sir,' said a middle-aged woman, 'but Bloomingdale's does not have a sporting goods department.' She turned to Berry. 'However it does have a department of clothes for the full-figured woman, which is located on the Metro level.'

Berry gave her a suspicious look. 'What's the Metro level?'

The escalator decanted Susan right in front of Berry. The two ladies glared at one another. 'The Metro level is the basement,' Susan informed her. 'And "full-figured" means "queen-sized". In other words, fat.'

All three Bloomingdale employees paled. 'Bloomingdale's has no basements,' the authoritative young woman declared.

'And we never use the word "fat",' the middle-aged woman added.

All three kept their eyes fixed on Berry. She put the gun back in her handbag. Susan moved to the side, out of earshot of the Bloomingdale bunch. She indicated with her head that Berry was to follow her, which Berry did with the utmost reluctance.

'I don't know why you want to kill me,' Susan said in a low voice. 'I've never done anything to you.'

'Never done anything!' Berry's voice rose. '*Never done anything! Do you call ruining my life nothing?*'

'Shhh, we're attracting attention.'

Berry lowered her voice, probably recollecting that this was not Gandistan, and it was wiser not to engage openly in heated argument with someone whom you were planning to kill shortly. 'You came between Buck and me. Do you know, I never saw him again after that time you interfered!'

Susan was glad to know it. She had never been sure.

'He told me on the phone that it would be too dangerous for us ever to meet again now that you knew about us. I

431

begged and pleaded but he said no, it was all over, but he would treasure my memory forever. I've hated you ever since.'

Her face swelled with the effort, she was making to keep her voice down. 'And you've hated me, because you were jealous. You wanted him all to yourself. You had an Electra complex, or whatever they call it now.'

'They don't call it anything, because there isn't any such thing—at least not any more.'

'Of course, you'd say that. But it's true.'

'You're crazy, do you know that? Mad as a hatter. Besides, I don't hate you. I merely dislike you more than words can say.'

'People don't try to kill each other just because they dislike them. And I know you came here to kill me—no use denying it.'

'I'm not denying it. People do kill other people who are threatening to kill them, and you threatened to kill me if I didn't join the Rundle House board. What else can I do? Besides, you're a menace to society.'

Berry's voice was incredulous. 'You want to kill me because you think I'm a menace to society? And you call *me* crazy!'

The authoritative young man approached them. 'Pardon me, ladies, but I'm afraid you're blocking traffic. If you could just move to some other part of the store. The restaurants are open for breakfast,' he added.

'I'm so sorry, I didn't realize we were in the way,' Susan said. Berry looked as if she were going to spit at him.

He backed away from them. The two ladies backed away from each other, like a pair of cats with uncertain territorial imperatives. Once she was sure she was well out of range of Berry's gun, Susan began to turn; then wheeled, in case this was some kind of feint on Berry's part.

But, no, she was walking away as briskly as she could—rather, waddling away. She'd had sense enough not to wear stilt heels for the occasion, but even two-inch heels were too high for her to manage a rapid getaway.

Seen from behind, she was even more outlandish than

from in front, and an above-the-knee skirt, however fashionable, was simply wrong for someone with knees like hers. There seemed to be some sort of sticker on the back of her stole with a printed legend on it that Susan was too far away to be able to read. 'Plain old Berry Rundle,' Susan thought, was a lot more conspicuous than the Begum in full regalia.

Susan went over to the bank of elevators, which fronted upon a long, deserted corridor—a good place for a shoot-out, she thought, as she glanced warily at both ends. Since she appeared to be alone for the moment, she took the opportunity to remove her jacket, take out her gun, and drape the jacket over it.

She pressed the elevator button with her free hand. She felt more confident now. Whichever came first, the elevator or Berry, she was ready for either.

The elevator came first. Going up. Up was as good as down, especially since she had no idea where Berry might be. Hadn't she said something about needing to buy glasses? The 'Main Course'—china, glassware, housewares—was on the sixth floor, Susan recalled. She decided to make that her destination. If she did not find Berry there, she would take the elevator back down, floor by floor. Anyone riding down on an escalator made too good a target.

There were only two passengers in the elevator. One was a middle-aged woman who gave the usual stony stare to the newcomer. The other was the young man who had been following Berry.

Susan pretended not to recognize him. He appeared not to recognize her. Perhaps he really didn't recognize her. He couldn't have seen her coming down the escalator. He might not even know what she looked like. It all depended on whether he had been at the trustees' tea or not.

She got off at the sixth floor. The young man remained on the elevator. Either he was going to bedding and linen on seven or whatever it was they had on eight; she couldn't remember. Or he didn't know where he was going. He looked as if he didn't know where he was going.

There were so many fragile objects on the sixth floor that navigation was hazardous, complicated by the fact that there were so many mirrors around. Even the wariest shopper ran the risk of either crashing into a mirror or into a delicate display. There weren't too many people around; and they were visible sometimes as themselves, sometimes as reflections. But neither reality nor reflection wore purple, so, unless Berry was a quick-change artist or lurking somewhere behind a partition or in the corridor off which the elevators opened, she was not on the sales floor.

Susan walked past an army of arcane kitchen gadgets that would have had Michelle drooling, over to the escalators. Banks of TV screens were promoting a special purchase of Ruritanian crystal in insinuating continental accents. She looked down to the fifth floor, while trying to keep an alert eye behind her—not as difficult as it might seem, because she was bound to see a purple flash in the mirrors if Berry were suddenly to appear.

All she could see below was furniture. No sign of Berry downstairs (down-escalator?) unless she was hiding behind that overstuffed couch. For a moment Susan thought she saw Berry peering out between the shelves of an étagère—but, no, it was only a large and particularly hideous Toby jug.

She knew that looking for Berry in Bloomingdale's was like looking for the proverbial needle (notions) in a haystack (beauty salon). Her confidence was beginning to ebb. You could be lost in Bloomingdale's for days and no one would find you. The only reason she felt she had any chance of finding Berry was that she knew Berry would be looking for her.

She was not going to give up now. She would proceed in her quest. The next step would be to check the fifth floor on its own level. She started to head in the direction of the elevators; almost walked into a mirror which was reflecting the area in which she thought she was going; swerved and came within a hair's-breadth of colliding with a table full of Chinese rice bowls.

'Susie!' a voice called out behind her. 'Susie! I been lookin' all over the store for ya!'

She turned. There was the Bat, Carlo Battaglia, C. Montague himself, with a burly man on either side of him. In fact, there were two Bats, with four burly men. Behind them she could see two hangdog young men carrying cellular telephones; no, four hangdog young men with four cellular telephones; and, if she looked in the wrong direction, an infinite number of hangdog young men carrying cellular telephones.

She didn't know which were real and which were reflections. She didn't care. Whichever they were, they were in her way. If only they would all prove to be illusory and vanish.

No such luck. 'I thought I'd give you two ladies a surprise and join ya,' the Bat beamed. 'I wanted to look over the place before I made 'em an offer, so I says to myself what better way to do it than in such classy company.'

'So that's why he was following me,' Susan said, gesturing at Nicky—or was it Nicky's reflection? Whichever it was turned red and stumbled into a display of huge copper pots which clanged but did not topple. The Bat frowned. 'You wanted to know where in the store we were going to be?'

'I tole him not to letcha see him,' the Bat said. 'But even if you din't, you were bound to smell him. Phew, he stinks to high heaven!'

Nicky sounded near tears. 'I cooden help it. A lady downstairs sprayed it on me. And it isn't a stink; it's the latest in fashionable masculine scents. She give me a little card that says so. See!'

The Bat shook his head. 'I'm afraid Nicky's not good for much. Not that Tony's much better.'

Tony gave a nervous leap. A tray of crystal goblets swayed and shattered.

The display might be a reflection, but the crash was real.

435

A saleswoman strode towards them, blood in her eye.

'He let the queen chase him away, but at least he saw ya in the elevator and tipped me off where ya were heading. Well, whadda you want?'

The saleswoman opened her mouth, but seemed incapable of speech. She pointed to the smashed crystal.

The Bat waved his hand. 'Oh, that! I'll take care of it.' He reached into his breast pocket.

Good heavens, Susan thought, he's going for his gun. If he shoots her, the store will be filled with police. All my plans will go down the drain.

But all the Bat brought out was a charge card. 'Put it on my tab,' he said.

The saleswoman accepted it frostily. The store might forgive him but she had her reservations. She retired with the card to the secret recesses of the store to do whatever it was salespeople did with charge cards.

Susan was surprised to find that card-carrying members of the Mafia were also card-carrying members of American Express or Master Charge. No reason why she should have been, she thought, upon reflection. You could get a credit card as long as you could establish a good credit record— by fair means or foul. Good character didn't enter into it.

'Well, that's taken care of,' the Bat said. 'An' it's gonna come out of your salary,' he said to the miserable Tony. 'Teach you to be more graceful.'

He turned back to Susan. 'You're lookin' real good, Susie. Don't forget we're steppin' out tomorrow so put on your gladdest rags.'

The bewilderment must have shown on her face. 'You haven't forgotten our dinner date for tomorrow night?'

'How could I forget?' As a matter of fact she had forgotten, though 'blocked it out' might be the more apt phrase. Having dinner with him was going to be awkward. Perhaps she could call it off under what she hoped would be the circumstances. If things didn't turn out the way she hoped, there would be no need for her to worry. It would be called off automatically.

*

'So what have you done with the queen?' the Bat demanded jovially.

She couldn't help a nervous start. 'Nothing yet. What I mean is, we seem to have gotten separated. I was just going to look for her. When I last saw her she was on the third floor. Maybe she's still there.'

'Well, let's go look for her together,' the Bat said, offering her his arm, only it was her reflection to which he made the gesture. He laughed. 'This store's like a fun house. I like it, I like it.'

Susan certainly didn't want the Bat to accompany her while she flushed Berry out of whatever covert she might have gone to earth in. 'She did say something about going to the ladies' room. It could be embarrassing if we all went down there, especially after what happened when Nicky was waiting outside the ladies' room.'

The Bat frowned. 'What did happen?'

Nicky gave Susan a reproachful glance. 'Nuthin' happened,' he said. 'I jus' knocked over a rack of clothes. They weren't breakable or anythin'.'

'Oh, Nicky, Nicky,' the Bat sighed, 'sometimes I think I shoulda let you go to cookin' school, the way your Mama wanted.'

'Why don't I go see if Berry's in the ladies' room,' Susan said, 'and, if I find her, I'll bring her back up here.'

Without waiting for the Bat's reply, she started towards the corridor off which the elevators opened. Behind her she could hear him saying something, but, as she was turning the corner, she couldn't make out the actual words.

An elevator door opened. Berry burst out. 'So there you are! Enough of this playing hide-and-seek all round the store. My feet hurt. I'm going to finish you off once and for all.' There was a gun in her hand.

Susan backed away from the elevator corridor. She lifted her gun. From the angle at which Berry was pointing her gun, Susan saw that it was her reflection at which Berry was aiming, not Susan herself.

But there were no mirrors behind Berry. It was Berry,

the real, live Berry in the considerable flesh, at whom Susan was pointing her gun.

'Ladies, ladies . . . !' the Bat's voice said, close behind her. Very close behind. He sounded alarmed, as well he might.

Susan and Berry fired at the same time. Susan's gun hit its mark. Berry crumpled to the ground. But not before her bullet had hit a mark—but not the one she intended.

There was a loud cry, followed by a thud. Susan did not turn to see whom Berry's bullet had hit, but she had a suspicion it had been the Bat.

An elevator door opened just ahead. She went towards it, circling Berry's body. The fur stole lay across the purple silk like a banner. She could read the sticker on the stole now. 'Animals have rights, too,' it said. Well, she wasn't going to argue with that.

Inside the elevator two ladies dressed in the height of fashion were carrying on an animated conversation. They ignored Susan's entrance. They ignored the screams and the sound of further gunshots as the doors closed behind her. They ignored the people who entered as the elevator stopped, time after time, on its maddeningly slow crawl to the ground floor.

Susan left, trying to look as if she were part of a group. Passing a clump of people who were waiting for the elevator to go up (was that Andy Mackay she glimpsed among them or was it just another illusion?), she moved as swiftly as she could, consonant with a decorous shopping pace, towards the front doors and the street.

As she came out, she could hear the sound of sirens approaching. No time to stop and try to get a cab. She walked up Lexington Avenue until she had covered six blocks or so, far enough to take her away from the scene. She was about to hail a taxi when she asked herself: why take a taxi on a fine day like this? She would walk back home. She had plenty of time now.

CHAPTER 27

Michelle was surprised and not at all pleased to see her employer return so soon. 'Thought you was gonna be out a lot longer'n this.'

'My business didn't take as long as I expected, so I thought I might as well make my calls from here,' Susan said, wondering why she felt this compulsion to explain to Michelle, when it should be Michelle who explained to her —and there was plenty that needed explaining. 'Have you done the shopping yet?'

'I ain't had no time, okay? I don't think you realize how much there is to do around here.'

'Good, because there are a few more things I want you to get. And you'd better go get them now, because I am going to have lunch at home. Maybe even dinner. I'm exhausted.'

'But you were on'y gone an hour. What were y'doin'—weight-liftin'?'

'Something like that,' Susan said. Lifting a weight off her mind, anyway.

As soon as Michelle had gone, Susan turned on the radio to see if news of the shootout in Bloomingdale's had reached the airwaves. It had, but accounts were sketchy and confused. There seemed, according to a bemused-sounding WINS announcer, to have been a gang war in Bloomingdale's. Carlo Battaglia, also known as 'the Bat', head of the Puzzone crime family, had been shot to death, and so had a well-dressed middle-aged woman whose identity had not as yet been established. Several of his henchmen had been seriously wounded in the battle, and a female member of the sales staff had been grazed by a bullet.

She had to call the Waldorf fast, Susan thought, and explain why she apparently hadn't shown up at Bloomingdale's, before Berry's body was identified. She had her story ready. She would ask for the Begum. Obviously the Begum would not be there. Then she would ask for the king. If the police had already found out who Berry was, he wasn't likely to be accessible. However, if she did reach him, she would tell him that she had gone to Bloomingdale's and found the place cordoned off by the police. It was obvious, she would say, that something had happened, possibly a bomb threat. Department stores were always getting bomb threats. Probably Berry hadn't been able to get in, either, but, in case she had arrived early, Susan wanted her to know that she hadn't been stood up.

However, she couldn't reach Serwar, so she had to table her story for later. On the whole, she was relieved not to have to talk to him right then. It would be hard to talk to someone whose mother you have just killed, while pretending that you had no idea she was dead.

Later, after Berry had been identified, Susan would call Serwar with her condolences. Or he might call her to give her the news himself. Other people would call, too. Andy, without question. Probably Lucy, and, of course, the rest of 'the old gang', as Berry had termed them. She hoped she wouldn't be invited to the funeral. If it took place in New York, she was very much afraid she would be. And she would have to attend, no way out of it.

She probably wouldn't be invited to the Bat's funeral, but she would send flowers. After all, he had sent her flowers. She felt a twinge of regret and wasn't sure whether it was because the Bat was dead or because she hadn't been the one to kill him.

The phone rang. She picked it up, prepared to greet the news of Berry's death with, first incredulity, then shock. But it was nobody connected with the late Begum. It was Ralph Towers, the young man from the Foundation.

'Miss Melville, I've been trying to reach you for some time. I'm afraid I have bad news.'

He paused, apparently to give her a chance to steel herself. If the events of the morning haven't steeled me, she thought, nothing would. 'It's about Peter, isn't it?'

'I'm afraid so. Dr Franklin and a companion went off o

a side trip some weeks ago. When they didn't come back, a search was organized. Nobody could find any traces of them.'

Susan was silent, wondering how she felt.

'That doesn't mean all hope is lost, of course. There weren't any signs of any kind of—uh—accident or anything. But I thought you should be prepared for the—that you should be prepared.'

'That's very kind of you,' she said. 'Very thoughtful. Who was this companion who disappeared along with him? Anyone I know?'

'Katherine Froehlich. She used to work at the Foundation.'

Dr Froehlich! So Susan's suspicions had been true. It looked as if Peter had taken one side trip too many.

Mr Towers interpreted her silence as an inability to speak because of grief. 'If there's anything I can do . . . ?'

'Just keep me posted. I'm sure it'll all turn out to be some kind of a mistake. Peter and Dr Froehlich must simply have gone off in an entirely different direction from the one they were supposed to be taking. Or they left the country without telling anyone. Peter's always so careless about forwarding addresses. They're bound to turn up safe and sound sooner or later.'

'Of course they are,' he said. 'May I say you're being very brave, Miss Melville?'

She was tempted to reply, 'No, you may not, Mr Towers,' but she controlled herself. 'Let's keep in touch,' she said.

After he'd hung up, she sat for a while, trying to analyse *her* emotions. She was naturally sorry that Peter had disappeared and was presumably dead. At the same time, she was less sorry than she might have been if he'd had a companion other than Dr Froehlich.

Susan and Peter had been together for many years now, and, although she had found her impatience with him growing over the years, that was true of most couples she knew. Odd, she reflected, that she had never thought of Peter and herself as a couple before.

Mimi Von Schwabe, of course, dealt with the problem of having a relationship grow stale by changing spouses—for she was always in a state of marriage—from time to time. She had stayed with Gunther Von Schwabe longer than most of her previous husbands because, she told Susan, it was time she settled down. But Susan knew that Gunther had said, 'If ever my Mimmchen tries to leave me for another man, I will strangle her with my own hands. And also him.'

Susan picked up the phone and dialled Mimi's number. 'Mimi,' she said, after they had gotten through the usual amenities, 'do you remember when I was at your house for dinner a couple of weeks ago? There was a young artist sitting next to me. I'm afraid I don't remember his name. I promised I'd introduce him to some sympathetic gallery owners.'

Mimi said she'd given so many dinners with so many young artists as guests she'd forgotten which one Susan was referring to. Susan resisted the impulse to ask her for a list of all of them. 'Oh, I'm so sorry, Mimi,' she said. 'I know what a wretched memory you have. Perhaps Gunther will remember. I saw his face when you and that young man—whatever his name was—came in after that long conversation you had on the terrace. I'm sure Gunther will be able to tell me what his name was.'

There was no point in bothering Gunther with such a triviality, Mimi said. He was a diplomat; he had more important things on his mind. She was sure that, if she thought hard, she would be able to supply Susan with the young man's name.

'Think hard, then,' Susan said.